Praise for

the novels of the Nine Kingdoms

Spellweaver

"Kurland's flowing prose combined with a strong multibook story arc and complex, evolving characters come together to make *Spellweaver* one of the strongest fantasy novels welcoming in the new year."

—*Fresh Fiction*

"Kurland weaves together intricate layers of plot threads, giving this novel a rich and lyrical style. Not only does mystery and danger abound, but also the burgeoning of a love and trust that is wonderful to behold. Kurland is an elegant spinner of tales!"   —*Romantic Times*

"Beautifully written, this tale is filled with mages, witches, spells, and shape-shifting, but also with plenty of intricate details of the incredible world around them."   —*Romance Reviews Today*

A Tapestry of Spells

"Charming, romantic, and verging on the wistfully sweet . . . Kurland deftly mixes innocent romance with adventure in a tale that will leave readers eager for the next installment."   —*Publishers Weekly*

"Ruith and Sarah captured my interest from the very first page . . . Lynn Kurland's time-travel series might occupy a favored place on my shelves, but I think she truly shines in the Nine Kingdom books."

—*Night Owl Romance*

"Lynn Kurland takes her audience back to the Nine Kingdoms with a strong opening act. Fans will feel the author magically transported them to her realm."   —*Midwest Book Review*

continued .

D1014247

Princess of the Sword

"Beautifully written, with an intricately detailed society born of Ms. Kurland's remarkable imagination." —*Romance Reviews Today*

"An excellent finish to a great romantic quest fantasy . . . Readers will relish Ms. Kurland's superb trilogy." —*Genre Go Round Reviews*

"An intelligent, involving tale full of love and adventure."
—*All About Romance*

The Mage's Daughter

"Engaging characters—family, friends, and enemies—keep the story hopping along with readers relishing every word and hungering for the next installment. [A] perfect ten." —*Romance Reviews Today*

"Lynn Kurland has become one of my favorite fantasy authors; I can hardly wait to see what happens next." —*Huntress Reviews*

"*The Mage's Daughter*, like its predecessor, *Star of the Morning*, is the best work Lynn Kurland has ever done. I can't recommend this book highly enough." —*Fresh Fiction*

"I couldn't put the book down . . . The fantasy world, drawn so beautifully, is too wonderful to miss any of it . . . Brilliant!"
—*ParaNormal Romance Reviews*

"This is a terrific romantic fantasy. Lynn Kurland provides a fabulous . . . tale that sets the stage for an incredible finish."
—*Midwest Book Review*

Star of the Morning

"Terrific . . . Lynn Kurland provides fantasy readers with a delightful quest tale starring likable heroes." —*Midwest Book Review*

"Entertaining fantasy." —*Romance Reviews Today*

"An enchanting writer." —*The Eternal Night*

More praise for the novels of Lynn Kurland

Till There Was You

"Spellbinding and lovely, this is one story readers won't want to miss."
—*Romance Reader at Heart*

With Every Breath

"Kurland is a skilled enchantress . . . *With Every Breath* is breathtaking in its magnificent scope, a true invitation to the delights of romance."
—*Night Owl Romance*

When I Fall in Love

"Kurland infuses her polished writing with a deliciously dry wit, and her latest time-travel love story is sweetly romantic and thoroughly satisfying."
—*Booklist*

Much Ado in the Moonlight

"A consummate storyteller . . . Will keep the reader on the edge of their seat, unable to put the book down until the very last word."
—*ParaNormal Romance Reviews*

Dreams of Stardust

"Kurland weaves another fabulous read with just the right amounts of laughter, romance, and fantasy."
—*Affaire de Coeur*

A Garden in the Rain

"Kurland . . . consistently delivers the kind of stories readers dream about. Don't miss this one."
—*The Oakland (MI) Press*

From This Moment On

"A disarming blend of romance, suspense, and heartwarming humor, this book is romantic comedy at its best."
—*Publishers Weekly*

Lynn Kurland

GIFT of MAGIC

BERKLEY SENSATION, NEW YORK

THE BERKLEY PUBLISHING GROUP
Published by the Penguin Group
Penguin Group (USA) LLC
375 Hudson Street, New York, New York 10014

USA • Canada • UK • Ireland • Australia • New Zealand • India • South Africa • China

penguin.com

A Penguin Random House Company

This book is an original publication of The Berkley Publishing Group.

Library of Congress Cataloging-in-Publication Data

Kurland, Lynn.
Gift of magic / Lynn Kurland.—Berkley Sensation trade paperback ed.
p. cm
ISBN 978-0-425-24520-0
I. Title.
PS3561.U645G54 2012
813'.54—dc23   2011038763

PUBLISHING HISTORY
Berkley Sensation trade paperback edition / January 2012

PRINTED IN THE UNITED STATES OF AMERICA

10 9 8 7 6 5 4 3 2

Cover illustration by Dan Craig.
Cover hand lettering by Ron Zinn.
Cover design by George Long.

One

The spell slammed into him with the force of a score of fists.

Ruithneadh of Ceangail met the ground with equal force. He lay on his back, winded, and stared up into the darkness above him. He couldn't decide if the stars he saw were ones his poor wee brain had created for his pleasure or ones twinkling in the sky for their own purposes. It was still at least an hour before dawn, so he supposed it was possible it was merely the heavens still displaying their sparkling finery.

He realized after a bit that he hadn't noticed it had begun to sleet. Perhaps what was swirling in front of his eyes was less a vision of the heavens than it was the aftereffects of a spell he'd known was coming his way but had been unfortunately less prepared to counter than he would have liked. He would have blinked the stinging rain out of his eyes, but it was too much effort. Breathing was too much effort as well given that all that seemed to be left of him was a void in his chest where his breath was accustomed to reside.

That was his own fault, he supposed. He'd thought a little sparring with spells before breakfast might be a good way to begin his day. And why not? His opponent had been a worthy one, and he had himself been eager to take any opportunity to improve his rather meager magical strength.

But now that he had regained what good sense he'd lost somewhere on his way to the appointed field of battle, he was prepared to revisit the conclusion he'd come to years ago:

Magic and all its incarnations should be sent briskly along to hell.

'Twas a pity he hadn't clung to that very sensible belief as firmly as he should have.

In his defense, he had tried. He had spent the previous score of winters in a house on the side of a mountain, conducting his life by purely pedestrian means. His days had been amply filled by roaming through the woods near his home, occasionally sampling the local alemaster's delicate apple-flavored ale, and continually stretching himself to perfect his recipe for unburned bread. Any magic he might or might not have possessed had been nothing but a distant and unpleasant memory, a memory that had occasionally plagued his dreams but never his waking hours—

He pursed his lips, the only part of him that seemed to be capable of movement at the moment. Very well, so memories of magic had plagued his dreams more than occasionally and intruded more than he wanted to admit upon his daylight ruminations. He had made it his life's quest to ignore those memories and dreams and other things that made him profoundly uncomfortable.

At least he had until his peaceful if not exactly useful existence had come to an abrupt end one evening at twilight when a knock had sounded on his door. Answering it—against his better judgement, as it happened—had resulted in finding himself cast headlong into a rushing river of a quest that had carried him places he'd never intended to go again—

"Perhaps you shouldn't have asked me to check mercy at the edge of the field."

Ruith winced as his breath returned, followed rapidly by the feeling in most of his limbs. He imagined he wouldn't be overly happy to discover what was left of his back after its meeting with the rock-hard ground, but there was nothing to be done about that. It would take his mind off the road in front of him, a road he knew would include death, danger, and duels of spells with men who would no doubt continue to suddenly and without warning appear from his past. Such as the one leaning over him, frowning thoughtfully at him.

He found he had breath after all to at least wheeze out a vile suggestion as to what his opponent might do with his annoying observations.

Mochriadhemiach of Neroche only laughed, grasped Ruith by the hand, and hauled him up to his feet. He stood back and looked him over critically. "I think we should have another go."

Ruith thought quite a few things himself, namely that he had gravely underestimated the truly evil nature of the youngest prince of Neroche. They had spent a fair amount of time together as lads, slipping away from responsible adults to whisper along passageways as chill breezes only to regroup in private to have lengthy looks at books of spells housed behind sturdy locks. He was, if he could be permitted a bit of self-congratulation, a damned fine picker of sturdy locks, much better than Neroche's newly crowned king.

A pity he hadn't maintained the same sort of abilities with his magic.

Which was, he supposed, why he found himself standing unsteadily in the middle of a muddy field with sleet stinging his skin where it struck him, gritting his teeth and fighting to ignore the particular draining sort of weariness the weaving of heavy spells

caused, and finding it in him to be grateful for time spent with a
mage he was fairly sure wouldn't kill him as he stretched his own
powers of endurance.

At least there was no one there to watch him shake not only
from weariness but from revulsion over the disgusting nature of
the spells Miach was no doubt dredging up for his benefit alone.
He had no desire to know from whence Miach had unearthed
them. If the man hadn't looked so damned casual about spewing
them out, Ruith might have felt sorry for him that the like were
rattling around in his wee head.

"Perhaps you would rather return to seek out a soft seat and a
hot fire?"

Ruith shot Miach a look. "I think I will manage another few
moments without either, thank you just the same."

"Truly, you don't look well."

"I appreciate your solicitude."

Miach only lifted one shoulder slightly. "I'm altruistic."

Ruith could have brought to mind several other things he would
have preferred to call him, but the truth was Miach was a fairly
decent soul, his vile collection of spells aside. He had been willing,
after all, to abandon not only sleep but an inedible breakfast to
march out into the gloom and toss a few spells about. Admirable
traits, those.

He was also lazy, illustrated by the fact that he seemed content
to simply stand there and yawn for a bit. Ruith was happy to take
advantage of that to put off the torture for a bit longer, not only to
catch his breath but also to look about himself to make certain they
were still about their unpleasant labors unobserved. He noted
nothing, but that didn't surprise him. The inn was at least half a
league behind them and surely no one else would tramp through
heavy spring snow to reach the clearing Miach had noticed as he'd
come on wing from his home in the west.

And even if anyone had known the glade was there, they

wouldn't have been able to take a closer look given that it was now covered by a glamour provided by none other than that illustrious king of Neroche. That spell, Ruith suspected, had been poached from Ruith's grandfather. Ruith didn't remember having been there for that bit of thievery, though he'd certainly accompanied Miach on several other forays into Sìle of Tòrr Dòrainn's library under cover of darkness. To say Sìle had disliked Miach for those intrusions was to put it mildly.

"Ruith?"

Ruith pulled himself back to the present, then smiled briefly. "Sorry. I was just wondering when it was you filched that spell for my grandfather's glamour and what you did to ingratiate yourself so thoroughly with him that he didn't do damage to you for it when last you met."

"Oh, he wasn't at all happy to see me," Miach allowed with a rueful smile, "but I had brought your sister to Seanagarra which earned me a bit of forbearance. I suppose nothing but good manners prevented him from killing me once he'd recovered from his surprise at seeing her."

"Did Grandmother Brèagha prevent him from forcing you to sleep in the stables?"

Miach laughed a bit. "Aye, she did, thankfully. And as for all that unwarranted animosity toward me he'd entertained over the years, I daresay he thought I was corrupting you, though I'm not sure how that's possible."

"Perhaps he was soured by all the times he caught you in either his library or his private solar?"

"With you leading the way?" Miach returned politely. "No doubt. And whilst we're discussing who corrupted whom, I seem to remember your having taught me several spells I hadn't considered myself, most of them having to do with shapechanging so we could venture into other, more exclusive places mere mortals would have considered utterly unassailable."

Ruith smiled faintly. "Did I? I don't remember that."

"They weren't your father's spells, if that eases you any," Miach said. "I imagine they were things Rùnach had stumbled across in his endless search for the obscure and elegant. As for King Sìle's tolerance of me now—" He shrugged. "'Tis nothing I've done, I assure you. I enjoy his favor simply because your sister was good enough to insist on it."

Ruith only avoided wincing because he had enormous reserves of self-control. He had just recently learned that his sister lived still, which had been startling enough. Standing five paces from her betrothed was substantially more wrenching. That Miach had passed so much time with her when he had still been laboring under the belief that she was dead—

He took a deep breath, but that left him coughing miserably. It was several uncomfortable moments later before he regained control enough to wheeze out a few words. "Stubborn, is she?" he managed, because he had to say something. "My sister, I mean."

Miach smiled. "It is a characteristic that has served her well in the past, though I haven't managed to convince her she doesn't need it any longer. She has very definite opinions on quite a few things."

"Then I'm surprised she stayed at Tor Neroche, instead of coming here with you on your little jaunt to lands not your own."

"Well," Miach said slowly, clasping his hands behind his back, "let's just say I wasn't entirely accurate about my reasons for the journey."

Ruith blinked. "You lied?"

"I hedged," Miach corrected. "I told her I needed to make a brief visit to Léige to discuss a trade agreement Adhémar had initially negotiated with King Uachdaran. Of course I had actually considered doing just that, though I was much more interested in several things going on elsewhere, things I thought merited my attention."

"And again, not within your borders."

Miach smiled grimly. "I find myself suddenly feeling responsible for things I could have easily ignored in years past."

"I doubt that," Ruith said with a snort. "You were always poking your do-gooding nose into places it shouldn't have gone. Obviously that gaudy crown of Neroche hasn't changed you any, though I will say that in this instance, I'm grateful for it. I need every opportunity I can find to stretch what feeble powers I have left."

"I won't flatter your enormous ego by choosing another word besides *feeble*," Miach said dryly, "though I'll concede that lazing about for the past score of years in your luxurious accommodations in Shettlestoune didn't do much past coming close to turning you to fat. I'm not sure we can remedy that in the next pair of days, but we can try." He started to turn, then paused and looked at Ruith closely. "What did you tell your lady you were planning on doing this morning?"

"I told her the truth, but I gave her strict instructions to remain at the inn."

"Best of luck with that."

Ruith shook his head. "She had her reasons for not wanting to watch us this morning."

Miach nodded. "I imagine she did. And I imagine her sight makes mine pale by comparison."

"I suppose you two could spend the day trying to decide if that's the case or not," Ruith said, "though I'm not sure Sarah would oblige you. As for what she does see, aye, it is quite a bit. I locked her out of Uachdaran of Léige's lists for that reason alone." He suppressed a shiver. "I wish I'd locked *myself* out of his lists, for I'm heartily sorry I saw a fraction of what he threw at me."

"How were his spells?"

"Very old," Ruith said, "old and more tangled than anything my father had ever done, to be sure."

"More powerful, would you say?" Miach asked, looking more

interested than was polite. "I wouldn't know, of course, having only scratched the surface of his collection myself."

Ruith pursed his lips. "You can continue to bleat out that tale as often as possible in hopes that someone will eventually believe you. But as for the truth of it, I'm not sure there's a way to qualify his spells. If you're a weary traveler, are you more intimidated by a sheer mountain face jutting up hundreds of feet into the sky or a mighty river tumbling over man-sized boulders and fells?"

Miach's ears perked up. "I wouldn't presume to offer an opinion, and I don't suppose you memorized any of those very tangled spells—"

"I suppose I did," Ruith said shortly, "but I haven't the stomach to teach them to you right now. The material point is that Uachdaran seemed determined to crush me under the vilest of the lot, no doubt as retribution for our having sneaked into his solar that one evening whilst our mothers and siblings were enjoying the delicate entertainments of his minstrels."

"I never stay long enough at Léige for any invitations to the king's lists, which I can see now has worked in my favor." He frowned. "I had no idea he even *had* lists, though now I wonder why it never occurred to me. I can't imagine they were very comfortable."

"They weren't," Ruith agreed. "I was very happy to leave Sarah in his solar, enjoying the fire. Much as I'm hoping she's doing at present."

"Whilst you stand here in the mud, shaking with weariness and fear?"

Ruith snorted. "I'm not afraid of you."

The look Miach gave him made him wonder if he might have spoken too soon.

"Then I'm obviously doing something wrong," Miach said mildly. He turned and walked away. "I'll rummage about in my memory and see if I can find things equal to keeping you awake."

Ruith took a deep breath, then quite suddenly found he couldn't even do that any longer. Miach's enthusiasm for the task at hand was matched only by his boundless imagination and what Ruith soon realized had been only the start of what he could do. Where Miach had dredged up those spells . . . well, it was likely best not to speculate. It was all he could do to keep himself from being crushed beneath things he couldn't see coming at him, though he could certainly feel them when they arrived.

A bit like his life, actually.

Not that his life should have been shrouded in that sort of mist. The quest that lay before him was rather simple, all things considered. He was going to find all the scattered pages of his father's private book of spells, put them back together, then destroy the whole bloody lot of them. There were several people he could bring to mind without effort who might want a different outcome once the spells were gathered, but with any luck he would have his task completed before any of them caught up with him.

He studiously ignored the fact that he wasn't entirely confident that would be the case.

He wrenched his thoughts away from unproductive paths and concentrated on fighting off what Miach was throwing at him. He recognized the occasional spell, but he was the first to admit Miach seemed determined to keep him off balance with things Ruith imagined had come from places his future brother-in-law likely wished he hadn't gone. Unfortunately, he could readily envision when and for what purpose he himself might need those very things.

He began to wonder, after a bit, why it was that he recognized not so much what Miach was sending his way, but how he was arranging the battle. Of course Miach had trained with his father, no mean swordsman himself, but somehow Miach's skills in using spells as a sword had improved to the point that Ruith wasn't sure he could credit that to happenstance.

"You haven't been studying swordplay with Soilléir, I'm sure,"

Ruith managed when the barrage paused long enough for him to gasp out a comment, "given that he wouldn't know which end of the sword to point away from himself if his life depended on it. Who has improved your paltry skills to such a degree?"

"You talk too much."

Ruith would have argued the point but found speech was simply behind him for quite a while. He would have considered it mean-spirited of Miach to leave him in such a state if it hadn't been so useful. As he'd noted before, anyone else he faced would have absolutely no reason to show him any mercy.

Time wore on in a particularly unpleasant way. Ruith suddenly noticed a streak of blue out of the corner of his eye, but supposed he was just imagining things. Considering how many spells Miach was flinging his way, seeing unusual things was perhaps nothing more than he should have expected.

He froze, then frowned. There was something about that flash that seemed . . . off. It was perhaps unreasonable to assume he could tell as much given the alarming nature of what was assaulting him, but he couldn't dismiss the impression. He countered a trio of very vile spells of Olc, then quickly held up his hand.

"Did you see that?"

"See what?" Miach asked, sounding not at all out of breath, damn him anyway.

"That blue flash."

"You're stalling."

Ruith would have protested, but he didn't have the chance. He continued to fight off an alarming number of increasingly powerful spells until he realized that at some point during the past few moments, he had crossed the line from scarcely managing things to being completely overwhelmed. As unpleasant a conclusion as it was to come to, he realized that if he didn't do something drastic very soon, he was actually going to perish.

That was a dodgy place to be given that Miach wasn't paying attention to him any longer.

He opened his mouth to point that out only to watch Miach's spells disappear as if they'd never been there. He looked up from where he'd fallen to his knees in the muck to find the king of Neroche trotting off the field.

"Where are you going?" Ruith gasped.

Miach paused, then swore just before he disappeared.

Ruith supposed that was answer enough, then he froze. Miach hadn't run off the field to search for a drink, he'd gone because there was something more in the surrounding woods than wildlife. Something Ruith had feared would find them.

He cursed and crawled unsteadily back to his feet. The next time he left Sarah behind at an inn, he was going to either put a better spell on the door or spend more time pointing out the dangers of walking in woods that might potentially contain more than just the usual complement of man-eating creatures.

Because the sinking feeling he had in his belly told him that Sarah had just encountered just that sort of thing.

Two

❧

Sarah of Doìre stood in the middle of a fairly well-used road that cut through a heavy forest of pines, facing what looked to be certain doom, and wondered where it was that morning that she'd taken a wrong turn. The possibilities were numerous, actually, and surely merited further investigation lest she make the same mistake again in the future.

Assuming, that was, that she had a future in which to make those same sorts of mistakes.

She turned her mind back to an hour ago when she'd woken from sleep with the feeling that there was something very foul going on in the world. Looking back on it now, she supposed that had simply been the smell of a breakfast that someone—or two someones, apparently—should have pitched onto the compost heap instead of leaving on the table. Instead of ignoring the smell and simply turning over to go back to sleep as she likely should have done, she had given up on any more rest and gotten up to face the day.

She had tended a fire that had been still burning thanks to a spell left there by some enterprising mage or other, then spent a few minutes pacing quietly so as not to wake the other occupant of the large gathering chamber. She had stopped more than once to look at him, on the off chance that the king of the elves had felt something amiss and woken from sleep because of it, but apparently he'd felt safe enough in his surroundings to continue on with his very sensible rest.

She wondered now if it had been a mistake to breakfast on bread that was almost free of bits of sand and butter that was still a few days away from rancid, or the extremely vile ale that tasted more like water that had merely been favored with a passing view of a few hops instead of enjoying a more substantial relationship with them. Not only had it not eased her hunger, it had left her looking desperately for any sort of distraction.

Perhaps she had chosen poorly when she had ventured into her pack, for instead of putting her hand on a pair of knitting needles and a ball of perilously soft blue wool, she'd come up with a book. And once she'd taken the book in her hands, it had fallen open to a page she hadn't asked for. At that point, there hadn't been any reason not to read, had there?

My dearest Sarah, I have given you the history of my people, but it is also the history of your people. Your mother was Sorcha, your father Athair, who was my cousin. I grieve for you that you didn't know her for she was a very lovely gel, full of laughter and joy and dreams that were easily read in her eyes.

She had shaken her head yet again because that's what she'd been doing since she'd read those words a pair of days earlier. She was obviously going to need more time to accept that her mother was not the witchwoman Seleg as she'd been led to believe for a score and five years, but instead a dreamweaver who had also apparently taken a wrong turn at some point during her life and wound up in the sights of Queen Morag of An-uallach, whose lust for magic and power was the stuff of legends. Sarah was certain she would have been familiar with those legends if she hadn't grown to womanhood in Doìre where the only tales told down at the pub were about how many attempts had been made so far that year to poach Farmer Crodh's painstakingly bred milch cows and how much rain a farmer might reasonably expect during April. The last wasn't even very interesting. The only things that grew successfully in Shettlestoune were scrub oak, sagebrush, and rumors about mages living in mountain cabins.

If Morag had known you were alive, she would have carried you back to An-uallach without hesitation, out of spite, if for no other reason. She has never realized that Seeing is not a blood magic, but a magic of the soul that cannot be given to another—nor taken from the one who sees.

Of course, Sarah wouldn't have had any idea about that particular sort of magic or what it might mean to her if she hadn't, several weeks earlier, marched off into the gloom after her alleged brother Daniel of Doìre to keep him from destroying the world. It had seemed so straightforward at the time, that marching, because all it promised to lead to was finding the fool, clunking him over the head to subdue him, then tying him up until she could deliver him to the place where ill-behaved mages were taken to be scolded into displaying good manners.

She supposed it was more Fate than simply bad luck that she'd been plunged into all manner of adventures she hadn't bargained for. She had traveled to Buidseachd to meet a particular master of wizardry named Soilléir, hobnobbed with the king of Léige, and most recently escaped from Morag of An-uallach's castle on the back of a horse who had shapechanged himself into a dragon and carried her and Ruith off to safety.

> *I am sorry, my dear Sarah, that the reading of this will grieve you. Know that you were—and are still—loved by those who have been watching you unseen over the years.*

Unseen, seen, seeing—all of that had left her thinking on things that made her truly uncomfortable. It had been one thing to discover early on during the journey that Ruith hadn't been the ancient curmudgeonish wizard living like a hermit several leagues from her home, but instead Ruithneadh of Ceangail, youngest son of the most notorious black mage in the history of the Nine Kingdoms; it was another thing entirely to find out hidden details about herself. If those things discovered would have been limited simply to a new set of relations, she might have emerged from the experience unsettled but relatively unscathed. But unfortunately those revelations had included learning that not only could she see, she could *see*.

The pages of Gair of Ceangail's highly coveted book of spells, among other things.

It didn't matter where she was or what she was doing, she could see those pages. She could do something as simple as draw a map with her finger in the dust on a table and suddenly there in front of her would spring up the locations of those pages, as if they'd been little fires that burned without consuming anything but her imagination. She had verified that for herself that morning in the dust on the table where the remains of breakfast had resided.

And it was what she'd seen when those little fires had sprung up that had convinced her to leave King Sìle sleeping happily in front of the fire and take her chances with what lay outside the door. A pair of spells had been laid there, one to protect and one to trigger an alarm. The first had been created by Ruith and was the sort of thing she was accustomed to from him: beautiful on the side she was to see and terrible on the side meant to repel intruders.

The other spell had been nothing more than a thin blue line laid across the threshold. She had readily seen that it had been fashioned by Miach of Neroche. Its purpose was to warn him if any mage crossed over it into the chamber, which she approved of. But since she hadn't been a mage but instead a woman with a pressing need to deliver very unsettling tidings to her comrade-in-arms, she had carefully lifted Ruith's spell, stepped over Miach's, then thought nothing more of either.

She had slipped out of the inn, then paused and considered her direction. She supposed if she were lucky, she would eventually run into Ruith and Miach. In preparation for that—and because she knew they were using spells she wouldn't want to see—she had whispered a particular spell under her breath.

She had no magic of her own, so spells were always nothing but words for her. The only reason she had any confidence at all in the spell she'd used that morning was because it had been one of Soil-léir of Cothromaiche's spells and his spells seemed, at least in her case, to come with power of their own. She had no idea how he managed that, but he managed several things she had no desire to investigate further.

And once she'd whispered that spell and had it come with a power she hadn't provided, her sight . . . well, there was no accurate way to describe what had happened to her. It wasn't as if she stood in a chamber where a torch had been suddenly extinguished or a candle snuffed out, leaving her in the dark. She could still see her surroundings; she could simply see less.

Less of things she shouldn't have been able to see in the first place.

She had enjoyed that diminishing of her sight for approximately twenty paces before she'd run bodily into something immobile and leapt back, an apology on her lips, assuming she had run into Ruith or perhaps the king of Neroche.

But she hadn't.

That had been an indeterminate amount of time ago. Now, she supposed if she survived what lay before her, she might look back at the moment she had bolted from the inn and wonder if she were prone to finding herself in the wrong place at the wrong time or if she, the very unmagical daughter of Sorcha and Athair of Cothromaiche, had been destined to spend her life trying to avoid being found and murdered by Queen Morag of An-uallach.

Who it seemed might manage the feat yet.

That very determined queen now stood five paces from her, not even looking at her, as if she had been a regal sort of kitchen cat too majestic to acknowledge the poor brown creature cowering next to her, its small heart beating with terror.

Sarah had never been fond of mice. They nested in her wool and chewed through her finished garments. She hadn't felt sorry for them when she'd seen them between the paws of her quite useful barn cats, though now she supposed she might have to revisit her opinion on that.

The queen glanced at her then, her eyes glittering in spite of the shadows.

"Well," she said softly, "out for a stroll, are we?"

Sarah considered bolting but discarded the idea immediately. She might manage a few paces, but no more. She wasn't sure screaming would serve her given that she had no idea how far away Ruith was, but perhaps it was worth a try.

She didn't manage so much as a squeak. It was odd how a spell of what she could only assume was silencing managed to completely obliterate even the veriest hint of sound before it was made. She could still breathe, but she supposed that was only because Morag wanted her in full possession of her wits as she was about her long-delayed and unhappily denied work of killing her. She would have attempted to explain exactly how it was that she had nothing Morag could possibly want, but she couldn't speak. Even if she'd been able to, she doubted Morag would have believed her.

She glanced without hope at the clutch of guardsmen standing behind the queen. They were, to a man, hard-eyed and stone-faced. Nay, no aid from that quarter.

She wished desperately that she had asked Ruith's grandfather to accompany her. She wished she had stayed at the inn. If she were going to be completely honest, at the moment she wished she had never left Shettlestoune. Now she would die before she could tell Ruith in great detail how she felt about him, perhaps find kin she belonged to but had never met, and use that third spell of Soilléir's she'd found in the book he'd given her but hadn't dared try yet—

She blinked, then realized abruptly that Morag hadn't begun circling her for the sheer sport of it, she'd been winding spells around Sarah herself, so tightly that Sarah couldn't move.

Which made it everlastingly too late to do anything at all.

Morag came to a stop in front of her and watched her with cold, glittering eyes.

"I should draw this out," she said, "but I've waited long enough. And don't think I give credence to that utter rubbish about your having no power of your own. *Everyone* from Cothromaiche has some sort of magic." She smiled condescendingly. "Perhaps even you, the least of Seannair's line."

But I don't, Sarah would have gasped out if she'd been able. Soilléir had said the ability to see was something that was woven into the soul, and Sarah had no reason not to believe him. Morag would slay her, then attempt to pick her as clean magically as another might a feast-day goose, but she would still have nothing to show for the effort.

Sarah looked up, unable to even wince at the spell that suddenly appeared over her head, a spell of death that formed itself into spikes that dripped with poison that burned her where it fell.

"You won't die quickly," Morag said with absolutely no emotion in her voice, "for that would defeat my purpose. You must die slowly, that I have time to catch your soul at the moment it has one foot in this poor world and the other in the world to come. It is only then—"

Sarah couldn't hear her any longer. She couldn't struggle, couldn't cry out, couldn't scream for help. All she could do was stare up at what was hovering over her, gathering itself together to fall upon her and crush her.

A wind, terrible and bitter, rushed past her so suddenly, she almost fell over. It sent the queen stumbling backward into the arms of her startled guardsmen. Sarah stared at what the wind had left behind, gold and silver runes that sparkled with painful bright-ness in the air in front of her. They were suddenly dispersed by a blue flash that streaked through the predawn gloom a single moment before the entire glade exploded in light, as if a thousand flaming arrows had been shot into the air only to stop and linger a hundred feet above her head.

Suddenly, out of nothing stepped a woman of about her own height with long, dark hair that was tangled from the breeze that still swirled around her. The woman raised a sword that glowed with that unearthly blue light and, with unnerving efficiency, sliced through the spell above Sarah's head as if it had been spider webs. It fell to pieces on the ground and writhed there like snakes.

Three more gusts of wind unspun themselves into men, rum-pled from their journey but looking terribly lethal nonetheless. Sarah supposed that since they had resumed their proper shapes closer to her and her rescuer than the queen, they could be consid-ered rescuers, not foes.

One held a bow loosely in one hand and an arrow tipped with werelight in the other. The second man, who held a sword in his hand, looked enough like the archer that they had to have been brothers, save the first one was dark-haired and the other fair. The third simply stood there with his hands empty, no doubt intending to intimidate with his terrible elvish beauty alone.

Sarah would have paused to thank them for the timely arrival, but the spell still wrapped around her had begun to tighten. She would have gasped out in pain at its sudden constricting, but she couldn't. The woman with the sword turned just the same and frowned in surprise.

Sarah would have warned her rescuer that Morag had more than one spell at her disposal, but the woman seemingly didn't need to be told that. She spun around, an eminently useful spell of defense accompanying her sword that blazed forth with renewed vigor. Sarah could see that whilst the spell the gel had spoken was strong enough on its own, it had been strengthened by something else. The runes that had preceded her, runes of Fadaire perhaps, though to be quite honest she couldn't tell. She was having enough trouble just breathing.

Morag laughed suddenly and the spell of death halfway out of her mouth fell to the ground, as if it had been shards of a broken mirror, easily discarded and trodden under heavy boots. "You, against my power with naught but that insignificant bit of provincial elven magic? Surely you jest."

"I'm afraid," the young woman said, "that I left my sense of humor a day or two behind me. Now, why don't you stand down before I plunge my very sharp sword through your breast and spare us all any more of *your* insignificant magic?"

Morag drew herself up. "Why, you disrespectful chit—" She stopped suddenly, and her mouth fell open. "If I weren't seeing this with my own eyes, I would never believe it. I almost mistook you for Sarait of Tòrr Dòrainn. But you aren't."

The woman standing in front of her didn't lower her sword. "Nay, I am not. My mother is dead."

"Oh, I know that," Morag said with another small, unpleasant smile. "Poor little Mhorghain."

Sarah would have gasped, but she still had no breath for it. This was Ruith's younger sister? Soilléir had told them she was alive, but this was quite frankly the last place Sarah had ever expected to encounter her.

"So I am," Mhorghain agreed. "Who are you?"

"I am, my rustic little miss," Morag said crisply, "Morag of An-uallach. I hold the ninth and most coveted seat on the Council of Kings, which perhaps you didn't know having grown to woman-hood who knows where. Obviously not at Seanagarra, else you would be better dressed. Now, if you'll excuse me, I have business to finish with the little coquette who stands behind you, business that should have been seen to long ago."

Sarah watched Morag's guards draw their swords. She would have warned Ruith's sister that she was about to be assaulted by them, but Mhorghain had apparently noticed as well. She also apparently didn't need any help.

It was almost appalling, the ease with which she fought the handful of very frightening warriors. Sarah looked quickly at Mhorghain's companions, but they were only standing there, obvi-ously feeling no need to offer aid. Sarah would have given them a brisk lecture on the virtues of exercising a bit of chivalry, but she saw the spell of death pouring again out of the queen's mouth and realized that the guardsmen had been nothing more than a distrac-tion from the true business of the day.

Mhor— was all she could even begin to think before Morag's spell was countered by a flash of blood red that was terrifying in the extreme.

She blinked and found herself suddenly with her nose pressed to a back that hadn't been there a heartbeat before. She realized immediately that the back belonged to Ruith. She found herself invited to step backward, which didn't go very well considering she was bound in spells that cut into her as she began to tip over. She cried out silently, but that was seemingly enough to draw

Ruith's attention. He spun around and caught her, then pulled her knife from her boot and cut where he apparently thought Morag's spell might be residing.

It fell from her, slithering down to disappear at her feet. Ruith replaced her knife without comment. Sarah would have thanked him, but he'd already turned back around to face Morag. She soon found herself joined by Mhorghain, who had been thrust behind her brother. Mhorghain resheathed her sword with a hand that wasn't all that steady, truth be told. Sarah doubted that had anything to do with a battle avoided, but quite a bit to do with the fact that Mhorghain was looking at Ruith as if she'd just seen a ghost. He seemed to feel her gaze boring into the back of his head because he looked over his shoulder at her briefly.

"Ruith," Mhorghain managed in a garbled tone.

"Later," he suggested, with a quick smile.

Mhorghain only shut her mouth and nodded, which Sarah suspected wouldn't have been her reaction under different circumstances. Sarah smiled at Ruith's sister and had that same look of astonishment in return before Mhorghain managed a weak nod. Sarah left Mhorghain to her digesting of events she obviously hadn't foreseen and looked around Ruith's shoulder at the king of Neroche, who was standing in front of them all, apparently not inclined to put away his sword bathed in that unnerving crimson light. Ruith stepped up beside Miach only to be elbowed aside with an ease that said they had done the same thing to each other a time or two in the past.

"This will require diplomacy," Miach said, not entirely under his breath.

"And you have any?"

"More than you do, I imagine," Miach said, stepping fully in front of Ruith. "I'd see to my lady, were I you. And mine, if you wouldn't mind."

Ruith didn't go willingly, but he seemed to agree with the

sentiment if not the execution of it. He sighed, then backed up a few paces, leaving Sarah no choice but to back up as well. She didn't mind, actually, because it put her yet a bit further away from Morag. Mhorghain went along only because her brother gave her no choice. Sarah exchanged a brief smile with her, then shifted slightly so she could see past Ruith's shoulder without putting herself in Morag's sights.

The king of Neroche had put up his sword and was standing there with his hands clasped behind his back, maintaining a polite but certainly not deferential pose. He inclined his head so slightly, it could have been mistaken for nothing at all.

"Queen Morag," he said politely. "What a pleasure."

"I heard the king of Neroche managed to get himself killed," Morag said, sounding as if she weren't unhappy in the least about that.

"Aye, he did," Miach agreed, "and is already laid to rest, but of course you knew that. It was a great loss to us not to have you at his funeral, though King Phillip represented—"

"He is not the king!" Morag shouted, then she took a deep breath. "He is the prince consort, which you know very well, King Mochriadhemiach. Before Phillip's father, King Sicir, died, he was wise enough to choose someone with the strength to rule An-uallach." She shrugged. "Phillip has his duties."

"I meant no slight, of course," Miach said. "I was simply honored to have your husband travel such a long distance on such short notice. I know that for you it must be difficult to do the same when neither shapechanging nor riding on the back of winged steeds is possible. It is very time-consuming to simply trot off on a horse, but if that is the only alternative open to you . . ."

"I am not afraid of heights," Morag snapped.

Miach only shrugged delicately. Or, Sarah realized, he might have had his shoulder lifted because his other had been bumped firmly by none other than Sìle of Tòrr Dòrainn, who had appeared out of nowhere and nudged the king of Neroche out of his way. Sarah caught sight of Morag's expression and suspected that Ruith's grandfather had appeared none too soon.

"Morag," said the king of the elves smoothly, "what a delight to see you again. You're looking well."

Morag looked as if she would rather have chewed on glass than answer politely, but apparently she could manufacture a pleasant look when pressed. She favored the king with a gracious smile.

"Sìle, it has been too long. How are the glories of Seanagarra?"

"My hall is dimmer without your beauty to adorn it," Sìle said. He gestured expansively behind him, almost taking off Miach's head in the process. "And whilst the nearby inn behind us is hardly worthy of your patronage, it does provide at least the hope of rude shelter. I should have brought my own kitchen staff, of course, but one makes do with less when circumstances demand it. Let me escort you out of the rain, my dear. Did young Miach tell you how greatly you were missed at Adhémar's funeral? And the lad's crowning, of course. The royal banquet was filled with far too many craggy faces and no queen to mitigate the unfortunate sight."

"Aye, the king of Neroche intimated as much," Morag said, though she sounded none too pleased about it.

Sarah was happy to hide behind Ruith's back as Sìle led Morag away back toward the inn. The queen's guards fell in behind her, but the men who had come with Mhorghain trailed after the small company at a safe distance, so Sarah supposed the king of the elves would be safe enough. She might have felt equally safe if she hadn't caught sight of the look Morag threw over her shoulder.

At her.

Not even Ruith's arm suddenly around her shoulders lessened the profound chill that came over her. Nay, Morag hadn't forgotten about her.

Not at all.

Ruith cleared his throat. "I believe, my love, that we should discuss at length what lurks in the woods that you might avoid in the future."

"We should," she said, deciding that what she had to tell him about their map could certainly wait for a bit. "Right after you see to more pressing business."

He looked rather pale in the pre-dawn gloom. "I hadn't expected to see her."

"If it makes you feel any better, your sister's looking rather misty-eyed herself. I don't think she'll notice if you find yourself in the same state."

He let out his breath slowly, then nodded before he turned to face his sister. He looked absolutely shattered, which Sarah could understand. To know she lived still had been a joyous revelation for him, but to see her in the flesh? If he remembered his name after he'd finished falling apart, Sarah would have been surprised.

She would happily help him pull himself back together after the fact. Perhaps that would be enough to help her forget a thing or two, namely her recent encounter with the queen of An-uallach who obviously hadn't forgotten one particular task she'd left undone.

That of making certain Sarah didn't live to see many more sunrises.

Three

Ruith supposed there were several things in his life that had truly left him past speech, most having to do with his family, many that unfortunately hadn't been pleasant. At the moment, though, he could safely say his speechlessness was due to a happy circumstance.

He had to admit that the first sight of his sister standing there between Sarah and Morag had almost knocked him quite fully upon his arse. He had followed the impetuous king of Neroche off their training field as something not altogether human—wind, he thought—then been brought up abruptly at the sight of what Miach had apparently noticed before. Finding Sarah facing Morag would have made his heart stop if he'd had one, but it had been realizing that there was someone standing between Sarah and the queen of An-uallach that had shocked him so abruptly back into his own shape.

He'd thought, at first, that it had been his mother.

He had grasped frantically for the remaining shreds of his wits, put himself between Sarah and Morag, then realized he needed to pull Mhorghain behind him as well. It had been simply good manners to put off giving Sarah a thorough lecture on the virtues of staying in inns where he'd put her until after he had attended to the less pleasant but necessary business of pitting himself against that viperess from An-uallach. Perhaps it was for the best that Miach had inserted himself into the situation. Ruith was absolutely certain he wouldn't have been as polite as his future brother-in-law had been.

Now, though, he was facing not his love but his sister and he found himself quite robbed of both his breath and his usual ability to find something useful to say no matter the amount of duress.

Admittedly, he'd known Mhorghain was alive, which should have given him an edge in the current situation, but somehow it didn't. The last time he'd seen her, they'd both been standing on the edge of a glade in a forest draped in the very vilest of spells of illusion and distraction, watching their father stride out into the clearing to demonstrate for them his unprecedented power by uncapping a well of evil, then containing it. Ruith's mother had given him the charge of keeping Mhorghain safe.

Looking back on it from the slightly less devastating position of having his sister again within reach, he could say that he had made the best decision he could have at the time. His mother had put herself in mortal danger to save them, and he'd released Mhorghain to try to save their mother.

He'd ended up losing the both of them.

He'd been washed away by the contents spewed by that monstrous well. When he'd managed to crawl back to the last place he'd seen his family, he'd found only his mother lying by the well, dead, and the rest of his family gone. He had assumed Mhorghain had been washed away to her death with the rest of them. He'd been wrong.

Mhorghain was looking at him as if she'd just seen a specter of some kind. It occurred to him, with a flash of dismay, that she might have mistaken him for their sire.

"Do I look so much like Father, then?" he asked.

"Don't be an ass," Mhorghain said promptly, "of course not."

Miach laughed briefly, then sobered abruptly at the look Mhorghain shot him. Ruith only shook his head. She looked like their mother, but she was obviously not their dam. He was fairly sure he'd never heard Sarait of Tòrr Dòrainn call anyone an—

"You look like *you*," Mhorghain was saying. "I simply hadn't expected to see you here, and that because *no one* bothers to tell me anything interesting before he flaps off into the night."

"Your betrothed has been hedging again," Ruith managed.

Mhorghain pursed her lips. "Aye, he does that."

"Outright lies now and again, I'd imagine," Ruith supplied helpfully.

"I don't lie," Miach said mildly, "though I will admit to leaving the truth undisturbed when necessary."

Ruith imagined so, which would make him a very good king indeed. Discreet and politic, two things his deceased brother wouldn't have recognized if those qualities had broadsided him. Ruith would have said as much, but he realized his sister was looking at him still, as if she just might have had enough surprises for the day. He winced, then reached out and pulled her into his arms.

He thought he might have wept. He was fairly sure Mhorghain had cursed quite a bit more than was ladylike. He supposed that in spite of the litany of curses he was fairly certain she hadn't learned at Nicholas of Diarmailt's knee, she had shed a tear or two herself.

She finally pulled away, dragged her sleeve across her eyes, then glared at him. "Where have you been?"

"Hiding," he said, intending that the word sound offhanded and casual. He failed rather spectacularly, actually.

She closed her eyes briefly, then shook her head. "You can't blame yourself for any of it, Ruith."

"The well," he asked politely, "or letting go of you?"

"Either," she said impatiently, "or both. You couldn't control the first and you had no choice in the last. You did what was needful. Not that I remember much of it, thankfully." She rubbed her arms suddenly. "I don't suppose we have to stand out here and chat, do we? It seems like either you or Miach could quite easily build us a fire in some secluded glade."

Miach laughed a little. "Morgan, the entire place is either still frozen solid or dripping with rain that should be solid—" He looked at her, then shut his mouth around what else he apparently intended to say. "I'm not comfortable with the exposed nature of a fire in the midst of a field. Perhaps we could seek out a comfortable corner of the stables instead." He paused. "If that suits you, of course."

Ruith suppressed a smirk and stopped himself just before he bawked like a chicken to mock Miach's utterly henpecked state, partly because he could see his sister was thoroughly undone but mostly because he was no longer a ten-year-old boy. He contented himself with the thought of poking Miach about it later, then realized what Miach had called his betrothed.

"Morgan," he murmured. Miach had told him that's what they had called her for most of her life, but it was still very odd to watch her respond to that name.

Mhorghain shot him a look he couldn't quite decipher, but there was a fair amount of discomfort in it. "You may call me what you like. Just don't let Grandfather hear you."

He took a deep breath. "I'm not sure I can call you anything save Mhorghain."

"I wouldn't expect anything else." She turned to Sarah and held out her hand. "I believe you must know my brother, and I'm guessing that harpy my grandfather just took away knows you, but we haven't met properly. I'm Morgan."

Sarah took her hand. "Sarah," she said politely. "And I appreciate the rescue. I needed it."

Mhorghain looked at her thoughtfully. "You remind me of someone. Not so much in looks, actually, but in the air about you . . ."

Miach leaned close to Mhorghain. "She won't tell you, but I will and face her wrath later. She's Soilléir of Cothromaiche's cousin, but she only recently discovered it. You remember that ageless, bright-eyed keeper of the spells of essence changing who roams the halls of the schools of wizardry, terrifying the masters and keeping the workers of evil in check."

Mhorghain looked at Sarah in surprise. "Then you have a mighty magic."

Sarah shook her head quickly. "I don't have any at all."

"I'm not sure how that's possible, but you can surely count yourself fortunate," Mhorghain said, with feeling. "'Tis vile stuff. I'm happy enough to watch Miach have as much of it as he likes, but I don't care for it."

Ruith suppressed a smile. The seventh child and only daughter of the black mage of Ceangail disavowing any claim to his power? Nothing would have wounded their father more.

"I imagine," Miach said dryly, "that you two might have several things in common."

Mhorghain lifted her eyebrows briefly. "I daresay. Perhaps we might discuss them later in front of a hot fire. For now, I'll be satisfied to know how it was you met my brother."

"In Doìre," Sarah said looking briefly up at Ruith. "He was pretending to be the ancient mage living in the mountains whose reputation was so terrifying no one dared disturb him."

"I'm unsurprised," Mhorghain said, rubbing her arms suddenly, "though I'm suddenly not so sure I want to hear the rest out here. Let's find shelter where you might tell me the rest."

Ruith realized abruptly that he shared the chill that had

suddenly overtaken her. He shared a brief look at Miach who immediately reached for Mhorghain's hand.

"A fine idea, my love. I'll make sure we have a bit of privacy from listening ears and conjure you up a decent blanket." He exchanged another look with Ruith. "I don't think Morag is the only thing haunting these woods."

Ruith didn't either, but he couldn't bring himself to speculate on who else that might be. The list was too long for his comfort. He looked pointedly at his sister's hand in Miach's, then glared at the man who thought he was going to actually drag her in front of some species of priest. Miach only returned his look steadily, without even so much as a hint of a smirk.

"If you kiss her in my presence," Ruith said, just so Miach was clear on where he stood, "I'll make it so you can't walk to your wedding—which I'm still not convinced isn't just a detail left over from a bad dream."

"Is it too late if they're both wearing Fadairian runes about their wrists?" Sarah asked with a thoughtful frown.

"Everlastingly," Miach said cheerfully before he walked away with a woman he obviously adored.

Ruith sighed and put his arm around the woman he shared that same sort of affection for. He only hoped he would manage to keep himself alive long enough to make it a permanent arrangement. Given the morning he'd had and how close he'd come to losing her to Morag of An-uallach, he was honestly afraid to hope too much for it.

"How are you?" she asked, as they followed the king and future queen of Neroche.

He supposed there was no point in not being honest. "I'm not sure unsettled begins to describe it."

"She looks so much like your mother, then?"

He blinked, then realized she was talking about Mhorghain and not the list of things potentially haunting the woods around them. "Aye, she does, but they are very different." He took a deep breath. "'Tis very difficult to think on how many years have passed since I saw her last."

"I suspect she feels the same way," Sarah said quietly. "And I imagine she doesn't hold you responsible for it."

"Can you see that?" he asked.

"I heard it in her voice, actually, but it would have taken no especial powers of sight to see in her face that she meant it." She looked up at him and smiled. "It's good to know that, wouldn't you say?"

He could only manage a nod, which he supposed was better than unmanning himself again by a display of untoward emotion. He also decided that lecturing Sarah on the perils of walking through the woods in the dark could be saved for later. After all, she'd had a rather busy morning trying to avoid being killed by the queen of An-uallach and then watching him fall apart whilst greeting the sister he hadn't seen in a score of years. Perhaps there was something in particular that had driven her from the inn in the first place.

He wasn't sure he wanted to speculate on what that something might be.

So he walked with her, feeling rather more content than he deserved to feel no doubt, and listened to the conversation going on in front of him between his wee sister who was not so wee any longer and the fig-eating, spell-poaching boy who seemed to be torn between his pleasure at seeing her and an intense desire to shout at her.

"You promised you were going to remain behind," Miach said rather calmly, all things considered. "You *promised*, Morgan."

"I brought guardsmen," Mhorghain returned without hesitation.

"Guardsmen," Miach echoed, sounding as if he were very close to choking on the word. "Is that what you call them?"

"Aye, that is what I call them. I was in no danger."

Miach opened his mouth to say something, then apparently thought better of it.

"*You* promised you would be gone three days," Mhorghain said tartly, "and you were gone *five*, which I thought was overlong, all things considered."

"I had business—"

"So did I. And part of that business was to find out where you were. Interrupting that shrew's morning sport was merely a happy coincidence."

Miach looked at her in silence for a moment or two, then sighed deeply. "I suppose I cannot fault you for doing what I would have no doubt done as well, but the least you can do is tell me how you knew where to find me and why you felt the need to look in the first place."

"Nicholas arrived shortly after you left and did me the favor of telling me where to look. He also had a suggestion or two about things I hadn't considered." She paused and gave her betrothed a look that Ruith couldn't quite identify. "As for the why of my journey, I did have a particular reason."

"I hesitate to ask what that might be. Well, past an intense desire simply to be in my arms again."

"There was that," she agreed, "but there was something else as well, something I had to bring you." She paused. "A particular something that you and I acquired in Lismòr, actually."

Miach looked winded enough that Ruith almost stepped forward to force him to sit and put his head between his knees. Miach recovered admirably, closed his eyes briefly, then reached out and tucked a wildly curling lock of hair behind Mhorghain's ear.

"I understand now," he said quietly.

"I imagine you do."

Miach exchanged a long look with her that Ruith envied. It was passing strange that Miach should know his sister so much better than he did—and substantially more wrenching than he'd suspected it might be. But before he could think on that overlong, Miach released Mhorghain's hand, then turned and smiled at them.

"The path here is wide enough for four, I daresay. Shall we walk together?"

Ruith checked his first impulse, which was to ask Miach what he was hedging about at present, and instead took the opportunity to walk for a bit with both Sarah and Mhorghain within easy reach. Miach drew Sarah into a conversation about the weaving guild in Neroche, which left Ruith walking alongside his sister, wondering where to even begin with her. He finally mustered up enough courage to look at her.

"I'm sorry, Mhorghain," he said quietly, "that I didn't know you were alive."

"'Tis hardly your fault—"

"But I would have come to look for you," he said. "If I'd known."

She started to speak, then shook her head. "There is no point in trying to refight yesterday's battle, Ruith."

"Is that one of Weger's strictures?"

"He is pithy," Mhorghain agreed. "And he would say the same thing to you. What's done is done and nothing can change it. I have no regrets for the course my life has taken."

Ruith sighed. "I suppose I should thank Fate that she didn't send me stumbling into Weger's thorny embrace."

"It is a bit austere," Mhorghain conceded, "but rather bracing, when looked at in the proper light."

He couldn't imagine, but he wasn't going to argue.

He studied her a bit longer in silence, storing up the sight against the possibility that he might not see it again.

She blinked in surprise. "Why are you looking at me that way?"

He lifted his eyebrows. "I haven't seen you in a bit, Mhorghain."

"Nay, you're looking at me as if this might be the last time." She looked at him narrowly. "What are you about?"

He thought very seriously about leaving the truth undisturbed, as Miach would have no doubt advised him to do. After all, what good would it do for his sister to know the madness he contemplated? It wasn't as if she could do anything to help him—not that he would have accepted her help if she'd forced it on him. She had, from what Miach had told him over a bracing cup of barely drinkable ale earlier that morning, closed the well their father had opened. Ruith had no illusions about what that had likely cost her.

But if he didn't tell her what he was about, he suspected she would investigate on her own and perhaps even insert herself into a battle that wasn't hers to fight.

He took a deep breath, then let it out slowly. "I'm collecting the pages of Father's book of spells."

"His what?" she asked in surprise, then she shivered. "Oh, that."

"Aye, that," Ruith agreed.

"And how do you propose to acquire these pieces of absolute evil?"

"Sarah can see them."

Mhorghain looked at him in astonishment, then she closed her eyes briefly. "The poor gel."

"I couldn't agree more," Ruith said quietly. "When we began this quest, she was hunting her brother to keep him from destroying the world and I was coming along to protect her. It was very shortly thereafter that I realized what we were really hunting was Father's spells and that I needed Sarah more than she needed me."

"For more reasons than just the seeing, I imagine," Mhorghain said, scrutinizing him a bit more than he was comfortable with.

"Aye, there is that," he said, "but I won't frighten her off by talking about it. And there you have it. I would leave her behind and do the best I can on my own, but—"

"She won't stay behind." Mhorghain shook her head. "Sometimes, Ruith, there are tasks that only you can do, no matter who or what you are. If this is Sarah's burden to bear, not even you can take it from her."

He rubbed his hands over his face before he could stop himself. "I don't want to hear that. The only mercy in all of this is that at least I had no idea you were going to that damned well with only Miach of Neroche as protection."

"And Grandfather," Mhorghain said, "and Sosar, Keir, and a contingent of elves. But in truth, all I needed was Miach. And if it eases your mind any, Miach told me just a moment or two ago—"

"Once he stopped shouting at you—"

"He didn't shout," she said primly. "He was simply expressing his joy at seeing me in a place where he hadn't expected to."

"Loudly."

"He's overprotective, and you're changing the subject." She shot him a look. "I think I remember this about you."

"I haven't improved over the years."

She laughed a little and the sound eased his heart more than he would have imagined it would. He couldn't bring to mind many memorable times with his sister—he had, after all, been singularly obsessed with looking for useful spells—but he could remember her laughing at Seanagarra. Never at Ceangail, of course, but often as she ran through their grandfather's halls. Her laughter hadn't changed all that much over the years.

She put her arm through his. "As I was trying to tell you, you need have no fear of my following you. Though I would ignore him if circumstances warranted it, in this I think I will humor Miach and leave you to see to your quest by yourself."

"Aye," he agreed, "you will. Your turn is finished for the moment."

"Which is probably just as well. I don't know anything about magic and that sort of rot." She patted the Sword of Angesand affectionately. "I'd rather best my enemies with steel."

"I have the feeling Mehar of Angesand would approve of you," he said.

"She claims she does," Mhorghain agreed. "You can ask her when you come to Tor Neroche after you and Sarah are finished with your task."

"I think I will," he said quietly.

Mhorghain nodded, then walked on with him in silence for so long, he wondered if she would ever say anything again. She seemed to be chewing uncomfortably on a thought she couldn't bring herself to voice. She finally looked up at him, her expression very grave.

"Do you think," she asked slowly, "that spells are all you'll find? In your search for that book?"

"What else would there be?" he asked in surprise.

"Oh, I don't know." She was silent for several more very long moments before she looked up at him. "You might find someone you didn't expect to find."

"Father?" he asked easily.

She looked profoundly unsettled. "I don't know. I've been surprised by so many things over the past few months, I think I might be prepared to find just about anything."

"I won't say that the thought hasn't occurred to me," Ruith admitted reluctantly. And it had, and not just the night before when Miach had suggested as much. In fact, making sure Ruith was acquainted with that unthinkable thought was what had sent Miach on his very long journey east. "I'll also not admit to all the useless hours I spent in my youth, wondering if he were alive and inventing terrible ways to repay him for his evil. But as for the truth of it?" He shrugged. "There is no conceivable way he could have survived, no matter what Miach thinks he suspects."

Mhorghain closed her eyes briefly. "Still, I don't envy you this task."

"And I don't envy you," Ruith said with a mock shudder. "Trapped in that rustic lean-to in the Nerochian hills for the rest of your life? Do they cook the meat these days or simply eat it right off the bone raw?"

Mhorghain blinked in surprise, then laughed a little. "You're insulting my adopted country. You'd best cease with that before I take you out to the lists and beat respect into you."

He imagined she would be able to quite easily if that mark over her brow was what he thought it was. He attempted a look of mock horror.

"Better that than being forced to face your betrothed over spells. He has a substantial collection of very nasty ones."

She looked at him with a slightly wistful expression. "Did you filch them together?"

"A goodly number of them, if you can believe it," Ruith said, "though I daresay you wouldn't remember it. You were very young and Miach and I were too busy poking our noses into places they shouldn't have gone for him to have made much of an impression on you. Well, that and Grandfather was determined to keep you out of the reach of any foul influences—and I imagine I don't need to tell you whose influence he considered foul. If you saw Miach more than twice from a distance in your youth, I would be greatly surprised. But, because I am a generous brother, I will tell you all manner of embarrassing tales about your betrothed when we have time later." He felt his smile fade. "I just hope your future will be repayment enough for a past not spent at Seanagarra."

She nodded. "It will, I daresay. If I hadn't walked that thorny path, I wouldn't have Miach."

"And the future crown of Neroche."

"I didn't say it was all perfection," she said with a snort, then she smiled. "As strange as it seems, I find myself willing to endure quite a bit to have him. He makes time to train with me in the lists and ride our superior Angesand steeds. And he flies with me almost every day."

Ruith clucked his tongue. "Elves do not shapechange."

She shot him a look. "Don't think I won't be asking him all the shapes *you* taught him before the day is out, though I will do it out of Grandfather's hearing lest your evening prove uncomfortable because of it."

He nodded, then watched her surreptitiously for several minutes. He finally cleared his throat. "Are you happy?"

She looked up at him, and he had the oddest feeling of time layering his past over his present and finally settling itself where it should have been. She was still that fearless lass of six summers who had been as willing to follow him into any number of adventures as she had been to sit next to their mother and, well, not stitch, but submit to having her fingernails inspected and her pockets checked for substances that should have been left behind in the woods. Ruith didn't know, never having thought to ask, but he had the sneaking suspicion that their mother had collected her share of interesting-looking rocks and sticks in her own pockets.

He also suspected that Mhorghain would be the same sort of mother their mother had been: willing to tromp about in the mud when called upon yet equally capable of drawing children onto her lap and wrapping them in copious amounts of safety and affection.

"Am I happy?" she echoed, then she smiled. "Very. And you?"

He took a deep breath. "Aye, happier than I deserve."

"And determined to have a lifetime in which to enjoy it with your lady."

"That too."

"Does she love you?"

"I like to believe she might have some small bit of affection for me," he conceded. "In spite of my heritage, it should be noted."

"I'll watch her today and see if I can find ways for you to improve your chances with her."

"That's good of you," he said dryly.

"My pleasure." She looked up at him suddenly. "You haven't changed, you know."

"Haven't I?"

She put her arm around his waist and hugged him as they walked. "Nay, you haven't, for which I'm very grateful. I assume Rùnach hasn't either."

"Nay, he's still the same as he ever was. Well, save for all the untoward habits he's acquired, having been in such close quarters to Soilléir all these years."

"I daresay."

Ruith looked up at the inn that was now but a hundred paces away, then stopped with the rest of them. "I don't suppose Morag will start a battle in the common room, do you think?"

Miach shook his head. "Not with Sìle there, I don't imagine." He looked at Mhorghain. "I think our other business is better conducted outside the inn, however, wouldn't you agree?"

Mhorghain nodded gravely. "I imagine it is."

Ruith watched them exchange a look that he had to admit bothered him more than perhaps it should have. There was something going on, something unspoken that they understood which he didn't. And that something had to do with him.

Mhorghain took a deep breath. "It is why I came, after all. Well, to find you as well, but mostly because of . . . well, that other business. But now that it comes down to it, however, I'm not sure I can do this."

"I think, my love," Miach said very quietly, "that you haven't any choice. In fact, it wouldn't surprise me that this meeting was predestined."

Mhorghain pursed her lips. "I've little liking for that sort of thing."

"I doubt you are the first one to say that," Miach said with a faint smile, "but you know that already."

Ruith would have asked them what in the hell they were talking about, but he was surprised enough by the tears in Mhorghain's eyes not to. She smiled very briefly at Miach—a smile that was actually rather strained—then turned to look at him. He suppressed the urge to bolt. He was, after all, a man, not a lad, and he had faced worse things than whatever his sister might have to tell him.

Surely.

"I have something of interest," Mhorghain said, putting her shoulders back and lifting her chin. "Miach's been keeping it, actually, for a pair of months." She paused. "I just didn't realize he was keeping it for you."

"What is it?" Ruith asked, feeling rather pleased that he sounded no more interested than if he'd been sitting down for tea and the hostess had announced the sort of sandwiches they might be looking forward to. At least it wasn't some dreadful piece of news. It was likely some trinket she'd kept from her youth, something she thought he should have.

Mhorghain dug about in a purse at her belt, then pulled out something wrapped in cloth. She unwrapped it, then held it out.

He supposed he would look back on that moment and quickly bring to mind several things that would explain several other things. It had been a very long winter. He had come within a hairsbreadth of losing Sarah to Morag of An-uallach's very utilitarian spell of death. He had spent the previous several fortnights facing things he had thought to have put happily behind him. But mostly, he'd had a tremendously nasty morning in the lists after an equally disgusting breakfast followed by the shock of seeing a sister he had for most of his adult life supposed to be dead.

All of that had left him feeling less than himself.

That was surely the only reason he fainted.

Four

✳

Sarah stood to one side of the window that overlooked the back garden of the inn and was grateful that all she saw was dirt, last year's rotting vines, and the occasional weed hardy enough to have survived the winter. She looked up at the late-morning sky, heavy with clouds and spitting a combination of rain and snow, and was relieved to find it also was just sky and not full of spells and things she wouldn't normally have expected to see.

The only thing unusual was that owl perched just on the other side of the stables, but perhaps that was more ordinary than it appeared. After all, Soilléir of Cothromaiche had gifted her and Ruith two horses—two shapechanging horses—who were prone to restlessness. No doubt one of them had wearied of standing in his stall and decided to take a bit of air. Perhaps the air was better fifty feet off the ground than it was below.

She was half tempted to join him. At least then she might be able to catch her breath, something she'd been struggling without much success to do all day. And that had everything to do with the company gathered and the conversation going on behind her.

She glanced over her shoulder to see if things had changed any in the previous handful of moments. Ruith was still sitting there in front of the hearth with his face buried in his hands whilst his sister sat across from him, looking no less unsettled. Miach was still standing behind Mhorghain's chair with his hands on her shoulders, his expression very grave. Sarah watched Mhorghain reach up and put her hand over one of his briefly, then go back to rubbing her fingers on her knees as if her hands pained her. Perhaps they did, and that seemed to have everything to do with the ring she'd handed Ruith.

The one that had left him with his eyes rolling back in his head as if he'd just witnessed his own death.

Miach had caught him, for the most part, before he'd hit the ground. Ruith had recovered his senses quite quickly, though his color hadn't returned. Miach had taken one side, Mhorghain the other, and they had half carried him the rest of the way to the inn and up the stairs. Sarah had followed them, gingerly bearing a ring that didn't cause her the same distress that it had Ruith but did, she had to admit, leave her feeling slightly uneasy.

She turned back to the window and opened her hand. It lay there, that flat onyx stone set in silver, innocently presenting itself as nothing more than what it seemed to be. Even looking at it, *looking* at it with more than just her natural sight, revealed nothing unusual—which she supposed in itself was unusual. She whispered the spell Soilléir had given her to augment her sight and, to her surprise, she found that she saw nothing more than she'd seen before.

Or . . . perhaps not.

She lifted it up to see if the dull light from the window might aid her, then felt herself beginning to fall into an endless darkness—

"Sarah?"

Sarah jerked herself back from the abyss she had almost pitched into, then hid the ring behind her back. She wasn't sure why she was so unwilling to have anyone see her with it in her hand, but she was.

She looked at the man standing near her and assumed he was a cousin to Ruith and Mhorghain, but she couldn't have said for sure. She attempted a casual expression as she slipped Gair's ring onto her finger. It made her feel slightly ill, so she took it off and wished desperately for some sort of pocket. She couldn't shove the damned thing down her boot and putting it in the purse attached to her belt would have been too conspicuous. All she could do was hold it behind her back and hope she didn't look as panicked as she felt. How Miach had carried it with him for so long she couldn't have said. There might have been nothing to see in its depths, but it definitely possessed a power she could feel pulsing up her arm. Indeed, her arm bearing the wounds left by Gair's spell began to hurt her so badly, she thought she just might have to sit down soon.

She forced herself to focus on her companion, then realized with a start that he did indeed look a bit familiar. She had encountered another man who looked a great deal like him in Slighe at the end of a long, unpleasant afternoon that had come after an equally unsettling journey on the back of a horse-turned-dragon across the plains of Ailean. That man had been Thoir, the youngest son of the crown prince of Tòrr Dòrainn. Sarah would have bet money if she'd had any that the elf standing next to her was one of his brothers. She cleared her throat.

"I believe I've met your brother, Thoir," she ventured.

"And I believe I've met your mother," he said politely.

She was very grateful for a trunk pushed up under the window, conveniently put where she could sit on it abruptly instead of copying Ruith's earlier actions and landing on the floor. The elf sat down next to her just as quickly, as if to spare her any embarrassment, then looked at her gravely.

"Forgive me," he said quietly. "I thought you knew."

"Oh, I know about her," she said faintly, "I just don't know very many people who knew her."

"You might be surprised," he said with a smile. "Of course, I didn't know her well, but I did have the pleasure of encountering her a pair of times at Seanagarra." His smile faded. "I heard tell of her fate, of course, but I had assumed that King Seannair had taken you back home. I begin to think I assumed where I shouldn't have." He smiled briefly. "You needn't elaborate, if you don't care to. I'm nosy by nature and tend to ask questions where I shouldn't. A bad habit I share with Thoir, who is indeed one of my younger brothers."

She started to tell Thoir's brother that she didn't mind talking about her past, but the truth was, she minded it very much. Thinking about who she was rumored to be whilst still feeling herself living quite fully in the skin she'd grown up with . . . well, it was a bit like having a tooth that was perfectly behaved until it encountered the wrong sort of supper and made itself unmistakably known. She was able to carry on as just Sarah, daughter of the witchwoman Seleg and a father she'd didn't know, until she bit down on memories of someone who had known her true parents.

Painful, that's what it was. Painful and unexpected and impossible to either ignore or hope would go away.

"I understand Ruith was lingering in Shettlestoune," the elf said, and he almost managed the last name without a shudder. "Beastly country."

"The worst," she agreed.

"I'm Iarann, by the way, Thoir's elder, much more responsible brother. I can tell you of your mother, if you like. She and Athair visited my grandsire's hall only a pair of times, but they were lengthy stays. Your parents were very welcome guests."

"Ah," Sarah began, because she couldn't say aye but she wasn't sure how to refuse without sounding ungracious. She'd almost decided to plead the excuse of a headache when the door opened and Sìle strode inside. He slammed the door behind him with a curse.

"That ill-mannered, ill-bred, uncouth—" He walked over to the fire and cast himself down into the chair next to Mhorghain. "If I could find a way to toss her off the Council, believe me, I would. Nemed, be a good lad and fetch me some wine."

Sarah shook her head as she watched the blond man who'd come with Mhorghain earlier make Sìle a low bow, then go off to find wine. She couldn't say that she had been particularly giddy as a girl, but she had, with Franciscus's help, learned all the names of the princes of Neroche on the off chance that she might have the opportunity to drop them a curtsey. The thought of actually meeting one of them had never been one she'd ever seriously entertained. Sìle had, the night before, refused to put any of the Neroche lads on the list of noblemen he thought Sarah might want to look over before she made a final decision on Ruith, leaving her laughing at the ridiculousness of the thought. A prince of Neroche not good enough? That she should be considering a liaison with the grandson of the king of the elves was even more difficult to believe.

She suppressed the urge to shift uncomfortably. She was fairly comfortable with Ruith and Miach and, if she were to be completely honest, even King Sìle. If it had been just the three of them, she thought she might have been able to at least make polite conversation. But now there were too many people in the chamber for her comfort, too many souls whose lineage and importance so overshadowed hers that she could scarce look at them. No matter who her parents might have been, she was still an obscure girl from an even more distant village in a country all sensible souls avoided. Associating with creatures from legend and even a pair of the very eligible princes of Neroche as well as the king and future queen of that realm was something she wasn't sure she could ever do with any degree of enjoyment.

It was tempting to see if she could slip down to the kitchens and head out the back door.

She realized with a start that Ruith was looking at her. She was rather glad she was already sitting down, for she would have needed to do so very quickly if she hadn't been. Ruith was every bit as handsome as any of the lads there, but there was something about him that left her feeling a bit weak in the knees. Perhaps it was that in addition to that elvishness that ran through his veins, he had magic to match anyone else in the chamber. If she'd been the sort of gel to admire that sort of thing, which she wasn't sure she was.

Nay, it was more that along with all that magic, he could start a fire without a spell, or feed whoever he was traveling with by his wits alone, or rummage through a stall in an obscure little city in the south and lay his hands upon a pair of knives that had been fashioned years earlier for a dreamweaver whose daughter would subsequently have a use for them.

Or it might have been just because he loved her.

"So, that's how it is."

Sarah had a brief smile from Ruith before he turned to listen— through a haze of pain she could see hovering around his head—to what his grandfather was trying to say to him. Sarah turned to Iarann and found him watching her with a smile.

"How what is?"

"You and Ruith."

Sarah took a deep breath. "We're friends."

Iarann only laughed a little. "Good friends, I would say, but 'tis none of my business. I think your great-great-grandfather Sean-nair might find Ruith almost worthy of you, but then again, he might not. You'll have to ask him when next you meet. Now, whilst my grandfather is voicing his complaints about the illustrious and ill-mannered queen of An-uallach, why don't you distract me with tales of Ruith's bad behavior? I will admit years have passed since I saw him last."

Sarah smiled in spite of herself. "And how did he behave then?"

"He and young Miach of Neroche were, as you may or may not know, troublemakers of the first water. I daresay the only reason they didn't pull Mhorghain into their schemes was that my aunt Sarait kept Mhorghain close to her so she wouldn't run afoul of trouble before her time. Miach and Ruith, however, seemed to find themselves together more times than was good for either of them. And when he was without Miach to spur him on, Ruith spent most of his time either terrorizing the librarian downstairs or fighting in the lists with his brothers."

"With swords?" Sarah asked in surprise.

"Rùnach obliged him as often as he wished with steel," Iarann conceded, "but for the rest, 'twas mostly spells." He paused. "For obvious reasons, I suppose."

Sarah nodded, because she didn't need any explanation. Ruith and his brothers had obviously been trying to prepare themselves to fight their sire. She was only surprised to learn of Rùnach's fondness for steel. How terrible for him, then, to have his hands be so much less than they had been.

"How was it you and Ruith met?" Iarann asked. "Crossing blades or spells?"

Sarah managed a smile. "I have none of the latter and no desire for the former." She started to explain the rest, then hesitated. She had no reason not to trust Iarann, but perhaps Ruith wouldn't want any of his secrets revealed. And the truth was, she found herself having difficulty trusting anyone at the moment.

Well, save Ruith.

"I won't betray you."

She smiled, though it felt pained. "Why would I think you would?"

He chewed on his words for a moment or two. "Because when you're thrust into a world where you don't know the players, you tend to look twice at everyone you meet. Worse still is when you know many of the players and one has betrayed you."

"Or when you're the eldest son of the crown prince of Tòrr Dòrainn and you're watching every shadow?"

"Aye, there is that," he agreed. He paused, then looked at her very seriously. "Though I cannot force you to trust me, I promise you, Sarah of Cothromaiche, that I will never do anything to betray either you or my cousin who sits over there carrying burdens he is loathe to reveal. 'Tis entirely possible that I might have some detail that would aid you."

She looked into his eyes, eyes that had no doubt seen several lifetimes and innumerable betrayals, and saw nothing in them that made her uneasy. She paused again, then glanced at Ruith. This time he was watching her.

He looked impossibly tired. She supposed, watching him as he was watching her and trying to listen to his grandfather at the same time, that they shouldn't spurn whatever help came their way. But there was no sense in not making very clear just what the price of betrayal would be. She smiled briefly at Ruith, then turned to Iarann.

"I don't have any skill with a blade," she said seriously, "nor any spells of death to wield, but I think I would guard that man's back with just my hands if I had to."

Iarann's eyes widened briefly, then he smiled. "Oh, so you're *that* sort of friend."

She shifted uncomfortably. "We're good friends," she conceded, "and I am fonder of him than I like to admit. I also don't know where to turn or whom to trust save Ruith, so I've decided not to trust anyone until I'm sure of them. You aren't interested in Olc, or that sort of thing, are you?"

Iarann's look of revulsion hastily stifled was answer enough.

"I wouldn't sully my soul thus. I'm only sorry Sarait and her children were forced to be witness to any of it."

Sarah supposed that was answer enough. She took a deep breath and took a chance. "We're looking for spells."

"Gair's spells?"

She nodded.

"That's a bit like looking for—how is it they say it in Shettlestoune?—an honestly won guinea in any grubby pocket, isn't it?"

"I hadn't heard that one," Sarah said, smiling in spite of herself, "though I fear it's very accurate."

Iarann leaned back against the edge of the window frame and frowned. "So, is it possible that Gair left all these vile spells in a tidy pile, or . . ."

"Or," she agreed.

Iarann studied his cousin for a bit, then looked at her. "How do you intend to find them?"

"We have a map."

He looked at her in surprise. "Gair left a map? I understood that he never allowed them to leave his person, but perhaps I know less than I think."

"Gair didn't make a map," Sarah admitted. She had to take a deep breath. "I did. Well, I haven't made it yet, but I have it in my head."

Iarann froze. "And how is it, my lady," he said very carefully, "that you know where these things that never should have been written down, much less conceived, lie when my cousin does not?"

Sarah felt the last of her very minor doubts about Ruith's cousin vanish. If Iarann could suspect her—even politely—of nefarious deeds, then perhaps he might be on their side of the battlefield after all.

"I can see them," she admitted. "Where they lie in the Nine Kingdoms."

He blinked in surprise, then a look of profound pity came over his features. "Ah, you poor child." He cleared his throat. "So you've gone from a bucolic existence in the south to accompanying Gair's youngest son on his quest to find spells of pure evil that only you can see."

"Aye."

"And when Ruith gathers them all up, what then?"

"Well, I don't imagine he plans on using them."

"No," Iarann said slowly, "he wouldn't. I think there are many things Ruith might do in this world that would lead elder statesmen to shake their heads, but using his father's spells isn't one of them." He shot her a look. "Do you doubt that?"

She smiled. "He has his faults, I suppose, but the desire to plunge face-first into endless pools of evil isn't one of them."

"Nay, he knows firsthand where that leads." He put his hands on his knees. "Well, I think before you march off into darkness, you should have a decent meal, don't you think?"

"Not in this inn, we won't."

Iarann laughed a little. "I'll see if I can't spell what's brought into edibility. I'm sure the effort will put me in bed for a solid fortnight. Miach's already been complaining about the disgusting nature of the offerings, but he always had a discriminating palate. Then again, once his mother was no longer there to charm his way out of trouble for him, he was relegated by my grandsire to eating in the kitchens. Perhaps he has cause."

Sarah nodded, then watched him go. She supposed she might come to regret no more opportunity to make polite small talk, because it left her thinking about what she'd told Ruith's cousin . . . and what she hadn't.

Such as the fact that the spells were laid out, if she considered their places on a map, in two lines that grew closer together as they carried on north until they converged upon a single point. Or that the spells were covered, strangely enough, with some sort of magic that seemed to enspell anyone who touched it.

Or that she and Ruith had begun to find, in the vicinity of those spells, scraps of another spell, as if there were someone who knew exactly what they were doing and wanted them to know he knew. The list of who that might potentially be was long and varied, ranging from her fool of a brother who wasn't in truth her brother to any one of a clutch of Ruith's bastard brothers.

Or, worse still, what she had left the inn that morning to tell Ruith: that she feared that the spells had begun to move on their own.

Iarann walked over to the hearth and inserted himself loudly into the preparations for lunch. It was a ploy, she could see, to distract others from things they were currently mired in. It seemed to be working less well with Sìle than she supposed Iarann might have hoped. The king of the elves was currently gaping at his granddaughter.

"You brought him *what*?" he asked incredulously.

Mhorghain didn't answer her grandfather. She exchanged a look with Ruith that sent chills down Sarah's spine. It was as if their meeting had been predestined to happen at just such a time and place, as though happenstance had nothing to do with it.

Sarah supposed the conversation carried on, but she couldn't hear it. She was suddenly too distracted by what she saw glinting on the ground thanks to the light from the fire. She remembered the runes that had appeared in the air just before Mhorghain had unspun herself from her wind-like shape, runes of gold and silver that had sparkled with a light of their own. Those runes, or more of them, were no longer in the air but had settled themselves in an orderly circle around her feet.

What lay around Ruith's feet were thorns.

Or, rather, thorns that were trying to intertwine themselves with the Fadaire that was suddenly swirling around him, as if it had been a shield, perhaps created by his own magic even. She quickly looked at Ruith's face, but he was too busy arguing with his grandfather to see what was trying to wrap itself around him.

She realized with an equal amount of alarm that there were thorns wrapped around her wrist, because she could feel them. She pulled her hand from behind her back and looked down. They were rooted in Gair's ring, rooted so deeply that she couldn't begin to ascertain where they began. All she knew was that they ended around her wrist.

She looked up and found Ruith watching her. He pulled a chair up next to him and held out his hand toward her.

She hesitated. She had once told him that she wouldn't have anything to do with him of a more romantic nature until he'd at least chatted with ten princesses. He had wended his way with shocking dishonesty down to one, then announced he was finished with the exercise. In return, she had demanded ten instances where she might get out of uncomfortable state suppers. He'd given her three and she thought she might have already used one in Buid-seachd. She was tempted to use another at the moment so she could go hide and stay out of sight, but if she did she would have only one left, which might leave her in terrible straits at some point in the future.

And the truth was, she was very fond of Ruith. If he wanted her to come and sit next to him in that company full of kings, princes, and a princess, she was a fool to resist. No matter what lay entwined about his feet and what she could feel wrapping itself around her wrist.

She had the sinking feeling that there was more to Gair's ring than either of them knew and that escaping its effects until it had served its purpose was going to be impossible. If only she knew a spell of containment, or had the power to use it . . .

She pushed the thought aside, because it didn't serve her to entertain it. She put Gair's ring on her finger, closed her hand around it so it wouldn't be seen, then rose. She walked across the chamber and sat down next to Ruith, ignoring spells and thorns that cut into her, and hoped she might find some sort of distraction in the conversation there. She would perhaps tell Ruith about what she'd seen the spells doing when they had a moment of privacy.

But she wouldn't tell him anything else about his father's ring.

Five

R uith hovered at the back of the chamber, restless and uneasy. Whilst he'd been very happy to see his sister and sit with Sarah for a bit in front of the fire, he simply couldn't discuss his plans any longer.

No one else seemed to share his unease. He stopped just outside the light cast by the fire in the hearth and looked at his grandfather and Miach grimacing over the wine that had been sent as refreshments and arguing companionably about what produced a more drinkable vintage, the vineyards on the lush rolling hills of Penrhyn or the exposed, rocky outcroppings of Ainneamh's most southern border. He preferred either cold water from a pure stream or something from Franciscus's kegs, but the others were welcome to their discussion. It was such a normal, everyday thing—to sit before a fire and critique the wine—that he wished he could join in and forget why he was where he was and what he faced.

Or he could have perhaps distracted himself with the sight of the other souls in the chamber, a collection of persons he'd never imagined he would see again alone much less together. He wanted to gape at his sister, but since he'd spent the majority of the morning doing just that, he supposed she might want a bit of relief from his scrutiny, so he looked elsewhere.

His cousin Iarann hadn't changed, but he wouldn't have expected that. Ruith honestly had no idea how old he was, or why he hadn't found himself a wife already and fashioned a dozen sons between them. He was Làidir's eldest, so one would have thought his father would have put pressure on him to produce a few heirs. Then again, Iarann's youngest brother Thoir couldn't enter a room that he didn't immediately draw every gel in it to him, so perhaps Iarann was simply waiting for the time when Thoir was otherwise occupied to go find himself a woman to love.

Miach's older brother Nemed, who was masquerading as Mhorghain's guardsman, had most assuredly changed over the years. Ruith wasn't sure he would have recognized him if he'd seen him walking down the street. At least Mansourah was still out scouting. Sìle had complained loudly about his arrows in the side of his stables, but then again Mansourah had been famous for shooting arrows into all sorts of things that inspired outrage.

Nemed was older, but Ruith suspected no different in either temperament or interests. It was rumored that he could weave melodies in the wind that would leave dreamweavers weeping, though Ruith suspected that rumor had been started by Nemed himself.

He looked at Miach, who was, it should have been noted, sitting far closer to Mhorghain than was polite. Who would have thought that a nine-year-old whose only passion had been unearthing an impolite number of spells from wherever their owners had hidden them would not only live to manhood but apparently make something useful of himself?

Ruith considered the last time he'd seen Miach at Seanagarra. They had spent the morning in his grandfather's library, breathlessly memorizing spells whilst hiding under a table. He'd looked up and found his mother and Desdhemar of Neroche sitting by the fire, talking in hushed voices. At the time, he'd assumed they'd been mourning the fact that they'd been thwarted in what he could readily admit was an admirable search for the obscure and useful. Having been on his own hunt, he had understood that very well.

Now, though, looking back on the memory as a man, he was fairly sure those had been not tears of frustration, but rather the tears of two lifelong friends who realized that one of them was about to step into a place she might not emerge from.

He wondered if Queen Desdhemar had had any idea, sitting with his mother who was facing a certain trip into darkness, that she would be soon taking her own journey to a place where she would give her life for her child.

And now that child of Desdhemar and Anghmar of Neroche had earned himself a crown on his head that he likely never wore and runes around his wrist that sparkled faintly in the firelight when he reached out and took the hand of the woman he loved.

Ruith sighed in spite of himself. Obviously there was nothing he could do to stop his sister from shackling herself to Miach. If Sìle of Tòrr Dòrainn could unbend far enough to give a grudging blessing to the upcoming union, Ruith supposed he couldn't withhold it. Besides, he had the distinct feeling his sister wasn't going to listen to him long enough to have him change her mind.

It was a little startling to look at her and realize he was looking at his sister and not his mother. But she wasn't his mother. She was much as she had been, if he could venture an opinion, at the tender age of six. Fiercely determined, terribly brave, ready to pick up a sword of any type and defend whichever brother needed defending against another. Ruith could bring to mind several times when he'd found himself standing behind his wee sister as she brandished whatever makeshift weapon she'd had to hand against Gille or Brogach when they'd been after him about spending too much time looking for spells and not enough time practicing the ones he'd already known.

He sighed, then turned his mind to much less comfortable things, namely to what Mhorghain had tried to hand him earlier that morning.

An onyx ring set in silver.

It was his sire's ring, that ring of silver that never tarnished that he had taken from Sarah's hands a pair of hours earlier and was currently keeping in his pocket. Ruith had never seen his sire without it on his finger. In fact, the last time he'd seen it was on his father's hand as he'd had that hand stretched up toward the heavens, grasping for that towering geyser of evil he'd unleashed.

Ruith supposed that perhaps his sire had fallen, rapped his head smartly against the stone of the well, and lain senseless long enough for the mercenaries who had rescued Mhorghain to slide it off his finger. Those lads had obviously been wise ones, for they'd deposited the ring along with Mhorghain herself on Nicholas of Lismòr's front stoop, apparently happier to rid themselves of the ring than the gel. Nicholas had no doubt recognized it immediately, having been a friend of Gair's for centuries. According to Mhorghain, Nicholas had given her the ring several se'nnights ago to convince her of the parentage she hadn't remembered.

Ruith couldn't deny that he envied her that forgetting, if only in regard to their father. There were several recent events—well, only one, actually—that he would have happily forgotten, namely his having been so horrified at seeing that ring again that he'd promptly fainted.

Miach had endeavored to save his pride after he'd slapped him back awake by pointing out to both Mhorghain and Sarah that he had thrown more disgusting spells at Ruith than was polite already that morning and that he couldn't blame him for surrendering to a well-deserved swoon of aversion. Mhorghain had only put her arms around Ruith and held on to him, matching his trembling more thoroughly than he would have thought possible.

It was more than a little strange to think he now had two siblings with whom to discuss his memories of his youth. Not that Mhorghain would remember all that much perhaps, but she might have a detail or two to aid him in his quest.

Mhorghain had told him that when Nicholas of Lismòr had shown her that ring, she'd had a slightly more violent reaction, going so far as to say that the only reason Miach lived still was that he'd rid her of all her weapons first.

Ruith had wished that the damned thing had been lost down the well, truth be told.

He woke from his reverie to find Sarah sitting in a chair nearest the fire, wincing as she brushed her arm against the wood of the chair. Sìle leaned forward.

"Sarah, my dear, you've hidden that away long enough." He took her hand gently in both his own and lifted her sleeve away from her flesh. "Tell me again how you came by this?"

Ruith shrugged helplessly at the look Sarah quickly threw his way. There was no hiding the truth of what had happened to her. She took a deep breath, then looked at his grandfather.

"I touched one of the pages of Gair's book," she said with the slightest of shudders. "It leapt up and wrapped itself around my arm."

Sìle stared at her for a moment, then looked at Ruith. "And what caused yours?"

Ruith looked down at his hand where only the ending trails of the same sort of wound could possibly have been seen, though given that he'd earned them in a dream, they shouldn't have been visible at all. He looked at his grandfather. "I touched the same thing, only in a dream."

Sìle pursed his lips. "I'm not sure, lad, that I can do anything for you. But tell me what's been tried with your lady and we'll hope for more success."

"I tried a healing spell of Camanaë, as did Sgath," Ruith said with a sigh, "but to no avail. Soilléir attempted a change of essence, but that only caused the lines to fade. There is something in the wound that will not give up the hold it has on her."

Sìle studied the black trails that were edged with red, then looked at Miach. "I believe, my boy, that I will try Fadaire. You may as well add a bit of your power to mine, if you think you can do it with any finesse."

Mhorghain shifted uncomfortable. "I'd rethink that, Grandfather, and it isn't his finesse I would worry about."

Sìle lifted an eyebrow. "I believe, missy, that you've acquired an overly inflated opinion of your betrothed's strength and forgotten about mine."

Mhorghain leaned over and embraced him briefly. "I haven't, Grandfather, nor have I forgotten who you are. Miach, take my seat. I'll catch whoever first feels as though half the Sgùrrachs have been dropped atop him."

Miach laughed uneasily and traded spots with her. Ruith supposed he would be wise to make certain Sarah wasn't the one to hit the floor first. He had a fair idea of what his grandfather could do, and he could guess, based on time spent sparring with him, just what Miach was capable of. He stood behind Sarah's chair and put his hands on her shoulders. Sìle shot Miach a look.

"Gently," he stressed.

"Of course, Your Grace."

"We'll try removing the evil first, then heal the wounds," Sìle said. He bent over Sarah's hand, then shook his head. "There are things there I cannot see clearly, but we'll make the attempt anyway." He smiled briefly at Sarah. "This won't hurt, Sarah, my dear."

"I'm not afraid, Your Majesty," Sarah said.

Ruith imagined she was, but she was the sort of gel not to admit it. He squeezed her hand, then held his breath whilst his grandfather wove his spell over her arm. It was an eminently functional Fadarian spell of healing. Ruith was sure his grandfather had used it countless times over the course of his life to great effect.

Sìle paused just before he spoke the last word and looked at Miach. Miach took a deep breath, let it out slowly, then put his hands over the king's and spoke the last word with him.

Sarah squeaked. Ruith caught her only because he'd been expecting the like. He kept hold of her, then lifted her up in his arms and sat down in her chair with her. She was, as he'd suspected she would be, completely senseless.

Sìle looked at Miach and rubbed his forehead crossly. "Damn you, boy, when will you learn to have a care for those you're aiding?"

Miach smiled briefly. "I'm working on that, Your Majesty." He took Sarah's hand from Sìle and frowned at it thoughtfully before he looked at Ruith. "What did you say you'd tried before?"

"Camanaë," Ruith said. "Soilléir used spells of healing and containment in Caochladh, but they made little difference. Well, the spell of containment took the red away for a bit, but even that proved unequal to the task of removing the true hurt."

Miach considered for a moment or two, then looked at Iarann. "I believe I will try that myself, but not alone. If you would aid me, Your Highness?"

Iarann smiled. "I'm flattered."

"Don't be," Ruith said. "He just wants you for your magic, and Miach, you've gone this long without using any of Soilléir's spells. You may as well go a bit longer. I'll do it."

"How?" Miach asked pointedly. "It isn't as if you know any of his spells."

"I know three of them, thank you, and am not above using them when necessary. I think Soilléir was very proud of you that you'd been so discreet. He never held out any hope for me in the matter."

Miach considered him for a moment or two in silence. "You'll be sorry you did this," he said slowly, "when you have no strength for the next fortnight."

"Am I to simply allow Sarah to flinch every time she brushes her skin against something?" Ruith said. "One spell, with your power behind mine. How much can that possibly take out of me?"

"I wouldn't ask," Mhorghain said pointedly. "I would lay Sarah down somewhere so when you fall over in a faint she won't land on the floor as well."

Ruith nodded, because Mhorghain was right. He laid Sarah on a blanket near the fire, then knelt near Sarah's right hand. He glanced at the very grave-looking king of Neroche, who knelt gingerly on the other side of her. "Don't kill me."

"I'll try not to."

"Don't believe him," Mhorghain said with a shiver. "He's overly modest about his abilities."

Ruith only had a smile from Miach before he turned his attentions to the task at hand.

He had to admit, if he could have been permitted a moment of unease, that there was something about the thought of using one of Soilléir of Cothromaiche's spells that gave him pause. Spells of essence changing were . . . well, they were so damned permanent. He had no qualms about binding someone who deserved it with invisible cords that could eventually be unraveled, or changing a ruffian temporarily into a mouse and watching him scamper off from all predators, or entertaining himself with thoughts of any of his bastard brothers serving however briefly as a footstool. Turning a fool into a rock, though, and knowing that fool would remain a rock for the rest of eternity was something else entirely. If he wove a spell that changed Sarah's flesh into something else and wove it badly, the damage would be terrible. And permanent.

He took a deep breath. Whatever he intended to do could be no worse than what Sarah endured already. Even if all he managed was to purchase a few days of ease for her, it would be worth the risk.

He considered the words of the spell he intended to use a final time, then began to weave it under his breath. He was fairly confident he would find it nothing more than the usual bit of magic under his hands.

And so it seemed, for a moment or two.

And then he realized he was dealing with something entirely beyond his scope of experience.

He could see the words hanging in the air as he breathed them out, waiting for their full complement to join them before they marched downward toward Sarah's arm. If he'd expected them to aggressively seek out what they were to contain, he would have been wrong. They very carefully and gently flanked the redness that had spread from the remains of Gair's spell on her skin and gathered it into an exceedingly fine line.

And then they set up a perimeter that could not be breached.

Ruith saw where Soilléir's spell wrought in Buidseachd had done the same thing, for there, visible to Ruith only through the filter of Caochladh, were the battle lines Soilléir's spell had drawn before. Ruith frowned. So, it wasn't that Soilléir's spell hadn't worked as it should have, it was that whatever was buried in Sarah's arm was continually mounting new assaults.

As if it had a mind of its own.

Ruith shook aside the absolute horror of that thought and watched as the last particle of the spell fell into place.

Sarah sighed.

Ruith couldn't have agreed more. He felt as if he'd run for days without end. He bowed his head for several moments to catch his breath, then looked at Miach in surprise.

"I forgot to ask you for aid."

"I didn't think you needed it," Miach said with a faint smile, "or I would have offered it."

Ruith took a deep breath and shook off his weariness. He imagined he wouldn't manage the feat overlong, but he would carry on for as long as he could just the same. He yawned suddenly and rubbed his hands over his face.

"I need either a walk or a nap," he said wearily.

"Let's go fetch more wine," Mhorghain said, rising suddenly.

Miach looked up at her calmly. "Not without a guard."

Mhorghain rolled her eyes. "I'll take my brother. He'll snarl at anyone who tries to vex me."

"Not in his current condition he won't," Miach said seriously. "I think, my love—"

Ruith supposed Miach and Mhorghain would have found much to discuss if they hadn't been interrupted by Mansourah suddenly regrouping himself in front of the fire. Or, rather, in the fire. He stumbled out of the hearth, leapt over Sarah, then patted himself frantically. Sìle rose and stamped out a few stray sparks, then shot Miach's brother a disgruntled look.

"You could have knocked."

Mansourah shivered. "Forgive me, Your Majesty, I didn't think."

"There are several unpatchable holes in the wood of my very fine stables that could vouch for that same flaw," Sìle grumbled as he resumed his seat. "You can see to them if I let you through my gates for my Mhorghain's wedding to your youngest brother. Iarann, move our sweet Sarah a bit and stand guard over her. Now, Mansourah, I can see you have been about a useful labor for a change. What have you seen?"

Mansourah set aside his bow and quiver, then accepted a cup of wine from Nemed. "Thank you, Nem," he said, then gulped a bit of it down before he managed anything further. "I will start by say-ing that whilst I saw nothing out of the ordinary, I didn't like the feel of the air."

"Too cold for his delicate backside, no doubt," Nemed said plac-idly.

Ruith suppressed a smile at the slap against the back of the head Mansourah delivered without looking at his brother, though his amusement hardly made up for the chill he felt sliding down his spine at Mansourah's words, expected though they had been. He didn't doubt there was at least one someone watching the inn. For all he knew, there were several someones. He imagined he would be damned fortunate if he didn't encounter the lot of them a quar-ter hour after he walked out the front door.

"It wasn't that," Mansourah said pointedly, "though I thank you for your concern, brother." He looked at Ruith. "Something watches the inn. I have no gift of sight past how to place an arrow where I want it to go, so perhaps I'm not the best one to judge such things."

"In my bloody barn," Sìle groused, "again, but we'll leave that for now. Was the lad well hidden?"

"Very," Mansourah said, "in the forest behind bits of spell, vague but assuredly there, that were cast about purposely to deceive and distract." He paused. "They were fashioned from Olc."

Ruith sighed and looked at Sarah to find she was now sitting up, watching him. He admired her resilience in recovering so quickly from that piece of magic he'd used. He wished he could say the same for himself.

He had no trouble reading her thoughts. The longer they stayed, the more danger they would put not only themselves but the rest of the company in. He looked at his grandfather.

"Perhaps we might be best served to slip through the kitchens whilst whoever—and however many of them there are—is watching us could possibly be distracted by watching other things," he said.

Sìle sighed gustily. "Very well, I shall send word to Morag and request her company for a formal supper tonight. If she thinks all will be in attendance—including you and Sarah, Ruith, if perhaps she won't be looking for you to leave this afternoon." He paused. "If you think 'tis she who watches the inn. Though I suppose it might easily be someone else."

And Ruith supposed the list could be long and the characters on it unsavory in the extreme. Morag would have been first, followed by Droch of Saothair if he could have been persuaded to leave his comfortable roost at the schools of wizardry, Droch's brother Urchaid, who wouldn't have been caught dead within a hundred leagues of his brother but might value quite highly a collection of Gair of Ceangail's spells, and last but not least, any number of his own bastard brothers who had their own reasons for wanting their natural father's life's work.

He rubbed his fingers over his forehead, trying to contain the pounding. "I'm not sure who—"

"I imagine you are," Sìle countered briskly, "and I believe it might be useful for us to know who those souls are you don't want to tell us about. That way, we might be able to eliminate a few possibilities for you."

Ruith looked at his grandfather blearily. "Would you?"

"Of course, I would," Sìle said without hesitation. "Nemed, see to more wine whilst Ruith makes his list. Sarah, my dear, how are you feeling?"

Ruith watched Sarah chat quietly with his grandfather for a moment or two, then rise to go rummage about in her pack for what he hoped might be herbs to ease his head. She didn't seem to be favoring her arm as much, so perhaps the spell had been worth the price. But if a spell of essence changing couldn't rid her of the aftereffects of touching his father's spell, what could?

He honestly wasn't sure he wanted to know.

Instead, he accepted parchment and ink conjured up by some

enterprising relation or almost-relation and set to making his list. It was easier than thinking on Sarah's arm, their quest, or who was lying in wait for them outside.

Because he was very afraid that someone might be a soul he hadn't dared consider.

Six

❈

S arah put away the herbs she'd used to brew Ruith a bit of tea, then looked at the rest of the contents of her pack placed in tidy piles under the window. She had things one might eat in a pinch on a long journey as well as a bit of cream-colored roving that was softer than anything she'd ever felt in her life. The only other things of value she had were a bit of wool, a pair of knitting needles, and a collection of books she couldn't bring herself to open at the moment.

She started to pack everything away, then looked at the spindle still lying next to her. It was cunningly carved, true enough, but it had been given to her by the king of the dwarves, so perhaps that told her all she needed to know about it. She touched the hidden lever she'd been shown and the wooden length of the spindle sprang away from the whorl to reveal a slim, terribly lethal-looking dagger. *Very handy for a weaver in a tight spot,* King Uachdaran had told her with obvious delight as he'd handed it to her.

He'd also told her she could spin all sorts of things she wouldn't expect with that spindle, but she hadn't had time to ask him what he'd meant by that.

She was tempted at the moment to try her hand at the whisper-soft roving Ruith's brother Rùnach had provided her, but that seemed a little frivolous considering the seriousness of the conversation that was going on over by the fire.

Well, perhaps calling it a conversation was putting a bit of gloss on it that it didn't deserve. It was a rather lively—and she used that term loosely—discussion about Ruith's plans for the future.

She repacked her gear quickly, ignoring what she was hearing, then set her pack aside. She took a deep breath, then pushed herself to her feet so she could look out of the window. The scene was much as it had been earlier that morning. The owl she'd seen earlier was still perched there in the tree above the stables, no doubt continuing to take the healthful air, and the sky was still full of clouds. Only now, she forced herself to take a closer look at the forest beyond that stable, to see if she could make out any untoward spells. Or, more importantly, who might be laying them there in the boughs of those mist-topped trees—

She jumped at the touch of a hand on her arm, but it was only Iarann.

"You shouldn't be standing here," he said quietly. "Not in the open."

She couldn't deny that he had a point, but she was also not enthusiastic about giving up any of the light the window provided. She didn't argue with him when he pushed the shutters to. At least he was kind enough to set a dozen recently created candles alight. He offered her a seat, but she shook her head quickly. She wouldn't pace in front of the window, but she couldn't bring herself to sit.

She looked at Ruith. He was grey, though she supposed that since she still felt as if he'd dropped a load of bricks on her, it was entirely possible he was feeling the aftereffects of wielding that magic himself. He was watching Miach's brothers argue over the list he'd provided of souls who might have wanted Gair's spells. Nemed looked over that list, handed it to Mansourah, then sat back with a sigh.

"Unpleasant," he said.

"And no doubt incomplete," Mansourah said, shooting Ruith a look. "As I said before."

Ruith blew the hair out of his eyes. "Then let's begin again with those sitting here. I think I can almost guarantee that I have no stomach for wielding my father's spells. I also think I can safely say that neither Sarah nor Mhorghain would be likewise tempted."

Sarah found the eyes of all on her, so she held up her hands quickly. "I couldn't use them if I had them."

Ruith looked at his sister who shook her head slowly, then he looked at Miach. "And you, Your Majesty?"

Miach tapped his forehead. "I already have them all here I'm very sorry to say, thanks to an unpleasant conversation with your brother Keir. As for my brothers—" He looked at Mansourah and Nemed, had a sharp shake of two heads in return, then turned back to Ruith and shrugged. "I think we can safely exclude all in this chamber, for your grandfather and cousin, I imagine, have neither the need nor the desire to possess them."

Iarann shuddered. "I wouldn't have them if they were all that stood between me and saving the world from destruction." He started to speak, then paused. "And forgive me for going back to this yet again, Ruith, but it seems to me that for most mages, those spells would be rather dangerous. I've heard they have minds of their own and take a great amount of power to use. Who would dare attempt it?"

"Lothar, for one," Miach said without hesitation, "but thankfully he's safely ensconced in Gobhann. Wehr of Wrekin might have found them to his liking, but he's almost assuredly dead.

Droch would have them gladly, and the thought of what he would do with them makes me very nervous indeed."

"Add his other brothers to that list," Nemed said, "if he has any of them left, which I doubt."

"Urchaid is alive and well," Ruith said with a sigh. "Or he was a fortnight ago."

"Was he?" Miach asked in surprise. He frowned thoughtfully. "His power isn't insignificant, but he's not likely now to be anywhere where Droch might find him." He looked at Ruith seriously. "And as unpleasant as this is, I think you should consider your father's other sons. I would only be surprised to learn they aren't already looking for his spells. Perhaps you should consider them whilst planning your route lest you find them waiting for you at a most inopportune spot."

Sarah suppressed a shiver. She had already encountered Ruith's bastard brothers and had no desire to meet them again. Ruith looked at her and smiled grimly, as if he understood exactly what she was thinking, then he turned to Miach again.

"They can't see the spells," he said wearily, "nor can Droch, for that matter, so they'll have no idea where we're making for. Even if Droch knew, his paltry scraps of power would not be equal to using my father's most treasured pieces of magic."

Miach laughed, apparently in spite of himself. "I don't think he would appreciate that assessment of his skill."

"He didn't," Ruith said, "but I felt I had no choice but to tell him as much when Sarah and I saw him at Buidseachd. Fortunately, Soilléir rescued the both of us—and more than once, as it happened."

"Good of him," Sìle said gruffly.

Ruith smiled at his grandfather. "Since he has so little to do to occupy his time, I didn't consider it an imposition. As for Droch finding my sire's spells—" He looked back at Miach. "I fear that effort would necessitate Droch's leaving his very comfortable nest at Buidseachd. The lack of adulation and terror inspired by venturing forth from his well-stocked larder wouldn't be worth the effort."

"What of the queen of An-uallach, who has already tried to slay your beloved?" Nemed asked pointedly.

Ruith sighed deeply. "Morag wants more than just the spells, but there is little use in thinking on it. The truth is, it matters very little who might make use, even poorly, of those spells. I must gather them up, then destroy them. Anyone who found them would wreak more havoc on the world that I can bear to watch."

Mansourah leaned back against his chair and folded his arms over his chest. "Perhaps I missed this part of the conversation, but how is it you intend to find them? Surely you have no more idea where they lay than anyone else. Do you intend to walk blindly into the dark—"

"Not blindly." Sarah realized she'd interrupted him only because she saw the words hanging there in the firelight, as if they'd been spider webs, fragile and easily destroyed. The company seated in front of the fire turned as one to look at her. She cleared her throat and tried again. "I can see the spells."

Sìle's face was full of pity, as was Iarann's, for they already knew that, as did Miach. The rest were looking at her with varying degrees of surprise. All save Ruith. He simply looked greyer than before, if possible. But they'd already had all the discussion about her part in the quest she imagined he was willing to have. He didn't want her to come.

But he knew he had no choice but to allow her to.

Mansourah looked at Ruith in surprise. "Surely you don't intend to walk into the darkness with Sarah and no one to guard your backs."

Ruith shook his head. "We have aid, though the quality of it could perhaps be called into question. We encountered Thoir wandering about with Ardan of Ainneamh whilst we were in

Slighe looking for our former companions. They don't know our errand, of course, but they were willing to bring us tidings—"

"And just what was my brother doing with that pompous arse?" Iarann asked sharply.

"They were off gathering information for their respective fathers, or so they claimed," Ruith said. "I'm sorry to say this, but I don't trust Ardan as far as I can throw him, which isn't far. He's going to burst the seams of his very finely wrought tunics if he doesn't push away from table sooner than he has been. I didn't tell them what I was looking for specifically, just that we were seeking tidings about things amiss in the world."

"Ardan will find ample material there," Iarann said with a snort, "given that nothing pleases him. Very well, so you have at least two on your side—well, let's not give credit where it isn't due—*one* on your side, that being my brother. I'm not sure that inspires confidence."

Miach cleared his throat. "Nay, but perhaps making a few extra preparations would. Perhaps, Prince Iarann, you could add to Ruith's list by naming all the bastard brothers he should make sure aren't following him. Mhorghain and I will write down which spells we remember Keir having told us—not the spells themselves, of course, but which ones they were—and perhaps Sarah would care to make Ruith a map of where she's seen the spells." He glanced at Ruith. "On the off chance you change your mind in the end about taking her with you."

Ruith's color hadn't improved and Miach's words didn't add to that. "You, my friend, would know, I believe, what it is to take your lady to a place where you wouldn't lead your worst enemy."

"But his lady had her own quest," Mhorghain said pointedly. "One I could not turn away from. I daresay Sarah feels the same way."

Sarah found Ruith's sister looking at her. She nodded, because she agreed with her. Mhorghain's task had been to shut Gair's well. Her task was no less daunting, at least to her, but it was one only she could manage.

She smiled briefly at Mhorghain, then busied herself tidying up luncheon dishes that had already been put on a table just inside the door, because it took her mind off what she was attempting to not listen to. She reached for a pewter cup, then paused when she caught sight of her arm.

She had to admit that whatever Ruith had done had definitely improved things, though the magic had left her feeling as if she'd been dropped off the parapet of Buidseachd. If she closed her eyes, she still had the feeling of falling she'd enjoyed when Sìle's spell on her arm had pulled the world from under her feet. The only thing she thought she could say for the experience was that she'd felt as if she were falling into a lake made up entirely of Fadaire. If she'd had to land somewhere, there was no sense in not landing there.

"I still don't like the thought of leaving you two to face Morag of An-uallach," Sìle said in a low voice. "Especially Sarah."

Sarah turned to find him looking at Ruith, his expression very grim. Ruith didn't look any better than he had, but perhaps that had to do with whatever magic he'd used. She cleared her throat carefully. "I have nothing she could possibly want."

Sìle looked at her with pity. "Sarah, my dear, you are not simply a village witch's daughter, regardless of how long you considered yourself such. And no matter how loudly you tell her, Morag will never believe you don't have magic she might have for her own with enough effort. And," he added, looking at Ruith, "I feel strongly that it isn't wise for the two of you to simply roam about without a guard. Morag might not be able to shapechange, but she has very powerful magic. And I fear she might be the least of those who may eventually find you."

Sarah watched glances be exchanged. She would have found it

an interesting exercise at another time, watching those who had known each other either for centuries or in a different locale discuss things without words, but not at the moment. She had been in Morag's sights more than once and had no desire to be there again. It was enough to be forced to search for Gair's spells. Having to look over her shoulder for a murderous queen was almost more than she could bear to think on.

Never mind who else might be looking for them.

Finally, it came down to Miach and Sìle indulging in a wordless conversation before Miach took a slight breath, let it out, then looked at Ruith.

"Iarann could come with you—"

"Ridiculous," Ruith interrupted with a snort. "The eldest son of the crown prince of Tòrr Dòrainn?"

"Then Nemed—"

"I'll go."

Sarah looked up to find that Mansourah had spoken. He looked at Ruith, then folded his arms over his chest in a way that said he'd spent his share of time arguing with brothers about various things and found that physical intimidation worked the best.

Nemed sighed gustily. "You're daft. You don't have—"

"Your magic," Mansourah finished for him. "Aye, I know that. I don't have magic to equal any of you, to Mother's eternal dismay, which is why she and Father were kind enough to teach me other things." He looked at Ruith. "I can at least scout for you. And conjure up a bit of werelight if necessary. And stand behind you and look fierce if absolutely necessary."

Sarah watched Ruith look up at a man who, his deprecating words aside, was a prince of Neroche and likely had much more magic than he was claiming. Ruith was silent for several very long moments, then he frowned.

"You might miss the wedding."

"I was there for my brother's crowning," Mansourah said with a shrug. "I think he can do without me for the next occasion of state."

Ruith considered a bit longer. "I'll think on it," he said finally. "I can't say we wouldn't be grateful for the extra pair of eyes."

Sarah couldn't decide if Ruith was happy about the situation or not, but she knew he wasn't happy when the conversation returned to the making of a map.

"We don't need one," he protested. "I have it memorized."

"And if something happens to you?" Miach asked pointedly.

"Then Sarah knows where to go."

Miach looked at him in silence for a moment or two. "And if something happens to Sarah?"

Ruith closed his eyes briefly, then blew out his breath. "Very well, make the damned map. I'll keep it down the side of my boot where that sort of thing goes."

Nemed rose. "I'll see to it."

"I'm the better cartographer," Mansourah said.

"You couldn't draw your way to the nearest full keg of ale," Nemed said with a snort. "Come with me, Sarah, and we'll have this unpleasant business over with as soon as may be. I'd like to discuss the state of your family tree before Mansourah starts rattling the branches. Do you have any cousins?"

Ruith caught Nemed by the arm. "I'll give you the locations—"

"Nay," Sarah said, though she feared it had come out as more of a croak than anything else, "I can." She smiled at Ruith. "I'm fine. Truly."

He hesitated. He continued to hesitate until she shooed him off and turned her back on him. She knew he didn't believe her. She didn't believe herself. The thought of having to think about, much less mark down, where Gair's spells resided was enough to turn her stomach. But the sooner 'twas done, the sooner she could think about other, more pleasant things.

Though she wasn't sure at the moment what those might be.

She took the chair Nemed offered her at the table he pushed under the window. She supposed that since he'd opened the shutters only far enough to let in a small bit of light they were safe. He conjured up pen and paper, then looked at her.

"The entire Nine Kingdoms?" he asked.

"You might as well," she said, "though I don't think the spells are south of us. Well," she amended, "I didn't see them there when I marked them on King Uachdaran's map."

"I can scarce believe he allowed Ruith anywhere near his solar," Nemed said with a faint smile.

"Ruith was on his best behavior."

"Oh, I imagine the king was being polite as well," Nemed said with a bit of a laugh, "not for Ruith's sake. He and Miach were only there once as lads, but I understand they made quite an impression. My mother sent numerous gifts after the fact, to soothe the king's offended pride, but I think it was some time before even she dared a visit, despite her immense amount of charm."

"He did grumble at Ruith at first," Sarah admitted, "and he spent perhaps more time with him in his lists than necessary. I'm not sure it was entirely altruistic."

"I imagine it wasn't," Nemed agreed. "I also imagine he favored you two with a meal or two simply for your sake. He and Seannair of Cothromaiche are very old friends."

Sarah wondered if the day would come when she wouldn't find herself winded by those sorts of revelations. "Are they," she managed. "I didn't know."

"I imagine he didn't tell you," Nemed said. "He's not much for chatting, that dwarvish king. But if he allowed you in his solar, especially given the company you were keeping, you might count it as a very great honor. I think my mother managed the feat a pair of times, but I doubt he left her there alone."

"I suppose that's where your brother learned his, ah—"

"Craft of poaching spells?" Nemed finished. "Aye, I daresay it was. I can't say Princess Sarait was any less devious, so you can imagine the things she taught Ruith."

She nodded, and the thought of mothers unable to see how their children had grown caught at her heart in a particularly painful way—

"I, on the other hand, have never seen the inside of King Uachdaran's solar," Nemed said, interrupting her thoughts, "though I have often traveled to Léige to guard whatever cloth and necessaries first my mother, then Miach and my now eldest brother Cathar have sent over the years, but I'm generally confined to the formal hall. If I can dredge up a satisfactory ballad or two, His Majesty will feed me in the kitchens."

Sarah smiled. "I'm sure he's teasing you."

Nemed pursed his lips. "He isn't, so consider yourself more fortunate than I've been. You think on that good fortune whilst I'm about this work here."

Sarah considered that, then watched the Nine Kingdoms come to life beneath Nemed's hand. She didn't want to think about the same sort of map she'd seen in King Uachdaran's solar, but she couldn't help herself. It was difficult to deny what she could see when the little pinpoints of light began to hover over the map where she knew Gair's spells lay.

If she did nothing else that day, she would use that spell Soilléir had given her to turn off her sight. Even if it only lasted for a few hours, that would be a relief.

She quickly told Nemed where to put marks indicating spells—including where the two spells had moved to—then turned away before she had to look any longer.

"Sarah?"

She realized, with a start, that Ruith was holding on to her arms. She frowned up at him. "What?"

"You looked as if you might faint."

"I never faint," she blustered, purposely ignoring the fact that when Sìle had attempted to heal her arm she had promptly fallen out of her chair. She supposed the only reason she hadn't landed on the floor had been because Ruith had caught her.

"What is it?"

She pointed toward the map. "Look at that and tell me what you think."

Ruith released her, then looked over Nemed's shoulder. He studied the map for a moment or two, then blinked in surprise. He looked at her sharply. "Am I mistaken in what I'm seeing?"

She shook her head. "I noticed it this morning. It's what I came to tell you whilst you and Miach were training."

He put both hands on the table, apparently to hold himself upright. "There are a pair of those that aren't where you marked them previously." He paused. "Unless we were mistaken in Léige as to their location."

She shook her head. "I have no pride to save in this, Ruith. I marked the spells in the king's solar exactly where I saw them. And aye, they have indeed moved."

"On their own?" Nemed asked in surprise.

Ruith shrugged. "I'm not sure how that's possible. I imagine someone is finding them." He looked at Sarah. "And carrying them off to have a closer look at them, perhaps."

She thought about the strange light that had come into her brother's eye that morning in Doìre when he'd looked at the half of one of Gair's spells he'd had on his table. It wouldn't have surprised her if others were finding the spells. It would have surprised her even less to learn that they'd picked up those spells and found themselves unable to release them.

"Then you'd best hurry before those mages run off with them where you can't follow," Nemed said.

Ruith nodded, then looked at his grandfather who had come to stand next to him. "I think perhaps we should leave now, if you could convince Morag to advance her supper schedule."

Sìle sighed deeply. "I will, of course. And I'll say this one last time: if I could retrace my steps, I would have killed Gair the first time I clapped eyes on him."

"And lost your grandchildren in the bargain," Sarah said quietly. She listened to the words come out of her mouth, but found it too late to take them back.

Sìle sighed deeply. "Aye, my gel, there is no going back, nor would I in truth. I simply grieve that there is so much darkness in the world."

"But there is light," Sarah said, because apparently she just couldn't keep herself from talking. "Obscured, perhaps, but there if one looks for it."

Sìle looked at her for a moment or two in silence, then walked behind Ruith to put his hand on her shoulder. He leaned over and kissed the top of her head.

"I'll remember that, lass, whilst you're about your business. Then you'll come to my hall and only look at loveliness." He stepped back. "I believe I'll go myself to push up my dinner invitation to that harpy Morag. Ruith, you and your gel should make good use of my sacrifice."

Sarah took herself out of the midst of the preparations, happy to simply sit on a bench under the window and stare at the floor. It was better that way, for she had less to look at.

She wasn't alone for long, though. She looked up to find Ruith's sister sitting next to her.

"Ruith will keep you safe."

Sarah smiled in spite of herself. "And here I was going to tell you I would keep him safe for you."

Mhorghain smiled wryly. "I don't know that you won't, in the end. Those are quite useful-looking daggers you have down your boots."

"If only I had your skill in using them," Sarah said with a sigh, "but I don't and I have no time for any instruction."

"I suggest using womanly wiles," Mhorghain said, "which Ruith said you used to great advantage in the woods near Doìre. I can't say that will work against all mages, but it's been my experience that they generally have poor opinions of those who they think are powerless. There is no shame in allowing others to underestimate you."

"Is that one of Weger's strictures?"

"Miach's favorite ploy," Mhorghain corrected with another smile. Her smile faded. "I would like very much to have the chance to speak at length." She paused. "I understand what it is to discover that your past is not what you think it is."

Sarah realized her nails were digging into the wood of the bench where she was holding its edge. "And how did you survive it?"

Mhorghain shrugged. "It galls me to admit as much, but I leaned on Miach. Far more than I should have, but there you have it." She smiled faintly. "He has mud on his boots, if you know what I mean."

"And your brother bakes a very decent loaf of bread, if you can ignore the burned outsides."

Mhorghain laughed a little. "They are, to my surprise, very much alike." She smiled. "Lean on him. I don't think he'll protest. In fact, he might be pleased to have you do so before you have a look at that very long list of suitors my grandfather thought you might want to have a look at before you considered Ruith. He said he'd discussed it with you already, but thought you might like him to write the list down so you might have it to study at your leisure."

Sarah couldn't help a smile. "And where is this lengthy list?"

"Ruith threw it into the fire."

"Aye, I did," Ruith said, nudging Sarah over a bit so he could sit down. "I thought it prudent to remove any distractions until I can present my suit to her grandfather Franciscus. I fear if I take any liberties before the fact, I'll find myself changed rather permanently into a boot scraper."

Ruith chatted companionably with his sister for quite some time, discussing things of no consequence, then was silent when Mhorghain went to see if the small meal that had been brought could possibly be any less disgusting than everything they'd eaten up to that point. Sarah watched her for a moment, then looked at Ruith. His eyes were bloodshot and he looked as if he could have used a decent nap.

"We'll leave within the half hour," he said quietly.

"Am I going to carry you?" she asked.

He smiled, then leaned over and kissed her very briefly. "I'll sleep after this is all finished, but you can close your eyes now for a bit if you like."

"I don't think I can," she said seriously.

He hesitated, then nodded, as if he understood.

She imagined he did.

The spells weren't where she'd thought they were, and they had no idea who was moving them.

Seven

❧

Ruith walked swiftly but silently through the forest with Sarah, wishing he dared make werelight. Fortunately he wasn't unused to stumbling through the dark, even the semi-dark of twilight, and apparently neither was Sarah. He wasn't sure he wanted to think about why she'd learned the skill. He already knew the answer for himself.

They'd left the inn just after Sìle commandeered the keeping room below for the queen of An-uallach and her advisors. The ensuing chaos once the innkeeper had learned just how many members of royal houses he was entertaining under his roof had allowed them to slip out of the kitchens. Sìle had promised he would make certain dinner lasted at least three hours. Ruith was grateful for the head start, and he hoped that once Morag realized that he and Sarah were missing, she wouldn't simply excuse herself and go

running after them. Ruith planned to be far enough away that even
if Morag rode like the wind, she wouldn't manage to catch them.

They'd left the inn by way of the stables in order to fetch their
horses, who they'd subsequently asked to change into something
discreet. Ruith had objected to the ferocious-looking spiders they'd
chosen, not because he was particularly squeamish but because he
had no desire to find himself as a repository for the fangs he'd been
able to see from several paces away. The horses had marched off in
something of a huff on eight legs apiece, then changed themselves
into mighty owls and flapped up into the trees.

Ruith had settled for dragonshape himself after half a league in
the twilight, and that only after having told Sarah that he would be
even less likely than her horse to allow her to fall off his back.
Apparently she'd been as eager as he to leave Queen Morag behind,
for she had agreed almost without hesitation.

To his surprise, he'd forgotten how much he'd missed shapechanging. He hadn't changed himself into anything more exotic
than either a mouse or night air in the past pair of fortnights. Feeling the dragon wildness coursing through him had left him rather
hard-pressed to remember that he had a rider atop his back he had
promised not to terrify.

He had landed an hour ago where Sarah had told him to, then
walked with her, trying to shake off the intense desire to change
himself again into something with wings and hurtle through the
rather breezy evening sky.

Perhaps he was slightly more grateful for his magic than he'd
been willing to admit.

Sarah had stopped him at one point, then pointed down at his
feet. He'd looked, then cursed under his breath. It was a piece of
the first half of his father's spell of Diminishing. Of all the things
he would have wanted to see, this was the last.

It wasn't that the spell itself was so powerful, though he had
very unpleasant memories of watching his father use it on fully

coherent mages who knew that every drop of their power was about to be drained from them and added to Gair's own considerable store of the like. It also wasn't the thought that someone was possibly aware enough of his movements that he was able to predict where Ruith would go before he went there and thereby leave a little surprise for him when he arrived.

It was that Ruith had had the second half of the spell of Diminishing stolen from him and he wasn't entirely sure that the mage responsible for that theft wasn't the one tearing up the *first* half and leaving it behind.

The question was, why?

After all, why would anyone with sense give up any part of that spell unless he had the bulk of it in his possession and could part with a bit of it with the apparent intention of making Ruith himself quite mad? Ruith supposed there were a variety of other reasons a mage might be doing the like, but he cared for none of them for they all led him to the same conclusion which was that there was someone out there, someone he couldn't see, who knew he was alive. Whether or not that mage realized what Ruith was searching for, Ruith couldn't have said.

He wasn't looking forward to the moment he discovered the truth.

Sarah put her hand suddenly on his arm. "It's over there. The spell we're seeking, not just a scrap of Diminishing."

Ruith pulled himself back from his useless thoughts and nodded, then followed her off the road and into darkness. She was unerring in her ability not to plunge them into ravines, though, and soon they were standing in front of a handful of stones. Well, they were actually boulders, but they looked as if they'd been there for centuries, grouped together unremarkably thanks to some heaving of the earth in distant memory. He looked at Sarah in surprise.

"Here?"

"Under there."

He considered his sword as a lever, then dismissed it and looked for something else. He didn't suppose even a sturdy branch would serve him any, so he settled for magic to move things to his satisfaction.

And there, under the rubble, looking rather worse for the wear, was one of his father's spells.

"Which is it?" Sarah asked.

He rolled it up without looking and stuffed it into his pack. "I don't know and couldn't care less. We'll lay them all out at the end of our road and see what we're missing. For now, I just want to be away from here. I don't like the feel of these woods."

She nodded and followed him away from the rock that had been rolled away from the others, then stopped with him when he pulled her into the deeper shadows of the forest. He leaned against a tree to catch his breath for a moment, then reached for her hand.

"How are you?"

"Terrified," she breathed.

He laughed a little. "Well, you're honest, at least."

"And you?"

"I'm trying not to think on it," he admitted.

And he wasn't. He had spent a score of years on his own, propelling himself into manhood without the guidance of anyone. Well, he supposed he'd had aid from the books in his library—heroic tales had been very well represented, as it happened—and the occasional lecture from Franciscus offered over initially very watered-down ale, but for the most part he'd relied on himself. Any uneasiness he'd experienced as a youth, he had faced and overcome by himself. And despite how lovely it had been to sit recently in a circle of family and friends, he certainly didn't need aid—

He stopped and looked at the remarkably beautiful woman standing next to him shivering with cold but watching him steadily, and it occurred to him that perhaps he needed more aid than he wanted to admit.

Aid, or perhaps affection.

He closed his eyes briefly, then reached out and pulled her into his arms. That she came willingly was perhaps one of the sweeter moments of his life.

"We'll be about our business as quickly as possible," he said finally, "so we might retreat to Seanagarra and perhaps even manage to witness what will be the most overdone and under-attended wedding in a century."

"Will no one come to Mhorghain's wedding?" she asked, her words muffled against his shoulder.

"My grandsire won't let them in," Ruith said. "He's notoriously inhospitable to those who don't meet his exacting standards."

She lifted her head and looked up at him. "Are you telling me Soilléir won't be on the guest list?"

"Miach will put him there, I daresay," Ruith said. "Whether our favorite spewer of simple words and purveyor of rudimentary observations slips discreetly past the gate is another matter entirely."

She studied him in silence for a moment or two. In fact, she looked at him for so long in such silence that he shifted uncomfortably.

"What?" he asked.

"I was just wondering what it was you and Miach were whispering about over in the corner before we left?"

Nothing he wanted to discuss with her, but he supposed that out of all the things he'd discussed with her, it was perhaps the least perilous. Why he hadn't thought to have that particular conversation with his future brother-in-law earlier in their visit he wasn't sure. Weariness, perhaps, or the distraction of seeing Mhorghain, or watching Sarah's dark red hair by the light of the fire and wondering how it was he could be willing to allow her to walk into such peril—

"Ruith?"

He cleared his throat. "We were making a list of my father's spells. Their number, as it happens."

"And what did you decide?"

"That Miach knew two more than I remembered."

"That's good," she said, then she froze. "Or perhaps not. How many spots have I marked?"

"Including the spells taken from me outside Ceangail?" Ruith asked. "A score."

"And how many spells did Miach remember?"

"A score and two."

She looked up at him in astonishment. "But how is that possible?"

He shrugged, though he felt anything but casual about it. "Miach could be wrong. Mhorghain didn't know, of course, and when I asked Rùnach when we were at Buidseachd, he feared to trust his memory. I understand that Miach and Keir had had the opportunity to discuss them at length. Miach, being Miach, memorized them all, of course. And by his count there were twenty-two."

"And what do you think?"

"I think I'll look at the list of them I made and stuck down my boot, then rack my wee head for any Keir might have missed."

She frowned thoughtfully. "Does the number strike you as inaccurate?"

"My father was terribly suspicious," Ruith admitted. "He wouldn't have chosen a number that didn't have a meaning for him. Trying to divine what that might be, however, is a daunting task." He tightened his arms around her briefly, then released her. "We should walk again, I think. 'Tis too cold to stand about."

She nodded and followed him for a bit until the path became wide enough for them to walk together. He reached for her hand and laced his fingers with hers. Sarah walked alongside him for several minutes in silence, then looked up at him.

"Do you have any idea what number would have had meaning for him?"

Ruith shrugged. "I'm not sure where to begin speculating. It could have been anything. He lived for a thousand years before he wed my mother."

"He had seven children."

"Aye," he agreed, "and there are seven rings of mastery, seven founders of the schools of wizardry, and seven points on the crown of Neroche."

"But nine kings—including Morag, of course—on the Council of Kings," she said with a faint smile, "ten languages of magic, and fifteen bickering farmers on the town council of Doìre."

Ruith laughed a little in spite of himself. "The last should likely shake the foundations of the world."

"It should," she agreed.

He considered the numbers, but none of them made any particular impression on him. The only thing he was certain of was that his father had never written anything in his book that hadn't been absolutely perfect down to the final syllable of each particular spell. That Miach could only remember slightly less than two dozen wasn't a surprise. Gair had had spells for everything, but it wouldn't have done to have gathered any but the most spectacular in a single tome.

Ruith could see the book now as clearly as if it had been in front of him. The cover had been finely crafted leather, dyed black. The only thing of note had been the lock, which Ruith had never had the chance to examine closely enough to determine how it might be bested. No doubt it required the most important spell of all, recited crisply and with authority.

Then again, the book could have simply required a key, but at the moment he couldn't have said which it was. Perhaps the most reliable thing he could say about it was that most if not all the pages had been ripped out. When that had taken place, Ruith couldn't have said. Surely not before his sire had attempted to best the well.

It was possible, he supposed, that his sire had left the book in the library at Ceangail and his bastard sons had fought over it, then scattered the pages out of spite. Or, perhaps more likely, his father had been the one to do the scattering, on the off chance that someone would gather up the pages of the book and use his accursed spells. Ruith had just never suspected that the spells would find themselves being called by someone.

What if that someone was his sire?

He could hardly bear to entertain the thought, but he had to admit he'd considered the possibility a time or two over the previous score of years. Anytime the idea had cropped up like a noxious weed in the garden of his tranquil existence he'd plucked it up and burned it without hesitation, but aye, he'd considered it a time or two. To know that Miach had whipped himself into a bitter wind and blown for two solid days to find him to suggest as much . . . well, it lent the idea a credence Ruith didn't care for in the least.

Gair of Ceangail, alive?

"Perhaps knowing the exact number isn't as important as we'd like to believe," Sarah said suddenly. "Could he have written spells that your brother might not have remembered?"

"I wish I knew," Ruith said, happily abandoning thoughts that bothered him more than he would ever admit. He dragged his free hand through his hair. "With my sire, anything was possible. I certainly didn't pay attention to his book as I should have in my youth."

"How were you to know what he was truly capable of?" she asked. "I'm sure you mother tried to keep it from you as best she could."

"Aye, until she couldn't deny it any longer." He sighed. "I suppose the worst part is, I entertained from time to time the idea that if I could reason with him, I could convince him to be other than he was." He smiled briefly. "I daresay my mother entertained the same notion, from time to time."

"There must have been something redeeming about him, else she wouldn't have wed with him."

"Oh, he could be charming," Ruith agreed, "when it suited him. My mother was no fool, so I imagine he had been charming enough, long enough, that she considered his nature changed. Or perhaps she was simply dazzled by his good looks."

Sarah laughed a little. "I'm sure the get of elf and wizardess had material enough there to dazzle."

"I daresay." Ruith shook his head. "He is an enigma I'm not sure I will ever understand completely. He had lived so long before he wed my mother I imagine his character was fixed beyond any repairing. But my mother obviously saw things I didn't."

"Or she had a tender heart," Sarah said with a smile, "like her son."

He laughed a little uncomfortably. "You give me credit for things I don't deserve. I'm as hard-hearted as the next black mage's son. I suppose I'll need to remember that if I ever see my father again . . ." He stopped speaking only because he realized that Sarah had come to an abrupt halt. He looked at her in surprise. "What is it?"

"If you ever seep your father again?" she echoed. "What do you mean by that?"

Ruith took a deep breath. "We haven't had a chance to talk—"

Her fingers suddenly digging into the back of his hand made him wince hard enough that he stopped speaking. And once he stopped thinking long enough to pay attention to his surroundings, he realized what she was telling him.

"We've been followed," he murmured, half under his breath. "Damn it anyway."

"Aye, I daresay," she breathed, "and so soon. What now?"

He was slightly surprised to find his first instinct was to turn into something difficult to contain and cast himself onto the first available wind. All those years he'd spent in the mountains without magic had been more easily left behind than he would have suspected. He let out his breath slowly.

"I think we should simply continue on. I've been laying spells of protection around us, though I haven't been as thorough as I could have been."

"Because we have Tarbh and Ruathar to keep watch for us?" she asked with a faint smile.

"What is the use of having shapechanging horses if they can't turn into watch owls for us?" he asked lightly. "So, since they've expressed no objection to what seems to be trailing us, I say we continue on as we have been. I'll lay an extra spell or two as a snare, and we'll see who winds up caught."

"I'll leave you to it."

She said it with a tone matching his, but he could tell by the chill of her fingers that she was less casual than she claimed to be. Perhaps he could have asked her if she could see anything, but he suspected he could narrow down quite quickly who their uninvited traveling companion could be. It was either Morag, escaped early from supper with Sìle, or perhaps one of his bastard brothers. The rest of the cast their assorted relations had identified honestly had no idea where he was or what he was about.

He continued on with Sarah, in silence, and stretched himself to see if he could gain a sense of who was behind them. He was fairly alarmed to find he didn't care for the whiff of magic the soul carried with him. It wasn't Morag, for it wasn't Caol he sensed.

It was Olc.

His first thought was that his father had come to haunt him, but he immediately dismissed that as the workings of an overwrought and overtired mind. He considered each of his bastard brothers in turn, but whoever was stalking them was very good at a spell of concealment, which left them out.

Nay, it was someone else. Someone with a powerful knowledge of a very dark magic.

He walked out into a clearing with Sarah almost before he knew what he was doing. He had to admit that was a fortuitous turn of events, for it made laying a spell of protection much easier. He quickly cast that net over himself and Sarah, then set spells of ward along the perimeter. And then, because he supposed that all that effort he'd expended memorizing Miach's most vile spells shouldn't go to waste, he used a few extra things guaranteed to make life rather unpleasant for anyone who drew too close to him.

And then he simply looked at Sarah. She wasn't, he could tell, any more comfortable with their location than he was, but she wasn't bolting.

"And now?" she asked, finally.

"We wait and see."

"I was hoping for a different answer," she said grimly.

He smiled. "Did you memorize Soilléir's spell before we left? The one to dim your sight?"

She nodded. "I've used it a handful of times already in the past several days."

"You might want to use it again fairly soon." He felt the presence of something behind him and it wasn't either an owl or a recently restored horse. "Does that other spell increase your sight, do you think?" he asked pleasantly, "or just clear away spells of concealment laid before you by others?"

"I don't think it affects anything anyone else does, because that would mean I had magic and we both know that isn't the case." She looked up at him bleakly. "I think it affects just me. I don't want to know the particulars right now, if it's all the same to you."

"Of cou—"

The word didn't make it past his mouth because he was interrupted by the annoyed bellowing of a mage who had run up against a spell that wasn't so much dangerous as it was painful. Ruith spun around, his sword drawn, to find Ardan of Ainneamh swearing profusely and trying to brush off several thorns that drove themselves further into his flesh with every brush. He finally looked at Ruith and swore again.

"Get these off me!"

Ruith wiped away not only his spell but the remainder of the thorns industriously working their way into Ardan's flesh. Thoir was standing a pace or two behind him with his hand over his mouth, no doubt striving to keep from laughing.

Ruith dissolved the rest of his spell without delay, then waited for his cousin—and cousin by marriage—to approach. He wasn't terribly surprised to see them there. After all, they had promised him they would do a bit of scouting, then find him and give him reports of what they'd seen.

He listened to them argue about who should have gone first in order to have been the one to have best enjoyed Ruith's spells for quite some time before they seemed to find the bickering too much effort. Ardan looked down his long, aristocratic nose at Sarah.

"Ah, the witchwoman's get from Doìre. Still."

Ruith opened his mouth to correct him only to have two elbows in his ribs. One, he knew without looking, had been Sarah's. He was surprised to find that the other was Thoir's.

"Shut up, Ardan," he said shortly, "and use your extensive knowledge of all the inns throughout the Nine Kingdoms to see if we're anywhere close to a hot fire and decent victuals or if we'll need to send Ruith off hunting for something to put in a stewpot."

"There is nothing for leagues," Ardan said with distaste, "and nay, Ruith will not go hunt. I shall, for at least I'll recognize what I find for supper. I'm not sure I would recognize anything he found, his having been out of polite society for so long, of course."

"Then be about it, please," Thoir said politely.

Ardan cast them all a look of disgust, then turned and walked away. He melted into the darkness and was gone.

Ruith frowned. He wasn't altogether certain Ardan wouldn't look for the nearest inn and poach whatever was bubbling over the fire, but he wasn't going to say anything. He had other things to think on, such as why Thoir was looking at Sarah as if he'd never seen a woman before.

He nudged his cousin gently in the ribs. "Stop it. She doesn't like scrutiny."

Thoir looked up at him. "And you don't like others scrutinizing her?"

"Nay," Ruith said shortly. "I don't."

Thoir only frowned at him, then turned back to his study of Sarah. "You look familiar."

"That's because you saw me in Slighe," Sarah said politely.

"Nay," Thoir said, shaking his head, "that isn't it. I'm not sure why I didn't see it before—and I can't believe I'm saying this—but you look a great deal like Sorcha of Bruadair." He glanced at Ruith. "She was a dreamweaver, you know. Very powerful, those gels from Bruadair. She wed Athair of Cothromaiche, if memory serves."

"How would you know that?" Ruith asked in surprise.

Thoir pursed his lips. "You forget how often I'm away from home, seeing to this and that. 'Tis surprising what you can pick up in even the seediest of pubs. And as unpleasant as the memories are, I have even ventured places that Grandfather would shrink from. Such as Cothromaiche."

"Are you insulting my lord Soilléir's homeland?" Sarah asked pointedly.

Ruith wondered if he might stop being surprised by things that came out of the mouths of those around him. If he hadn't known better, he might have thought Sarah was preparing to draw one of her blades and use it on the fool standing to his left.

Thoir only looked at her as if he were seeing her for the first time.

"Hmmm," was all he said, then he turned to Ruith. "Since we're waiting for Ardan to return with breakfast—"

"Supper," Ruith corrected.

"Aye, that," Thoir said, rubbing his hands together, "let's make ourselves comfortable and rest. I'm interested in what King Uachdaran had to say about your quest."

"You assume he let us inside the gates," Ruith said.

"Grandfather had been there less than a fortnight earlier," Thoir said with a shrug. "I assumed he had paved the way for you. But don't describe what you found at his table. I'm not sure I could bear it given the unpalatable things I've eaten over the past se'nnight. Here, I'll make a fire to warm our hands against."

Ruith left him to it, for he was more interested in staying aware of his surroundings than he was making in his cousins comfortable, though he wasn't above seeing Sarah seated comfortably in front of flames that sparkled on rather damp wood thanks to Fadaire. He made certain Sarah wasn't going to be gawked at, listened to a few words of conversation to make certain she wasn't going to be insulted, then put his hand on her shoulder briefly before he started a slow circle of the glade.

He felt nothing, which suddenly struck him as odd, for he'd definitely felt a goodly bit of menace not a quarter hour ago.

But he felt it no longer.

"Ruith, stop glowering and come over here," Thoir called. "I have gossip you'll be interested in."

Ruith considered the surrounding environs once more, then shrugged aside his unease. He'd obviously been awake too long. Awake or suspicious, he wasn't sure which. Thoir was his father's son and like Iarann, wouldn't have touched Olc if it were all that stood between him and death. Ruith couldn't say he was as confident in Ardan's scruples, but he could certainly vouch for the elf's disdain for anything that didn't come from within his borders. Nay, it had to have been someone else.

He set spells of ward about the glade, leaving Ardan's name out of them for the sake of friendly diplomatic relations, then walked back over to the fire. He would have a bite of supper when it arrived, then have another look around whilst Sarah slept. Hopefully she wouldn't mind spelling him for an hour or so. He didn't want to ask, but he was more tired than he should have been, with no end to that in sight.

He stared out into the darkness one last time and felt the faintest hint of Olc. But was it something new or merely an echo of things gone before?

He wasn't sure he wanted to know.

Eight

❈

Sarah woke abruptly and sat up, realizing only then that she'd fallen asleep. She looked over her shoulder to find Ruith sitting on a log behind her, watching someone that she discovered subsequently was Thoir sitting on the other side of a very lovely but rather inadequate fire. Ardan sat up as she watched, scowled, then brushed the dirt off himself with angry strokes. Apparently the rustic accommodations didn't suit him at all.

She supposed there was little point in trying to feign sleep any longer, so she inched back until she was sitting against the log, not because it was more comfortable to be further away from the fire, but because she didn't want to be in the middle of any of the conversation going on at present. She didn't particularly care for Thoir or Ardan, no matter how they were related to Ruith. Ardan was a fine example of every terribly arrogant characteristic generally associated with elves, and Thoir was . . . well, he was simply too

handsome. All that male beauty made her nervous. It wasn't that
Ruith wasn't handsome, it was just that in addition to his unwholesome good looks, he had some useful skills. She suspected Thoir's
only skill was leaving all maids in his vicinity swooning.

She had no desire to swoon, so she was more than happy to
simply let Ruith make all the polite conversation he cared to. Why
he put up with those two was a mystery, but she supposed the
answer was likely simply because his mother had taught him decent
manners. And there was something to be said for another pair of
eyes—two, even—looking in places Ruith couldn't go himself.

"Perhaps I should have been there," Thoir said thoughtfully,
obviously continuing a thought he'd had earlier. "I've only encountered the queen of An-uallach at state functions, of course, but I
might have been of use to Grandfather. After all, I am the son of
Làidir, grandson of—"

"Oh, aye, we know all that already," Ardan said with a gusty
sigh. "Second in line to the throne, or you would be if Sìle hadn't
wrapped those runes around Miach of Neroche's wrists, but let's
not discuss that or you'll stomp about in a snit again."

"I never stomp about in a snit," Thoir said, shooting Ardan a look.

"And you aren't second in line to the throne," Sarah said. She
heard the words come out of her mouth and wondered when it was
she was going to be able to control her tongue. First Sìle, now his
grandson. She wondered if it were simply a lack of sleep or a lack
of safety that had left her blurting out what would have been better
left unsaid. She started to apologize, but Thoir waved away her
words before she managed them.

"Nay, I'm not," he agreed, apparently unoffended. "I am my
father's youngest son not his eldest, which Ardan would remember
if he didn't have such trouble counting. That inability to follow
consecutive numbers makes for interesting, if not taxing, journeys." He looked at Ruith. "Where were we, cousin?"

"You were discussing that hag from An-uallach," Ardan said

with distaste, "and why she didn't squash Ruith like a bug." He shot Sarah a look. "Surely Morag didn't want anything to do with *her*."

Sarah didn't dare look at Ruith. She heard his sharp intake of breath, which was enough.

"Perhaps, Prince Ardan," Ruith said in a low, careful tone, "there are glittering palaces which are calling to you to add to their spring-time splendor. I suppose 'tis too much to hope for that in such locales you might learn even the basic manners a well-bred lad should call his own, but perhaps you *and* Thoir might benefit from at least attempting to gain entrance."

Thoir laughed a little. "I think I'll stay and keep my mouth shut. You can improve my manners all you like, Ruith."

Sarah didn't look at Ardan, but she didn't miss his very gusty sigh. He pushed himself to his feet, muttered another curse about the primitive nature of their outdoor accommodations, then, instead of stomping off which she fully expected him to do, turned and made her a slight bow.

"Mistress Sarah," he said, sounding not precisely contrite but slightly less arrogant than usual, "if I might apologize?"

Sarah looked up at him. He was, as she had noted before, almost difficult to look at, and that not just because of the fairness of his face. She had no idea what sort of magic ran through the streams in Ainneamh or flowed through the veins of the elvenkind there, but it was a very complicated, very formal sort of magic. Perhaps Ardan resented the necessity of traveling about in the world when he could have been at home, surrounded by the very stately, formal beauty she could see reflected in his soul.

She put on the best smile she could manage. "There is no need—"

"But there is," he said. He considered, then made a very low, formal bow. "I apologize. I am, as anyone who knows me will tell you, a great arse. Being away from the edifying influence of my mother has only augmented the problem."

"Well, now that is cleared up for us," Thoir said dryly, "why don't we turn to other things. Ruith, don't you think you should tell us what you're truly about? You know I hate mysteries."

Sarah found that Ardan was waiting for her to accept his apology, so inclined her head at him and hoped that would be enough. He seemed to think so and resumed his seat by the fire with a grunt. Thoir was still looking at Ruith expectantly, waiting for details she wasn't sure Ruith would give him. She felt Ruith's hand come to rest against her back, as if he either strove to give himself something else to think about or wanted to keep her from jumping up and plunging a knife into the chests of their company. She looked up briefly at him, had a grave smile in return, then turned back to watching Thoir and Ardan.

"Ruithneadh said he was hunting black mages," Ardan was saying, "or had you forgotten? Perhaps he's decided his bastard brothers at Ceangail have lived too comfortably all these years and need to be vexed a bit. Amitán was certainly looking a little worse for the wear when last we saw him."

Sarah flinched in spite of herself. She felt Ruith do the same thing.

"You saw Amitán?" he asked casually. "Where?"

"Just outside Léige," Ardan said, "wandering aimlessly. I didn't engage him." He wrinkled his nose. "He smelled, truth be told."

"Which you would notice," Thoir said. "I didn't see him myself, but Ardan and I have been searching separately over the past fortnight. I haven't seen anything unusual save you, which leads me to ask again, what is there that you're not telling us?"

Ruith shrugged. "Nothing of import."

Thoir sighed. "Ruith, you've been too long in Shettlestoune. Not every soul you meet is an enemy. Well, you could think twice about Ardan, but not me. Your mother was my aunt." His smile faded. "I am on your side, cousin, for I know what your mother faced. If you're trying to eradicate what was left behind—which

I very much suspect is the case—you can know with a surety that I *understand*."

Sarah shifted so she could look at Ruith as well. He dragged his hand through his hair.

"I imagine you do—" he began.

"Imagine?" Thoir interrupted in disbelief. "Ruith, *think*. If I could slay what Gair spawned at Ceangail and not have it stain my soul, I would have done so years ago. If you're hunting black mages, as you very carefully suggested you were—for your own perverse reasons, no doubt—why wouldn't I throw my lot in with yours? Why do you think I do nothing but roam the Nine Kingdoms? For my own pleasure? I would much rather be home, dressed in fine silks and enjoying the pleasures of Seanagarra. But I don't because I am willing to go places even my father dares not tread and I do so *because* I want Seanagarra to be free of demons like Gair. And if that is what you hunt, I have very good reason to want to hunt with you."

"Count me in as well," Ardan agreed heavily. "For the same reasons."

Sarah found Ruith looking at her. She wasn't about to offer any opinions. The two across the fire were his kin, true, so there should have been no reason not to trust them. She realized with a start, however, that she had become just as wary as Ruith had. She would have trusted his family back at the inn, but . . .

She took a deep breath and reached for reason. Those were his cousins there, his painfully beautiful, terribly powerful cousins who might have been slightly annoyed at their situation in life, but they surely had no love of darkness. There was no reason not to consider them friend, not foe.

Ruith looked at her for another moment or two in silence, then lifted his head and sighed. "I am hunting pages from my father's book of spells."

Sarah looked at their companions. Ardan was blinking, as if he hadn't heard him. Thoir's mouth had fallen open and he was gaping in a most unattractive fashion.

"Why?" he managed.

"So I can destroy them."

Thoir closed his mouth, apparently with difficulty. "Why waste the effort? Even if someone finds the pages of that accursed book, who would have the power to use the spells?"

"That doesn't matter," Ruith said grimly. "My task is to gather up all my father's spells, then destroy them. Then at least whatever black mage next steps up on the world's stage will have to start from scratch with his evil."

Ardan shrugged. "Seems reasonable to me."

Thoir hadn't moved. "And do you have any idea where these pages might be hiding, or are they all in the same place?"

Ruith rubbed his hands over his face. "I have a map," he said wearily. "A map of where the spells can be found."

Ardan rubbed his hands together. "Let's see it." He made were-light that sparkled in a particularly elvish way, then nodded encouragingly. "There you go. Produce the map."

Sarah watched Ruith lean over to pull the map from his boot, then make a production of freeing it. He shot her a look whilst he was about it, a look which she had no trouble understanding. He was going to lie and do it without a moment's hesitation.

He straightened, then rose and handed the map to Thoir.

"Those are where we know the spells to be at the moment," he said carefully. "How they came to be there is a mystery we haven't yet solved."

Ardan peered over Thoir's shoulder. "Perhaps 'tis only because I see things where others do not, but there appears to me to be a sort of pattern here."

"Is there?" Ruith asked politely.

Ardan shot him a look. "Aye, there is. And it points to this spot here."

"He has that aright," Thoir said, peering at the map. "See you how there is a mark here and another at the same latitude, though seemingly several leagues away. They proceed northward, these marks, growing closer and closer together until they terminate at the same point." He looked at Ruith. "Why not just go there and see where they've led you?"

"Because that's not the point," Ruith said calmly. "I need the spells themselves."

"To destroy them," Ardan asked skeptically, "or to keep for yourself in the end?"

Ruith shot him a warning look, but said nothing.

Ardan merely shrugged. "I had to ask."

"Prince Ardan, if I wanted to use my father's spells, I would have done so already," Ruith said evenly. "I'm sure it occurs to you that I might have them memorized already."

"Yes, it does indeed occur to me," Ardan agreed. "And again, I had to ask. And I'll ask something else: how did you discover where these spells lie?" He looked at Ruith and blinked innocently. "Just out of curiosity."

"That is a curiosity I have no intention of satisfying," Ruith said. "Just trust me that they're there."

"The spots are rather vague," Thoir said thoughtfully. "How are we to recognize the particular location when we come upon it?"

"I hadn't intended that you go look for them," Ruith said, sounding very surprised.

"Well, it isn't as if you can go do it all yourself," Ardan said. "Not with Morag of An-uallach in a fury behind you. For once I agree with Thoir. Let us help you with this madness of yours as quickly as possible, then you can scurry home to wherever you feel most comfortable, and I'll return home to beauty and elegance you can't possibly imagine. In your case, you can perhaps hope that Morag fears a journey south of Slighe might wreak havoc on her complexion."

Sarah watched Ruith hesitate, which brought an immediate reaction from Thoir, who rolled his eyes and made a noise of impatience.

"What do you think, Ruith?" he asked with a snort. "That we want these vile bits of business for ourselves? Don't be daft. Tear the map in half, give us the more difficult route, and we'll meet you at the final spot. I think even Ardan could find that."

Sarah watched Ruith consider. She supposed she knew what he was thinking, for they had been her thoughts as well. They had spent much of the past few fortnights relying on the kindness of strangers whilst never knowing who might betray them. She couldn't imagine Thoir would want Gair's spells for himself. Not even Ardan seemed capable of sullying his hands with the things, especially given his obvious love for himself and his disdain for anything not elvish.

Ruith looked at her finally. "I'm not opposed to the aid, if you aren't."

She nodded, then rose and reached over the fire to take the map from Thoir. She looked down at it, backlit as it was by the light of not only the flame but Ardan's werelight, and flinched, because the fire was not only lighting the map, the spells had lit little fires themselves *on* the map. The sight startled her so, she dropped the sheaf of parchment. Thoir rescued it from the fire, blew out the edge that was burning, then handed it back to her slowly.

"Are you unwell?" he asked quietly.

"Weary," she said without hesitation. She hesitated. "Do you want the map itself, or shall I just tell you where to look for the spells?"

"You?" Ardan asked in surprise. "The witchwoman Seleg's daughter? What could you possibly have to tell *us* about any of this?"

Thoir clucked his tongue at Ardan, then looked up at Sarah. "I think I would prefer to have half the map, if it's all the same to you."

Sarah nodded, tore the map in half lengthwise, then handed half of it to Thoir. "Those spells lie at the feet of the Sgurrachs. I hadn't intended this to be more than just general directions, but I can be more specific about the locations if you like."

"Can you?" Thoir asked seriously. "And how is that, lady?"

She found the words surprisingly difficult to utter. "I can see the spells."

"And how is that possible?" Ardan asked, his words dripping with skepticism. "An unnamed by-blow of a witch with no power and who knows who else can see anything but the nearest pub—"

Sarah put herself in front of Ruith as he launched himself to his feet and halfway across their hastily made camp. She stopped him, but found herself in the midst of the fire as a result which necessitated Ruith's beating out flames on the edge of her cloak. She shot him a look.

"Don't."

Ruith considered, then very carefully put his hands on her shoulders and set her aside. He turned to face Ardan. "There will come a day, my lord Ardan, when you and I will find ourselves without cooler heads to restrain us and then you will indeed learn a few manners. I only refrain now out of respect for my lady's wishes."

Ardan blew his hair out of his eyes. "I believe it is likely best that I refrain from comment from now on."

"Very wise," Ruith agreed shortly.

Sarah found Ardan looking her way. He made her yet another very low bow, straightened, then visibly clamped his lips shut. Thoir only laughed.

"I'm not sure why you two seem to rub each other the wrong way, but it indicates to me that dividing this map in half is the safest thing for both of you. Now, perhaps we should have more precise directions." He looked up from the map in his hands. "If you wouldn't mind, my lady."

She shook her head. "I wouldn't."

"And I won't ask you how it is you can see these."

"Thank you," she said simply. It was one thing to trust them with her map; it was another thing entirely to trust them with her . . . well, whatever it was she had. Her past. Her past that she still had trouble accepting. She supposed she could have presented herself to Seannair of Cothromaiche, watched him present her with portraits of her parents as proof, and she would have still had difficulty accepting who she was. Discussing the like with the two facing her was something she absolutely could not do.

So instead she spent half an hour telling Thoir all he wanted to know about the location of the spells, feeling rather more grateful than she likely should have that Ruith was breaking camp and gathering their things, for it meant she would soon be free of his cousins.

By the time she had finished, Ruith was ready to go. She took her pack from him and handed him back their half of the map. He rolled it up and stuck it down the side of his boot, then paused and looked at Thoir seriously.

"There's something else."

Thoir only lifted his eyebrows briefly. "I can scarce wait to hear what."

"Someone is leaving bits of my father's spell of Diminishing near each spell. Or, rather, near where Sarah and I have been traveling, but that might have been naught but chance."

Sarah was slightly surprised he had admitted any of that, but perhaps he had his reasons. Thoir didn't look particularly surprised, but Ardan was gaping. Again.

"What?" Ardan said incredulously.

Ruith looked at him evenly. "Bits of my father's spell of Diminishing, in locations where Sarah and I have traveled."

"But who has known where you were?"

"The list is unfortunately quite short," Ruith said grimly. "My bastard brothers, perhaps. Sarah's erstwhile brother Daniel, possibly. Someone we haven't thought of, no doubt."

"Who would want Gair's spells?" Ardan asked with a fair bit of distaste. "Such ugly things."

"And you would know?" Ruith asked sharply.

Ardan looked down his nose at him. "I am not unaware of what passes in the world, Ruithneadh. I had the serious misfortune of encountering Díolain in Slighe once. He tried to use your father's pitiful spell of fettering on me. Unsuccessfully, I might add."

"Then he must have sampled a bit too much of what passes for ale there or you wouldn't have escaped him."

"Rather my superior magic left him looking like a foolish child," Ardan shot back. "Olc and Lugham and whatever other bilge your sire was perfecting does not last long against the mighty sources of power that flow naturally through the woods and mountains of Ainneamh, sources that have found particular home in yours truly."

"Or 'tis merely that Díolain's an ass," Thoir offered, "but let's leave that be. I think the identity of who is teasing you with bits of spell is less important than gathering the rest of them together, though I'm still not convinced of the necessity of that. But since, Ruith, it seems to be your current obsession, I'll lend you my aid as I may." He folded up the map and stuck it into the purse at his belt. "Ardan, let's be off and leave these two to their own devices for a bit."

Ardan sighed. "Are there any pubs marked on that map? I didn't notice."

"There weren't, but you can use your nose to its best advantage whilst we fly," Thoir announced. "Come along, Ardan, there's a good lad."

Ardan shot Thoir a murderous look that made Sarah flinch. It was gone as quickly as it had come, however, which almost made her wonder if she'd been imagining things. She watched Thoir and Ardan until they were gone before she turned to Ruith.

"That was interesting."

His expression was inscrutable. "Very."

"Do you trust them?"

He pursed his lips. "Ardan? Nay. Thoir?" He smiled briefly. "Almost. But I do trust you, my lady, so what say you we be off? I think we lingered here overlong."

"Not that it served you any," she said, shouldering her pack. "You didn't sleep, did you?"

"I wasn't tired," he said easily. "Perhaps we'll find a comfortable hollow this afternoon and I'll snatch an hour or two. For now, I think we should travel quickly. I don't like what the daylight reveals."

And considering that all daylight would reveal would be them, she had to agree. There was something that bothered her about the conversation, but the moment she reached for it in truth, it was gone.

She shrugged. It would either come to her or it wouldn't. There was enough in front of her to worry about without adding to it.

She shouldered her pack and followed Ruith out of the glade.

S arah dreamed.

She realized as she walked, not getting anywhere on a road that never changed beneath her feet, that she couldn't see anything. Or, rather, she couldn't see anything. She was surprised at how accustomed she'd grown to seeing things that others couldn't. Spells. Names written on souls. Music hanging in the air.

She could see none of that at present. All she knew was that the road didn't vary in its incline or composition. It was flat, running endlessly under her feet, leading her through a fog that was so thick, she could have put her hand out and touched it if she'd had the strength.

She thought she might have been caught up in some sort of unpleasantly monotonous spell, but there was nothing enticing about where she was, not as it had been when she'd been walking in Droch's garden. No flowers, no comfortable place to sit beckoning her, no pitchers of cool water to ease her thirst. It was nothing but terrible darkness, terrible hunger, with no end in sight.

She continued on until she felt the darkness finally give way to something less dark though no less unsettling. She looked around herself but found nothing there.

She was absolutely alone.

Or, perhaps not.

Sarah woke and realized she hadn't been dreaming. She knew that only because she was standing on a well-worn, partially frozen road and her feet were freezing even in her boots. She was wearing her cloak, but she was so cold that she had to suppose there was more than just nasty weather at work. She had obviously been walking for some time in her current condition.

And she was alone.

She drew her hand over her eyes, but the gloom didn't abate. The trees that flanked the road were nothing more than vague outlines of themselves, scarcely hinted at through the fog.

She considered, then murmured the spell to sharpen her sight. She decided abruptly that it worked all too well. There were times when not being able to see what was before one was better than seeing it too clearly.

Such as the current moment.

She realized that what she'd thought were trees huddled in the fog were actually men-at-arms, grim-faced and silent. Some carried pikes, others wicked-looking maces sporting numbers of spikes that were surely beyond what was considered polite, and still others simply stood with their hands on their swords.

Sarah wondered why it was she merited such attention, then realized there was a very good reason.

They didn't want her to escape.

For the first time in her life, she wished so desperately for magic, she felt physical pain. Unfortunately, the truth was that she had none so all she could do was stand there, her feet numb and completely useless for any hasty sort of flight, and wait for her doom to arrive.

It did, parting a pair of guardsmen with long-fingered, slender hands.

Morag of An-uallach's slender hands.

Sarah would have put her shoulders back and swallowed her fear, but she was past that. It was one thing to have been caught in a trap by Droch. He hadn't known who she was—or so she assumed—and had only been toying with her for the sport of it. With Morag of An-uallach, there was no sport involved. The queen was interested in revenge.

Or worse.

Morag stopped a handful of paces from Sarah, so close that Sarah could see that there weren't so much as even the beginnings of faint lines around her mouth or eyes. She wondered, absently, how old the queen was, how she managed to look as young as any of her daughters, how many innocent people she had slain in her quest for power. She wondered how it was that Prince Phillip ever managed to walk through the halls of his keep without looking over his shoulder to make certain Morag wasn't about to cast a spell of death over him just because she could.

"Now," Morag said softly, "let us be about finishing this unpleasant business, shall we?"

"What business?" Sarah asked, her mouth completely dry. She knew she was squeaking, but since she was back again in the position of mouse facing cat, perhaps that was fitting.

"The business of my taking your power," Morag said with a smile.

But I have no power would have been the first thing out of her mouth if she'd dared speak, but since it was always the first thing she said when Morag was trying to kill her, she supposed there was no point in saying as much any longer. Morag wouldn't believe it until she'd finally succeeded in killing Sarah and found there was no power there to take.

"Where's Ruith?" Sarah asked, because when she opened her mouth, it was what came tumbling out.

"*Prince* Ruithneadh," Morag said sharply, "who is so far above you in station, you can't possibly think to have him consider you anything but a chambermaid, is happily wandering about in a spell he doesn't realize I've cast over him."

"But he set spells of ward—"

Morag's laughter was like claws across her skin. Sarah flinched in spite of herself, which seemed to please Morag all the more.

"Spells," she said with a disdainful half laugh. "Is that what he calls them?" She leaned closer. "Let me share a secret with you, young Sarah: he may be Gair of Ceangail's youngest son, but he inherited none of his sire's power. He certainly wouldn't have the power to use his sire's spell of—what was it Gair called it?"

"Diminishing," Sarah whispered.

Morag fixed her gaze on Sarah. "Aye," she said softly, "Diminishing—not that Gair's spell was nearly as useful as he thought it was. You see, 'tis at the instant a soul leaves this world that power is best taken, something even Gair didn't understand. He was too greedy, too impatient to wait for the proper moment. And yes, my little innocent, I have my own spell for that sort of thing." She lifted an eyebrow. "I used it on your parents, to great effect—"

"I hope it hurt you," Sarah blurted out.

The change in Morag's mien was terrifying. Sarah had known she was walking along a knife's edge as it was, but to see Morag in a full-blown rage was something else entirely. A spell came rushing out of her mouth, a spell full of barbs and clawing fingers, a spell designed to tear open her soul and have what Morag wanted as her final breath left her body.

And she could do absolutely nothing to keep it from falling on her.

Nine

Ruith caught Morag's spell of death and wrenched it away from falling upon Sarah even though taking hold of it was like grasping the fangs of a score of asps. He fell to his knees, gasping in pain.

"Well," a voice purred, "if it isn't the handsome prince of Tòrr Dòrainn, who was clever enough to free himself from confusion in time to come rescue his little dreamweaving trollop from death."

Ruith shoved himself back to his feet and jerked Sarah behind him. He would have told her to run, but he didn't imagine she would be safer away from him than she would be near him. At least he could keep her out of Morag's sights with his body alone.

He looked behind Morag to find half a dozen guardsmen who looked as if they shared not only their queen's foul humors but perhaps her magic as well. He was appalled to find his first instinct was to finish them all with a spell of death. He shoved aside the thought, then laid a spell over them that turned the falling rain into stinging insects. The mayhem that immediately ensued would have been entertaining if he hadn't been so unnerved. A mage underestimated Morag at his peril.

Hadn't he had proof of that not half an hour ago? He'd been walking with Sarah alongside him only to realize at some indeterminate point that he was no longer walking beside her. Worse still, he couldn't have said when he'd lost her.

He had thrown off the spell he'd realized had been cast over him, then frantically searched for Sarah, cursing the fact that he didn't have her sight. He'd finally resorted to hawk shape, skimming the tops of the evergreens, desperately looking for Sarah before something befell her.

To his horror, he'd found her covered by what he'd originally thought was a spell of death.

Only to discover that it wasn't.

She had been under a spell of . . . well, he couldn't call it Diminishing. It had been something else he hadn't been able to name, but it had been terrible. He didn't want to know what sort of things Morag dreamed up in the bowels of her castle, stewing over what she didn't have, restlessly searching for more efficient means to remedy that.

And though that piece of evil had been destroyed, he was sure it was just the beginning of what Morag could do. For all he knew, she had others just waiting to join in the battle. He looked behind Morag's frantically dancing guardsmen and realized that they weren't the only souls watching the goings on. There was a wagon there, a well-used ale wagon being leaned on by four lads he recognized.

The youngest of the lot was gaping at Morag as if he'd just had a peep into the deepest pit of hell and thought the slightest push might leave him lingering there for an eternity or two. That was Ned, Sarah's farm boy, whose only skill in life lay in escaping either peril or his father's barn.

The much shorter man to the right of Ned was Master Oban, wizard extraordinaire, who had faced Daniel of Doìre and come out much worse for the wear. He was gaping in much the same way Ned was, only his open mouth was partially covered by his wand, as if he feared to blurt out any expression of terror. His most obvious sign of distress was that his pointed wizard's hat had fallen so far forward and to the side, it had completely obscured one of his eyes. Ruith thought it might be best for Oban and Ned to scamper behind one of the wagon's ale kegs for the duration of the morning's events, but he suspected he wouldn't have the chance to say as much.

Next to Oban stood Seirceil of Coibhneas swathed in a simple dark cloak and wearing not so much an expression of dismay as one of satisfaction, as if something he'd suspected earlier had just been verified. Ruith was fairly sure he knew what that something might be. He hadn't been exactly forthcoming with the details of his life to any of his company earlier in the winter, and he had outright lied to Seirceil about his identity. No doubt the jig was up.

Then again, the fourth member of that little group behind Morag's frantic guardsmen hadn't been exactly forthcoming about *any* of his details, so Ruith supposed he might be considered the lesser of the two offenders there.

That fourth man, Franciscus, the alemaster of Doìre, was leaning negligently against the side of the wagon, looking for all the world as if he'd just stopped to water his horses and decided a nap on his feet was a good way to pass the time. Quite a pretty sight for a man who was in truth the grandson of King Seannair of Cothromaiche. Franciscus's hood was pulled over his face and his arms folded over his chest. He certainly didn't look as if he spared any concern for the fact that the dragon queen of An-uallach was about to kill him, Ruith, and then quite possibly Franciscus's own granddaughter, Sarah.

Morag didn't seem to have noticed anything that was going on behind her or noted who might have been watching her. Ruith was happy to leave it that way. He wasn't above asking for a rescue from old friends if the need arose.

"You don't look well, Prince Ruithneadh," Morag said with exaggerated concern. "Why don't you go have a little rest until you feel more yourself. I'll pass the time very pleasantly with the lass hiding behind you."

"I don't think you will," Ruith said, promising himself at least a solid handful of hours in a safe place to recover from Morag's initial salvo at Sarah. He could only imagine what she would throw at him.

"You don't," Morag said sharply. "You *don't*? Why, you arrogant, foolish *boy*, who do you think you are? Coming to my hall uninvited, leaving me with a *hole* in my wall, assaulting my guards, *stealing*—"

"Stealing?" Ruith echoed, dredging up his own bit of disdain. "Surely you can't be serious. We were guests in your hall when we were assaulted by *your* spells—"

"Which were nothing but a pale foreshadowing of what magic I have to hand now," she spat.

"One would hope," he said, affecting a look he imagined Sìle would have been proud of, "considering the spells in your keep weren't all that impressive."

"Will you shut up?" Sarah hissed from behind him.

"If you think you'll get in the way of my prize," Morag said, drawing herself up, "then you are sorely mistaken, my young princeling."

Ruith shrugged. "I don't think I am. And I am usually right about these kinds of things—"

He didn't gasp, but it was only because he didn't have the wind to. Her spell slammed into him with even more power than Miach's had toward the end of their little tête-à-tête. He remained on his feet only because Sarah's hands were buried in his cloak, keeping him upright. He planted his feet apart and prepared to face a woman who was, in the end, just a woman. Those of An-uallach had lifespans that far outstripped the average farmer in the south, but certainly didn't stretch out unendingly like those of elvenkind. She had power enough, but nothing, in the end, to equal any of his forebearers.

He suspected that annoyed her quite a bit.

It was no doubt why she had spent so much of her time trying to invent a way to copy his father's spell of Diminishing. Perhaps she thought that if she could steal power, she could steal life as well.

And then he had no more time or space for leisurely thoughts. Morag wasn't his father, but she had her own store of very vile spells that she didn't hesitate to use. The only thing in his favor was that those spells were no worse than what Miach had thrown at him—and a handful of them were ones he wasn't entirely sure Miach hadn't possessed himself—so he countered them if not with ease, at least without drawing back in revulsion.

And then she turned to things he realized he truly did recognize.

It took him a moment to identify them as magic akin to what Uachdaran of Léige had used. He didn't want to know where either of them had learned those spells for they were full of shadows from nightmares and depths better not peered into. He had a strong stomach, but he found that even he flinched a time or two.

He noticed after a bit that there hadn't even been a change in Morag's breathing, which worried him. He certainly couldn't say the same for himself. He dragged his sleeve across his eyes and fought with renewed determination. But he felt himself beginning to slip

Just a bit.

And then he realized suddenly that Morag was being quite a bit more devious than he'd imagined she would be. She was hurling spells at him at an alarming rate, true, but she was also weaving something behind him.

Something meant just for Sarah.

He countered that spell—a spell that was far too much like his father's spell of Diminishing for his taste—as best he could, but just the effort of that wore on him in a particularly inconvenient way. Then, as things took a turn for the worse, he found himself contemplating a few less savoury things. He had to physically stop himself from spewing out a spell of essence changing. That the bloody thing came so easily to his mind was alarming, but what kept him from using it was the thought of Morag hearing it. He could only imagine what she would turn others into without hesitation. For all he knew, she was less interested in whatever magic she thought Sarah might possess than she was in Cothromaiche's most powerful spells—

Diminishing.

He hesitated, then brushed the thought aside as if it had been an annoying fly buzzing round his head. As tempting as it was to rid the world of Morag, he couldn't do it that way. He *wouldn't* do it that way, not if that was the only means left him to do her in.

But that didn't seem to keep the thought from continuing to tug at him.

He realized, with a start, that it wasn't just his imagination or his sense of self-preservation that was making untoward suggestions to him in the less-than-quiet of his mind.

It was the bits of spell in his pocket.

"Ruith!"

He looked up in time to see a wave of evil geysering up into the sky.

And in that moment, he knew he was lost.

He was once again standing at the edge of a particular glade, watching his sire uncap a well of evil, watching the precise moment occur when his sire knew that he had no hope of containing it. He listened to his father spew out spell after spell in an effort to contain what he'd loosed. He watched as his father stretched up his hands and spat out his most treasured, most closely guarded, most potent spell.

Diminishing.

Ruith realized the words were half out of his mouth—nay, half the *spell* was out of his mouth—only because something connected very sharply with his ribs and he abruptly lost his breath. He found himself shoved aside so hard that he almost went sprawling. He made a grab for Sarah because he saw Morag's spell beginning to descend. It was obviously going to fall on someone, but he was going to make certain that someone wasn't going to be Sarah.

It was apparently going to be Franciscus.

The man said nothing as he stood there, facing Morag in her terrible rage, but the spell above them was changed abruptly—and quite permanently—into a soft, gentle rain that healed as it fell.

Ruith supposed it might not be politic to point out to the grandson of the king of Cothromaiche that those sorts of spells weren't to be used lightly, so he kept his mouth shut.

Morag had begun to swear in a most unattractive fashion. Ruith looked at her fists, clenched and held down at her sides, and wasn't entirely sure she wouldn't reach out and strike Franciscus. It took her but a moment, but she recaptured her mocking expression and looked down her nose at the man standing twenty paces from her.

"And who might you be, come at such an opportune moment?"

Sarah's grandfather considered for a moment or two, then lifted his hood back off his head and faced Morag without any disguise.

Morag blinked in surprise, then threw back her head and laughed. Ruith didn't see anything humorous about it, but he was beginning to suspect that Morag was not in full possession of her wits.

"Well," she gasped, dabbing at her eyes with a snowy white

handkerchief she produced from her sleeve, "if it isn't Prince Fran-sciscus of Cothromaiche, back from the dead."

Franciscus only inclined his head slightly. "So it would seem."

"This is unexpected," she said with a smile. "It has been many years, my friend."

"It has been many years," Franciscus agreed, "but you and I, Morag, were never friends."

"Oh, come now," Morag cajoled, "you aren't going to hold a small and insignificant disagreement against me, are you? After all this time?"

Ruith stopped listening to her only because he realized he was being beguiled by her words. He watched her hand weaving some-thing and was on the verge of calling out a warning to Franciscus only to realize that wasn't necessary. Franciscus batted her spell away as if it had been eiderdown, only the spell became fluff in truth. Ruith imagined Soilléir wouldn't have approved, but he also imagined Soilléir didn't have the cheek to tell his uncle what to do with his magic.

"Why don't you speak those spells aloud?" Morag taunted. "Afraid I'll memorize them?"

"I wouldn't give you the pleasure," Franciscus said without any inflection in his voice.

And that was the last thing either of them said for quite some time.

Ruith thought he had seen quite a few things that would have shocked most polite mages, but he found himself watching, open-mouthed, as what had been a fairly polite discussion between dig-nified members of some exclusive club turned into a full-on battle between two mages who had no intention of giving any ground to the other.

And then Morag used spells that made Miach of Neroche's look pleasant by comparison.

Sarah gasped. Ruith stepped back in front of her and pulled her hard against him. "Don't look."

"But—"

"Repeat the spell," he said, keeping her turned toward him. He looked over his shoulder, winced, then bowed his head to shield Sarah's face. "The one Soilléir gave you to shut off your sight. Dimming, or whatever rot we're calling it."

She was trembling badly, but she said the words. His sight was nothing compared to hers, and it did occur to him that he was perhaps imagining things, but he could have sworn he saw a shadow fall over her. It wasn't an evil thing, but instead merely the shadow that came over the ground when a cloud obscured the sun. Sarah sighed deeply, put her arms around his waist and buried her face against his neck.

He would have drawn her away from the fray, but a darkness sprang up so suddenly, he couldn't see his hand in front of his face—and that was no pleasant effect of one of Soilléir's spells. He didn't dare move for fear he would walk them into Morag instead of ushering them toward escape. His sense of direction was normally very good, but along with that darkness, Morag had added a fair amount of confusion—

And then, suddenly, the sky above them burst into light thanks to a thousand arrows that had been shot up to linger above their heads, arrows tipped with werelight that was almost too bright to look at it.

Mansourah of Neroche, obviously, doing what he did best.

"Let's go," Ruith said, pulling Sarah with him. The only direction he knew was *away from Morag*, so that was the one he took without hesitation.

"But Franciscus—"

"He'll manage." Ruith put her in front of him and gave her no choice but to run on. He looked back and saw the bulwark of spells

Franciscus had been weaving around both himself and Morag. If things truly went south, Francicus could likely hop over that and leave Morag enclosed in something that would take her a year to unravel.

Mansourah stood behind that magical wall and grimly picked off Morag's guardsmen one by one, until only one poor lad remained standing there, looking as if he was close to puking his guts out at any moment. Ruith paused next to Miach's brother.

"Leaving that one to tell tales?"

"Prince Franciscus bid me leave him alive," Mansourah said with a shrug. "Did you not hear him?"

"I've been distracted."

"With good reason. I think we should go quickly."

"We can't leave Franciscus," Sarah croaked. "I can't lose him too."

"You won't," Ruith said, praying that would be true. "I don't think we've begun to see what he can do—and that is how he wants it. Trust him, Sarah. He has no intention of losing this battle."

"But Morag—"

"Is an overdressed, vain, vexatious wench," Mansourah supplied loudly. "Don't know why they let her on the Council."

"They keep her there for pity," Ruith said just as loudly.

Morag glared at them, but apparently had no energy to toss any spells their way. Ruith took the opportunity to stumble on with Sarah along the side of the road, trying not to slip on the less-than-pristine snow that had apparently survived what passed for spring in the surrounding environs. He gave Morag a wide berth, though he soon saw that was unnecessary. She was too distracted by the spells Franciscus was using, no doubt torn between fighting them off and wallowing in her anger that such spells were not hers.

He shot a look at the lone guardsman who had fitted an arrow to the string and was pointing it at them. The man considered, then lowered his bow. Ruith continued his ungainly run with Sarah toward the lads who had, very wisely to his mind, abandoned the wagon and regrouped under the trees on the side of the road.

Ruith looked up in time to find two owls flapping down out of a tree only to land as jet-black dragons, adorned with nothing but saddles and a bit of smoke wreathing their nostrils.

Ned squeaked and fainted. Oban looked at Ruith in astonishment but managed to reach down and slap Ned awake just the same. Seirceil looked at Ruith and smiled.

"I think we're short a mount or two," he said easily. "I don't mind wearing dragonshape, if you don't mind putting it on me, Prince Ruithneadh."

Ruith was too exhausted to even manage to snort. "You have a keen eye."

"And you look rather less like your sire than you might fear," Seirceil said with another smile. "Perhaps at first glance, but a closer look says you resemble your Uncle Làidir on your mother's side and your Uncle Miadhail on your father's side."

"A fact for which I am most grateful."

Seirceil shrugged. "Gair was an exceptionally handsome man, it could be said, though I'm not much of a judge in those matters. Out of all of you, I daresay your brother Keir looked the most like him. Before," he added quietly.

"Then you know of his passing?" Ruith asked in surprise.

"There have been tales of the closing of your father's well a pair of fortnights ago borne by many creatures who speak only to those who are listening. I thought it best to keep those tidings to myself."

"I imagine you did," Ruith agreed. "Very well, if dragonshape suits you, I'll see to it." He paused and looked over his shoulder at the battle still raging behind him. "We need to go quickly, though I have no idea where we should make for."

"If I might suggest a place," Mansourah began slowly, "Taigh

Hall lies not far from here. It is the last decent hall on the road north before one must either press on and hope for entrance to Bruadair or take his courage in hand and make the long, arduous trek for Gairn. No traveler is refused there, though the best we could hope for would be a scrap of floor in the outer gatehouse."

"Agreed," Seirceil said. "I think we would be tolerated at the very least—unless one of us had any sort of connection to those in Bruadair?"

Ruith wasn't about to divulge secrets that weren't his—which he was fairly certain he'd heard Soilléir say on at least one occasion—so he simply shook his head.

"None that we're able to claim," he said easily. "Perhaps we'll have to simply arrive and take our chances."

"What's that place, again?" Ned asked, looking as if he'd had another look into hell. "Somewhere with more of these magish sorts?"

"Bruadair is the home of the dreamweavers, Ned," Seirceil said patiently, "not goblins or ogres. Taigh Hall is nothing more than a waystation for weary travelers. You'll be perfectly safe. Now, Ruith will change me into a dragon, then you'll climb on just as you'd do with one of your father's horses. I won't let you fall off."

"Oy," Ned breathed, drawing back from Seirceil in horror. "A dragon?" He took another step back. "I'd best fetch my gear from the wagon."

"Be quick," Ruith warned, then turned back to Seirceil who was still watching him with a faint smile. He managed a weary smile in return. "A pleasant journey here?"

"Hellish," Seirceil said, "and made for the most part with only spotty appearances by our good alemaster, who is definitely more than he seems."

"Is there anything you don't know?" Ruith asked sourly.

Seirceil only smiled. "I am an obscure son of an obscure lord, Your Highness. That anonymity permits me to observe things that others might not be privy to. So, aye, I knew who you all were, including Lord Urchaid, but discretion dictated that I keep silent. And to answer what you haven't asked, our journey has been uneventful in all the ways that count, for we are very unimportant players in a grand drama. And thankfully we are players who are missing two hounds that Oban turned into birds and sent flapping off to Lake Cladach to put themselves in the care of Prince Sgath."

"Thank heavens," Ruith said, with feeling.

"I thought you might feel that way." Seirceil turned and walked away. "Dragonshape, Your Highness, if it isn't too much trouble. I'm afraid I might turn into something unrecognizable if I do it myself."

Ruith obliged him, shot Ned a warning look he correctly interpreted as a command to go mount up, then looked at Oban. He gestured toward to Tarbh. "If you don't mind, Master Oban. We're in a fair bit of haste, I fear."

Oban shoved his sleeves up above his elbows, straightened his hat, then marched over to the dragon, trailing spells that turned into wee dragons and flapped off behind him. Ruith looked at Mansourah.

"And you?"

"I think I can manage wings myself," Mansourah said dryly, "though I thank you for your concern." He paused and lowered his voice. "I didn't say this before, but I think we should tread carefully at Taigh Hall."

"Why?" Ruith asked.

"Because we're in the north and traveling even further north," Mansourah said. He seemed to consider, then shrugged. "Things are different there."

"If they have a hot fire and scrap of floor we can use, I'll allow them all the strange happenings they want."

Mansourah only nodded and walked away. Ruith turned and found Sarah standing next to him, watching what was still a very unpleasant though relatively contained battle between her grand-father and the queen of An-uallach. She glanced briefly at him.

"He'll win, won't he?" she asked very quietly. "Franciscus, I mean."

"Your grandfather is centuries old, love," he said just as quietly, "and cannier than either of us can imagine. I think I can safely guarantee you that if things become too dodgy, he'll turn Morag into something humiliating. A skunk, or a mangy racoon, perhaps. Or a stone in the road that's endlessly cursed for laming horses and breaking carriage axles. But he won't be vanquished by her. And if I might suggest the same thing he would suggest, we should be on our way. He'll be along soon enough."

Sarah nodded uneasily, but walked with him to where Ruathar crouched, waiting patiently. Within moments, they were airborne, hidden by Ruith's most potent spell of glamour.

He spared a grateful thought for the fact that Morag couldn't shapechage, then hoped they had seen the last of her. He imagined if Franciscus had anything to say about it, they had.

One enemy crossed off the list, an indeterminate number of others still to go.

He had the feeling the rest of them might not be dispatched so easily.

Ten

Sarah wondered if the day would ever come when she could climb off the back of a dragon and find her legs steady beneath her. She leaned on Ruathar, clutching the saddle he had so thoughtfully provided for her until she'd stopped shaking. She didn't realize he had turned himself back into a horse until she lifted her head and looked at him.

He stared at her from limpid eyes that were full of stars and wildness. She supposed she would eventually grow accustomed to his and his brother's changing themselves into whatever suited them, perhaps in the same distant year when she'd grown accustomed to the fact that her life was not at all what she'd expected it would be.

"Well, this is interesting."

She realized Ruith was standing next to her. She half expected him to tell her to hop back up in the saddle because safety was definitely not to be found where they were.

Instead, he was simply frowning at what looked at first glance to be an enormous hunting lodge. It was protected by no more than the same sort of rock wall surrounding the homesteads she'd seen below her as they had made their way north. There were stables tucked into the corner to her right and what looked to be a guardhouse near those, all surrounded by a thick forest of stately pines. If the lord of the hall had delusions of it being any sort of grand palace, she couldn't see it. She looked up at Ruith.

"What had you expected?" she asked.

"I have no idea," he said frankly. "I'm not even sure what this place is, and I don't mean merely where it is on a map. Mansourah was particularly closemouthed about it all." He paused and looked at her. "What do you see?"

"I don't think there are any nefarious mages waiting behind that wall." She shrugged. "I don't see anything, really. It certainly feels nothing like An-uallach."

"We can be grateful for that—"

Sarah found herself suddenly pulled behind him, but since that wasn't an unusual thing, she didn't protest. Their horses backed up behind her, as if they thought it might be wise to remove themselves from a fray which Sarah saw might become reality very soon thanks to the men suddenly pouring out of not only the front door but the surrounding forest as well. They didn't seem to mind so much about the humans standing in front of them, but they were obviously not at all happy about Seirceil who was still crouching ten feet away from them in glorious dragonshape. Mansourah caused a bit more commotion as he suddenly unspun himself from whatever brisk breeze he'd been traveling as. He turned and looked at Ruith, his eyes full of delight and something else not nearly as tame, and pointed at Seirceil.

"You should do something about him."

Ruith stared at him evenly. "Is there any point in that, or are we going to be taking wing again right away?"

"Shapechanging doesn't go over well here."

Sarah started to point out that he likely should have said something about that earlier but Ruith beat her to it.

"And you couldn't have told me this sooner?" he asked incredulously.

"You were distracted. Do something about Seirceil, then we'll see about the rest."

Ruith cursed him succinctly, then turned Seirceil back into his own shape. The ragtag group of guards came to an abrupt halt some thirty paces away, but they didn't put away their swords and their archers didn't take their arrows away from their strings.

"Let me pave the way," Mansourah said, half under his breath. "With some success, I hope."

"Mansourah, if you've led us into a trap—" Ruith growled.

Mansourah looked at him with a bit of a smile. "Now, Ruith, why would I do that?"

"Because you're responsible for several episodes in my youth that resulted in my grandfather shouting me half deaf, which means I don't trust you."

Mansourah put his hand over his heart. "I'm hurt, Ruith, truly hurt."

"You will be in truth if this turns into something foul."

Sarah found Mansourah winking at her before he turned and walked away. She would have smiled at the list Ruith was making not entirely under his breath of the things he would do to Miach's brother if he had a free quarter hour, but she was suddenly too busy trying not to wring her hands. If they had escaped one piece of peril only to plunge themselves into another . . .

Mansourah kept his hands in plain sight as he contined to walk forward. He stopped a discreet distance away from the captain of what apparently passed for guardsmen at Taigh Hall.

"Mansourah of Neroche," he said politely, "with friends, here to see Lord Cuirmear, if you please."

"His Lordship isn't receiving anyone at present," the man growled.

"Then perhaps you would be so good as to let us rest ourselves in your gatehouse until he decides to," Mansourah said smoothly. "Unless courtesy no longer has a place here."

The man snorted. "Courtesy to a cluster of shapechanging demons and the beasts you've brought with you? I'd say we aren't obliged to do anything at all." He peered at Mansourah suspiciously. "Where're you from?"

Mansourah clasped his hands behind his back. "Neroche, as I said before, and I'm happy to just stand here until your lord tires of his luncheon and comes out to see us. You might whisper in his ear that I bring greetings from not only King Sìle of Tòrr Dòrainn but my brother Mochriadhemiach, who as you may or may not know is the newly crowned king of Neroche."

Sarah watched the man consider, then purse his lips. "Very well, you may go sit yourselves down on those benches over there. Take your beasts with you and keep your rabble together. I don't like to think what'll happen to you otherwise."

"I wouldn't either," Mansourah agreed frankly. "Thank you for your graciousness."

The captain walked off, muttering unintelligible things, and Mansourah turned and smiled.

"Well," he said brightly, "that went well."

Ruith blew out his breath. "Remind me not to put you in charge of my life again, Buck."

Sarah stepped around Ruith so she could look at him. "Buck?" she echoed. "Is that what you call him?"

"I've called him much worse," Ruith said sourly. "*Mansourah* is a bit of a mouthful and *fathead* was already taken by another of his brothers, so Miach and I were left with that." He pursed his lips. "It became something of a common name amongst us."

Given that he'd used it at Buidseachd to get them in the front gates, she had to agree with the truth of that. She looked at them both in surprise. "I didn't realize you knew each other so well."

Mansourah sighed lightly. "I don't admit to it often, for obvious reasons. The truth is, I was much fonder of Eglach—Ruith's older brother, you know—than I ever was of this lump of refuse here, but aye, I know him well enough. As lads, Eglach and I were generous enough to allow our younger brothers to come with us from time to time, to admire our adventures and heap praise upon our heads at their successful conclusion. But take part in glorious escapades? They weren't worthy of it."

Ruith glared at him. "I hope Miach grinds you to dust all the days of your life."

"I imagine you do," Mansourah said, raising his eyebrow briefly, "though I imagine he'll do it so sweetly that I'll never notice. Now, before you think too long on past brotherly injuries, let's be about herding our lads over to where we've been directed before we lose even that concession." He paused, then looked at Ruith, suddenly serious. "I would, if I could make a suggestion, shield your face, my friend."

Ruith blinked. "Why?"

"Just trust me. We'll be safe enough if we can get past Lord Cuirmear's first impressions of us—or so I'm hoping—but until then, I would beg you to simply do as I ask. Sarah, you should do the same."

Sarah found that her hands were trembling too badly to be of any use at all, but fortunately Mansourah had turned away to watch the hall and he didn't notice. Ruith did her the favor of pulling her hood up over her hair. He leaned in as he fussed with the clasp under her chin.

"If events spiral out of control," he murmured, "I will change us both into wind and pull you after me. Our ponies will follow, I'm sure."

"And the rest?" she asked, her mouth suddenly very dry.

"That damned brother of Miach's can fend for himself. As for the others, I don't think two damaged mages and a farmboy are going to be any threat to anyone here, so I'll turn them all into snakes and they can slither their way out onto the road after we're safely away. We'll rescue them when we can."

She shivered as he took her hand and nodded for Mansourah to walk on the other side of her as they made their way toward the gatehouse. She looked over her shoulder to find the rest of their company trailing after them, wide-eyed and silent.

She wondered as she approached what apparently served as a refuge for travelers—outside the rock wall, as it happened—why Mansourah would have chosen this place when there had been a dozen others just like it all along the feet of the mountains. She also wondered, because it helped to take her mind off her unease, if gardens were possible in such a climate or they simply lived on mutton and potatoes. She had seen copious numbers of very wooly sheep, the occasional plucky field of cultivated grain, but not much else save enormous swaths of evergreens.

Which were, she had to admit, gloriously beautiful. It had reminded her once again how desperately ugly Doìre had been and how grateful she was to know she would never have to see the place again.

She soon found herself sandwiched between Ruith and Mansourah on a bench pushed up against the wall of the guesthouse. Ned and Oban made themselves at home on another stone seat, though they looked no more comfortable than she felt.

Sarah leaned closer to Ruith. "Do you know anyone here, or are we at Mansourah's mercy?"

Ruith wrapped his hand in both his own and studied the enormous lodge behind the low rock wall. "I could hazard a guess, but I believe I'll allow our illustrious guide to give us the details instead."

Sarah looked at Mansourah, who was only watching them with a smile.

"Where we are?" he asked, shaking himself out of his thoughts.

"Taigh Hall, which I believe I mentioned before, where Cuirmear of Bruadair is the self-styled lord. He is actually a decent host, but only because entertaining travelers is how he keeps his folk fed. As for the souls who find themselves here, I suppose you could say this is something of a halfway house for disaffected dreamweavers."

"Troublemakers, you mean," Ruith corrected.

"Aye, I suppose so," Mansourah said with a bit of a laugh. "I think the rabble that trickles down from the north is a bit on the subversive side. This is also, as it happens, a popular destination for adventurous travelers who would like to catch a glimpse of a dreamweaver but aren't so adventurous as to attempt entry into Bruadair itself."

Sarah shivered. "That doesn't sound like a very pleasant place."

"I've never been inside Bruadair's borders," Mansourah admitted, "so I can't say what the truth is. Those who have escaped won't talk about it and those who live there still but have dealings with the outside world are equally closedmouthed. I *have* heard that it is a glorious place, almost too beautiful to look at."

"Or too ugly," Ruith muttered, "which is what *I've* heard."

"Well, I doubt either of us will know the truth of it any time soon," Mansourah said cheerfully, "given that we would never get inside the borders alive." He shot Ruith a look. "If you think your grandfather is particular about who comes into his land, you should meet the current king of Bruadair."

"Have you met him?" Ruith asked in surprise.

"Not him," Mansourah said cryptically. "His predecessor, aye, but not him. I think I'm rather grateful for that, actually."

"Details, Buck, to keep us awake," Ruith said with an enormous yawn.

Sarah listened to them discuss rumor and heresay and found herself wondering a thing or two. If rumor were to be believed and her mother had in truth been a dreamweaver from a land too glorious to be believed, why had she left it? Or, more to the point, how had Athair of Cothromaiche gotten inside its borders to convince her to leave with him?

Those were questions she decided abruptly that she didn't need to have answered, so she leaned her head back against the cold stone of the house behind her and enjoyed the fact that she was sitting on something that wasn't moving. And to keep herself from paying attention to the trading of insults that was now going on over her head, she forced herself to study the enormous hall in front of her.

Now that she had the leisure to look at it for a bit, she saw that it wasn't quite as close to the mountains as she'd thought it was, and she wondered what lay behind it. As an afterthought, she murmured her spell of seeing under her breath. Ruith looked at her briefly, smiled, then said something particularly vile to Mansourah. That was likely why he didn't realize her mouth had fallen open.

Then again, perhaps he had. He leaned over to whisper to her.

"What do you see?"

She wasn't quite sure where to begin. The enormous lodge was still there, but it was as if a great tapestry had been laid over it, fashioned of colors she had never seen before much less imagined could exist. But it was a living thing somehow, as if the scenes that played out in front of her were being captured by master weavers as they occurred, then the cloth rolled up and a new scene begun as events changed or the players came and went. She watched for another moment or two, then looked at Ruith.

"I'm not sure I can describe it."

"Well, the place gives me the bloody shivers," he said with a smile, "so perhaps 'tis best you don't."

She looked into his very lovely bluish green eyes and thought she just might have a few fond feelings for him. It had nothing to do, she told herself firmly, with the fairness of his face, or that he could put himself in front of her and defend her from all manner of terrible mages or vicious queens, or that he could put all that magic aside and build her a very lovely fire.

It was that she loved him. Beyond reason, beyond any sense, and beyond any lists that either she or his grandfather had made of suitable matches for either her or Ruith.

He lifted an eyebrow in question, as if he wondered just what she might be thinking, leaned closer to her, then kissed her. All without so much as a by-your-leave.

"Oh, please," Mansourah groaned. "Not that."

Ruith pulled away just far enough to look at her. "We will be jettisoning that bit of rubbish as quickly as possible, I assure you."

Mansourah snorted. "Don't think I intend to come all the way with you to the bitter end. I've rethought it and decided I have a wedding to attend. I think there might be a handsome lass or two there with nothing more pressing to do than dance with me. I'll stay until I'm sure you can carry on without me, then I'm off with the first brisk breeze—"

Sarah watched in surprise as he leapt to his feet and strode forward a handful of paces. She would have asked Ruith what he thought of that—and told him that she was rather glad, all things considered, that she and he were such good friends—but Ruith had jumped to his feet as well and had pulled her up behind him. She put her hands on his back, but they were trembling so she wrapped her arms around herself instead. Ruith reached behind her with his left hand and felt for her hand, then laced his fingers with hers.

She glanced at the rest of their company to find them perfectly still, then took her a deep breath and looked around Ruith's shoulder. She couldn't imagine what the fuss was about—

Until she saw the man walking without haste but with definite purpose toward them and realized the lord of the hall had indeed finished with his meal. At least he had no magic that she could see. After her morning's encounter with Morag of An-uallach, that came as something of a relief.

He stopped a handful of paces away from Mansourah and folded his arms over his chest.

"Yes?" he asked briskly. "And make your answer brief and to the point. I have things to do."

Mansourah bowed slightly. "I am Mansourah of Neroche, Lord Cuirmear, and bring you greetings not only from my brother the king but also Sìle of Tòrr Dòrainn."

"Did you bring me anything more—shall we say—substantial?"

Sarah watched Mansourah make a production of reaching inside his cloak which sent Cuirmear's guards into a frenzy of renewed bristling, but Cuirmear only waved them aside negligently. Mansourah presented a rather substantial bag of something that made a very soothing clinking sound. Sarah had no doubt Mansourah had simply conjured it up at that moment for His Lordship's pleasure.

"Unfortunately our journey was in haste and a more suitable gift was not possible," Mansourah said regretfully.

Cuirmear hefted the bag with a practiced hand. "Of Neroche strike?"

"Of course, my lord."

Cuirmear tossed it to one of his aids, then nodded toward the rest of their company. "And who are these?"

"Friends," Mansourah said easily. "We're seeking shelter for the night. We'll be on our way in the morning."

Cuirmear looked at him shrewdly. "Running from something, are you, Your Highness?"

"Morag of An-uallach," Mansourah answered frankly.

Cuirmear grunted. "Fortunately for you, I don't mind vexing her every chance I have, though you'll regret it if she makes trouble on my front stoop."

Sarah supposed, given the tone of his voice, that he wasn't particularly worried about that. She looked around Ruith in time to see the lord of the hall turn away.

"My servants will find a chamber for you," he threw over his shoulder. "Put on decent clothes for supper, if you have them."

Sarah suspected she should have felt relieved, but Mansourah wasn't relaxing and neither was Ruith. Cuirmear was well on his way back to his front door, his guardsmen either trailing along behind him or returning to their posts, but she had the distinct feeling they weren't completely out of the woods, as it were. She looked at the remaining servants, no more than a handful of them, who remained behind. She likely wouldn't have thought anything of them if it hadn't been for a man and a woman who stood in front of the little group. She looked more closely at them, then struggled to identify what it was about them that didn't seem quite right.

And then she realized what it was. They were part of the tapestry as well, yet at the same time . . . not.

Because they were the weavers of that tapestry.

She focused on them with difficulty, for everything was in continual motion. They were a man and woman dressed in simple homespun, then a crowned king and queen dressed in velvet purple robes trimmed with ermine. Surrounding them was a riot of color, thousands of hues, innumerable variations in saturation that she had never imagined could exist. She clutched the back of Ruith's cloak with the hand he wasn't holding and hoped she could keep herself upright.

The other servants were given permission to take the horses away and see to their stabling. There were yet other guardsmen standing a fair distance away, no doubt left there to make sure no one got into any trouble, but Sarah immediately dismissed them. All she could do was look at the pair most immediately in front of them, those two who were definitely not what they seemed to be. They continued to stand there, as if they'd been frozen in place.

Mansourah stepped forward and greeted the man first with words Sarah couldn't quite hear. He turned to the woman, made her a bow—which surprised Sarah quite a bit—then straightened quickly. The woman smiled, as if she'd seen Mansourah before and the memory had been pleasant.

"Here you find us in less than ideal surroundings, Prince Mansourah," the man said in a low voice, "though it could be much worse. Could it not, my love?" he asked the woman.

"It could," she agreed. She looked at Mansourah. "It grieved us to hear about King Adhémar, but we understand that Mochriadhemiach now wears the crown."

"He does," Mansourah said quietly, "and very well, if I might offer an opinion."

"I don't doubt it," the woman said. She looked past him with interest. "We'll find places for you and your friends—our situation does have its advantages when seeing to the housing of guests—for you look as if you've traveled here in great haste."

"You do look a little windblown," the man agreed with a bit of a laugh. "Now, my lad, who do you have with you?"

Mansourah stepped aside. He gestured first toward their companions, naming Ned and the mages. Then he looked briefly at Ruith before he turned back to the pair Sarah had begun to suspect were not servants at all.

"I believe," Mansourah began carefully, "that you'll find no introductions will be necessary here." He looked at Ruith. "If you would, Your Highness?"

Sarah felt Ruith pull her forward to stand next to him. She had no idea what Mansourah was doing, but she was the first to admit that the niceties required of royalty were not anything she was accustomed to providing. Ruith was still for a moment or two, then he slowly reached up to pull his hood away from his head.

The woman gasped, then fainted.

And then things took a turn for the worse.

The man had a spell of death tumbling out of his mouth before Mansourah had even stretched out his hands to catch that same man's wife.

"Stop, Fréam," Mansourah said sharply, "before you do something you'll regret."

The man named Fréam was obviously not interested in what Mansourah had to say. Ruith swore at Miach's brother—no doubt for putting them all in danger unnecessarily—then fought off the servant-now-turned-mage's very vile barrage of spells that assaulted him from all sides. Sarah would have stepped in front of Ruith, but he pushed her out of the way and continued to counter the attack with nothing more than rather benign spells of defense. That seemed to be sufficient, for the other man's magic seemed to be nothing more than echoes of true spells.

Sarah frowned. It was very odd, that magic.

Sarah started to relax, but then noticed the single, unremarkable black thread that slipped past Ruith's defenses. She might have thought it innocuous enough, but it began to wind itself around him. She looked at him to see what he would do but realized immediately that he hadn't noticed it. She tried to call out a warning, but he was obviously too busy to hear her. Waving her hands and shouting didn't garner any attention either.

It was as if he had stepped into another world where she couldn't touch him.

If she hadn't been panicked before, she was then. She drew the knife out of her boot and turned toward him only to have him look at her, then blink in surprise.

"Where did you come from?"

"I've been here all the time," she said, reaching out toward him.

He backed away with a look of horror on his face. She took hold of his arm and reached out to try to cut the thread, but he spun away from her, looking at her as if he'd never seen her before. That was perilous enough, but the mage king's spells were also falling on him and wrapping themselves around him too quickly for her to do anything but watch them so obscure Ruith's vision of the real world, he obviously couldn't see what was truly in front of him. She took a firmer grip on her knife, then turned to the perpetrator of the attack. She stepped in front of Ruith, pushed her hood back off her hair, then glared at the man.

"Stop it," she demanded.

The king—for she couldn't deny the crown she'd seen atop his head and the velvet robes wrapped around him—gaped at her, openmouthed. Fortunately for her—something she promised herself a good think on later—his spells fell to the ground like piles of waste yarn that lay there, still and useless. Sarah glanced briefly behind her to see that black thread still wrapping itself around Ruith, forming a barrier between him and where he stood in the world truly. She turned back to the king and frowned fiercely.

"That as well, Your Majesty."

The king spoke a single, very garbled word, and all the spells disappeared as if they'd never been there.

"Sorcha," he gasped, then he looked at her more closely. "Nay, you aren't . . . but then that would make you—"

"Sarah," she said, because the blood rushing through her veins with such violence left no room for caution, "and I insist that you leave that man behind me alone."

"Sarah," the king repeated, sounding as if he hardly dared give voice to the name. "They told us you were dead." He gestured weakly behind her. "What are you doing with that mage?"

"I'm helping him," she said. "And he isn't who you think he is. Look again."

The king of a place she couldn't yet name had another look at

Ruith, then drew his hand over his eyes. He looked suddenly very ill.

"Forgive me, lad," he said hoarsely. "I mistook you for your father, but I can see I was gravely mistaken."

"I am his son," Ruith conceded, "but that is where any similarities end."

"And you are . . not Gille—"

"Nay, Your Majesty," Ruith said. "I am Ruithneadh."

Sarah watched the king study Ruith for another minute, look at her just as closely, then shake his head, as if he hadn't expected to see anything like them in his courtyard—though Sarah supposed it wasn't his courtyard if he were relegating himself to simply being a servant.

"I can see there is a tale here," he said faintly. "I would be interested in it, if you care to give it, but perhaps later when we might have a bit of privacy." He turned to Mansourah and took his senseless wife from him. "Thank you for catching her. I think she's had a bit of a shock."

"I daresay," Mansourah murmured.

The king shot him a dark look. "You know, little Sourah, there will come a day when you go too far with me. Emissary of your king or not, your love of drama is ill-concieved and excessive."

Mansourah smiled. "In this instance, Your Majesty, it was less drama than it was necessity. There was no time to prepare you. We are being pursued by dangerous souls, seen and unseen, and needed a safe place to rest. I sacrificed niceties in favor of expediency."

The king pursed his lips. "I'll consider that an apology, though a poor one. I'll have one of these lads here lead you to your chamber." He looked at them all briefly. "I would like to come to you later, when I can manage it."

Sarah nodded, because he seemed to be looking at her for some sort of permission, and she didn't dare deny him. She watched him walk off, then realized tranquility hadn't been completely restored for Ruith was in the process of threatening Mansourah with bodily harm.

Mansourah only shrugged. "I did what I thought best."

"And almost got me killed in the process!" Ruith exclaimed. "A little *warning* next time would be greatly appreciated."

"Neither of you was in any danger. Well, you were perhaps, but you have magic enough to defend yourself." He blinked owlishly. "Or am I mistaken?"

Ruith growled at him. "We'll discuss that at our earliest opportunity over blades, Your Highness, in the lists—if they have lists in this rustic hunting lodge, which I sincerely doubt. But since that is what you're accustomed to, living in that flea-infested barn you call a palace, I imagine you'll be able to lead us to the field without any trouble."

Mansourah pursed his lips, then looked at Sarah. "He has very bad manners."

"I don't think he'll take kindly to your trying to improve them," she offered. "He hasn't been sleeping well."

"He'll sleep less well with what I leave of him," Mansourah said. He slung his arm around Ruith's shoulders. "Let's take advantage of what I'm certain will be very luxurious accommodations and have a wee rest. It will perhaps be your last decent one for the next day or so, Ruith my lad, so you should take advantage of it—"

He stopped speaking abruptly thanks to Ruith's elbow in his ribs. Ruith looked over his shoulder with a warning look on his face that Sarah didn't mistake. She gathered up the rest of their company immediately and pointed them in the right direction. She didn't want to be out in the courtyard any longer than necessary.

"Oy," said Ned, sounding as if he were choking.

Oban made no comment but pulled his hat down further on his head, took a firmer grip on his wand, then marched off purposefully behind Ruith and Mansourah, who were exchanging pleasantries—if that's what they could be called—she could hear from where she stood. Oban stopped and beckoned imperiously for Ned to follow him. Sarah watched them go, then looked at Seirceil who had come to stand next to her.

"Well?" she asked.

"Well, what?" he replied politely.

She pursed her lips. "I think, my lord Seirceil, that you know a great deal more than you're telling."

"And why would you think that?"

"Because you don't talk enough," she muttered, then she couldn't help but smile at him. He was a man that inspired that sort of thing. "I assume you know about Ruith."

"And Franciscus, as well," Seirceil offered. "And several other things, actually, that might interest you. I'll tell you of them as we walk, if you like."

"I would," she said, starting across the courtyard with him. If he could take her mind off what she'd just seen, she was happy to chat all afternoon. "Beginning with what Mansourah was thinking to almost get Ruith killed here a moment ago."

Seirceil seemed to consider his words rather carefully. "Let's just say," he began slowly, "that Prince Mansourah's thought was that this was a good place to pause and refresh ourselves. It is close enough from our recent battlefield that a return to that spot is possible if necessary, but not so close that we couldn't press on quite easily should word reach us that Morag has not been dissuaded from further pursuit." He paused. "As to anything else, I can only suggest that it never hurts to make new friends."

"I'm not sure Ruith made any just now."

"Perhaps not," Seirceil conceded. "There are those here in this part of the world who have no love for certain other mages. No manner of flowery introduction will change that."

"Then it was best to just toss Ruith into the fray and see how he came out?" she asked tartly.

Seirceil smiled. "Prince Mansourah does have a flair for the dramatic, and it served him well here. King Fréam will regret his actions and likely offer aid in repayment whereas if he'd simply been introduced to Ruith without fuss he might have been less interested in helping us."

"How do you know all this?" she asked in surprise. "And how do you know all these people?"

"I was, if you can fathom this, a student at Buidseachd once," Seirceil said with a smile. "One learns all sorts of useful things there."

Sarah shivered in spite of herself. "I'm not sure the learning is worth the price of having to learn it there, but that's just me. How long were you there?"

"Six years. I had gone with the hope of apprenticing with Master Soilléir, but the seventh ring eluded me." He shrugged. "I was unwilling to do what was required to earn it, so the fault is purely mine. I was fortunate enough, however, to have many long conversations with Master Soilléir about the philosophy of magic. I will admit that I share his belief that ofttimes for a mage, 'tis preferable to limit oneself to expressing simple thoughts and single words rather than attempting to dazzle the world with mighty deeds of magic."

"It seems to have served him well enough."

"That sort of thinking tends to engender an attitude of humility," he said dryly, "for it keeps a mage from thinking he knows better than those around them." He glanced at her and smiled. "You look a great deal like your mother, you know."

Sarah had assumed there would come a time where that sort of thing would leave her wanting to find somewhere to sit down abruptly, but apparently that time wasn't coming soon. "Do I?" she managed.

"You do," he said easily. "I saw her at the schools of wizardry once, visiting Soilléir of course, long before she met and wed your father. She was in the back of Soilléir's chamber, weaving on a loom he'd had fashioned for her. I'm not sure what she was weaving into that cloth, but then again, dreamweavers have threads at their disposal that the rest of us do not." He paused for a moment or two, then looked at her gravely. "I understand she wore flowers in her hair for her wedding instead of a crown."

Sarah smiled in spite of herself. "Why are you telling me that?"

"It was just a simple thought I suspected you might want to know." He shrugged. "Put it away for the spring and see if it serves you then."

Sarah closed her eyes briefly, then looked at him. "Thank you."

"'Tis my pleasure, my dear." He nodded toward their company in front of them. "We should hurry before your lord flattens Prince Mansourah to be free to come fetch us."

Sarah nodded, then hurried with him to catch up to Ruith and Mansourah, who had apparently traded the exchanging of insults for keeping their thoughts to themselves and marking the details of the hall.

She stopped at the doorway to the enormous hall and looked back over her shoulder. She wasn't one to give credence to an overactive imagination, but she couldn't deny that she had the feeling there was something out there, watching. She wondered if it might be Morag, freshly come from vanquishing Franciscus.

Or it might have been someone they hadn't considered.

She wasn't sure what would have been worse.

Eleven

❧

Ruith paced in front of the fire not because he was restless, but because he was afraid if he sat, he would sleep, and whilst he was grateful for the refuge he wasn't entirely sure they were any safer where they were than they would have been in an open field.

Mansourah had assured him there was nothing to worry about. Cuirmear was arrogant and condescending, but he was also a pragmatist. If he thought there was more money to be made in the future by offering them any sort of hospitality at present, he would do so. Grudgingly, but there it was. And they weren't exactly in a position to be choosy.

Ruith unfortunately hadn't been in the position to take Miach's brother out to the lists and beat manners into him either, but he had been granted a bath, so he supposed he would have to be satisfied with that for the moment. He might have been if he hadn't been so uneasy. And the list of things to be uneasy about was very long.

First and foremost, Sarah was not within arm's reach. She had been escorted to points unknown to have her own bath. Whilst he was pleased that she might have a bit of comfort along a seemingly endless and uncomfortable journey, he wouldn't truly breathe easily until he could see for himself that she was well.

Second, he had left Franciscus of Cothromaiche battling Morag of An-uallach when he should have finished the thing himself. He consoled himself with the fact that he'd had more to worry about than his own pride, but he did not care for allowing others to finish his battles for him. He was half tempted to leave his company safe within Taigh Hall's rustic embrace and have a little look around to see if Franciscus still breathed.

But that might leave him too dead to address the most pressing of the problems, which was to reach the end of his journey and have the wherewithal to best whatever lay there.

He dragged his hand through his hair, then turned at the knock on the door. Mansourah shot him a look, then walked over to it and opened it. He opened it wide and allowed two souls into the very small gathering chamber they'd been granted to use for the night. The door was shut quickly behind them, Mansourah made them a low bow, then led them over to the fire and proceeded with formal introductions.

"Prince Ruithneadh, if I might present King Fréam and Queen Leaghra of Bruadair? Your Majesties, Ruithneadh of Tòrr Dòrainn. And aye," he added, "he is the son of Gair and Sarait, which, Queen Leaghra, you already surmised."

Ruith dusted off his unused court manners and hopefully did credit to his mother. It was readily apparently, however, that whilst Queen Leaghra was willing to concede he was not his father, she was still very unsettled by something.

"Where is the girl?" she asked, looking around and utterly failing to conceal an expression of concern. She looked at Ruith. "That wasn't, well, I'm not sure how it could be, but I'm wondering . . ."

She took a deep breath and her eyes filled with tears. "It isn't possible that it was Sorcha, but I'm not sure who else—"

Ruith shook his head slowly. "I'm sorry, Your Majesty. Sorcha is dead."

"Then who—"

"Her daughter, Sarah."

"A daughter," she breathed. "Fréam said as much, but I didn't believe him." She looked up at Ruith. "Sorcha was my niece, you see. Well, Fréam's younger brother's daughter, if we're to be perfectly accurate, but I loved her dearly." She paused. "We have no children of our own."

"Nor any thrones," Fréam said in disgust, "thanks to my *youngest* brother, may he find the seat uncomfortable all the days of his very long life." He held out his hand to Ruith. "Forgive me again for my unpleasant greeting, Prince Ruithneadh. I won't hide the fact that I mistook you for your father, though if I'd looked more closely, I wouldn't have made that mistake. Though there is a fair bit of Sgath in you, if I might offer an opinion."

"Thank you, Your Majesty," Ruith said seriously. He considered, then supposed there was no reason in not having answers to his questions. "I hesitate to ask this, but did you know—"

"Your father?" Fréam finished for him. He made no effort to hide his distaste. "I'm afraid so, and the memories, though few, are unpleasant ones." He started to speak, then turned at the sound of the door opening. He frowned fiercely. "You!" he exclaimed.

"Aye, me," Franciscus said, shutting the door behind him. "Sorry I'm a bit late."

Ruith put his hand on the mantle not because he'd worried about Franciscus, but because it had been a very long day. He was, however, very relieved to find that Sarah's grandfather was alive and apparently undamaged by his morning's labor.

Franciscus walked wearily across the floor, gestured pointedly for Ned to move, and cast himself down into Ned's chair. "I don't

suppose there is any ale in this hovel, is there? Ned, be a good lad
and fetch me a mug." He looked up at the king. "'Tis good to see
you, Fréam."

Fréam didn't seem nearly as delighted to see him. "You stole my
niece!"

Franciscus rolled his eyes. "Of course I didn't, you great ass.
My son and your niece met—and I will admit to being a bit sketchy
on those particular details—they fell in love, and they wed after a
proper courtship where you had ample time to object to the marriage. Which you did not. Neither did any of my kin."

"Because you were trying to steal my niece, and they were pro-
tecting you!"

Ruith didn't particularly want to insert himself into the conversation, but he needed at least an indication of how the battle had
finished lest he be required to put their company back in the air
sooner rather than later. He cleared his throat, which seemed to be
enough for Franciscus. He smiled wearily.

"All is well, Ruith—"

"Discuss it later," Fréam interrupted briskly, folding his arms
over his chest and glaring at Franciscus, "for I'm not finished here.
There is something new afoot here and I have the unpleasant feeling you're to blame."

Franciscus ignored him and heaved himself to his feet. He
reached for Queen Leaghra's hand and bent low over it. "My dear
Leaghra, it has been too long. You are, as always, a vision of loveliness wrought from a particularly memorable dream."

Ruith watched the queen actually blush and had to hide a smile
behind his hand. The widow Fiore had always been resistant to
Franciscus's charms, but he could see now that that had only been
because the man hadn't truly put them on display.

"Franciscus, you are a rogue," she said with a delicate laugh.
"Look at me in these rags—"

Fréam took his wife's hand out of Franciscus's and glared at him. "He's not a rogue, he's a blackguard. He stole—"

"Your niece," Franciscus said, "aye, you've already said as much, and it is still untrue. My son is the one who stole her, not me." He accepted a cup of ale and smiled at Ned. "Thank you, Ned my lad. I can only hope this is drinkable."

"It can't be any worse that the swill Seannair produces," Fréam muttered.

Franciscus resumed his seat, tasted, then drained the rest in a single draught, apparently so he wouldn't have to taste it. He lowered his cup and looked at the king of Bruadair.

"If you want to be completely accurate, Athair didn't steal her—"

"Nay, you did!" Fréam bellowed.

Franciscus laughed a little in exasperation. "Fréam, I had nothing to do with their meeting, their courtship, or their marriage, though I was overjoyed that my son should have a lass who was the embodiment of pure joy. And," he added, shooting Fréam a look, "I did everything in my power to keep them both safe, which you well know."

"Well," Fréam said with a bit of a huff, "be that as it may, you may rest assured that I will see that the same thing does *not* happen with Sorcha's child. I might not have a throne any longer or an army of mages at my disposal, but I am not without plans to regain both. Sarah will enjoy all the luxuries her mother was denied."

Ruith supposed it might not be the right time to point out to the king that Sarah might not be looking in a direction he would approve of at all. Ned and Oban were perched very uncomfortably on two halves of the same stool and were both looking too terrified to speak. Seirceil was watching him with a faint smile on his face, but Ruith supposed he was too discreet to say anything. Mansourah was standing on the other side of the fire, looking untrustworthy, but Ruith shot him a look of promise that he couldn't have misunderstood. He was just considering following that up with a fist under Mansourah's jaw to render him pleasantly unconscious when he found himself interrupted by a soft knock on the door.

All conversation ended abruptly, and Mansourah immediately started across the room. He peered carefully out the door, then quickly opened it to allow Sarah inside. He shut it and slid the bolt home.

Ruith had assumed he was past losing his breath where she was concerned, but he realized he was most certainly not. He wasn't sure where Cuirmear's servants had unearthed the gown Sarah was wearing, but it was fit for royalty. Ruith had never considered himself a connoisseur of women's fashions except to note when they were ridiculous, but he had to admit that the deep blue of the gown was the perfect setting for the true gem.

Sarah walked halfway into the chamber before she came to a stumbling halt. Ruith took a step toward her only to find that Mansourah had reached her first, damn him anyway.

"I have the feeling," he said, obviously putting on his prettiest manners for the edification of all, "that introductions need to be made." He offered Sarah his arm, then turned toward Oban and Ned. "You two have perhaps been in the dark longest of all, so we'll begin with you. Lads, this is Sarah of Cothromaiche. That is her grandfather over there, Franciscus, who is the grandson of the king of Cothromaiche, Seannair."

Ned gulped. "But that makes her a—"

"A princess," Mansourah said pleasantly, "aye, so it does. And that leaves her with the necessity of investigating a very long list of suitable princes before she settles on just one."

"Which list won't contain anyone in this room, thankfully," Fréam said pointedly. "Mansourah, bring her over to this side of the chamber where she belongs."

Ruith watched Mansourah completely ignore the ousted king of Bruadair in favor of continuing a very lengthy and purposeful turn about the room. He watched, feeling a very uncomfortable burning behind his eyes, as Sarah was presented to her grandfather. He found himself truly finished at the look Sarah shot him just before Franciscus enveloped her in his arms.

Tears were shed, by more than just him.

Mansourah came to stand next to him and offered a bit of deliverance by means of a very sharp elbow to the ribs.

"Sentimental sap," he said cheerfully.

"It has been an extraordinarily long winter," Ruith said roughly.

"In case you hadn't noticed, my dear Ruithneadh, 'tis spring. And you're still a blubbering fool."

Ruith glared at him, which made him feel much more himself. "I am counting the hours until we meet in the lists."

Mansourah only smiled. "I am as well. I'm always happy to school novices in the rudiments of swordplay."

"Since you can no longer school your youngest brother," Ruith said with a snort. "I noticed he wears Weger's mark."

"Aye, well, that is true," Mansourah said, shifting uncomfortably, "but I try not to discuss it with him. And since it wouldn't do for me to humiliate my liege by besting him with steel, I keep myself discreetly withdrawn from the field of battle."

"Then I would suggest, Your Highness, that you continue on with that discretion by keeping yourself withdrawn from the field of amorous adventures. Lest you find yourself dispatched without regret."

Mansourah turned bright blue, twinkling eyes on him. "She might like me better."

"She wouldn't."

"I think we should give her the choice."

"I think we shouldn't bother her with lesser goods."

Mansourah only lifted an eyebrow and slithered away, apparently to be on hand if Franciscus ever released Sarah. Ruith didn't suppose he dared insert himself between Sarah and reunions with the rest of her relatives, so he remained where he was by the fire and clasped his hands behind his back where he wouldn't be tempted to do anything untoward with them.

Though he supposed the most useful thing he could do with his fist was not plow it into Mansourah of Neroche's nose, but use it to help him find the nearest exit.

Which he would do the first chance he had.

The day dragged on with a slowness that only someone who had grown to manhood in Shettlestoune where the scenery never changed no matter how many leagues were traveled could possibly appreciate. Ruith had only vague memories of the afternoon, which mostly included sitting in that very small chamber and speaking of nothing. Sarah had been pale and grave, Mansourah overly solicitous, and Franciscus apparently unwilling to discuss anything but the most trivial of matters with Fréam and Leaghra. Ruith would have escaped with Sarah and at least gone for a walk, but he wasn't sure he wanted to draw any more attention to them than they had already just by arriving. So he'd sat to the side of the hearth, felt too tired to even nap, and wished the day would end.

The sun had set eventually, and they had been summoned to a supper that hadn't been terrible but certainly wasn't anything he would have thought about for months afterward. Now he limited himself to watching the goings-on in the midst of the hall with a jaundiced eye.

Which goings-on included Mansourah of Neroche, that bumbling oaf, dancing with that glorious, grave, Sarah of Cothromaiche, whom he was fairly certain he had indicated he wanted to wed.

He hoped she'd been listening.

"Easy, lad."

Ruith glanced at Franciscus who was sitting next to him. "I am well, my lord. Thank you."

Franciscus laughed softly. "Surely you aren't jealous of that whelp out there. After all, it isn't as though he's handsome, or disgustingly wealthy, or walks about the world's stage with a deprecating air that belies his magic, his skill with a bow, or his ability to dance and leave every maid in the hall swooning with delight."

"Are you helping me?" Ruith asked sourly.

Franciscus laughed a little. "Seeing where your heart lies, I suppose."

"I believe you're painfully aware of that already, Your Highness, aren't you?"

"Aye, Ruith," Franciscus said, his smile grave, "I am."

"I would ask you for her hand, but at the moment I'm not sure I could pry it away from that prancing fool out there."

"I wouldn't worry about him," Franciscus said mildly, "though if you want my suggestion you'll remind her of your ability to survive without a valet—unlike young Mansourah out there. I would also suggest a walk in a moonlit garden, but I'm not sure I would venture outside the hall tonight." He sobered. "I don't like what I feel there."

Ruith sighed and rubbed his hands over his face. "Neither do I."

"You should also know that it is with a great deal of trepidation that I come along with you as merely a disinterested observer and leave the actual solving of this tangle to you."

"If that is the case, then where does saving me from Morag this morning fall under that vow?"

"I was saving you *and* Sarah, and I was continuing a battle begun long before you were born that was mine to fight, not yours." He looked at Ruith inscrutably. "Yours will come later, I fear. And that is one I wouldn't fight for you even if I could."

Ruith took a final opportunity to make certain Mansourah was keeping Sarah at a discreet distance from his sorry self, then, momentarily satisfied that such was the case, turned in his seat and looked at a man he had assumed for two decades was nothing more than a simple village alemaster. A talented one, to be sure, but an obscure one.

"I'm not sure I want to know all the details at present, but I am curious how things finished with Morag this morning. I assume you bested her somehow, else you wouldn't be here."

Franciscus rubbed his fingers uncomfortably. "I can't say it was a pleasant encounter, for I had much to repay her for. But I found, in the end, that I had no choice but to treat her far differently than I would have had she been a man."

"How polite of you."

Franciscus shot him a dark look. "You would have done the same thing, I imagine."

"I would have," Ruith agreed. "So, given your impeccable manners and undeniable chivalry, how did you leave things?"

"I wrapped her up in a selection of very elegant spells then settled her most comfortably in the back of my ale wagon. I healed a pair of her guardsmen whom Mansourah had only wounded and not slain, and turned them into pair of sturdy if not exactly fleet oxen. I suggested to Morag that a few hours spent with her minister of protocol would serve her very well in the future, after which I took a few minutes to lecture her on the folly of pursuing Sarah any further. A simple girl with no magic couldn't possibly be a worthy trade for a seat on the Council of Kings."

Ruith leaned back. "She won't see that."

"Probably not," Franciscus agreed, "but I was very good at maths as a youth and I illustrated for her how few rulers it would take to give her the boot, as it were. She is already on shaky ground with young Miach of Neroche and certainly King Sìle has no love for her. Uachdaran of Léige is very fond of you and Sarah both. He told me so himself, and in your case that came as quite a surprise to him."

"Thank you," Ruith said dryly.

Franciscus smiled. "You should stop stealing spells. You're gaining a reputation."

"I haven't poached a spell in twenty years," Ruith said with a snort. "It seems that I will never live down the foibles of my youth."

"And that because your escapades with your friend Miach were the stuff of legend, no doubt," Franciscus said. "So, with those three men firmly against her, as well as whatever support I could gin up from other sources without difficulty, she was looking at least seven kings willing to force her out of her seat. I think Allaidh of Gairn might stand with her, but only because his land borders hers. He's realistic and his army is weak." He shrugged. "By the time I was finished with my list, she was quite a different lass. I don't doubt that she'll continue to look for other victims wandering across the border from Bruadair, but I think I can say with a fair bit of certainty that Sarah is safe. Especially if you're there to keep her safe. Morag was, I will tell you freely, unhappily impressed with your spellweaving this morning."

"How lovely," Ruith said dryly. "I will admit that I wasn't being polite."

"She would have been insulted if you had been," Franciscus said wryly. "She was furious at the care I was taking with her." He shook his head. "How Phillip lives with that woman, I don't know. You can imagine how horrified we were when instead of leaving the crown to Phillip, his father left it to Morag. This might be difficult to believe, but there have been times over the centuries when An-uallach was a pleasant and welcoming place."

Ruith was spared trying to imagine that by the dance ending and the dancers being released briefly to refresh themselves. He excused himself from the conversation and trotted around the table to place himself most advantageously near the wine. There was no time like the present to elbow any potential competition out of the way.

Mansourah was, as Ruith had remembered very distinctly, not

one to give up easily. Ruith supposed only superior breeding and reams of manners instilled by his mother kept him from brawling with Miach's older brother right there in front of the high table. He supposed things might have descended into that if it hadn't been for Sarah who put her hand on Mansourah's arm and smiled.

"Thank you for all the lovely dances," she said politely. "Ruith will kill you, however, if I don't dance with him for a bit."

"I'm not afraid of him," Mansourah said with a snort.

"Then be afraid of me, because if he doesn't do you in, I will."

Ruith only managed to keep from smiling because he had, along with those reams of good manners, enormous amounts of self-control. Mansourah laughed, apparently in spite of himself.

"Very well, I can see when I'm bested. Off with you two, then, and enjoy. I'll go content myself with keeping Master Oban from filling the chamber with flowers and bumblebees." He shook his head. "There is something quite seriously amiss with his magic."

Ruith didn't want to say what that something was, so he didn't. He merely held out his hand and waited for Sarah to put hers into it. She did, then looked up at him.

"I'm not sure I can take much more today."

"I know."

"There isn't a place to escape to here, is there?"

He shook his head slowly. "I think, however, that we might create our own little spot of ordinariness here. Have you used Soilléir's spell of Dimming?"

"Repeatedly." She took a deep breath. "It doesn't seem to last very long, but perhaps that's because we're . . . well . . ."

"Close to Bruadair?" he supplied carefully.

She winced. "I'm afraid that might be the case. Or perhaps there is something else afoot that I don't understand."

"I've heard there are many Bruadairian expatriates here. I have the feeling they didn't leave willingly, for the most part, but I could be wrong. In any case, perhaps 'tis their magic you're seeing."

"I suppose that's possible."

He danced with her a bit longer, then noticed a circlet on her head. He stared at it for some time, trying to decide what it was made of.

"Ruith?"

He met her eyes and smiled reflexively. "Aye, love?"

She reached up and touched the circlet. "It came with the dress."

"It's lovely."

"It's made of dreams."

He stumbled in spite of himself. "How do you know?"

"Because they're my dreams."

He looked at her, expecting to see her wearing an expression of distress, but she was only looking back at him steadily.

"Does that bother you?"

She considered for a moment or two, then shook her head. "They're good dreams. And I think some of them are things I haven't dreamed yet. Those are even better."

He wondered if there would ever come a time when she didn't leave him winded. Her beauty, her courage, her willingness to simply do what needed to be done, no matter the cost. That she was not only able to accept her birthright, but embrace it . . .

He promised himself a good falling apart over it all later, then danced with her until the music stopped. Fortunately for his peace of mind, the set had gone on for quite some time. He stood with her in the middle of the great hall and did his damndest to ignore not only everyone around him but the way his eyes were burning unmercifully. He met her eyes.

"Anyone interesting in those dreams?"

She looked down, perhaps at her hands that he was still holding. He decided that it might be better to know sooner rather than later what she was thinking. Perhaps seeing one of those bloody Neroche lads up close had led her to wonder if that list Sìle wanted her to make might be a good idea after all.

He realized only as she pressed her lips against the back of his hand that she had raised his hand up to her mouth.

Then she smiled, turned, and pulled him away from the middle of the floor.

"Sarah," he managed.

She stopped and looked over her shoulder. "What?"

"Are you going to tell me what was in your dreams?" he asked.

"If I told you, you'd be impossible to live with."

"I am already, I'm fairly sure."

She turned back, kissed him far more quickly than he would have liked, then sank back down to her heels and pulled him along after her.

He went, because she gave him no choice. And he didn't argue with her, because he understood. The last thing he wanted to do was sully his distant future with what his immediate future held.

For he had the feeling that Morag was simply a foretaste of what was to come.

And if he failed to best her, what did that say about his hopes of besting anyone else?

He wasn't sure he could bear the thought of finding out.

Twelve

S arah sat in the chair closest to the fire and held the crown she'd been given in her hands. She had told Ruith it was made of dreams, but she wasn't sure at all how those dreams had been spun into anything that could possibly be woven. All the otherworldly bits aside, it was made of a material she honestly couldn't identify. It wasn't silk—for she knew what that felt like—nor anything else of a more pedestrian nature such as wool or cotton. It was made of something so soft and so fine, she found that she almost had to use her imagination to feel it.

She looked up and wished she had other things to think on, but there wasn't anything in the chamber that didn't lead her back to having to face uncomfortable things.

At least the former king and queen of Bruadair had left them and gone to bed. Sarah had managed to put the knowledge of her heritage behind her after they'd done so, along with the gown she'd been given for supper. She was back in her comfortable leggings and tunic, though she hadn't been able to find a decent place to stash the crown. She wasn't happy with keeping it on her lap, but she wasn't quite sure what else to do with it.

She looked at her companions to see if anyone else had noticed her discomfort. Ned was happily snoring on a blanket near the fire. Oban had also succumbed to the lure of that warm fire. Sarah couldn't blame them. If she'd had any sense, she would have joined them. Unfortunately, she was too unsettled by the conversation going on before her to even attempt it.

"You could have warned me, you know," Ruith said with a frown.

Sarah realized he was talking to Mansourah, who didn't look nearly as repentant as he likely should have.

"The truth is, I wasn't entirely sure the king and queen were still here," he said with a shrug, "so there was little point in getting your feathers ruffled unnecessarily. We didn't exactly have a large selection of bolt holes, did we?"

Ruith pursed his lips. "I suppose not."

"Besides, given the particulars of your map, I thought it might be interesting to see what they might know."

"And did you discover anything over supper," Ruith asked, "or were you otherwise engaged?"

Mansourah laughed a little. "I had all the conversation possible with them beforehand, that I might spend my evening in more enjoyable pursuits. As for anything else, your lovely lady there was singularly uninterested in my admittedly numerous charms."

Sarah couldn't help but smile a bit. "Oh, they were impressive enough."

"But 'tis hard to vie against the painful beauty of the elves of Tòrr Dòrainn," Mansourah conceded, "though I will warn you, Sarah, that if you have anything to do with our lovely Ruithneadh, you'll fight him for time in front of a polished glass."

"At least we have polished glasses," Ruith said with a snort, "and aren't doomed to gazing at our likenesses in horse troughs."

Franciscus laughed briefly. "Ruith, I should have thought so many years away from your grandfather would have cured you of his disdain for others not of his ilk, but I can see 'tis lodged somewhere in your blood. Mansourah, lad, why don't you tell us of your conversation with Fréam. I would have attempted speech with him, but he wasn't overly pleased to see me. As usual."

Mansourah shrugged. "I know you won't take it personally, my lord, as you know he is vexed by many things. As for anything else, let's just say that he has little love for Gair."

"So he knew my sire?" Ruith asked in surprise.

Mansourah hesitated. "*Knew* is too strong a word. *Knew of him* is closer to the mark." He paused. "I understand Gair was seen as an undesirable neighbor."

Silence descended. Sarah felt it fall, then wrap itself around the four of them, muffling heartbeats, leaving a stillness behind that was less unpleasant than it was unexpected. She watched Ruith set his cup very carefully on the floor.

"What did you say?" he asked carefully.

"King Fréam said they weren't at all happy about the thought of having your sire as a neighbor."

"And they thought this might be a possibility?" Ruith asked.

Mansourah only returned his look steadily. "Have a look at your map, my friend, and see what you think."

Ruith pulled the map from his boot. Sarah was rather impressed that his hands were steady. She knew hers weren't, but she had them buried under her crown, so perhaps no one noticed.

Ruith pulled over a low side table and spread the map out, turning it so Franciscus and Mansourah had the best view. He pointed to the spot where the two trails of spells converged.

"Where would you say that lies?" he asked hoarsely. "On what boundary?"

Franciscus sat back with a deep sigh. "Bruadair's southernmost tip, as it happens. I don't think there are many who inhabit that corner of their kingdom, for 'tis very rugged." He looked at Ruith. "There is no denying, however, where that point lies."

"Then in exactly what country does that point find itself?" Mansourah asked. "We aren't in Uachdaran's kingdom any longer, nor Morag's I'll warrant. Or are we?"

Franciscus shook his head. "The land belongs to the kingdom of Gairn, though Allaidh has been fighting off claims to it from those at An-uallach for scores of years. It has been many years since I traveled there, but I imagine it looks much as it always has: stripped of anything useful. I know Allaidh tries to make it as unattractive a prize as possible and when he isn't doing that, Morag is razing it out of spite."

Ruith rubbed his hands over his face, then blew out his breath. "I'm not sure why they would have worried about him, given that he is surely dead."

"Likely because his acquisition of that land wasn't a recent one," Franciscus said. "I can't say I knew much about your sire, Ruith, but as you might imagine, I have had the occasional dealing with Fréam over the years. He complained endlessly about Gair's plans to escape to the north if necessary—and that was three centuries ago. I didn't have a chance to talk with him tonight about whether or not that opinion has changed in the ensuing years."

Ruith stared at the map for another moment or two, then sighed deeply. "Very well, we'll carry on. I've no idea what we'll find there, but I can't help but believe there is something there. At the very least, we'll gather up the spells we find along the way. I think we should leave well before dawn. The less fuss we cause, the better, no doubt."

"Do you think," Seirceil said slowly, "that we'll manage to gain this particular spot without interference?"

Ruith looked at him in surprise. "What do you mean?"

Seirceil exchanged a look with Franciscus, then looked at Ruith carefully. "I have not traveled extensively, but I have unfortunately met Queen Morag more than once. Whilst I would like to believe that Prince Franciscus was successful in warning her off, I wonder if she might find a little harassment to be to her taste. Not enough to warrant an all-out repudiation of her by the Council, of course, but enough to cause us grief."

Mansourah sighed gustily. "I wouldn't put it past her. She could make trouble for you all in a score of annoying little ways."

"I'll see to her—"

"Nay," Mansourah said suddenly, "I'll make the journey." He smiled. "As I said before, I wasn't intending to go much farther with you anyway. I need to get inside Sìle's gates before he knows I have, lest he lock me out and I miss out on the wedding victuals. I'll fly south by a very circuitous route, make certain that Morag is behaving herself, and then be on my way."

"But she is dangerous," Ruith began.

Mansourah snorted. "And so are we all, in our various ways. At least you can shapechange. I don't think she can do much more than hurl about a few unladylike curses. Besides, I'll be as invisible as the wind and as annoying as a good gust in an inconvenient place."

Sarah watched Ruith consider. He looked at her and smiled wanly.

"Help from unexpected places."

"That is our lot," she agreed quietly.

"So it seems to be," Mansourah said. He put his hands on his knees, then rose. "I believe I'll go wander through the halls for a bit and see what mischief is afoot. I suggest sleep for the three of you sooner rather than later. My road is quite comfortable when compared to yours."

Sarah watched him go, then listened to Seirceil plead exhaustion as an excuse to roll up in a blanket and drift off into dreamless slumber. Sarah watched the fire in the hearth for a bit, then looked at the crown in her hands.

It was a lovely thing, actually, made of whatever stuff it was and braided with four strands. She turned it around until she found the end of it, then couldn't help but fuss with it a bit. One side of it detached itself so easily from the other, breaking the circle, that she couldn't help but wonder if it possessed a mind of its own. She started to unbraid the strands not because she wanted to destroy someone else's work, but because the crown seemed to want her to do so.

It also gave her something useful to do instead of looking at either Ruith or Franciscus. Ruith, as always, almost hurt her to look at. She could remind herself a score of times that thanks to a quirk of Fate at her birth she was indeed worthy of being put on a list of potential princesses to court, but in her heart she would never believe it.

That was made all the worse by the fact that her grandfather, a man she had loved like a father for the whole of her life, *was* actually a prince of a noble house, grandson of a man who held spells in his hands that were so dangerous that he never gave them out—and if she ever saw Soilléir again, she would ask him how he'd managed to escape Cothromaiche with those spells and not had his great-grandfather chase after him, catch him, and slay him for his cheek. And that her grandfather was sitting across from her, no longer just the alemaster she had loved because he had always and without condition loved her.

She hadn't spoken to him of her heritage or his. The truth was, she'd hardly spoken to him at all. She'd only wept in his arms.

She looked up briefly to find him watching her and wondered if the time might come soon when she would have to discuss with him things she wasn't sure she wanted to.

He smiled, pained, as if he knew her thoughts. "Forgive me," he said quietly.

"For wh—" she croaked, then she cleared her throat. "For what?"

"For leaving you with Seleg and that damned Daniel for so long."

"And what else were you to do?" she asked. "Make a fuss?"

Franciscus looked down at his hands for a moment, then back at her. "I suppose you know why I made the choices for you I did."

"Soilléir told me," she said. "Well, he didn't tell me. He wrote it all down in a book."

"Because he's a coward," Ruith supplied without hesitation.

Franciscus smiled at him briefly. "You know, Ruith, one day you will poke him too hard, and then he will put you in your place."

"Never," Ruith said, picking up his mug of ale and waving away Franciscus's words with it. "He knows I love his cousin. Whether it would grieve her or not to lose me is still unclear, but it might vex her and that he wouldn't have. Besides, he loved my mother."

"He did," Franciscus agreed. "Very much. Very well, so Soilléir gave you what I'm assuming were the barest of details about your past, Sarah." He smiled wearily. "I would give you more, but I fear this isn't the time or the place. Our journey from here will be arduous, I fear, and the end unpleasant. I will, however, tell you everything you want—and deserve—to know when we're again at our leisure."

Sarah nodded, because she was happy to put off that conversation a bit longer.

"There are a pair of things I would have answers to," Ruith said, "before you nod off into your cups. What have you been doing since you kicked up a fuss at Ceangail?"

Franciscus shot Ruith a look. "I will tell you that much only after I tell you that you were ill-advised to go inside your father's keep with no magic, lad. Unfortunately I came too late to stop you."

"It isn't as though I would have thought to ask your opinion," Ruith said with a snort, "not having sensed any magic in you over the years."

"You aren't the only one who's been inside Léige," Franciscus said with a faint smile.

"Are you telling me," Ruith said with mock horror, "that after

King Uachdaran allowed you to use his forge for the sword I wear, you abused his hospitality by filching one of his spells?"

Franciscus only lifted an eyebrow. "'Tis a *very* good spell, my lad."

"Aye, it is," Ruith agreed. "And apparently a very popular one."

"Well, if it eases your guilty conscience any, I've heard rumors that he leaves it lying about in plain sight, ripe for the picking, whilst he hides a much more potent version of it somewhere else in his hall. I haven't had the chance to investigate where that might be, but I'm quite sure it would be worth the effort for the right mage."

"Which isn't me," Ruith said without hesitation. "Very well, so you unearthed your very rusty magic and trotted off into the sunset to effect a rescue of your granddaughter and the fool who loves her. How did you know where we would be?"

"Because you are so unlike your sire, I had no trouble realizing that you would do the most noble thing possible which was doing whatever it took to rid the world of your father's legacy. You aren't the only one who has wondered if that book of spells might still be in his library."

Sarah watched Ruith out of the corner of her eye. His face was expressionless, a sure sign he was struggling with emotion he didn't want to reveal. He glanced at her, smiled faintly, then turned back to Franciscus.

"Where did you leave the lads whilst you were off on this errand of mercy?"

"Slighe," Franciscus said with a fair bit of disgust, "which I didn't want to do, but I had no choice. I hastened to Ceangail, arriving just behind you unfortunately. I expected the battle, but I was taken by surprise by one of the occupants of the hall."

"Sarah?" Ruith asked.

Franciscus shook his head. "Urchaid of Saothair."

Sarah shivered. "Seirceil recognized him, I think," she said. "During our earlier journey."

"I thought he looked familiar myself," Franciscus admitted, "but I had other things on my mind during the journey and didn't study him as I should have. I didn't dare look, if you take my meaning, lest he know who I was, and he looks nothing like his father. I can safely say that Dorchadas wouldn't be caught dead with lace dripping from his cuffs."

"And Urchaid didn't recognize you?" Ruith asked in surprise.

"You flatter me, Ruith," Franciscus said dryly, "but nay, I daresay he didn't. I have been out of circulation for some time and uninterested in extensive travel before then. Well, that and I'm older than Urchaid and Droch both. I was surprised enough to find Urchaid at Ceangail, watching the two of you, to be thrown off guard for a second too long. I had scarce recovered before all Gair's spawn were upon me." He shot Ruith a look. "You shouldn't underestimate them, lad. They aren't your father, but their power, especially when combined, is significant."

"Lesson learned," Ruith agreed, "and rescue appreciated. What did you do then?"

"Dragged myself out of the rubble, hid in the witchwoman of Fàs's garden shed for a full fortnight until my head had cleared, then I realized I had no idea where you'd gone. I didn't dare reveal myself, not knowing who might be watching, so I've been searching by more pedestrian means. I will admit that I was grateful for the brief flash of the Sword of Neroche—how long ago was it? A se'nnight ago, almost? I was standing on the walls of Buidseachd when I saw it."

"You were?" Sarah asked in surprise. "How did you get there?"

"Soilléir gave me a boost." He laughed a little, then shook his head. "He was also the one who pointed out to me that unpleasant red flash. I changed myself into a dragon and flew hard, but the distance is not small. That and your spell of concealment is very good, Ruith."

"It's Miach's," Ruith said with a sigh, "mixed in with a bit of my grandfather's."

"Well, 'tis damned effective." He paused and sipped at his ale. "I found the lads, then waited for you to catch up with us. I saw that Morag was hunting you and arranged for us to be in the right place at the right time, on the off chance aid might be needed."

Sarah didn't want to ask Franciscus what he saw on a daily basis or how it was he saw it. She supposed she knew the answer to both. She certainly didn't want to know how that answer might affect her and if there were things she could see that she hadn't realized yet.

She looked down at what was left of her crown, long stands of something that wasn't quite of the current world. She considered it as Ruith and Franciscus changed the subject to less weightier matters, then reached over and dug about in her pack for the roving Rùnach had gifted her and the spindle from Uachdaran of Léige. She rolled the spindle between her fingers for a moment, admiring the lever she knew would cause the shaft to fall away and reveal a slim, very useful dagger, then broke off a lengthy piece of yarn from other wool Rùnach had given her to use as a leader.

She didn't spin with a spindle as a rule, having preferred her spinning wheel that was now nothing but wood destined to turn to dust under a collapsed barn in Doìre, but she could make do with one in a pinch. She drafted out the snowy white wool and began to spin.

She was actually rather surprised to find that a single strand from her crown had caught itself up in the roving.

As if it had decided it would become a part of whatever she intended to take with her.

She spun for quite some time, drawing the strands of her crown into the roving, until she realized that she was being watched. She looked up to find both Franciscus and Ruith looking at her with their mouths hanging open. She froze.

"What?"

Ruith cleared his throat. "What are you spinning?"

She held up the wool roving. "This?"

He shook his head, looking profoundly startled. "Nay, the other business."

She held up the strands of, well, she hadn't anything good to call it. And she realized as she held it up, that she wasn't holding on to all that much. It had become less strands of stuff than it had images of dreams and visions and things she supposed she might see if she looked hard enough or dreams that she might remember if she thought about it long enough. But it was definitely not anything of substance.

She looked at Ruith. "It is as I said before: dreams."

"How are you spinning it?" Franciscus asked, frowning slightly.

She held up the spindle. "King Uachdaran gave me this. He said it would spin many kinds of things. I didn't think to ask him what those things might be."

"That was probably very wise," Franciscus said with a shiver. "The things that come from his forge—and, apparently, his woodshop—are sometimes better left unexamined too closely." He set his cup down and smothered a yawn behind his hand. "I think, children, that we should put ourselves to bed before any more of the night wears away. Sarah, you might keep that wee contraption handy. You never know when you might need it."

"Uachdaran said it doubles as a dagger."

"I imagine it does, my gel." He looked briefly at Ruith. "Bed down a discreet distance from my granddaughter, lad, if you value your pretty nose."

"How barbaric," Ruith said.

"I thought it better than turning you into a tapestry and hanging you in the garrison hall."

Ruith looked at Franciscus closely. "Do you know any of Seannair's spells?"

Franciscus rose and stretched. "Good night, children."

Sarah watched as her grandfather went and rolled himself up in a blanket on a rug on the other side of the fire. She waited until he'd closed his eyes before she looked at Ruith.

He was watching Franciscus thoughtfully, but he soon turned to her. "Aye?"

"What do you think?"

"About your grandfather?" Ruith asked. "I think I'd best be careful around him. Then again, he hasn't turned me into a rock yet, so perhaps I'm safe. For the moment, at least. And I daresay he knows far more than he'll admit to. What do you think?"

"I'm almost afraid to." She wound what she'd been spinning around the spindle along with the roving and dreams, then looked at Ruith.

"Can you not see this?"

He shook his head slowly. "But that doesn't surprise me."

She put it back in her pack, then took a deep breath before she looked at him. "What now?"

"Sleep," he said seriously. "I'll put myself discreetly by your head and hold your hand, if you don't mind. Perhaps we'll both sleep dreamlessly, though I don't hold out much hope for it in this place."

She nodded and decided that perhaps she would put her pack far away from her so her spinning didn't seep into her dreaming.

She had the distinct feeling that she wasn't going to be able to separate the two for very much longer.

Thirteen

Ruith wondered how it was possible for the sun to shine so relentlessly but for it to be so bitterly cold. He was beginning to wonder if he would ever again feel his toes. He was fairly sure he would never rid himself of the headache he had from the harsh sunlight above him.

They had been traveling for two days in various guises. After the first few leagues spent on their feet walking from Taigh Hall, they had fallen into particular patterns of shapes for those capable of assuming them and rides for those who couldn't. Ruith had taken to riding Ruathar with Sarah and leaving Tarbh for Ned and Oban. Seirceil had happily accepted aid with turning himself into whatever pleased him at the moment, and Franciscus had invariably disappeared into a gust of wind. They had landed wherever Sarah had instructed them to and retrieved spells that had clearly been hidden for many, many years.

Ruith would have suspected a score of years if he'd been a more suspicious sort of lad.

Their entire company was now hunting on foot, because he'd grown tired of flying and because it bothered him that the last spell hadn't been where the map had indicated it should be; it had been simply lying on the ground.

Not damaged by snow, mud, or half a dozen forest inhabitants who might have trampled it in their haste to be somewhere else.

Sarah seemed less troubled by that than he was, but then again, she could still see where the spells lay without the map. That some of them had moved . . . well, he preferred not to think about why that might have been.

"Ruith?"

He looked at Sarah but realized he couldn't quite see her. He drew his hand over his eyes, which seemed to clear his vision a bit.

"What is it, love?"

"What are we going to do?" she asked. "When we reach the end of the road."

He didn't ask her what she meant because he'd spent the whole of the morning thinking about nothing but that. He shifted his pack on his back, then dragged his hand through his hair. "I wish I knew," he said with feeling. "I suppose it depends on what we find once we get there. If anything," he added, not entirely under his breath.

She nodded, then simply walked next to him for quite some time in silence. "Do you think it's possible he's alive?"

Ruith would have happily put off discussing that indefinitely, but knew he couldn't. Sarah was going to be walking with him into darkness. She couldn't not know what he feared. He took a deep breath, then looked at her seriously.

"Miach suspects so."

"That was what he came to tell you?"

Ruith nodded.

"And you?"

He shook his head, then shrugged helplessly. "I don't want to believe it. I don't think it's possible that he could have survived that slaughter at the well, but what do I know? A pair of my brothers apparently have, along with Mhorghain and me. But if he had, I can't imagine that he would have remained in obscurity all these years. His enormous ego wouldn't have survived the lack of adulation." He continued on with her silently for a moment or two before he could spew out his next words, words that almost burned his mouth as he spoke them. "I'm not sure there is anyone else who would have scattered his spells, though."

"Not his natural sons?"

"Nay, they would rather have had the spells for themselves."

She frowned thoughtfully. "But if your sire is alive—which seems impossible—why would his spells be laid out in two separate paths?"

"I have no idea," he said honestly. "He was nothing if not logical about his method of carrying on with his life. It wouldn't be like him to simply scatter his book about without some sort of plan to gather it back up again, which leads me to believe that he can't have been the one to hide the pages hither and yon."

"Your future brother-in-law came a very long way to suggest differently."

He would have smiled if he'd had the energy. "Aye, he did, but he has a very vivid imagination so perhaps he'd had too much rich food at his crowning."

She looked up at him searchingly. "Do you think so?"

"Nay, but I'm not sure I can consider the other without becoming rather ill, so it seems the safer of the two possibilities at the moment. We'll press on and be careful."

She nodded and fell silent.

Ruith looked around him as they continued on, wishing he could ignore their conversation but realizing that he couldn't. He had spent the occasional happy hour as a lad perusing books of spells and wondering which of them might inflict the most damage on his father did he have the man immobile before him. But he had never seriously considered that he might have such an encounter.

He didn't like the fact that he was considering it now and that if he found his sire, he likely wouldn't find him helpless.

He looked about him as they walked, more to keep himself awake and alert than anything else. If that unnaturally harsh sunlight hadn't been shining down on him, he would have found their current surroundings quite beautiful. The mountains were magnificent, covered as they were with a heavy forest of evergreens capped with the last of winter white. There was a stream that ran alongside the path, tumbling endlessly over rocks and fallen logs.

Despite that, though, all was silent. He could hear nothing being whispered in the trees, no rills of delight from the rushing water, no sounds of birds venturing out to herald the potential arrival of spring.

It was as if the entire countryside had been silenced.

He pulled himself away from his uneasy contemplation of their surroundings in time, and looked at Sarah.

"What were we talking about?" he asked absently.

She shook her head with a grave smile. "I don't remember."

Unfortunately, neither could he. He took her hand, partly because he wanted not to lose track of her and partly because he simply wanted to have someone ground him where he was. He wasn't altogether certain he was walking where he was. In fact, he wasn't at all sure he wasn't dreaming. He looked at Sarah.

"Am I awake?"

"If you're not, then we're both asleep."

He was vaguely dissatisfied with that answer, but couldn't press her for a better one. He was too busy concentrating on putting one foot in front of the other. It was more difficult than he would have expected it to be. Unfortunately, there didn't seem to be any end to the current dream, though there was, apparently, an end to the road.

The road continued to run along the river, disappearing into the dark forest in front of them, but Sarah had stopped. Ruith stumbled to a halt next to her and looked at her blearily.

"Is this it?" he managed.

She bent over to look at a clutch of rocks that had been laid in a particular way to make an enclosure. Only the rock that should have acted as the lid was gone. Sarah straightened, then looked at him.

"This is where the spell should be," she said slowly, "and where it lay before."

"Is the spell still lingering in the area, do you think?"

She looked around her uneasily. Ruith saw nothing, but he hadn't expected to. That the spells were moving at all was unsettling in the extreme. He couldn't imagine they were doing it on their own, which meant—

"Ruith!"

Ruith spun around in time to see a man coming out of the trees and making straight for him, as if something left him powerless to do anything else but rush forward. Before Ruith could even open his mouth to demand to know his intentions, the mage, who looked as if he hadn't seen the business side of a comb in at least a month, started hurling spells at him.

Spells that made no sense, truth be told. Ruith fought them off easily, which allowed him time to examine them as they flew toward him. They were shards of spells, jagged, disjointed, having no pattern or organization about them. The mage seemed to find nothing amiss with them. He simply flung whatever came to hand at Ruith, frantically, as if he weren't quite in his right mind but had no realization of that fact.

And then the mage threw himself at Ruith. Ruith knew he shouldn't have been surprised at being assaulted not only by spells but by a sword the mage drew and seemed to know how to use, but he was. It was perhaps the oddest altercation—magical or not—he had ever found himself in. He studied the other man as he fought with an increasing desperation that was difficult to watch and wondered if perhaps it wasn't his own sweet self the other mage wanted.

And then something else occurred to him.

What if what the man wanted was the spells Ruith was carrying shoved down the side of his boot?

Ruith sent the man sprawling by means of his foot in the other's gut, then pulled the spells out of his boot and held them up.

The mage heaved himself to his knees, saw the spells, then shrieked.

Ruith tossed the spells to Franciscus, who certainly could have been of some use—calling out encouraging words or helpful suggestions—then waited to see what the mage would do.

The mage stopped in mid-howl, looked from one of them to the other, then charged Ruith.

Ruith had the unfortunate opportunity to look in the other's eyes at close range. There was no sanity there, nothing that could have even been called human. The man was nothing but unassuageable desire for something he couldn't have. It was with regret as well as a great deal of pity that Ruith forced the mage to meet his end on the end of Athair of Cothromaiche's sword.

The man died with a sob.

Ruith laid him on the ground, cleaned his sword, then resheathed it, feeling a grimness settle over him. He took a step backward and folded his arms over his chest. He had gotten rid of all his father's spells, yet still the man had come for him.

Why?

He studied the mage for several moments in silence, wondering if he had perhaps seen him before and the mage had been seeking revenge, but there was nothing familiar about him. Ruith could safely say he had been out of circulation, as it were, for enough years that the list of wizards he had offended was very short.

He considered a bit longer, then rolled the man over onto his belly and pulled away his cloak. He was wearing a pack, which wasn't surprising. Ruith riffled through its contents briskly, drawing forth something that surprised him not at all.

It was his father's spell for making werelight, a fairly useless thing, but Ruith had to admit Gair had taken the art to a new level. Not only could he light up an entire room with a handful of words, he could twist the light into all manner of shapes to delight and astonish. Or horrify, as had often been the case.

The spell itself was wrapped in remarkably clean linen and folded very carefully, as if it had been a great treasure. Ruith took it and walked over to where Sarah was standing with Franciscus. He looked at the older man and frowned.

"He didn't want me."

Franciscus nodded. "I'd have to agree."

"He wanted the spells, I thought, but that doesn't seem to be entirely the case, does it?" Ruith handed Franciscus the spell to put with the others. "It seems that if he'd wanted the spells, he would have turned to attack you, doesn't it?"

"You're sure there's nothing left down your boot?" Franciscus asked seriously.

"Nothing—"

"Ruith."

He looked at Sarah, who was very pale. "What, love?"

"The pieces of the spell of Diminishing," she said faintly. "Where are those?"

"In my—" Ruith felt himself sway. "In my pocket, but surely he couldn't have known that." He looked at her. "Can you see them on me?"

She took a deep breath, then nodded. "Aye."

"But no more clearly than the other spells, surely."

She swallowed with difficulty. "No more clearly," she said unhappily, "but there is something different about them."

"That damned spell is going to be the death of me," he said, dragging his hand through his hair. He looked at Sarah grimly. "Is there something specifically different about the spell of Diminishing, do you suppose, or is it just its usual destructive self?"

"It is more . . . compelling—if that's how to describe it. I didn't notice it before, but I don't think there was anything there to notice." She met his gaze. "I think something on the spells has awoken—"

"A visitor," Franciscus said suddenly, quite loudly, "and it looks as if we might know this one."

Ruith spun around to find none other of Amitán of Ceangail stumbling out into the clearing, blurting out a spell of death. Ruith listened to the garbled words and realized Amitán was intending it for him alone.

He was somehow quite unsurprised.

He fended off the spell without thinking, leaving Amitán gaping in surprise.

"You have your magic," he stammered.

Ruith had to think for a moment about what he meant, then he realized that the last time they'd met, his magic had been securely buried inside him, covered with that eminently functional and quite lovely spell of hiding created by Uachdaran of Léige. The lesser spell, apparently, but useful enough for the rabble. He shrugged his shoulders and smiled.

"I never lost it," he admitted. "It was just unavailable before."

Amitán's expression was inscrutable, but that might have been courtesy of the scars covering his face that were still an angry red. Ruith wasn't sure if he could say pity was what he felt for his bastard brother. He had, after all, been without magic and not precisely in a position to defend himself against a mage of Amitán's stature yet still Amitán had tried to slay him. The only reason he hadn't managd it was that he'd been assaulted by a spell of Olc that had been, ironically, laid over Ruith by someone else to protect him.

Ruith had given that spell a good deal of thought over the ensuing days. There had been something else attached to it, something that had taken the spell of death Amitán had thrown at Ruith, turned it into something quite a bit more vicious, and flung it back at Amitán. Ruith hadn't spared too much worry over Amitán's fate, though he seemed to remember having told his bastard brother how he might free himself. Apparently he had done so eventually, but not soon enough to save his now-ruined visage.

Amitán stared at him, nonplussed, then glanced to his left. His mouth fell open.

"You," he gasped, pointing with a trembling finger at Franciscus. "You destroyed my father's hall!"

Franciscus lifted a shoulder in a half shrug. "I thought a bit of rock on your wee head, lad, might knock sense into you. I can see I was wrong."

Ruith listened to Amitán begin to hurl insults and spells at Franciscus, all of which were absorbed by the spell of protection Franciscus had cast over himself and Sarah both. Oddly enough, it seemed to not only repel Amitán's spells but cast a bit of something back with them. Though the end results were different—Amitán was enveloped in the lovely smell of flowers and pines—the execution was exactly what had happened with the spell that had ruined Amitán's visage. Ruith looked at Franciscus in surprise.

"I was covered by a spell of Olc just outside Ceangail," he said, not sure how he felt about what he thought he now knew, "and it was sweetened—"

"If that's the word you should use," Franciscus interrupted dryly.

Ruith shot him a look. "Very well, it was *mixed* with something else that turned it into something else indeed. The same thing happened to a spell of protection that Soilléir cast over me—over me and Sarah, actually—in Beinn òrain. It is the same something you're using there."

Franciscus glanced him briefly. "'Tis nothing more than a piece of the more pedestrian magic of Cothromaiche, lad. I draped what I dared over you near Ceangail before I dragged myself off to hide in the witchwoman of Fàs's potting shed. If you saw it in Beinn òrain, you can be sure it was Soilléir to use it. And if you'd stop talking long enough to finish your business with your half brother there, I might teach you a few useful spells in that language."

"Who *are* you?" Amitán demanded, starting toward Franciscus, his ruined face contorted in rage. He froze suddenly, as if he'd run into a wall.

Ruith suspected he'd run into a very useful sort of spell of binding. Which seemed, unfortunately, to work on everything but Amitán's mouth.

"Where did you obtain that power?" Amitán shouted.

"From my grandsire," Franciscus said. "Seannair of Cothromaiche."

"That *farmer*?" Amitán said in astonishment. "I don't believe it. He can scarce find his way to the ale keg, much less the Council of Kings."

"You underestimate what you don't understand, Amitán my boy," Franciscus said seriously. "There is power from other sources than what your father dug up from wells he shouldn't have been drawing from. You might consider that the next time you look at the ruin that is your visage."

"It wasn't my father's power that did this to me," Amitán snarled. He glared at Ruith. "It was his."

Ruith shook his head. "I told you, Amitán, that it wasn't me, and apparently it wasn't Prince Franciscus either. It was nothing more nefarious than a quite lovely spell of Olc, cast by one I can't name. I suppose you could take yourself off to search for him, if you cared to do so."

"You *lie*," Amitán spat.

"Why would I?"

Amitán opened his mouth, then shut it suddenly, as if words had quite abruptly failed him.

Ruith studied his bastard brother. "Why are you here?"

"Release me and I will consider telling you."

Ruith returned his look steadily. "I'm not sure you're in the position to be demanding anything. Let's instead say that if you tell me what I want to know, I won't kill you."

"You wouldn't dare," Amitán bluffed, then he looked at the mage dead at his feet and seemed to reconsider. He looked at Ruith. "I want something for the tale. Besides my life."

"What?" Ruith asked.

"A restoration of my visage," Amitán said without hesitation. He nodded in Franciscus's direction. "Done by him, with those spells he knows." He looked at Ruith angrily. "They all know them, those barbarians from that hellhole in the north, so don't believe him if he tells you otherwise."

Ruith wasn't about to argue the point, but he did glance at Franciscus, who nodded just the slightest bit. Ruith turned to Amitán.

"Very well. Your handsome visage for the truth." He bit his tongue before he said, *if you can spew out the truth without it burning your mouth*, which he would have said under other circumstances. No sense in provoking the man unnecessarily, especially if there were details Amitán might have that would save him trouble further down the road.

Amitán looked about himself as best he could, then back at Ruith. His eyes were full of something Ruith couldn't quite identify at first. Not fear, nor triumph. Something a bit like what Ruith had seen in the eyes of the mage who lay dead at his feet.

Something unnatural.

"I was told," Amitán said in a low voice, "that if I found you—

which given that you've done an abysmal job of covering your tracks since you left Léige wasn't that hard—and killed you, the wench would lead me to a cache of our father's spells. The ones from his book. The ones that were *supposed* to be in the library but were apparently rescued by persons unknown and unauthorized after that fool Táir set the bloody place afire."

Ruith realized he'd flinched. He didn't want to speculate on which wench Amitán was referring to, but he didn't have to. Amitán was smiling.

"Aye, Ruith, that gel over there. The one who *sees*."

"You're imagining things," Ruith managed.

Amitán's expression didn't change. "As I said, you should have covered your tracks more carefully and kept your mouth shut more often."

"Have *you* been following us?" Ruith asked in astonishment.

A brief something flickered over Amitán's face, which led Ruith to believe he was about to tell an impressive lie.

"Well, not all the time. Not entirely."

"Who was, then?" Franciscus demanded. "Surrender the name if you want me to do anything for your face."

"I don't know, for I never saw him. Because I cannot *see*," Amitán said pointedly. "I just heard his voice."

"A ruffian, was he?" Ruith asked flatly. "Or a man of culture?"

"I believe," Amitán said, obviously taking quite a bit of pleasure in his secret, "that he was an elf."

Ruith kept his mouth from falling open only thanks to years of austere living and self-denial. He managed to simply look at Amitán dispassionately whilst at the same time his mind was racing furiously.

There were two possibilities: either Amitán was lying or he was telling the truth. If he were lying, that meant that the someone who was following them—and Ruith had to allow he fully believed that was happening—could still have been anyone. Well, save Morag, who was no doubt still traveling quite uncomfortably on her way back to An-uallach. The list of likely suspects then could include any of his bastard brothers affecting an accent that wasn't their own or Urchaid of Saothair, who knew Sarah could see because she'd seen him hiding behind a spell in the keep at Ceangail.

But if Amitán were telling the truth, who did that leave? Ardan of Ainneamh? That was stretching things a bit much. Ardan was annoying, not evil. As for anyone else, who could he possibly put on a list? His own relations? The very thought was preposterous.

Ruith considered Amitán a bit longer, then looked abruptly at Franciscus. "I believe we've had all the answers from him we'll get. If you wouldn't mind restoring him to his former loveliness, we'll send him on his way and be on ours. Surely Díolain has seen fit to put the keep at Ceangail back together. Our good lord Amitán will have somewhere to lay his head."

Franciscus nodded, then walked over to Amitán. Ruith turned away and found himself with Sarah's arms around his waist. He looked at her and smiled grimly.

"Afraid I'll fall over?"

She didn't smile. "He could be lying, you know."

"Aye, he could be," Ruith agreed. "Or not."

"How many bad elves do you know?"

"One," Ruith said shortly, "and his name is Ardan of Ainneamh, but I'm not sure I could credit him with mischief past mixing purples with red." He shrugged helplessly. "I don't know what to think. I'm not even sure whom to trust any longer, save our company and my family—with the possible exception of Miach of Neroche. He is always on the hunt for a few more spells to add to his unwholesomely large collection."

She smiled then. "You don't mean that."

"I do. He knows too many spells, and he is always adding to

them from sources he should leave alone. But given that he already knows all the spells in my father's book and does seem to love my sister, I think we can safely cross him off the list."

"Are you ready to do that with any others?"

"Not yet," he said with a sigh. "I'll think on it as we travel. Perhaps something will present itself that will clear up the mystery for us." He put his arm around her shoulders and turned to watch as a squirrel ran over and sat up in front of Franciscus.

Franciscus had some sort of conversation with the little beast, who then chirped and ran across the glade.

Ruith blinked and in the next moment, a large, sturdy horse stood there. Chirruping.

"I am *not* riding that," Amitán exclaimed. "I can tell already the gait will be dreadful."

"Come, Ruith, and let us hoist him up into the saddle," Franciscus said with a smile. "An uncomfortable ride home might be just the thing for him."

"I'll see you both dea—"

Silence suddenly filled the small clearing thanks to another of Franciscus's spells. Silence save the decidedly unhorselike comments being made by Amitán's mount. Ruith aided Franciscus in hoisting his more presentable but substantially more irritated half brother atop that rather unstable squirrel-turned-horse, then watched Franciscus secure the load, as it were. A slap on the rump sent the beast trotting off into the forest. After a fashion.

Ruith looked at Franciscus. "I think we should press on."

"Perhaps after you see to your new guests."

Ruith spun around, his sword halfway from its sheath, only to find Ardan and Thoir walking into the glade. He was surprised to see them, yet not surprised at all. All he could say for himself was that he was not paying his surroundings the attention he needed to. He put up his sword, slowly.

I believe that he was an elf.

Ruith took a deep breath and shoved aside Amitán's words. Thoir was his cousin and Ardan, while completely devoid of the smallest collection of good manners, was also his cousin. They would have sooner given up their lives than to have associated themselves with Olc or anything like it.

He wasn't, however, above making certain that Franciscus was standing next to Sarah before he walked over to greet his kin.

"Well met," he said, shaking their hands. "You look to have had a fair time of it."

Ardan sighed gustily. "I am counting the days, believe me, until I can sit in the hallowed halls of King Ehrne's palace and have first a decent meal, then a retreat to a long, hot bath. Of course, the company will be more suited to my station as well, but let's not dwell on that."

Ruith glanced to his left to find Ned and Oban gaping at the newcomers as if they'd just seen something from legend. Seirceil was only watching with no expression at all on his face, but that one rarely gave anything away. Ruith turned back to his cousins.

"How was your hunting?"

Thoir pulled a roll of scorched sheaves from within his cloak and handed them over without comment. Ruith didn't bother looking at what Thoir had found. He would go through them when he had the stomach. The collection was thick enough, but Ruith knew there was one thing missing.

The first half of the spell of Diminishing.

He glanced down at the topmost spell there. It was a spell of Summoning. 'Twas nothing special, that spell. It didn't call souls back from the dead or draw anything of a demonic nature to a mage. It was merely a spell of calling, quite useful if one wanted his boots to come find him, or his valet to bring him his tea on time without having to be reminded. The uses for it were benign and numerous.

A pity he couldn't have said that about the rest of his father's spells.

He looked up at the sky which was now a dingy grey with unnaturally flat clouds, and wondered why it was that his father had chosen darkness over light. Had it been a gradual thing, that choosing, or had he simply woken one day and announced to the world that he intended to become one of the most feared black mages in the history of the Nine Kingdoms?

Ruith could only imagine how his grandmother Eulasaid would have reacted to hearing that at the breakfast table.

He turned away from the thought, then took the remainder of the spells Franciscus handed him and put them in his pack. If they were attacked again, he could chuck his gear to Franciscus and have his hands free to see to the resulting chaos. If a potential attacker went for Franciscus instead, that would answer a question or two. Perhaps there was something on those sheaves of paper, something more powerful than just decent handwriting.

The same sort of thing that was apparently on the scraps of the spell of Diminishing he had in his pocket.

He looked at Ardan and Thoir. "We're going to carry on to the last spot on the map, if you care to come along. I assume you'll determine your own shapes?"

"Naturally," Ardan said, walking away.

Thoir only smiled, rolled his eyes a bit, and turned to follow after his traveling companion. Ruith watched Franciscus go to gather up their own company, which left him alone with Sarah. He found her watching him closely.

"Did they find them all?" she asked.

"Thoir didn't say he hadn't found what we sent him for, so I'll assume he did. I don't think I have the stomach to look through them right now."

"We'll press on, then."

"I think we must." He paused. "Do you think there is a spell there still, at the end of our road?"

She looked off into the distance for a moment, staring at things he couldn't see, then frowned. It took her a moment or two to come back to herself, but when she did, her expression was inscrutible.

"I'm not sure."

"Is there a mage there, do you think?" he asked. "Loitering with spell in hand, waiting for us?"

"That I can't say either."

And it was for damned sure he wasn't going to ask her to look any harder. He shouldered his pack, reached for hers, then turned and walked with her over to where Ruathar stood waiting for them.

And he tried not to think about what might be awaiting them at the last point on the map.

Fourteen

Sarah stood on the ground near Ruathar's head and held on to his neck, finding her legs less steady than usual. There was nothing in particular that inspired that weakness. Nothing past a general feeling of uneasiness, as if there were a mighty thunderstorm brewing and even the air held its breath waiting for something to break.

Not that she had all that much experience with thunderstorms. Doìre was, as it happened, famous for its habit of watching the clouds gather just beyond its borders, as if the entire county was simply too polite to ask the clouds to come any closer. She supposed that two or three storms in the spring and perhaps the occasional cluster of clouds in the fall overcame their shyness to venture inside the provincial confines, but the general condition of relentless sun could safely sum up the weather for every year she'd spent in that accursed place.

Perhaps all the unsettling things she'd been through over the past pair of months had finally pushed her over the edge of comfort into a place she wished she could leave as quickly as possible.

Or her unease could have come from the fact that she was standing on the edge of the most desolate patch of ground she'd ever seen. And given where she'd come from, that was saying something.

She was actually a little surprised that the countryside wasn't more beautiful. They were somewhere in the wilds north of Léige, a country full of impressive mountains, spectacular fjords, and more water than she'd suspected the Nine Kingdoms might be home to. The road that ran under her feet and traveled north was large, but not so wide that it cut an ugly swath through the trees, and the mountains to her left were covered with a forest of evergreens. There was a river to the right of the road, and the music of it should have been pleasing to the ear.

But somehow, it wasn't.

It was possible it was disappointment that soured her, disappointment over reaching the end of the trail and finding it nothing at all remarkable. Or it could have been because even though she had led Ruith to where a spell had been, the spell was there no longer.

Again.

She wished desperately for a place to sit down, but there was nowhere other than the middle of the road, and that was made very inhospitable by a combination of melting snow and mud. There were a few boulders languishing up against the mountain face in front of her, but she couldn't bring herself to go any closer. There was something about the rock there that bothered her, though she couldn't have said why.

She looked to her right to see if the rest of the company was equally as unhappy with the results of their journey. Ned, Oban, and Seirceil were standing together, watching with various expressions of curiosity—and alarm, on Ned's part—as Ruith simply stood in the middle of the road and looked at the mountain in front of him. Franciscus was standing a little ways apart from him, his arms folded over his chest, his expression inscrutable.

Ardan looked equally as disinterested, though she couldn't believe that was the case. He had spent the past pair of fortnights either looking for spells or looking for signs of black mages and had made no secret of his irritation that such had been his task. His boots were encrusted with numerous layers of mud, his cloak was travel-stained, and he looked hungry.

She shifted a little to ease a sudden pulling in her back, then turned her attentions to Ruith's cousin. She ignored the more quotidian things and looked at him. *Him* being who he was, not what he wore.

He was, as she had come to expect from full-blooded elves, difficult to look at it. Not only was he handsome, there was something surprisingly, painfully beautiful about his soul, as if he had sprung to life in a place where the ceilings were covered in stars and the floors glittered with a thousand facets of whatever rare and exclusive rock they'd been hewn from before being polished to glass. She had no idea how old he was, but his power was immense, descending into depths that refused to be plumbed by her paltry eye. She couldn't speak to his skill, but if he had taken a mind to challenge Ruith to a duel of spells, he wouldn't best Ruith because Ruith couldn't counter the words. It would have been because, as powerful as Ruith was, Ardan's roots went deeper.

The only thing that bothered her was that there was something slightly dark about him, as if he were a window that wasn't quite clear. She suspected it was less a fascination with evil magic than it was simply his sour personality clouding whatever he did, but she couldn't have said for sure.

He looked at her, blinked in surprise when he realized she'd

been staring at him, then lifted an eyebrow. His glance of supercil-
iousness would have been comical if she hadn't suspected he meant
it in full.

She looked away before she felt any smaller than she already did.

She turned to Thoir, who was standing to Ruith's right, there in
the middle of the road. She had to admit she hadn't had either the
time or the heart to look at him before either, and she couldn't say
she was particularly interested at the moment, but it took her mind
off the fact that they had reached the end of the trail and it seemingly had led them to nothing, so she carried on with it.

She expected him to remind her of his grandfather Sìle, and he
did. The magic that flowed through his veins was the same claimed
by all the elves of Torr Dorainn she'd encountered. He didn't possess the almost terrifying stature that his grandfather did, but she
could see how he had indeed grown from an acorn that had fallen
from that mighty tree. She had no idea how old he was—surely
older than Ruith. His magic was, again, not necessarily more substantial, but its roots went much deeper.

She almost turned away, then she found herself freezing. She
frowned thoughtfully as she turned back toward him and looked
more closely. There was something about him, something different
from his grandfather and his brother. The trails that Fadaire had
carved into their souls were crisp and defined, as if they had put
their hands on Fadaire alone

Thoir's magic, truth be told, looked a little bit like her arm. She
could see the traces of it, but the lines were blurred.

She found the sight of it . . . disturbing.

She came back to herself to find Thoir watching her. She smiled
quickly, as if she'd been about nothing any more nefarious than a
decent daydream. It was a surprising relief when he only frowned
at her and turned back to watch Ruith.

Ruith was currently removing sheaves of parchment from his
pack. If he felt revulsion at touching his father's hand-penned

spells, he didn't show it. He simply held them in his hand without comment.

"Well?" Thoir prodded. "What now?"

Ruith dragged his hand through his hair. Clouds were rolling in, which gave some relief from the dull flatness of the garish sun. "I have no idea."

"You know," Thoir suggested slowly, "you might ask if your lady could see something we have missed."

"Nay," Ruith said shortly, "I could not."

"Then are we to stand here all day and do nothing?"

Sarah watched Ruith turn on his cousin and say something to him, but she couldn't bring herself to listen. It had been a morning full of bickering, with Ardan complaining about the locale and Thoir poking at Ruith to do something sooner rather than later. Even Ruith was short-tempered, for he didn't hesitate to respond to his cousins with unusually curt answers.

She looked at the mountain in front of her and wished there was something there for her to see. A spell had been there, lying in a stone box beneath a scraggly bush, but it was there no longer. There was nothing left but the echo of Gair's handiwork.

In fact, the whole place was nothing more than an unremark- able spot where the feet of the mountain had given way, sheering off and leaving a smooth face behind. Piles of rock lay on the ground there, grouped—

She froze.

Grouped as if they were flanking a path.

She walked past Ruith, who was pacing and cursing, and Thoir, who was beginning to sound slightly impatient that more progress wasn't being made, and Ned, who only squeaked and ducked behind Seirceil. Sarah ignored them all and whispered Soilléir's first spell under her breath.

And then she saw.

She stood in front of a doorway. She looked up and realized

that the entire face of the mountain wasn't just rock that had lost its outer covering of greenery. It was the outer walls of a keep. Cut into the mountain like some sort of façade.

She heard someone—Ruith, perhaps—call her name, but she couldn't answer him. She put her hands on the face of the rock, then brushed aside what looked to be years of dirt and small, stubborn fauna, and a few bugs she didn't want to identify. It hurt her hands to do so, but she kept at it, because she had no choice.

flora

She soon had help. Hands brushed away the layers the years had placed upon what was soon revealed as a front door.

It wasn't a very impressive front door, as front doors went, but it was undeniably an entrance. Thoir elbowed her aside in his enthusiasm and ran his hands over the rock. He turned and frowned at her.

"Where's the key?"

She blinked. "How would I know?"

There was something halfway out of his mouth, words that were colored with an unpleasant sentiment, but he bit them off and they fell to the ground, unused. He took a deep breath, then smiled.

"Forgive me. It has been a very long journey." He ran his hand over the rock again, then looked at her with another polite smile. "Do you see any sort of lock here, my lady?"

"Well, she might be able to if you'd give her a bit of space to breathe," Ruith said, giving his cousin a friendly push.

Actually, that had been more of an unfriendly shove than a cousinly push, but Sarah supposed tempers were frayed all around. She waved everyone away and looked more closely at the stone.

And she saw the spell.

It was an unhappy combination of Olc and Lugham, Gair's signature magic. It started above her head near what she could see was a seam in the rock, traveled to the opposite side of the door, down almost to her knees, back over again, and then back up to the original point, forming a perfect square. The thread of the spell wrapped ever inward, becoming smaller and smaller until it terminated in the middle of itself. She supposed that if it could be unwound, it would reveal interesting things.

The thought of unwinding it, however, was one she couldn't bring herself to consider.

Ruith touched her arm, and she jumped in surprise. She let out a shuddering breath, then looked at him. His expression was very grave.

"What is there?" he asked.

"A spell." She paused. "I'm not sure I can touch it."

"Who laid it there?"

She met his eyes. "Your father, I think."

He nodded, as if he hadn't expected anything else. "Where does it begin?"

She drew her knife and pointed to the initial spot. "There. It ends in the center of the door."

"Well," Ruith said under his breath, "here goes nothing at all."

He flinched as he touched the end of it, but the pain was apparently not enough to keep him from carrying on. He unraveled, as it were, and as he did so, the true face of the door became clear.

There was one thing she could say about Gair: he seemed to be quite fond of riddles. The door was plain, unremarkable, and sporting nothing resembling a keyhole. There was, however, a spot in the middle of the door where the spell had finished that seemed odd, as if it didn't quite belong. She started to lean over to have a closer look at it, but felt Ruith pull her back.

"A false lead," he said regretfully. "I suppose we'll need to look elsewhere. Perhaps another spot farther up the path? Thoir, lead the way, why don't you?"

Sarah stepped away from the door only because Ruith gave her no choice. She continued to step backward until they were standing some fifteen paces from the spot she'd uncovered. She didn't dare look at him, for fear she might spoil some plan she hadn't been told about.

"There's an indentation there," she murmured under her breath when she could stand it no longer.

"I know."

She looked up at him then. "You do?"

"Aye, and I think I'm slightly more comfortable keeping that to myself for the moment." He cleared his throat and spoke up. "Keep a weather eye out for anything useful, lads. Press on with enthusiasm."

Ardan turned and shot him a look of fury. "And why don't you come sully your lily-white hands right along with us, Ruithneadh? Are you so far above this labor?"

"Not at all," Ruith said cheerfully. "Be right there." He tightened his arm briefly around Sarah's shoulders. "Wait for me."

She nodded, then watched Ruith walk back across the road and begin to brush away debris and rubble from another section of the house's façade just as enthusiastically as his cousins. Sarah watched the rest of the company join them, but she thought she might like to stay just where she was. It was true that the door looked as if it hadn't been opened in a decade, but who was to say that was the case? Gair was the most powerful black mage in the history of the Nine Kingdoms. Putting a little rubbish on the outer wall of his keep and ageing it wouldn't have been beyond his skill. And adding that little spell to the front door was easily done as well. She supposed even a child—

She would have squeaked at the feeling of being jerked off her feet, but a hand was clamped over her mouth before she could. It was so startling, she didn't think to reach for her knife or throw an elbow before Ruith had turned around with a frown. He looked at her in surprise, then put his hand out to presumably warn the rest of the company to stay where they were. He lifted an eyebrow.

"Daniel," he said smoothly. "What a pleasure."

"A pleasure," Daniel croaked. "You left me on the plains!"

"With water right there and your own tremendous amount of skill at your disposal," Ruith said with an indulgent smile. "Just a little test to see if you're worthy of what you want."

"Don't want your test," Daniel spat. "I've come for the other."

"What?" Ruith asked as he stepped away from the door and gestured to it. "This?"

Sarah was happy to have Ruith be a bit closer to her, but she wasn't sure that would make any difference. Daniel was trembling so badly, she could feel it in her bones. That, and he was leaning quite hard on her, as if he simply didn't have the strength to stand up. At least it was simply his forearm across her throat and not a knife. Things could have been worse.

"Give me . . . spells," Daniel wheezed. "Now."

Ruith walked another few steps closer, then froze when Daniel blurted out for him to stop. He slowly pointed to the pack in the middle of the road. "I put them in there but a moment ago. I'll need to fetch them out."

"Go . . . on, then."

Ruith continued to watch Daniel as he carefully walked forward and reached for his pack. He pulled the spells out, set his pack down, then held out the sheaves of parchment.

"Here they are, my friend. Come and get them, if you want them."

Sarah found herself dragged across the road, but only for a few steps before she felt her brother stop, then suddenly become an almost intolerable weight against her back. Ruith leapt forward and pulled her away before Daniel collapsed entirely.

She turned around in surprise and found Ardan standing there with a rock in his hand. He looked down at Daniel, looked down his nose at her, then shrugged and walked away. He heaved the rather substantial stone into the river where it landed without making a sound.

Daniel groaned. He suddenly shook his head, rose to his hands and knees, then staggered to his feet. He looked around himself frantically, then flinched at something he saw.

"You!" he gurgled.

And he threw himself across the road.

At Thoir.

Sarah wasn't surprised to find herself with her nose to Ruith's back, though she was going to have to tell him eventually that he was continuing to ruin her view of interesting events. Perhaps she would tell him at some distant point in the future when the most interesting thing happening to them would be trying to identify what sorts of musical notes were hanging in Uachdaran of Léige's great hall, or admiring a life-sized game of chess in Soilléir of Cothromaiche's solar, or perhaps even discussing the offerings for supper at some decent inn or another.

"—*you* told me to come here—"

She looked around Ruith's shoulder to try to catch Daniel's words and instead managed only to watch Thoir take his knife and plunge it mercilessly into Daniel's belly.

Daniel fell at his feet and didn't move again.

Thoir didn't clean his knife, he merely shoved it back into his belt and looked at Ruith.

"How do we get inside that damned door?" he demanded.

Ruith ignored him and went to check Daniel's boots—presumably for stray spells. There were none there, which didn't surprise Sarah. They had relieved Daniel of the single page he'd possessed when they'd met on the plains of Ailean well over a fortnight ago. It wasn't reasonable to believe that Daniel could have followed them, not with the twists and turns they'd taken, which meant that he'd known where they intended to wind up.

But how was that possible?

Ruith left Daniel where he was and walked back over to where he'd been working on the mountain face. Thoir followed him, seemingly untroubled by what he'd just done.

"Let's go over this again," Thoir said impatiently. "The runt of Neroche believes your sire wrote down a score and two spells—"

"Keir said there were a score and two," Ruith said, shooting him a dark look. "I don't know how many are here."

"Well, why don't you have a look?" Thoir said shortly. "Since we don't seem to have anything else productive to do."

Sarah watched Ruith merely look at his cousin in silence. Thoir returned his look, as if he sought to motivate Ruith with his gaze alone. Ruith lifted his eyebrows briefly, then walked to where Sarah found herself, standing near his gear. He took a deep breath.

"I suppose I don't have any choice but to look at these seriously now."

"I'm sorry," she whispered. "Truly I am."

He smiled very briefly at her, then took a deep breath before he retrieved the collection of spells and began to sift through them. She didn't particularly relish aiding him at that task, but she supposed it was the least she could do. She stood next to him and held her hands out to take the spells once he'd looked at them.

Or at least she did until she got too close to the first one and the wound on her arm burst into flames.

Ruith swore in surprise, then extinguished the flames with a spell. Sarah looked down at her skin and realized, to her profound surprise, that there were no scorch marks there. Either those flames had been naught but her imagination or there was some sort of spell in her arm that had a mind of its own.

"I'll keep them," Ruith said faintly.

"Thank you," she managed, putting her hand behind her back. "I think that would be best."

He nodded, then began to look through the stack, slowly and methodically. He finished, then stared off into the distance for several minutes without speaking. Sarah didn't say anything. For one thing, her arm was burning as if it had truly sported flames, and for another, she didn't want to distract Ruith. He finally let out his breath and looked at her.

"A score and one."

"A score and one," a voice said brightly from beside them, "how delightful. Which ones do we have?"

Sarah watched Ruith turn to look at his cousin. She listened to them speak—if that's what it could have been called—for several minutes about the number and names of the spells Ruith held in his hands. Something bothered her, but she couldn't lay her finger on what it was.

It occurred to her suddenly that Miach had said there were twenty-two spells. Given that he had traveled with Ruith's eldest brother Keir who had apparently known the number and kind of all the spells, she supposed there was no reason to doubt him.

"Why don't you list them and let's see what we have there," Thoir suggested, sounding as if he were recommending nothing more taxing than a stroll through the garden.

Sarah watched Ruith look at his cousin as if he couldn't quite see him, then bend his head and recite tonelessly the spells he held in his hands. Sarah listened carefully, then realized what was missing. She hardly considered herself an expert on Gair of Ceangail's most treasured spells, but given the one that Ruith had omitted, she felt fairly safe in identifying it.

"You didn't list the spell of Diminishing," she said.

Ruith looked at her in surprise. "What?"

"The spell of Diminishing." She felt her mouth fall open as she realized what else was bothering her. "You have twenty-one spells."

Ruith looked at her blankly. "Aye."

"But there were at least a pair that were stolen from you just outside Ceangail. We only recovered the spell of Un-noticing from Daniel on the plains of Ailean, which means—"

Ruith swore and flipped through the spells again. He closed his eyes briefly, then blew out his breath. He separated a single sheaf from the rest.

A sheaf that had been scorched along the edges and torn in half.

"The second half of the spell of Diminishing," Sarah said uneasily.

"So it would seem," he agreed grimly.

"But how is that possible?" Sarah asked. "That spell was taken from you outside Ceangail. As were two of the others you hold in your hands—"

The blood drained from Ruith's face. He held up the pages and looked at Thoir. "Where did you find these?"

Thoir waved his hand dismissively. "Where Sarah said to look. They were all there."

Ruith began to pace. Sarah watched him and shared the unease that was plain on his face. Someone had stolen spells from Ruith's boot, spells that now found themelves in his hands. Why steal them just to leave them lying about for Thoir to find—for it had obviously been Thoir to find them. Ruith hadn't looked closely at what he had discovered, but Sarah had and the second half of Gair's most prized spell hadn't been among the lot.

That led her to another very uncomfortable question. Every since they had left Buidseachd, they had been finding pieces of the *first* half of the spell of Diminishing left either near spells they had been recovering or along their route to a particular refuge. Who had been tearing up the first half of the spell of Diminishing and leaving it lying about?

And why was it they hadn't found any of those pieces since they'd left the inn behind?

Sarah began to feel the world begin to spin. They hadn't found any of those pieces since Thoir had joined the company—

"What are you missing still?"

Ruith ignored his cousin and continued to pace.

"I say," Thoir said, sounding for the first time as if he were truly annoyed, "Ruith would you bloody stop pacing and pay attention to me?"

Ruith shot him a disgusted look, but ignored him. Sarah watched his cousin grow increasingly angry until Thoir's face became a rather unattractive shade of red.

"Stop," Thoir commanded, "and tell me what we're missing."

Ruith whirled on him. "What I'm missing is a bit of peace and quiet for thinking," he snarled, "so either shut up or go away. If you stay and continue to yammer at me, you will leave me with no choice but to silence you myself."

His words hung in the air, sharp shards of anger that seemed particularly suited to their location. Sarah didn't blame him for them. If she'd been in his place, she likely would have silenced Thoir by means of a fist to his mouth.

There was something very odd, though, about the sudden feel in the air. The storm which had been brewing for the past hour was upon them and the air was thick with power that Sarah half fancied she could see was on the verge of exploding.

Thoir was perfectly still. In fact, he was so still for so long, Sarah began to wonder if he had been so shocked by Ruith's words that he'd lost his ability to speak.

And then she realized she was wrong.

"Oh," Thoir said, his tone suddenly soft, "I don't think you'll want to do that."

"Why the hell not?" Ruith snapped.

Thoir pulled something out of his boot and unrolled it. "Because of this."

Sarah saw what he had in his hands and realized just how badly they had miscalculated everything.

Fifteen

Ruith wished the buzzing in his ears would cease. It was making it very difficult to think clearly. That was the only reason he was looking at his cousin, who was holding on to a good-sized scrap of his father's spell of Diminishing. The *first* half of his father's spell of Diminishing. He could see without any trouble at all where bits of the spell had been torn away.

Those bits of spell were ones he had in the purse at his belt.

He looked at his cousin in astonishment. "Was that on Sarah's map?"

Thoir raised an eyebrow. "Why would you think that?"

Ruith suppressed the urge to draw his hand over his eyes. In truth, he wasn't quite sure of anything. "I don't know."

Thoir handed him the spell. "You can have it. You might as well put it with the rest."

Ruith looked at his cousin, dumbfounded. "Was it intact when you found it? And where did you find it?"

"I found it here, at this spot," Thoir said, nodding at the wall behind Ruith. "Hidden securely in a box that I uncovered with my own two hands. And aye, it was intact. Well, at least the top half of it."

Ruith shook his head, because he just couldn't understand how it was his cousin would have found the first half initially. "If it was intact, who has been ripping it into shreds? And why?"

"Well," Thoir said softly, "who do you think has been ripping it into shreds, Ruithneadh?"

"You?" Ruith said shortly.

Thoir only lifted his eyebrows briefly, but said nothing.

"How long have you had that spell?" Ruith demanded. "If I'm allowed to satisfy my curiosity about something you shouldn't have been stupid enough to touch much less carry with you."

"And why couldn't I see it with you?" Sarah asked suddenly.

Thoir shot her a look of disdain. "And just who did you think I was, my little country bumpkin?" he asked cuttingly. "The witch-woman Seleg's son? Not only did I have the first half of Gair's very useful spell of Diminishing, I had the second, which I removed from Ruith's boot whilst he was senseless in the glade near Cean-gail. That little scrap of velvet that Connail of Iomadh prized so thoroughly was something I spelled into oblivion." He looked at them, his eyes hooded. "And I took them to keep them with me because I could."

Ruith could scarce believe his ears. Thoir? He would have believed it of Ardan, but not his cousin. He hazarded a glance at Ardan, who was looking at Thoir as if he'd never seen him before. It was a genuine look of astonishment. Ruith knew the difference. He turned back to Thoir. The first question was why he had been so interested in those spells. The second was, how had he cut through that spell of Olc so easily? Ruith suspected he might like the answer to the first better.

"Why?" he asked simply. "Why would you want any of Gair's spells?"

Thoir conjured himself up a chair. Ruith realized, with a rather sick feeling indeed, that he'd done so using one of Gair's spells. It was almost impossible to believe, but he was beginning to suspect that Thoir had more than a passing acquaintance with his sire's magic.

"You see, young Ruith," Thoir said slowly and patiently, as if he prepared to launch into a discourse that might just be a bit too complicated for Ruith to understand, "the beginnings of my fascination with a more powerful magic than is found inside Tòrr Dòrainn's puny borders began, oddly enough, with a sincere desire to help my great-aunt." He looked at Ruith knowingly. "That would be your mother."

Ruith found himself with the almost overwhelming urge to walk over and plow his fist into Thoir's face. He resisted with difficulty. For one thing, it would rob him of the opportunity to find out just what his cousin was planning. Secondly, he himself was standing too close to Sarah. The last thing he wanted was for one of Thoir's spells of retaliation to go awry and strike her instead.

He forced himself to take deep, even breaths and move slowly and carefully. He conjured up a sturdy stool, shot Ardan a pointed look, which he was surprised to note his cousin seemed to understand without difficulty, then sat himself down with great ceremony. Ardan strode off purposefully, took Sarah by the arm on his way by, then pulled her along with him to join Franciscus's company. Ruith pretended not to watch them go and instead settled himself more comfortably on his three-legged, humble milking stool. Perhaps that would help Thoir feel even more superior, which he seemed already inclined to do.

"Go on," Ruith invited.

Thoir's look of loathing was surprising enough that Ruith flinched in spite of himself. He would have been happy for the luxury of a few moments to search back through his memory and determine when it was he'd neglected to suspect his cousin of truly vile deeds. Perhaps later, if he survived what he was certain would be an afternoon that would rapidly descend into madness.

"I was," Thoir said stiffly, "as I was attempting to tell you, trying to aid your mother. It was as I was about that noble work that I realized that whilst Gair's spells were disgusting, they were also extremely powerful." He shot Ruith a look. "Though you may not be intelligent enough to discern the difference, Ruith, I certainly am."

"Oh, I see the difference," Ruith said, with as much sincerity as he could muster. Of course he wasn't going to tell Thoir that when it came to black mages and their spells, there was no difference in the damage they could do.

"I began to look for ways to weaken Gair," Thoir continued, "which I knew would be very difficult. When I learned of Gair's book from Keir, I decided that it might provide me with the means to defeat him. I had been looking for it in the library at Ceangail when one of your bastard brothers set the whole bloody place on fire. If the witchwoman of Fàs hadn't offered me refuge, I'm not sure I would have survived."

Ruith couldn't find anything innocuous to say. He was beginning to think that woman was a keeper of more than just the most detailed history of the Nine Kingdoms in existence. He wouldn't have been at all surprised to find her library, covered as it was in cobwebs and dust, rivalled the one at Buidseachd. He shuddered to think of the notes she'd made about him.

"When I saw a black leather volume on her shelf, I thought it might contain the spells I was looking for. I considered it prudent to take it with me when I slipped out whilst she was napping."

Ruith didn't want to point out to Thoir that there were many black, leather-covered books in many libraries but not all of them were books of spells. The truth was that whilst the cover of his sire's book of spells had indeed been black, it had had a square on the cover—

A square that was about the same size as the indentation on the door to his right, actually.

He set that aside to think on later and concentrated on his cousin. Sìle's grandson. Sarait's nephew. An elven prince who should have known better than to dabble in dark arts.

"The cover proved to be empty," Thoir continued in sonorous tones better reserved for lecturing at the schools of wizardry, "but I considered that merely a reason to continue on. Years passed after your mother's death, and whilst I found the occasional bit of information, I found my search thwarted." He had been looking off into the distance, but he swung his gaze to Ruith. "Until a handful of months ago when I happened upon the intrepid Daniel of Doìre nosing about in places he shouldn't have been. I followed him home, naturally, because he continued to mutter to himself about Gair and spells and wells of power. How could I resist?"

How, indeed, Ruith thought.

"One thing led to another and soon I was eavesdropping on more conversations than just Daniel's with himself. Imagine my astonishment at finding out that you and your little country mouse there were going to do for me what I'd been trying to do for a score of years."

"Find my father's spells?" Ruith asked sourly.

Thoir shot him a look that Ruith supposed was answer enough.

"I'm still unclear as to why you would want them," Ruith said slowly.

Whatever mask Thoir had been wearing slipped. The glimpse was brief, but Ruith flinched in spite of himself. It took Thoir a moment to regain control of himself, but he finally managed to recapture his look of disinterest.

It was then that Ruith realized his cousin was mad.

"I realized, after I escaped from that unpleasant skirmish in

Ceangail where Prince Franciscus fair brought the entire place down upon our heads," Thoir said, continuing on as if he hadn't heard Ruith, "that I had been missing something. I will admit to having been slightly baffled as to how you and your little dalliance over there were finding the spells you'd found, for you seemed to follow no logic I could discern—especially after you left behind populaces large enough to merit their own wizards. All I knew was that if anyone could find Gair's spells, it would be his son. It was in my best interest to keep you safe."

"Then were you the one to cover me with that spell of Olc near Ceangail?" Ruith asked in surprise.

"Of course not. That lovely spell had been cast by Urchaid of Saothair. I merely stood to the side and watched events proceed unimpeded. After I had slit through his pitiful spell and relieved you of the burden you were carrying in your boot, of course."

Ruith nodded slowly. "I see. And then you followed us to Buidseachd?"

"I though it prudent," Thoir conceded, "if not a little unnecessary on your part. I watched *that*—" he pointed to Daniel's corpse—"attempt a little business with Droch's servant whilst you and your little trollop were in Buidseachd. Once I'd recovered from laughing myself sick over his foolishness, I dropped a piece of the spell of Diminishing there on the plains of Ailean with what his servant had ripped to shreds, then waited to see what you would do."

"And you've followed us ever since?"

Thoir shrugged. "Or led you, rather. When I realized you were making for An-uallach, I went ahead to leave you a marker there." He smiled, but it was a cold, unpleasant smile. "Always a step ahead of you, Ruithneadh, as I always have been."

Ruith wasn't about to comment on the direction Thoir had been taking, so he shrugged it aside. "As you say, cousin."

"You might, if you had the wit, imagine my surprise and delight when I discovered that your admittedly lovely but lowborn lass over there had the gift of sight. It was then that I hit upon the plan of leading you here. That she had seen the rest of the spells and their location came as a bit of a surprise, but once I realized that she was, as they say, sallying forth after them, I knew my work was being done for me. At that point, I knew I didn't need to leave any more clues for you. You were headed where I wanted you to go without my leaving you a trail to follow."

"I don't think I understand why here," Ruith said carefully. "Why this house?"

"Because after that unfortunate business at the well I listened to Díolain and his warty-nosed dam discussing where Gair might have gone if he'd survived. Of course Díolain was unable to get anything out of his mother and went off in a huff. I was masquerading as a potted plant in her library and found out all the details I wanted." He smirked slightly. "She talks in her sleep. Of course I'd always assumed that your sire had more than one bolt hole, but I'd never thought he would come this far north. I believe I was wrong about that."

Ruith felt something crawl down his spine. "This far north?"

Thoir looked pointedly at the house cut into the rock. "Must I lay everything out for you, Ruith? That unassuming spot behind holds more than cobwebs."

Ruith wasn't sure he agreed, but there was no sense in saying as much. "Any idea what?" he asked casually.

The light in Thoir's eyes was just a little too bright, as if he burned from within in a way that Ruith wouldn't have wanted for himself. "Why would I tell you?"

Ruith shrugged. "There isn't a good reason to, I suppose, except for the fact that you seemed to want us here so very badly. If you wanted what was beyind that door, why didn't you just look for a key? Or, even better, just knock?" *BEYOND OR BEHIND*

"I tried that," Thoir snarled. "What sort of fool do you take me for? If I'd managed to have what I think lies behind that door, why would I need you?" He scowled. "I found the first half of Gair's spell of Diminishing here behind that rock all by myself and only because I'd risked life and limb to eavesdrop on the witchwoman of Fàs—"

"You spend a goodly bit of time in her house," Ruith interrupted.

Thoir glared at him. "This was all during a single visit, you fool. Her house is so full of clutter, I doubt she would have noticed me if I'd been standing there in purple silks and a pointed hat. She had been muttering her displeasure over Díolain's conduct, then she ventured off into several unkind words about Gair and his stupidity in hiding his spells in rather pedestrian places. I gathered, as I sifted through the torrent of complaints, that she thought Gair was a fool to hide even part of one of his spells near his lair of escape. She was good enough to describe where that lair might be found whilst about her boasting that she had told him many times that he would live in this desolate place alone. She was perfectly happy tending her garden of poisonous plants near Ceangail and had no desire to live so close to any bloody dreamweaver."

"And so you came here," Ruith prompted, when Thoir seemed to become distracted by his memories of flora and fauna.

Thoir swung his gaze back to Ruith. "Aye, I did, and 'twas a bloody perilous journey."

"What did you find?"

"As I said, the first half of the spell of Diminishing, hiding behind that rock. I memorized it, of course, and took just a piece of it, to prove I had it should I need to. After I'd removed the second half from your boot, I tried the spell on one of your bastard brothers."

Ruith wasn't going to speculate which one it had been.

Thoir frowned thoughtfully. "It didn't work, which leads me to believe the spell isn't complete." He shot Ruith a look. "I don't suppose you would know what's missing, would you?"

"I don't suppose I would."

Thoir frowned. "I'll have to see to it myself, as usual. All I can say is it didn't work very well, for I haven't quite felt the same since." He put his hand protectively over his belly. "I think perhaps there's just something amiss with my digestion."

Ruith suspected there was more amiss with Thoir than his digestion, but he wasn't going to say as much. Trying to convince his cousin that Gair's magic would eventually be the death of not only his body but his soul and his reason was a futile exercise.

"So, now that I can see that that most coveted of spells isn't complete, I have decided that the answer must lie behind this door."

"And you think I'm going to help you find the key?" Ruith asked.

The look Thoir sent him was unpleasant in the extreme. "Not you," he said softly. "Her."

"Why her?" Ruith said quickly, desperate to draw attention away from Sarah. He could only hope Franciscus was having the good sense to ignore the instinct as spawn of Seannair of Cothromaiche to do nothing and instead stand in front of her.

"Because she sees," Thoir said. "Táir and Mosach weren't particularly willing to divulge the particulars, but I found new ways to inspire them. I believe that I will ask her very politely to determine for me how that door is opened. Which is, of course, the only reason I brought you both here."

"You could ask her, I suppose," Ruith agreed, though Thoir would speak to Sarah only after he himself was dead, "but I'm curious about another thing or two first. Why go to the trouble of finding my father's spells if all you wanted to do was come here to this hovel?"

"Because," Thoir said, holding the black leather cover aloft, "I suspected that given how assiduously Gair protected them, there must have been something else to his spells besides just the words. I still believe that, which means there's something missing here."

"One of the spells?" Ruith said slowly.

Thoir shot him a look. "Or several. Who knows? It is hardly my fault that neither you nor Keir seems to be able to count." He seemed to search for the right way to say what he wanted to, then finally gave up and threw the cover down on the ground. "I think there must be more spells *behind* that door. Once I have them all, they'll go into the cover, and then the book will be complete."

"And then you'll have what you want, is that it?" Ruith asked. "All the power you want?"

The light in his eye burned brighter. "The spells are the key, cousin, to all his power. I'm not surprised you can't see that, given your blindness where your father was concerned, but they are the key to it all."

"Actually," Ruith said mildly, "I think the key you're looking for needs to fit into that lock there."

"I know that too!"

Ruith didn't want to speculate on what might lie behind that door. It was enough for the moment to send his cousin off on yet another useful endeavor.

"Perhaps you should go have another look," Ruith said, "and see if something doesn't strike you. I daresay you have more experience with my father's methods than I could ever boast of."

Thoir looked as if he couldn't quite decide if Ruith were being serious or not, then rose carefully. He kept Ruith in his sights as he eased over to the door and had his look. He ran his fingers over the hollowed-out square that sat in the precise center of the door.

"We need something here," Thoir announced, though he didn't look particularly sure of that. "The hilt of a knife, perhaps, or the head of a staff. Something square."

"Something square did you say?" Ruith interrupted, feigning a look of utter bafflement.

Thoir shot him a look. "Do you know what a square is, Ruith-neadh?"

Ruith scratched his head, then pulled off his boot. He shook his father's onyx ring into his hand, then put his boot back on. No sense in not being prepared to fight if necessary, though he seriously doubted a battle with Thoir would be with steel. He looked at his father's ring, then held it up.

"I don't know, Thoir," he said seriously, "is this a square?"

"It is a ring, you fool."

Ruith turned the flat onyx stone just so. "And this?"

Thoir gasped.

Ruith was, he would readily admit, prepared for the spell Thoir threw at him. He wasn't, however, prepared for the same spell to encompass Sarah. He caught it—a very unpleasant spell of death initially conceived and thereafter perfected by none other than Gair of Ceangail, as it happened—and flung it back with added force at Thoir. He looked briefly over his shoulder to find Franciscus standing in front of the rest of their company. He knew without asking that Franciscus wouldn't help him, but he would keep Sarah safe.

Ruith turned back to Thoir. His cousin was not as powerful as their grandfather, but he was not a novice either. Ruith was immensely grateful not only for those impossible three days with Uachdaran of Léige, but the subsequent time spent with a ruthless and relentless Miach of Neroche. He found himself not only unsurprised by the nastiness Thoir dredged up—all too easily, as it happened—but unmoved. Even when Thoir added a bit of shapechanging to his display, Ruith remained unaffected.

And then, without warning, Thoir took Ardan's power.

Ruith knew that because he heard the words coming out of Thoir's mouth and saw they weren't directed at him. He stepped to one side—mostly so he would see things coming at him he hadn't realized were in the air—and watched Ardan fall to his knees, gasping in horror.

Thoir swelled up, as if he'd been a dragon drawing in an enormous breath to spew out fire that no amount of water could quench.

"Give me that ring," he commanded.

Ruith looked at his cousin. "No."

Ruith could see the spells gathering around Thoir. They weren't pleasant ones. They were also somehow not quite right, as if Thoir were using things he hadn't memorized properly. Ardan's power—however much of it he'd managed to steal—added to his own made him formidable indeed, but Ruith had the feeling things were not going to turn out quite like Thoir expected. He braced for the onslaught, grateful beyond measure that Franciscus was there to protect Sarah, then began to weave several spells of protection he'd learned from Uachdaran of Léige over not only himself but the rest of his company as well.

Thoir opened his mouth.

Then he froze, as if time had stopped. He looked at Ruith, then he began to list to the side, as if he'd been a boat that had had all its cargo roll to starboard. He continued to tilt until he had fallen completely over.

Ned stood there, a rock in his hands, trembling like the last courageous leaf clinging to a bare-branched tree in the depths of winter. He looked down at Thoir, blanched, then looked at Ruith.

"He did it first," Ned said, pointing at Ardan. "To Sarah's brother."

"So he did, Ned," Ruith said, feeling a rather unwholesome sense of relief. "So he did." He caught sight of Ardan, though, and sobered immediately. He turned and squatted down in front of the man he had suspected of such nefarious deeds.

Tears were streaming down Ardan's face. He looked at Ruith, absolute agony written on his features.

"He took my magic."

Ruith put his hand on his cousin's shoulder. "There's nothing I can say to make this any easier for you," he said quietly, "but I will tell you that I don't think he did it very well. I don't have any answers for you at the moment, but I think with enough looking we'll find them. Don't," he said sharply, "kill him in your anger. If you slay him, you'll never have your power back."

"At this moment, I'm not sure I care," Ardan said bitterly.

"You will later," Ruith said. "And there are worse things that could happen to you."

Ardan's look of disdain was perfection. "Aye, being forced to seek refuge at Seanagarra, or, worse still, Tor Neroche now that I'm too ashamed to go home. I think I would do better to lie down in a ditch and sob myself to death."

Ruith looked over Ardan's head to find Seirceil standing there. "Perhaps you might see to the mighty prince of Ainneamh for a few minutes whilst we investigate other things."

"Conjure us up a bench, Your Highness, and I shall."

Ruith did as requested, turned Ardan over to Seirceil and Oban, then turned to Sarah.

"I suppose we should try the lock," he said slowly.

"I'll stay behind you."

"I was just going to suggest that."

She walked over to him, put her arms around his waist, and hugged him tightly. "That was a great chance you took there, provoking him that way."

"He's a blustering fool," Ruith said with his own fair bit of bluster. "I think the real test lies ahead, wouldn't you say?"

"I don't want to speculate."

He couldn't say he did either. He simply took her hand in his, walked over to the wall, then pulled her behind him. He looked down at his father's ring that he'd put over his thumb, then took a deep breath and reached out to put it into the lock.

And for a moment, nothing happened.

And then, as easily as if the door had been opened the day before, it separated itself from the surrounding rock and swung inward.

Into total darkness.

But since Ruith had been putting his foot out into darkness whilst the light remained behind him for the past two months, he supposed there was nothing noteworthy about stepping across the threshold.

He only hoped he would feel the same way in a quarter hour.

Sixteen

Sarah stood behind Ruith at the doorway and hoped he wasn't stepping into a trap. There was absolutely no light inside, which she supposed shouldn't have surprised her. There had been no windows that she could see in the face of the rock. She wouldn't have been surprised to find the inside nothing more than a few crude benches pushed up against rough-hewn walls and perhaps a pile of blankets wadded up in a corner.

Ruith ventured in a pace or two, then stopped, no doubt listening for a sign of something alive inside. Sarah tried her spell of seeing, but that did nothing for her. She closed her eyes to see if her ears would serve her better.

Unfortunately, all she could hear was her own rapid breathing.

Ruith blew out his breath suddenly. "I think I must attempt a bit of werelight."

"What's the worst that could happen?" Sarah managed. "We see something we don't like."

He laughed a little. "Aye, I suppose so."

Sarah listened to the words of the spell that he spoke aloud—something he didn't often do, but perhaps it was fair warning to anyone who might be hiding in the dark.

Light exploded above them, instantly driving back shadows into corners. Sarah made her way to Ruith's side, blinked a time or two, then felt her mouth fall open.

She felt as if she'd stepped into a dream. They were standing in an entryway that seemed to stretch forever into the distance, with polished marble on the floor and gilt mirrors lining the walls. Chandeliers made up of a dozen tiers apiece hung from the ceiling, sparkling with faceted crystals that took Ruith's werelight and turned it into something worthy of any elven palace she ever could have dreamed up on her own.

Sarah couldn't help herself. She laughed.

Ruith looked at her, apparently fighting his own smile. "I'm not sure that's the reaction I expected, but I think I approve."

Sarah managed to contain herself, but she couldn't help a smile. "This is so far removed from what I thought we would find, I don't think words will do it justice." She watched Ruith light the chandeliers with a proper spell, then shook her head as the light leapt from fixture to fixture, changing the hallway from merely spectacular to something far more impressive. She had no means to describe it, so she simply stood there and laughed again.

"I'm not sure I want to know what's hiding in any of the rooms off this modest entryway," Ruith said dryly, "but I think I can safely guarantee that the place has been empty for quite some time."

"How so?" she asked, feeling faintly surprised.

He pointed down and lifted his boot. The print left behind in the dust was perfectly revealed thanks to the enormous amounts of light. Sarah looked more closely at the luxuriously upholstered sofas placed strategically along the walls—presumably so there would be somewhere to collapse should a guest become over-whelmed by his surroundings—and found that they were covered as well by a rather substantial layer of dust. She might have been tempted to have a seat, but she realized upon closer inspection that the dust was liberally mixed with droppings from animals she wasn't sure she wanted to have a closer acquaintance with.

She looked up to find Ruith wiping a finger along the edge of a stately side table. He frowned at the dust, then looked at her.

"I don't think anyone's been here recently," he said slowly.

"Years, I would guess," Sarah offered.

Ruith lifted his eyebrows briefly. "I think we might consider that a good thing, actually."

"What now?"

"A brief explore, perhaps, in this place that I must admit leaves me feeling slightly less kindly toward my sire than usual. I had no idea he possessed anything so opulent."

"Is Seanagarra not so grand, then?" she asked gingerly.

He looked at her in surprise, then laughed a little. "Oh, nay, 'tis far more lovely. My grandfather would immediately label this a hovel and demand better accomodations—or, I should say, he would have before he found himself as the regular traveling com-panion of the rustic king of Neroche. The indignities he has endured in the past several fortnights will no doubt find themselves described in great detail in some annal that will be read with hor-ror for centuries to come."

Sarah smiled. "I like your grandfather."

Ruith smiled in return and reached out to pull her into his arms. "He likes you. I, however, have slightly fonder feelings for you, but I might have told you about them before."

"And always at the moment of greatest peril for us both," she said, a little breathlessly. "Your timing, Ruith, is exceedingly poor."

"I'm an opportunist," he admitted cheerfully. "No spells of

death are being flung at us, no annoying cousins demanding attention, no crazed mages lunging at us from the dark."

He looked over her head briefly, perhaps to make certain that
was the case, then back at her with a smile.

She shifted, feeling slightly uncomfortable. "Ruith—"

"I courted my ten princesses."

"You didn't. You barely spoke to them, and there were most
certainly not ten of them."

"I danced with nine," he corrected her. "I then threatened to
kiss Miach and avoided any encounters with a barmaid I'm fairly
sure had a moustache which left me, if memory serves, finding you
in the stables of that disgusting inn and kissing you. And we both
know what you are."

She put her hands on his chest and looked up at him. "Do we?"

He smiled gravely. "Apart from everything else, Sarah my love,
you are a weaver of dreams. You have woven yourself into mine so
thoroughly I can't remember the last time I had a nightmare, or
dreamed of darkness, or woke in terror of things I couldn't name."

"Makes up for the daytime, then," she managed.

He smiled, bent his head, and kissed her softly. "Aye, love, it
makes up for the daytime. Hopefully the daytime will throw off its
unpleasantness as well."

She put her arms around his neck and held on tightly. She
couldn't tell him that she hoped so desperately for that to be true
because the thought of it was so tenuous, she wasn't sure she could
entertain it with any seriousness at all.

She had told him, all those many days ago that felt more like
years and in not so many words, that she wasn't opposed to a future
with him. She could readily see how the thread of her life might
wind alongside his for whatever length of life they were granted.
But, somehow, the thought of being Sarah of Cothromaiche, daughter of royalty, and not just Sarah of Doìre, uninteresting by-blow

of the witchwoman Seleg, was a leap she couldn't quite bring herself to make.

Not yet.

"You think too much," he murmured, just before he bent his
head toward hers.

"Why, there'll be none of that!" a voice bellowed from behind
them.

Sarah was quite certain she missed landing upon her—well, not
upon her feet—because Ruith caught her. He kept his arm around
her, then looked over his shoulder at Franciscus who was standing
just inside the door, wearing a very stern look.

"Forgive me, Your Highness," Ruith said politely. "I didn't mean
to take liberties."

"Of course you did," Franciscus said with a snort. "I can see I'll
have to do a better job of chaperoning you two until something
more formal is arranged."

"I think your time might be better used in chaperoning our
good Thoir outside."

"Oh, I swaddled the young git in a comfortable little spell of
binding and tied it with a pretty bow," Franciscus said, rubbing his
hands together and smiling. "He's not going anywhere. Why don't
we take the tour, children, and see if this little house provides any
useful clues." He looked at Ruith pointedly. "You might give her a
little room to breathe, lad."

Ruith reached for Sarah's hand instead, then looked steadily at
Franciscus.

Sarah found herself exchanging a shrug with her grandfather.

"You raised him for a goodly part of his youth," she reminded him.

"Very well, lad, keep her hand, but don't think you'll have it
permanently without a proper request. Let's go do a little investigating whilst we have the chance here."

Sarah smiled at Ruith, had a very brief kiss as her reward, then

walked with him after Franciscus, who seemed particuarly interested in seeing what sort of refuge Gair had provided for himself.

An hour later, she could honestly say she no longer cared how
many sitting rooms, salons, or ballrooms Ruith's father had built.
She wanted out of a place that for all its obvious expense was the
coldest, most lifeless and unpleasant place she'd ever set foot in.
She left Ruith with Franciscus as they considered a doorway that
seemingly required some manner of spell to unlock and made her
way without delay outside.

Or, almost outside.

She looked down as her foot was hoving over the threshold and
wondered if she were seeing things.

A single thread lay there, golden, glinting in the sunlight. She
leaned over to have a closer look at it only to have it fade, as if it
didn't want to be seen. She straightened and frowned, then stepped
over the threshold and looked back.

It was gone.

She started to go back inside, but had the distinct impression
that she shouldn't. She wasn't one to shun that sort of thing, given
that it had spared her untold grief over the course of her life, so she
shrugged and turned away to look at other things.

Thoir was, as Franciscus had promised, trussed up snuggly in
spells she could see weren't nearly as unpleasant as they could have
been. She couldn't say the same for the cloth someone had thoughtfully stuffed in his mouth. He was furious, but obviously very well
contained. She was tempted to point out to him that black mages
were never happy, but refrained. If he hadn't learned that yet, he
never would.

She looked the other way. Seirceil and Ardan were imbibing
something Oban was pouring out of a silver pitcher Sarah was
fairly certain she'd watched Oban snatch up as they'd all fled his
house several fortnights earlier. Ardan didn't look particularly
impressed with his brew, though the glance he cast at the silver

goblet in his hand was less critical than it might otherwise have been. Ned was standing behind them, his arms folded over his scrawny chest, looking fierce.

She smiled and turned away. Things had definitely changed.

She considered wandering about for a bit, then felt herself freeze before she could take a single step. Being inside had apparently left her feeling far too comfortable for it was only then that she realized she had let down her guard.

There was someone watching them.

She walked over to Ruith's pack, because it gave her something to do and perhaps might leave the watcher thinking she hadn't noticed anything amiss. She picked up the black leather bookcover Thoir had dropped and put it into Ruith's pack for safekeeping, then noticed that someone had helpfully removed Thoir's half of her map from his person and put it together with Ruith's half. She picked up both halves and made a production of smoothing them out. She yawned, patted her mouth in a ladylike fashion, then looked around her as if she searched for somewhere comfortable to sit and relax.

Urchaid of Saothair was standing under a tree some hundred yards away.

She considered what she should do, but decided that running screaming back into Gair's hideout was likely the worst choice. As long as he was simply standing there, watching instead of casting spells at them, perhaps he could stand there a bit longer. She looked up again at the sky, which had cleared a bit and saw nothing untoward, nor was there anything creeping along the ground toward her, so perhaps he was content to merely stand there and watch.

She made herself at home on Ruith's stool, then looked at the two halves of the map she held in her hands. She would have spelled it back together, but she had no magic. She would have sewn it back together, but she didn't have needle or thread. There was nothing she could do but stare at both halves and watch the way the sun either shone down or darkness fell upon them, depending on what the clouds were doing overhead.

She noticed, absently, that the fires were no longer lit on the map, fires she'd been able to see since she'd first begun to dream them after she'd left Doìre. The spots were now simply Xs on a map, plain and unremarkable.

She glanced at Urchaid to make certain he was still where he was supposed to be, then looked back at the map. She put the two halves together, facing each other lengthwise, primarily because she had nothing else to do. It was rather startling, actually, to see how well the locations of the spells matched up, as if they were two paths converging on the same spot.

And that spot happened to be Gair's refuge.

As she considered that, several other things occurred to her.

All Gair's spells were scorched along the edges, which meant they all had to have been in the fire at Ceangail at the same time, perhaps even still as part of Gair's book. That fire had happened *after* Gair had been to the well and was presumed to be dead, which meant the spells had to have been scattered *after* Gair was presumed to be, again, quite dead.

But who would have scattered them?

And why?

It wasn't possible that it had been done by Gair himself, mostly because she believed Ruith when he said he was sure his father had died at the well. And even if by some miracle Gair had somehow survived what had slain most of the rest of his family and subsequently been the one to hide those spells on his way north, why wouldn't he have hidden them all in the same place instead of moving from spot to spot on the same latitude whilst allowing those spots to come closer as he worked his way north?

She looked at the map again and tried to study it dispassionately. The only thing that made sense to her was that whoever had hidden the spells had taken one trail north, then another on his way back south. But the question was still why.

She couldn't bring herself to believe that the who was Gair.

She fussed with the map a bit longer, then folded it in half as she saw Ruith and Franciscus coming out of Gair's front door. They were deep in conversation, no doubt about more ballrooms and kitchens. They paused long enough to give Thoir a warning look before they came to stand in front of her.

"I also think it might be wise to be on our way before it begins to rain," Ruith said with a sigh. "Wherever it is we go from here."

"Any ideas as to where?" Franciscus asked him.

Ruith shook his head. "That is the piece of the puzzle I fear I just don't have. I thought we would follow the trail, then have all our answers. I'm not sure where the trail leads from here."

Sarah had risen, thinking that Ruith would be ready to leave right away, but it looked as if the pair was perfectly content to stand there and discuss possibilities well into the afternoon. She sat back down with a yawn, then attempted to focus on the map, just to keep herself awake.

"I have wondered," Franciscus said after a very long discussion about dwarvish trade routes, "why it was the spells were moving."

"Mages were picking them off and carrying them off?" Ruith suggested.

"To where?"

Ruith started to speak, then shut his mouth abruptly. "I have no idea. I didn't think to pay attention to where they were heading. It was unsettling enough to know they were moving."

Franciscus shrugged. "It likely means nothing. 'Tis a pity we don't have anyone nearby who might have answers we could use."

Ruith nodded back over his shoulder. "That one there?"

"Which one?" Sarah asked, looking up at them. "Thoir or Urchaid?"

Ruith blinked at her in surprise. "What did you say?"

"Urchaid is standing in the trees over there so don't make a fuss," she said in a low voice. "He's not casting any untoward spells that I can see, so perhaps he's not as dangerous as we think."

Ruith exchanged a look with Franciscus. "Let's see to Thoir first, then turn our attentions to intimidating other mages later. I don't want to terrify that fop back there in the trees unnecessarily."

Franciscus nodded and bent to remove the very filthy cloth from Thoir's mouth. He stomped out several nasty spells that Thoir immediately spat out, then used some sort of Cothromaichian spell of containment to help him keep his magic to himself. He hauled Thoir up into a sitting position, then stood behind him and held him there with his knee. He looked at Ruith.

"Ask away."

Sarah watched Ruith come to stand in front of Thoir. "You said you simply trotted up here—thanks to directions from the witch-woman of Fàs—and immediately laid your hands on a spell buried behind a rock. Somehow I find that last part difficult to believe." He folded his arms over his chest. "Who left that spell of Diminishing here, Thoir?"

Thoir looked at him with contempt. "Do you think I'll tell you anything you want to know?"

"Do you think I'll spare one moment's regret leaving you here, bound helplessly, to be devoured by wild beasts?" Ruith shot back. "Do you think I'll *ever* allow you to sully Seanagarra's glittering halls again? If you tell me what I want to know, I might beg Grandfather to show you mercy."

Thoir cursed him viciously, but seemed to realize rather quickly that he had very little room for bargaining. He looked at Ruith with absolute hatred in his eyes.

"Who do you think left that spell here, Ruithneadh?" Thoir asked flatly.

Sarah might not have noticed Ruith sway if she hadn't known him so well. His face certainly gave nothing away. His hands were now clasped behind his back, though, and his knuckles that she could see were white.

"My father?" he asked flatly.

"Of course your father, you imbecile," Thoir spat. "I followed him here just in time to see him tear the spell in half, roll up a part of it, and tuck it behind a rock over there."

"And then you just pulled it out and made off with it before he noticed, is that it?"

"Actually, nay, I didn't," Thoir said stiffly. "I found myself overcome by a spell I hadn't seen tiptoeing up behind me and was unfortunately rather senseless for quite some time." He paused. "I'm not sure how long."

"My father is a rather clever fellow," Ruith said. "You shouldn't feel embarrassed that he bested you. The first rule with him is to always watch behind you for what he doesn't intend that you see. So, he rendered you blissfully senseless and no doubt set some spell of ward over you that nothing ate you whilst you were dreaming of spells you shouldn't have wanted, then you awoke. What happened then?"

"I looked for the damned spell, that's what happened," Thoir snarled. "What else was I going to do?"

"Identify evil for what it was and leave it alone?" Ruith asked politely.

A light came into Thoir's eyes that chilled Sarah to the marrow. She thought she had understood, after the times she had come face-to-face with Olc, that the reasons Ruith wanted nothing to do with it was because of its inherent evil. Now, looking at the elf in front of her, his eyes full of madness, she suspected Ruith shunned it for other reasons entirely.

"You don't understand at all," Thoir said quietly. "You don't understand the power—"

"I do," Ruith corrected him. "I do, all too well."

Thoir made a sound of impatience. "Aye, as an observer. But to actually use Gair's spells, to feel their absolute perfection under your hands, to have their power rushing through you like a mighty wind that only you can control—"

"Illusion," Ruith said curtly. "'Tis illusion, Thoir, and distraction and a thousand other things that lead you to believe things that simply aren't true. His magic is evil, conceived in darkness—"

"It is beautiful!" Thoir shouted suddenly. "Beautiful and perfect in a way you couldn't possibly begin to understand." He took a deep breath and looked at Ruith pleadingly. "Can't you understand? I once thought as you do, that Gair was darkness embodied and that my task was to aid Sarait however I could in stopping him. I was wrong, though. The first of his spells I tried was a simple spell of reconstruction, but the way it took the elements and rearranged them, making them more beautiful than they had been before, fashioning something new and enticing from the old." He started to shake his head, then he froze. "Perhaps you do know."

"I don't," Ruith said without hesitation.

A look of profound suspicion came over Thoir's features. "You're lying. You saw his book, the *whole* of his book. You can't tell me you didn't memorize the spells you read there."

"Of course I did," Ruith said shortly, "and I've memorized scores of others I shouldn't have, but that doesn't mean I would ever use them."

"Then you're a fool," Thoir said. "A fool not to use the power available to you."

"I prefer to use that power for good—"

Thoir laughed derisively. "How noble of you, Ruithneadh. Always trotting off into the darkness to do the right thing, the praiseworthy thing, the thing that ingratiates you with our grandfather."

Ruith looked at his cousin steadily. "Far better to ingratiate myself with him than trade my soul for the madness that comes with Gair of Ceangail's spells." He paused and considered. "When did you take the first half of Diminishing?"

Thoir looked down his very aristocratic nose. "After you left Léige, for reasons of my own."

"Which no doubt included fear that I would find it first," Ruith said with a snort. He looked at Franciscus. "We have to do something with him. We cannot leave him simply roaming about the Nine Kingdoms in this state."

Sarah watched Franciscus draw Ruith aside, but she had no desire to listen to their conversation. She couldn't look at Thoir either. The look of pleasure on his face when he'd spoken of Gair's spells was a thousand times worse than the madness in his eyes.

She looked down at the map in her hands, desperate for a distraction. She could hardly believe that Gair might be alive, but she supposed it wasn't unthinkable. The well had been powerful, true, but surely he wouldn't have attempted to open it if he hadn't known he could contain it. Even if it had wounded him grievously, it was not beyond belief that he could have survived.

After all, Ruith had.

She looked off unseeing into the distance, hoping for a distraction, but finding only that unpleasant and unwelcome thoughts began to crowd in on her.

Perhaps the spell of Dimishing did call other spells to it. It certainly seemed to call other mages to it if the events of their journey north were any indication. She saw immediately the truth of that, for the other spells had remained in their proper places until Thoir had removed the first half from the crevice behind her. She thought back to the mage Ruith had been forced to slay on that morning they'd encountered Amitán. Hadn't the mage ignored the bulk of the spells Ruith had tossed to Franciscus and instead made straight for him? Hadn't Ruith had pieces from the spell of Diminishing on his person?

She wondered, with a fair amount of discomfort, what the

second half of the spell might have woven onto its surface. It had been covered with something—and that something had leapt up and wrapped itself around her arm.

Leaving a wound that simply would not heal.

"Oy, Mistress Sarah, will you look at that?"

Sarah looked up to find Ned standing over her. She frowned. "What is it?"

He pointed to the map. "Look there. 'Tis the exact shape of the highest window in my sire's barn." He frowned. "Don't know why he favors turning them on a point like that save it makes 'em more difficult to open."

"A point?" Sarah echoed, wondering why there was such an annoying buzzing suddenly in her ears.

"Like a square, only turned on a point," Ned said. He reached over and took the map from her, lined it up so the torn edges met, then showed it to her. "See? 'Tisn't a perfect square, more like one a bit squashed in its middle—"

Sarah stopped listening. She felt behind her for any part of Ruith she could lay her hand on. She tugged until he was standing next to her, then she simply pointed at the map.

"Look," she managed.

"Interest—"

He stopped abruptly. She understood. The spells, marked as they were with the ones she'd found in the south and the ones they and Thoir had found in the north, formed a square. Well, not an entire square, because there was one corner that should have lain in Tòrr Dòrainn but didn't. But if one were to count Gair's well as one point and his refuge as another and an unmarked spot in Tòrr Dòrainn as a third . . . that left a fourth as yet unmarked spot that made something of a square.

A fourth point that found home in a place where things were not visible.

In Dòire.

Seventeen

Ruith caught Franciscus as he swayed. He would have helped the man down onto the stool Sarah had just vacated, but he wasn't all that steady on his own feet and wasn't sure he wouldn't join Sarah's grandfather in an undignified swoon. Franciscus put his hand on Ruith's shoulder and attempted to catch his breath.

"Let's go over there," he said faintly. "Where we'll have a modicum of privacy."

Ruith looked at Sarah and found her visage ashen, as if she'd had a great shock. He understood completely. Though it should have been of no great import, somehow seeing a pattern made not only by the locations of his father's spells, but the significant locations in his father's life—especially the well—was unnerving in the extreme.

He put his arm around Sarah's shoulders, then walked with her and Franciscus far enough from Thoir that he wouldn't be able to overhear them. He looked at the map, then at Franciscus.

"Are you seeing what I'm seeing?"

Franciscus rubbed his hands over his face, then folded his arms over his chest, perhaps to hold himself upright. Ruith understood that, actually.

"It could be a random thing," he said.

Ruith wished he could have agreed. "We have two points representing two corners of a square, then marks on the map indicating the locations of my fathers spells which if connected would form two solid sides of the square and suggest two other sides of the same." He had to pause to catch his breath. "If Tòrr Dòrainn is counted as the third point and the locations of the spells we found at the beginning of our journey used to draw other lines—" He had to spend a bit more time simply breathing. "Tell me you're not looking at this map and thinking what I am."

The forth point lay in Shettlestoune, in Doìre.

Was it possible his father was *there*?

Franciscus looked rather green. "Let me give you details about your past—both your pasts—then we'll examine this tangle here." He looked at Sarah. "I am sorry, Granddaughter, if these tidings will grieve you. I will try to atone for my choices when our circumstances permit."

Ruith felt Sarah squeeze his hand. It was the first time Franciscus had called her that. It hadn't seemed inappropriate, rather it had sounded like something he had wished to call her for the past score of years but hadn't dared.

Franciscus sighed. "Briefly, here is a bit of history you need to know. There are those of my kin who have not only the gift of magic and sight, but of Foreseeing."

"Foreseeing," Sarah echoed faintly. She shot Franciscus a look. "You can't mean that you can see the future. Soilléir said nothing about that."

"As well he should have," Franciscus said darkly. "Most of us know how to keep our own counsels. And aye, that foresight has to do particularly with the future and events to be found lingering in its mists."

Ruith would have smiled, but he was too unnerved to. He could only imagine what sort of long periods of silence filled the halls of Seannair's palace if Soilléir was the most loose-lipped of the clan. Soilléir could be, he could say with certainty, counted on to remain silent on almost any subject under any inducement. To learn that his relatives were even more closemouthed came as no surprise at all.

"Very well, so you see the future but you're discreet," Sarah managed. "What terrible details do you have for us today?"

"Things in the past, fortunately," Franciscus said, sounding very relieved. "I would like to blame some of this on others—Sgath in particular—but I fear I must bear the responsibility for the choices I made for you both. You see, I knew what Morag was planning, and while I prepared Athair and Sorcha as best I could . . ."

"With steel," Ruith said when it looked as if Franciscus might not say more.

Franciscus nodded with a grim smile. "Uachdaran told you as much, I suppose. Aye, I made those knives you bear, Sarah, and your sword, Ruith. And whilst I could do that for my son and his lady wife, I could do no more."

Ruith saw Sarah close her eyes briefly and understood. Simple thoughts and single words were all that Soilléir would offer, and he gave those both sparingly. Ruith had thought he'd understood why before, but he'd been wrong.

"I could not wrench events surrounding them to my pleasure any more than I could convince your sire to stop being a fool," Franciscus said with a sigh, "though I will admit I said more to Gair than I should have. With my children, however, I could only watch and hope they would succeed."

"Even though you knew they would fail," Sarah said quietly, her eyes full of tears.

Ruith winced at the grief in Franciscus's eyes. He found himself quite thoroughly grateful that he was not one of those lads who belonged to Seannair. Their principles were too lofty and painful for him.

"Who am I to challenge destiny, my gel?" Franciscus asked softly. "I prepared them as best I could, then made other, more quiet preparations that your great-great-grandfather Seannair would have found . . . inappropriate."

"Would he?" Sarah asked. "Is it wrong to prevent suffering?"

"Who am I to change the course of Fate?" Franciscus asked. "Not all evil is final, nor is all suffering needless."

Ruith choked a bit in spite of himself. "I think I've heard Soilléir say the same damned thing in exactly the same way."

"They're the first words we learn," Franciscus said seriously. He turned back to Sarah. "Your parents were slain, Sarah love, three years before Gair took his family to the well. I had suggested to Phillip, Morag's hapless mate, that he might spare his conscience undue distress by sending you away with Seleg, and that if he suggested to her that Doìre would be a fine place to land, she would be able to keep you out of Morag's sights. I knew he would take my suggestion and that Seleg would travel south. She had her own reasons for wanting to disappear, not the least of which was wanting to be out of Morag's reach. I had already scouted out possible locales, of course, and decided that Doìre suited my purposes. There was the house on the hill, of course, and in truth there had been a mage who had lived there for centuries. I wasted no time ginning up his legend every chance I had. I knew it would suit Ruith perfectly when he came south."

"Did you know he would come south?" Sarah asked quietly.

Franciscus rubbed his hands over his face briefly. "Sgath and I had had numerous conversations about Gair, of course, and considered all possible outcomes, so aye, I had considered it."

"Considered it?" Ruith echoed. "Didn't you know?"

"Nay, I didn't know," Franciscus said, "not with certainty. Short of picking you up and carrying you to Shettlestoune, I couldn't control your destiny. I could attempt to see how it might play out, but that is the thing about Foresight that isn't always reliable."

"The freedom of the poor sap in question to choose a different path?" Ruith asked dryly.

Franciscus shot him an arch look. "I refuse to respond to that. All I *will* ask you is, didn't you wonder why every step you took seemed to feel as if you were going downhill? I went against every precept, every warning, every stricture my father and grandfather spent lifetimes pounding into my thick head to lead you south. Because my lady and your mother were very fond of each other and the same thing killed them both."

Ruith found he couldn't breathe all of a sudden. Sarah's arm was around his waist just as quickly, holding him up more than he cared to admit.

"I won't speak of it now," Franciscus said grimly. "Later, perhaps, when this tale is finished. Suffice it to say that Gair is the most powerful of the current crop of black mages, but there are others who share his vision for a world without light. And while I, unlike Nicholas of Diarmailt, did not promise your mother as much, Ruith, I vowed to myself that I would see you kept safe as I kept my granddaughter."

"Did Sgath know where I was?" Ruith asked. "Or what had become of the rest of us?"

Franciscus shook his head. "I told him that I would do what I could, but I gave him no particulars. He has no self-control, you know, and he might have put his oar in where it didn't belong. Once I'd landed in Shettlestoune, I didn't dare leave, not even to visit Lake Cladach. I occasionally ventured to Bruaih to see how the ripples of Gair's well were faring, but I didn't dare leave Sarah alone there for long with Seleg and I didn't want to draw any attention to myself from unseen eyes. So, aye, Sgath's surprise at seeing you earlier this year was genuine."

"And the house on the hill?" Ruith asked, because he was hav-ing answers to questions that had plagued him for years. Under-standing the particulars of the map could wait another few minutes as far as he was concerned.

Franciscus shrugged. "As I said, the house was there when I arrived hard on Seleg's heels and there had indeed been a mage there, but I embellished a legend of my own creation as thoroughly as possible. As you might expect, the locals had no trouble believ-ing it. There were several who told me that there was a darkness there in the forest, something that seemed to leave everything around it laboring under a particular sort of malaise that no one could explain."

Ruith found it very difficult to swallow. "The mage on the hill," he said, meaning it to sound like a statement of fact, not a question.

Franciscus met his gaze. "Nay, lad, not the mage on the hill."

"Who then?" Ruith asked thickly.

Franciscus lifted his eyebrows briefly. "That is the question, isn't it?" He paused and looked off into the distance, as if he saw things they couldn't. "I never imagined that there might be truth to the rumors." He looked at them both bleakly. "I will admit I was perhaps not thinking past what I could see, which wasn't much."

Ruith frowned. "But how is that, with your mighty gifts of sight? Could you not see the future?"

"Not when that future happens in Shettlestoune," Franciscus said frankly.

Ruith felt his mouth fall open. *"What?"*

"Just what I said, lad," Franciscus said. "Magic is possible in Shettlestoune—the sort you might have from the local witchwoman or wizard—but not serious magic. Not *seeing* magic. At least that was my experience." He shrugged. "To tell the truth, I never inves-tigated it past realizing during my first visit there that my sight was completely dimmed. 'Tis possible, I suppose, that I could have augmented that sight with a pointed spell or two, but I had no reason to and no stomach to see past the end of my worktable." He chewed on his words for a moment or two. "I'm realizing now that that was a mistake."

Ruith looked at the map in Sarah's hands. He looked at the location opposite the house where they now stood. And he couldn't deny that that corner of that square found itself in Shettlestoune.

In Doìre.

On the side of the mountain near his home.

He felt a shudder tear through him so suddenly and so strongly the only reason he didn't fall straightway upon his arse was that Sarah was holding up one side and Franciscus the other. He felt as if he had recently and quite narrowly avoided certain death but was now only realizing how closely he had come to having his life be ripped away from him.

He had explored the woods for leagues around his home, just to give himself something to do. There had been a particular house in the midst of a clearing, a clearing with a well-tended garden, animals in a pasture, a finely laid path leading to the front door.

And a well beside that path.

Ruith waited until the stars had cleared, then looked at Franciscus in horror.

"Impossible," he managed.

"Improbable," Franciscus said grimly, "and terrifying, but not impossible. Doìre isn't large, but the mountains are full of all sorts of places no one dares travel. You hid there for a score of years without garnering undue notice, didn't you? It isn't unthinkable that other mages could have done the same." He paused. "There's only one way to find out—"

Ruith nodded briskly, because he had no choice. The thought that his father might be alive had been troubling enough. The possibility that not only was he alive, he had been living for years less than five leagues from his own house was . . .

Devastating.

He turned and looked at Sarah. "I have to go."

"Without me?" she asked in surprise.

He shook his head sharply. "You cannot come on this—"

"Of course I can," she said, stepping away from him. "I'll pack my gear. How shall we travel?"

Ruith wanted to protest. Indeed, he opened his mouth to protest, but then it occurred to him that if he left her behind, he would be leaving her . . . well, he had no idea where he could leave her. Franciscus would no doubt wish to come along, which left her relying on a pair of damaged mages, a powerless elf, and a farm boy without any useful skills. He sighed.

"Very well." He looked at Franciscus. "What of Thoir?"

Franciscus looked behind Ruith, blinked, then swore. The vehemence of that swearing startled Ruith so that he looked over his shoulder.

To find Thoir of Tòrr Dòrainn nowhere to be seen.

Well, that wasn't precisely true. Ruith followed Sarah's extended arm and looked up to where she was pointing. There in the sky, quite a decent distance away and becoming smaller by the heartbeat, was a dragon frantically flapping its wings. In its talons was clutched a man who was struggling violently. Ruith looked at Franciscus.

"Well?"

Franciscus rubbed his finger over his mouth, as if he strove not to smile. "Forgive me, Ruith, if I find the humor in this."

"Help me see it," Ruith said sourly, "because I'm finding that difficult."

Franciscus laughed briefly. "I'm imagining that Urchaid thinks he'll carry his prize off to some pleasant locale and terrify a bit of information out of him. Sadly enough, he will have met his match in Thoir who is not only his grandfather's grandson, but half mad as well. If they wind up as anything more than two souls locked in an eternal battle to determine who is more worthy of disdain, I would be very surprised. Or," he said with a shrug, "they may find

themselves wanting the same thing and joining forces at least out-
wardly to have it."

"At least Thoir has no idea where we're going and won't be able
to see us to follow us," Ruith said, even though he didn't completely
believe it.

"So we could hope," Franciscus said his smile fading. "I'll
shadow them and engage them both if necessary. Or I might just
lead them in the wrong direction. I would suggest that you two
make haste and travel under cover. Consider this a final gift for this
quest that from this point on is yours alone."

Ruith sighed deeply. "You have helped us both more than we
could reasonably expect, and I thank you for it."

"What are grandfathers for," Franciscus asked seriously, "if not
to offer everything possible to prepare their charges to take their
own places on the world's stage?"

Ruith found that words were simply beyond him. He took a
step backward, then made Franciscus a low, formal bow. "Thank
you, Your Highness."

Franciscus only smiled, then clapped a hand on Ruith's shoulder. "The same was done for me, once upon a time, under not so
dire circumstances, lad. You'll do it in your turn, I'm sure." He
embraced Sarah briefly, then looked at her with rather misty eyes.
"We'll meet again, hopefully under more cheery circumstances. Be
careful with that lad there. My suggestion is to keep him at arm's
length more often than not."

Ruith pursed his lips. "Is this another selection from that grand-
fatherly code you seem to be so familiar with?"

Franciscus only smiled at him pleasantly. He paused, ran his
hand briefly over Sarah's hair, then smiled at her before he walked
away.

He vanished without a trace.

Ruith took a deep breath, then reached for Sarah's hand. "Well,"
he said, because that was all he could manage.

"We should finish up here," she said, looking easily as overcome as he felt, "and I'm not saying that to put the journey off." She paused. "Not entirely."

He understood completely. He took her hand, then walked over with her to the rest of their company. He put on a cheerful smile, because he didn't want to terrify them.

"My lord Seirceil, if you and Master Oban would be so good as to take Prince Ardan to Seanagarra," he said, shooting Ardan a look that said he would be wise to simply keep his mouth shut and go along, "I would appreciate it. Sarah and I have a small detour to see to before we join you there."

Seirceil inclined his head. "As you wish, Prince Ruithneadh."

"You can take our horses, of course," Ruith said, hoping that Seirceil would be able to manage them. "Ned, you make sure they're fed and watered properly."

"As dragons?" Ned squeaked.

"Seirceil will see if he can convince them to turn themselves back into horses when you reach Tòrr Dòrainn. I think I can safely promise you that no matter their form, they won't eat you."

Ned didn't look particularly convinced, but Ruith supposed after what the lad had seen he had good reason to be a little overwhelmed.

He thanked them all for the companionship on the journey, then turned away and wondered why it felt more final than he would have liked.

He was becoming sentimental in his old age, no doubt.

He walked over toward the doorway of his father's spectacular bolt hole with Sarah, picking up his pack as he did so. The spells were safely inside, as was the cover for them. He supposed the map didn't make any difference, but he thought he might rather have it than not, so he picked it up and shoved it down his boot.

"The door?" Sarah asked.

Ruith pushed it to, then considered for a moment or two. He

looked at the ring on his finger that he'd put there simply to keep it safe, then reached out and put the stone into what seemingly served as a lock.

The spell leapt up from where it had lain coiled on the ground and rewound itself over the face of the door. He pulled the ring away only because the end of the spell came close to tapping him on the back of the hand to get himself out of its way. Any hint of it no matter how faint immediately disappeared fading into an obscurity that matched the rest of the rock face. Ruith took a deep breath and looked at Sarah.

"Well?"

"I'm ready to go," she said, sounding rather unnerved. "How will we travel?"

Ruith considered. "Wind, I think."

Her mouth fell open. "Absolutely not."

"I won't lose you, I promise."

"Well," she said slowly, "you haven't before."

That wasn't entirely true, for he had indeed been bested, and by Urchaid himself, outside Ceangail where he had most certainly lost her. But that had been before, when he'd had his magic buried and only his nightmares to keep him company. Now he had spells at his disposal and strength he hadn't possessed before. He could at least manage to get them both to Shettlestoune in safety.

He could only hope he could manage safety for them both once they were there.

Eighteen

❖

Sarah dropped to her knees, gasping, and was immensely grateful she had knees to fall to. The fire to her right sprang to life in the hearth and candles lit themselves on the table behind her.

Well, that wasn't exactly true. The candles and the fire were lit thanks to the man who regrouped next to her and joined here there on his knees. She knew she shouldn't have been pleased to see him gasping for breath as well, but she was. She mustered up a glare.

"That is the very last time you turn me into wind."

"I thought you didn't want me to turn you into a mouse."

"I didn't want that either!"

He put his arm around her shoulders and rested his cheek against hers. "We'll try dragonshape next time. I think you might like that. You're feisty enough for it."

She would have elbowed him rather firmly for the wheezing laugh that accompanied his words, but she just didn't have it in her to do so.

She turned slightly and put her arms around his neck, partly because she was very fond of him and partly because she needed something to hold on to. It had been a very long journey from Gair's palace, a journey she wasn't sure she would recover from anytime soon.

"I don't feel well," she managed.

And that was the last thing she remembered saying.

She woke to find she was stretched out in front of the fire with Ruith's cloak under her head. She wasn't sure how she'd gotten there and thought it best not to ask. She simply watched him as he moved about what had been his home for a score of years, preparing supper, feeding the fire. He pulled two loaves of bread out of the oven to the side of his hearth, then smiled at her.

"Sleep well?"

"I'm not sure," she said. "Did I sleep long?"

"All night," he said gravely.

"Did you?"

He shrugged. "For a few hours. I had too much to think on to make a proper night of it."

She sat up, then had to put her hands to her head to keep it from spinning. Perhaps dragonshape was the best idea. It was sad to say, but she thought even riding atop a dragon was preferable to the past two days of blistering travel in a shape not her own. Perhaps if she'd had magic, she might have enjoyed it. As it was, it did nothing for her besides making her very glad she could spend most of her life on the ground in her own shape.

She breakfasted with Ruith, complemented him on his bread and eggs, and enjoyed a cup of Franciscus's lovely apple-flavored ale. She considered asking Ruith if it was wise to alert anyone to their presence there given that the smoke from the chimney was a telltale sign, but she supposed he'd already thought of that.

At that point, she supposed there was little reason in trying to hide.

She helped him put the house to rights, watched him bank the fire by very pedestrian means, then waited at the door whilst he looked about the house a final time. He walked outside with her, then pulled the door shut behind them. He stood with his hand on the latch for a moment or two, then looked at her with a weary smile.

"We should be off."

She could only nod. The last time she had stood at that particular doorway, she'd been oblivious to her heritage and equally as unaware of just how powerful mages outside Shettlestoune could be. Ruith had terrified her with his reputation alone, driving her away into woods that had been full of nothing worse than woodland creatures and Ruith himself following along after her. She hadn't known she could see, hadn't known what that gift would cost her, hadn't known just how much there was to fear.

She also hadn't known what beauty there was in the world to be seen by a rustic miss from the most barren part of the ugliest country in all the Nine Kingdoms.

Ruith took her hand and drew her away from the door. She walked with him, because there was no use in putting things off any longer. Their path was laid before their feet, a shining river of Fadaire that sparkled and sang as it flowed around them. She watched it in wonder until she and Ruith reached the end of the path that led up to his house. The Fadaire faded, then disappeared.

"Did you do that?"

He looked at her, apparently equally moved. "I didn't. I saw it first after I shut the door on you—"

"Threw me out of your house, you mean."

He laughed a little. "Aye, that. I walked outside, trying to elude my guilt, and walked into the middle of that stream." He was silent for a moment or two. "I think it has lain there, undisturbed, for twenty years." He shot her a look. "You know, 'tis possible you were the one to convince it to become visible."

"Me?" she asked, finding herself smiling uneasily. "I doubt that. I'm sure it was you. I just wonder who put it there."

Ruith shrugged. "It could have been any number of people, though my best guess is Franciscus. He certainly has the power to use that magic, and the cheek."

She shook her head. "You mages are so possessive of your heritages."

"We don't like lesser hands at the tiller," Ruith said dryly, "though even Sìle would conceed that Franciscus is not a lesser hand." He took a deep breath and looked at the path in front of them. "Right to Doìre, left to . . ." He was silent for several moments. "Well, to wherever it leads."

Sarah nodded, then turned to the left with him and started along the path that led, she was sure, to a place she would happily have avoided for the rest of her life.

She spared a thought, as she walked, for the rest of their company. The lads and Ardan would find their way to Tòrr Dòrainn with little trouble with Seirceil leading the way. Franciscus, she hoped, would have already given both Urchaid and Thoir a stern talking to and set them on a path to more productive endeavors. Perhaps her grandfather was now sitting with Sgath, discussing where the best fishing spots were on Sgath's pristine lake.

Unless the unthinkable had occurred and he had been overcome by either Thoir or Urchaid—or both. She hadn't thought about either of them on her journey south, but then again, she hadn't had much of a mind to think with. Now, though, it was hard not to worry about what could possibly happen if they appeared at an inopportune moment and made trouble neither she nor Ruith could fight.

She couldn't bring herself to even consider just what sort of trouble that might be.

She put those unpleasant thoughts behind her and simply walked next to Ruith, forcing herself to pretend they were out for a stroll through unremarkable woods with a very pedestrian afternoon stretching out before them. That stroll might be followed, if they were feeling particularly spry, by an evening down at the pub where they might enjoy a fine mug of Franciscus's ale and try to ignore whatever entertainment might have been on display for their amusement.

A pity she couldn't quite bring her rather decent imagination to grasp hold of any of that with any success. She found that the only thing each league brought her was a drier mouth, a more fiercely beating heart, and in the end, a terror that made it almost impossible for her to swallow. She could say with all honesty that when she reached a path that broke off from the main road and turned toward a deeper forest, she was almost relieved.

Until she realized what it meant.

Ruith stood there at the head of what was nothing more, in truth, than the faintest hint of a trail, for so long, Sarah began to wonder if he would be able to move forward again. He finally lifted his head and looked at her.

"I think we should go on without magic."

She felt her mouth fall open. "You can't be serious."

He smiled briefly. "How easily we've both become accustomed to it."

She would have blushed, but she couldn't muster up the energy. "Forgive me. I don't doubt your ability to keep us safe."

He pulled their bows out of his pack and restored them to their original size. He handed her a bow and a quiver full of arrows, then smiled.

"You would have every reason to at the moment, but I promise I won't let harm come to you." He paused. "I think, though, that I will make a brief change to myself."

She knew what he was going to do even before he whispered

the spell under his breath. She couldn't see it, of course, because she could see nothing. She wasn't sure that she wouldn't be able to at least see *something* if she tried Soilléir's spell, but she found herself hesitating. She wasn't sure it would work, which left her without any desire to try it.

She didn't want to think about what might happen if she desperately needed to use the spell and it didn't work.

"Well," he said finally, "by my count, we have twenty-two spells including Diminishing, and we have the bloody cover to the book. All we need to do now is to see if we can't pry the proper total number out of him, then find a way to dispose of the lot before he kills me." He paused. "Assuming he's there to be pried, of course."

Sarah tried to swallow, but it was impossible. "Do you think he is?"

Ruith blew his hair out of his eyes. "Sarah, my love, I have absolutely no idea. A sneaking suspicion, but nothing sure." He looked at her. "Shall we press on?"

She could only nod, because her mouth was too parched to allow her to manage speech. She watched Ruith pull his bow over his chest and sling the quiver of arrows over his shoulder. She tried not to notice that they were back to just two, marching on into the unknown with no magic at their disposal. Somehow, after all they'd been through over the past few weeks, it seemed a great deal more dangerous than it perhaps should have.

"Do you know where you're going?" she asked at one point, after they'd been walking for quite some time in silence.

"Aye."

She took an unsteady breath. "I wish we were anywhere else."

He stopped suddenly, pulled her into his arms, and held her close. She didn't protest the string of his bow pressing into her cheek or the way resting her cheek against his chest left her with an all-too-accurate knowledge of how hard his heart was beating. She didn't like being terrified, but she couldn't help it. She couldn't even bring herself to enjoy the fact that the grandson of Sìle of Tòrr Dòrainn was holding her in his arms. Not even the thought of dragging him along behind her to the home of Dierdhra Higgleton— Prunella's cousin—and watching the admittedly stunning but undeniably dim lass attempt to throw herself at Ruith and find herself rebuffed was any consolation.

"What are you thinking?"

"That Dierdhra Higgleton would poke my eyes out with hatpins if she thought it would earn her a turn where I'm standing."

He laughed softly. "You and I, my love, have had a very interesting few years."

She nodded, but she couldn't say what she was thinking, which was that she desperately hoped they would have something besides those interesting few years to carry with them past the grave. While she wasn't sure she wanted glittering elven palaces with sharp-eyed courtiers watching for any misstep, she was absolutely sure she didn't want to spend the rest of her life living in Dòire.

She didn't protest when Ruith pulled away and took her hand, though she would be the first to admit she would have happily turned and bolted in the opposite direction.

She realized as they continued on that she recognized her surroundings. She had roamed through those woods countless times over the years to escape her mother—

She took a deep breath. Nay, Seleg wasn't her mother. She couldn't even call her her guardian. She supposed she couldn't call her anything but what she had been: a woman who had been given charge of her and had fulfilled that charge grudgingly.

In time, she began to wonder if she were dreaming or awake, for she felt as if she'd walked the path before her not once but several times before, either in dream or waking vision. It lay first through unimpressive scrub oaks that eventually turned into taller, mightier trees as it climbed a fairly decent incline.

By the time they walked without warning out from the trees

and into a clearing, she was winded. Handy, that, given that what she saw took away the rest of her breath.

It was a modest, unremarkable house enclosed by a low fence, a house such as any woodsman might have built for himself. There was a well there to the side, a small barn huddled behind the house, a garden laid out to the side where it might best catch what sun it could. The path that wound from where they stood to the front door was paved with flat stone. Moss grew in the cracks, which was surprising given how little rain Shettlestoune as a whole enjoyed during the year.

There was no light pouring from the windows, but Sarah realized with a start that there didn't need to be. She had lost track of the time they had walked, or the brief pauses when she'd fallen instantly asleep, but she supposed now that they had walked through at least one entire night and a morning. It was noon, for she could see the sun overhead, but it was obscured by something. She wondered if perhaps there was a darkness that lived there in that glade that couldn't be dispelled by any amount of sunlight, however relentless.

And then the front door opened.

A tall, grey-haired man, bent and obviously crippled, leaned heavily on a cane as he carefully stepped over the threshold of his door. He inched a pace or two forward, then stopped and looked at them.

Sarah would have caught her breath, if she'd had breath to catch. He looked like Sgath, if Sgath had actually shown his age. She didn't dare look at Ruith, though she could certainly feel the tenseness in him.

The wizened man had eyes only for Ruith. He stared at him in silence for several minutes, his face betraying no emotion at all. And then he cleared his throat.

"I was wondering," he said in a ruined voice, "when you would come to tea, son."

Sarah imagined he did.

Nineteen

Ruith stared at the old man hunched there in front of a sturdy but very modest house and could hardly believe his eyes.

There was no denying, though, what his eyes were seeing.

It was his father.

Ruith was so surprised to see him—not just in Doìre, but at all—that he could hardly take it in.

"I'm wondering," Gair said in that same voice that sounded as if it had been caught between the stone cap of a well and its walls, then pulled out by force and left in his throat, "why it is you never came to call on me before."

"I didn't know you were here," Ruith said, because he could think of nothing else to say. Actually, he realized that wasn't quite true. There were several things that came readily to mind, beginning with *how the hell did you get here?* and ending with *how could you do what you did to my family, you heartless . . .*

He took a deep breath. There was little point in calling his father names only because he feared once he started, he wouldn't be able to stop.

"Ah, well, that is quite a tale," Gair said, sounding as happy as if Ruith had asked him to recount in great detail a magnificent day spent betting on horses in Cearracas. He shuffled to his left until he was standing in front of a bench pushed up against the house, then he sat with a deep sigh. He smiled. "Care to join me? You and young Sarah?"

Ruith pulled Sarah behind him, because it was profoundly disturbing to him that his father knew Sarah's name. And once she was there, he supposed there was no reason not to keep her there.

"Thank you, but nay," he said. "We'll stand."

"Suit yourself." Gair settled painfully on the bench, then rested his hands over his cane. "It is rather interesting, isn't it, how disaster turns to good fortune?"

Ruith could hardly believe his father was talking about the disaster at the well, for nothing good had come from it that he could see. Not even that his sire, the most powerful and feared black mage in the history of the Nine Kingdoms, should find himself crippled and keeping house in the ugliest country of the Nine Kingdoms was good fortune enough for the price it had cost.

Perhaps Gair had lost his wits along with his magic at the well.

Assuming he'd lost his magic.

"I was off on a walk through the woods hereabout, as is my custom," Gair continued, apparently needing no prompting to continue with his lofty conversation, "when I dropped something."

"What?" Ruith asked finally, when it looked as though his sire wouldn't continue on without prodding. Ruith thought it best to prod. Better that than giving the man time to consider things he shouldn't. The list of what those things could have been was one Ruith couldn't begin to consider, but he suspected how in the hell his father had known Sarah's name would begin and end it.

He forced himself not to shake his head, and not to continue to shake his head until it spun endlessly. He could hardly believe he was standing where he was, such a short distance from his house where he'd felt so safe. It was almost more appalling that Sarah had been so close for so many years, never dreaming that Gair of Ceangail was taking the air just up the way.

"The second half of my spell of Diminishing."

Ruith almost wished he'd taken his father up on that seat. "What?"

"You heard me."

Ruith frowned. "You had it?"

"Of course I had it," Gair said sharply. "How would I have dropped it if I hadn't had it to drop?"

Ruith felt himself shrinking right there before his father as if he'd been nothing more than a ten-year-old boy facing a man who towered over him both in stature and power. He tried to ignore the feeling but it was so strong, he was having trouble breathing. "What happened then?" he managed.

"Well, the spell was stolen, of course," Gair said crossly, "but only after I dropped it, which was an accident. It was picked up by that ridiculous boy, the witchwoman Seleg's son. No magic to speak of in him, but a vastly overrated sense of his own magnificence. That sort of thing is useful, if you didn't know, in helping weaker souls do for you what you don't particularly want to do for yourself."

Ruith imagined it was. He wondered why it was someone hadn't noticed that about his father and used it against him centuries earlier.

"Well?" Gair demanded. "Aren't you going to ask me what it was I didn't want to do myself?"

"What didn't you want to do?" Ruith asked dutifully, because he supposed since his father was being so verbose, there was no sense in not having a few answers out of him.

But he knew he needed not only to listen, but watch at the same time. With Gair, the attack rarely came from the place one expected.

"I didn't want to carry that spell out of Shettlestoune," Gair said impatiently, as if it should have been obvious, "but I couldn't leave it here any longer. It certainly wasn't going to awaken the other half if it loitered here under this magic sink."

Ruith frowned. "I don't think Shettlestoune is much of a magic sink. Not in the truest sense—"

"Oh, be silent," Gair said, waving his stick impatiently. "I don't want to know what you think it is. As far as I'm concerned, the whole damned place is a magic sink. The point is, I didn't want to stir myself to dirty my hands with such a menial task, so I sent that boy off to do it for me."

"He didn't do it very well," Ruith said.

"Nay, he didn't, did he? Got too high on himself, didn't he? I'd intended he merely go as far as Bruaih, which is far enough from this hellish country that the spell could do its work, but apparently the lad took it upon himself to collect the rest of my spells."

"Then you are the one who scattered them," Ruith said.

Gair made a noise of exasperation. "Well, of course I scattered them. What else was I going to do? Keep the book on my person and possibly have it stolen?" He shot Ruith a look that was so full of hate, Ruith almost flinched. "I needed time to recover from the betrayal my family perpetrated on me at Ruamharaiche's well."

"Betrayal?" Ruith echoed, coming close to choking on the word.

"Of course, betrayal," Gair snapped. "You turned on me, every one of you, just as I'd suspected you would." He lifted his chin. "One does not recover from that sort of mutiny in a fortnight. I suffered for years."

Ruith listened to his father carry on about the pain he'd endured, and watched him grow angrier by the word. And though his first instinct was to shrink back as he'd done countless times as a child, he realized with a start that that impulse wasn't coming come from himself.

It was coming from a spell his father was casting over him.

He would have spared a thought or two to wonder how often that had been the case in his youth, but he had more pressing matters to consider at the moment. He simply folded his arms over his chest, ignored the spell, and sifted through the threads of the spell to see his father for what he was. Not mad, not power-hungry, not selfish.

He was evil.

Ruith had known it, of course, but now he could see how his father had become what he'd chosen. Gair was a man full grown, with centuries of living behind him, centuries of opportunities to look at the world and fashion himself a destiny that could be looked back on by future generations and admired.

But his father had chosen differently.

He had chosen a path that demanded he be admired, not for his strength of character, but for all the evil he could loose into the world. He had chosen a destiny that left countless others shivering in fear when his name was mentioned, while still others worried that their peaceful lives would be irreparably damaged by actions that weren't simply an unthinking assault, but a deliberate campaign to eradicate anything good.

Ruith realized in that moment that one thing he'd tried to convince himself of as a youth and attempted to put behind him as a man was actually true.

He was not his father.

There was not a part of him that belonged to his sire. Not his anger, nor his disgust, nor his heart. Where his sire had chosen evil, Ruith knew he had chosen good. Where his sire had chosen darkness, Ruith had chosen light.

Where his father had chosen Olc, Ruith had chosen Fadaire.

He was not his father.

He would have sat down right there just inside his father's pretty wooden picket fence if he'd dared, just so he could allow the relief to wash over him, but the battle was not won and the time for reveling in success had not come. He permitted himself a very careful sigh, then resigned himself to a very long afternoon of listening to his father complain.

"None of you were loyal to me, but I have put it all behind me," Gair groused, huddling over his cane, "because after several years of suffering, I knew I couldn't bear the hurt any longer. And once that foolish Daniel stole the spell I'd inadvertently left behind, I knew the time to take my place in the world again had come."

Ruith decided it would be ill-advised to point out to his father that he didn't look as if he could walk to his garden much less walk back onto the world's stage.

"Daniel, being the weak-minded lad he is—"

"Was," Ruith interrupted.

Gair looked at him blankly, as if he had heard that there was only regular ale and not anything more delicate at the pub and couldn't quite understand why that was, then shrugged. "As you say, then. I saw him leave on his little journey to try to collect more of what he'd found, which then involved his do-gooding sister standing behind you, and then you trotting off to follow her." He leaned to the right. "You can come out from behind him, my dear Sarah. You need have no fear I'll discover your true identity."

"She'll stay where she is, thank you just the same," Ruith said, putting his arm out to keep Sarah behind him. That was unnecessary, he found, because she wasn't moving.

"No matter," Gair said with a shrug, though his eyes were glittering with anger. "'Tis a poorly kept secret by those with two good eyes that she has no magic. Though those from Cothromaiche have magic that isn't quite the norm, don't they?"

Ruith wished that he had left Sarah behind, anywhere, at any point on their way south. He cleared his throat and attempted a distraction. "What did you intend to do when Daniel collected all your spells?"

"Oh, I didn't intend that he collect them all," Gair said smoothly. "I intended that *you* collect them." He smiled, but there was no warmth to it. "You always were one for a good mystery, weren't you, Ruithneadh? I knew once you realized what Daniel had, you would trot out your chivalry and attempt to rescue the world from my spells."

Ruith inclined his head, conceding the point. "I suppose you're fortunate I have any chivalry at all."

"I am," Gair agreed, "though you can't be fool enough to suppose I didn't have something else in place."

Ruith frowned. "And what would that be?"

Gair laughed, a horrible scraping sound that set Ruith's teeth on edge. "Ah, well, have yourself a look there, my son, and you'll see who I'm talking about." Gair nodded to Ruith's left. "That elven princeling there, who thinks he was so clever in trying to ferret out my magic." Gair looked down his nose. "How arrogant, young Thoir, to think someone from that collection of mountain huts in Tòrr Dòrainn could possibly outthink me."

Ruith looked at Thoir standing ten paces from him on his left, looking very much the worse for wear. Or perhaps that was because he had looked into the face of the man he apparently admired to the depths of his soul and discovered that his idol was not exactly what he'd thought him to be.

Ruith lifted his eyes in time to see a magnificent owl come to rest in a tree just behind Thoir. That wasn't one of the horses, for he assumed they were safely tucked in the stables at Seanagarra. He didn't suppose it was Franciscus either, but he couldn't be sure. He suspected 'twas Urchaid of Saothair, come to enjoy the show and hopefully outlast all the players for a chance at the spoils.

All of which left him wondering where Franciscus was. He couldn't believe the man was dead, but it was a possibility.

'Twas also a possibility that Franciscus had done a bit of peeping into the future and decided that Thoir might have a part to play in the drama yet. Ruith wasn't sure what that said about that owl sitting a safe distance off the ground, but he promised himself a thorough questioning of Sarah's grandfather later.

He refused to consider the very real possibility that he wouldn't have that chance, either because Franciscus was dead or he himself soon would be.

Thoir didn't seem to be able to do anything but gape at Gair, so Ruith left him to it and continued with his plan to keep his sire talking.

"Why now?" Ruith asked, stepping a pace or two back so he could keep both his father and his cousin in his sights. "Why send someone to gather the pages of your book now?"

"Why now?" Gair echoed incredulously. "Have you been so long out of the world, Ruithneadh, that you're ignorant of the events passing there? That damned Lothar of Wychweald has been using my spells!"

"I don't follow—"

"You never did, so I'll explain it slowly, so you might. Despite what has been said, I wasn't vanquished at Ruamharaiche's well. I simply decided to retreat and reconsider my spell of opening. To refine it, of course, not replace it. I rested for a bit thanks to the hospitality of those who truly cared for me, then went to the keep only to find my sons had done the unthinkable and burned the damned library almost to the ground. I rescued my spells, then decided that perhaps I should spread them about, so the fools I had spawned wouldn't find them and destroy them in a fit of pique."

"So you did travel to the house cut into the rock," Ruith said slowly.

"Aye only to find I'd lost that bloody ring somewhere along the way and couldn't get inside." He scowled. "I hadn't wanted to sentence myself to a lifetime here, but I had decided I could endure it for a year or two. 'Twas a bloody inconvenience to come here, and by a different route, but I was afraid I'd been followed. That and I wasn't about to leave the rest of my spells anywhere near the first ones. Wise, don't you think?"

"I wouldn't think to offer an opinion," Ruith demurred.

Gair frowned, then continued. "I had spent a handful of years here, working on spells I had been considering before, when I heard from a very reliable source that Lothar had been using *my* well to fashion creatures whose task was to hunt down my descendants—if any lived—and carry them back to Riamh where Lothar could torture them until they revealed my secrets to him. Knowing the weakness of my progeny—and the deviousness of my children which led me to believe they knew more than I would want them to—I knew something had to be done. Unfortunately, I needed someone to help me counter the outrage, for I knew the moment of my full return had not come." He looked down his nose. "I suppose I should have been grateful at least one of my offspring survived."

"Did you know I had lived?" Ruith asked.

"Oh, aye," Gair said softly. "After all, Franciscus did a rather poor job of covering his tracks, didn't he? A pity I was left only with you. I would have preferred one of your brothers."

Ruith was tempted almost beyond what he could bear to tell his father his damned well had been shut by Mhorghain and Keir, and that Rùnach had spent the past twenty years searching for all the sources Gair had used for his spells and could likely improve upon all of them without any effort. If Rùnach had been willing to lower himself to use Olc, which Ruith was certain he wouldn't have been.

"So, when I recently saw that young fool there sniffing after my spells, I couldn't help but use him." Gair smiled at him. "Such a good fool you are, Thoir."

Ruith looked at his cousin, who had stopped staring at Gair with his mouth open and was now turning a rather robust shade of red.

Gair leaned forward. "I think he harbors a secret wish to be my apprentice," he whispered loudly. "I'm not sure he has the wit for it, but I'm willing to try him out for a bit." He frowned suddenly, then sat back. "I must assume that one of you has all my spells, else you wouldn't be here." He looked from Ruith to Thoir and back several times before he finally settled on Ruith. He pursed his lips. "You?"

"He does," Thoir rasped, sounding as if he'd been running for days without rest or drink. "He has them all."

"Thank you, Thoir," Gair said, waving him away. "You may go."

Ruith wasn't sure his cousin's face could darken any more, but he looked as if he were about to explode with rage. Ruith had to admire his ability to continue to stand there in spite of being so summarily dismissed. He kept his cousin in his sights and looked back at his sire.

"I'm not sure I understand why you wanted them. Surely you can write them down again."

"Your problem, Ruithneadh," Gair said shortly, "has always been your painful lack of imagination. Have you not noticed anything about the spells?"

"They're charred on the edges," Ruith said flatly.

The owl tittered. Ruith imagined that wasn't Franciscus, for he likely would have hooted with derision. Nay, that was Urchaid which meant that Franciscus had either been overcome fully or taken by a bout of altruism that had left both Urchaid and Thoir flapping off into the sunset. Ruith didn't dare hope that Franciscus was simply hiding in a different tree, disguised as a less showy bird.

"Those spells also contain, you stupid boy, vast amounts of my power," Gair said pointedly. "I imagine not even your little wench behind you could see that. And so aye, I had a rather compelling reason to collect them all, just as young Thoir there had a very compelling reason to want them for himself. Only our understanding of what they contain is far different, which I will show you if you'll be so kind as to give me back my life's work."

Ruith took off his bow and quiver of arrows and felt Sarah take them from him. He unslung his pack, keeping his eyes on his father at all times, and fished around in it for the black leather book. The spells were already inside it, for he'd put them there during that night at his house he'd considered such a safe haven for all those years. He continued to look at his sire as he held the book up.

"Good," Gair said, sounding far too pleased. "Let's see if they're all there, shall we?"

"I will," Thoir blurted out.

"Very well," Gair said benevolently. "Go and fetch them from my son, Thoir, and bring them to me."

Thoir strode over to Ruith and stopped in front of him. "Give them to me," he snarled. "Before I destroy you."

"You don't know what you're doing," Ruith warned.

"Neither do you."

Ruith shrugged, then handed the book over without comment.

"And my ring, Ruith?"

Ruith shot his father a look. "What ring, Father?"

"The one in your pocket." Gair looked at him evenly. "You've forgotten the extent of my powers, lad. I know what you have. And I know you think your magic is buried."

Ruith opened his mouth to compliment his father on his sight only to have Thoir throw Gair's spell of Diminshing at him. It sought for what was hidden, then slid away, useless. Thoir drew back and scowled, but said nothing.

Ruith threw his cousin a look of disgust before he pulled the ring from his pocket and looked at his father. "And you expect me to hand this over to you?"

"Aren't you at all curious as to what will happen?" Gair asked with a mocking smile. "You were so curious as a lad."

Ruith shrugged. He had no magic to take, nor did Sarah. The ones in true danger were Thoir and that damned owl sitting up in the tree, preening. He handed the ring to Thoir, then held his hands behind him for his bow. He felt Sarah put that and a handful of arrows into his hands, then steeled himself to use a more pedestrian means of protection.

Thoir made a production of starting across the glade, then stopped suddenly and shot Gair a triumphant look.

"I believe I'll have this now."

Gair only watched him, smiling faintly.

Thoir brushed aside spells Ruith hadn't noticed there before, then pressed the ring into the square indentation on the cover. If he'd expected something to happen, he was disappointed, but that didn't stop him from making several more attempts. He turned the ring this way and that, swore inventively for several moments, then looked at Gair.

"It doesn't work," he said incredulously.

"The lock's tricky," Gair said dismissively. "Bring everything to me, lad, and let me have a look. How many spells are there inside?"

"A score and two," Thoir said impatiently, finishing his journey across the glade to where Gair was waiting. "That's how many Miach of Neroche said there were."

"Well, Miach of Neroche doesn't know everything now, does he?" Gair said smoothly. "I wouldn't choose a pedestrian number such as a score and two. It has no stature, no style, no presence. Though we might give it a go and see." He took the book from Thoir with trembling hands, dropped the ring, then waited until Thoir had picked it up. He fumbled with the book and ring for another few minutes, then scratched his head.

"We might be missing something."

"What?" Thoir demanded.

Ruith watched as the owl flapped down from his perch and changed itself into Urchaid as he landed.

"Perhaps a bit of power," Urchaid said, brushing his hair carefully away from his face. "My dear Gair, why don't you let me help you with that."

Gair looked at him, then laughed. "The son of Dorchadas?" he asked incredulously. "What could you possibly help me with?"

"Taking your magic, for a start," Urchaid said smoothly.

Ruith watched the next handful of moments hang in the air there in front of him as if they intended to remain there forever, endlessly open to alteration, just waiting for someone with sense to say something useful.

Unfortunately, he didn't have a chance.

Twenty

❖

Sarah wondered, as she stood near the little clearing several leagues from the ruins of her mother's house, if she would ever stop shivering. She was standing near a house that she had seen scores of times, thinking nothing of it on those mornings when she'd been roaming far afield for particular plants to use for the dyeing of her wool. How odd that the rare woad she had sought was only to be found on the path leading to the very small, tidy house that contained the old man she had greeted occasionally as he'd been outside tending his garden.

Only now she realized who had been growing heaven only knew what in that garden.

It occurred to her, as she looked at that garden, that even within the dampening influence of Shettlestoune, she could still see more than she'd been able to before. She whispered Soilléir's spell in her mind and her vision sharpened far past what it ever had before, leaving her gaping at what she saw within Gair's low garden walls.

There were plants there that would have, with enough time, grown and blossomed into things she wouldn't have picked if they'd been the last things edible on the face of the earth. She didn't want to begin to identify them, for just the sight of them terrified her. She started to put herself behind Ruith only to realize that she was no longer behind him because he had stepped forward to try to stop events from spiraling out of control.

Or, rather, careening toward a destination she now realized she should have seen approaching.

Droch's spell of Taking was rushing out of Urchaid's mouth toward Gair, but slowly, as if time had ground to a halt along with everthing and everyone in it. Gair had the time to stand up and throw off the ruse he'd drawn about him like a cloak. In place of the old man stood a young man, scarred yet unbent by years and evil, full of energy and power.

She had to admit she could see why Sarait had looked at him more than once. He was almost as handsome as Ruith, which was saying something. And sadly enough, there was an edge to him that was . . . mesmerizing.

She looked away, because she realized it was a spell he was casting her way for precisely the purpose of distracting her. She realized at about the same time that her arm felt as if it had just caught fire. She had left her cloak on the far side of the glade, which left her arm bare to what little breeze blew through the clearing. She lifted her arm and looked at it.

There were little flickers of flame dancing again along the black trails.

She looked back in time to watch Gair bat away Urchaid's spell as if it had been an annoying fly. Gair dismissed Droch's brother with a snort of derision, then looked at Thoir.

"The book doesn't work, dear boy, because it is not complete."

Thoir gaped at him. Sarah knew Thoir was prepared to do anything to have Gair's spells, but she suspected, based on his inability to stop his mouth working like a dying fish, that he had never considered that Gair might have anticipated that very thing. But before she could say anything to Ruith or blurt out a warning to Thoir—not that he would have listened if she had—the chess pieces were put into place and the movements begun.

Gair produced from his person another spell, slid it into the back of the book, then placed his ring into the indentation on the cover.

"Twenty-three," Ruith said faintly. "It was a score and three."

His father shot him a look. "Divisible only by itself and one. You were always very good at maths, Ruithneadh. 'Tis fitting, isn't it? I needed a number that was unique to itself, for obvious reasons."

Sarah couldn't imagine what those reasons were except that Gair had an ego that was almost as vast as the limits of his power. Surely far beyond any attempt to control it.

"And which spell is the last one?" Ruith asked.

"I don't suppose you'll find that out," Gair said pleasantly, "until 'tis everlastingly too late."

He opened his book of spells and flipped through them frowning thoughtfully. Sarah would have tried to move closer and have a look at what he'd added, but she didn't dare. She watched him pause and look closely at one of the pages, then lift his head. He continued to frown as he looked around himself, as if he looked for something he'd lost.

And then he looked at her.

Before she knew what he intended, Gair had stridden over to her, caught hold of her hand and dragged her over to the house. He looked at her, smiled a smile that didn't reach his eyes, then reached out and took hold of the thread of magic his spell had left in her flesh.

"Last bit I needed, my dear," he said in a loud whisper. "You know, the spell doesn't work properly without this final word that you've been carrying for me all this time in your arm. The echo on Ruith's arm was just for show."

Sarah almost fainted from the pain as what had been buried in her flesh was pulled free. She managed to stumble away from him only because he obviously didn't need her any longer. She turned and fell into Ruith's arms, becoming momentarily tangled in his bow, then finding herself freed as he cast the bow aside. She would have told him he shouldn't, but there was no time for speech. Time remained at its excruciating crawl, but events took up even the time that was available to them, time that she supposed they should have used to stop Gair.

But it was too late.

He took the thread from her arm and wrapped it around his book.

And he smiled.

Magic swirled up out of the book, hovered in the air above Gair as he looked up and laughed, then poured into him as if he'd been parched earth and it a heavy, endless rain.

The spell of Diminishing was spewing out of Thoir's mouth almost before Gair was finished. Sarah watched it surround Gair, then pull to itself not only the magic still falling toward him, but the magic already in him. It gathered, in spite of the protests that were coming from Gair.

Or perhaps that was a spell. Sarah listened to Gair's murmured words, but her sight wasn't equal to seeing if he was creating anything, and the spell didn't sound familiar to her ears. He didn't seem overly troubled by his own spell that Thoir was weaving over him, which surprised her. Thoir laughed as he sucked all of Gair's power into himself.

All save a drop Sarah could see there, hovering on the end of one of Gair's fingertips, a drop that remained thanks to the spell he finished weaving before Thoir spoke his last word.

A spell of Anti-Diminishing.

She saw the name of it written there in that perfectly round drop of power clinging to that single fingertip. She couldn't imagine that was enough to save Gair from being stripped of what he held dear, but apparently she knew less about magic than he did. Before Thoir's cry of joy had even begun to ring in the glade, Gair had begun to smile.

Using that single drop of power left him, he began his spell of Diminishing, the crowning achievement of all his centuries of evil, the one spell that no one had ever been able to match. Sarah looked quickly at Thoir, but he was too busy exulting in his triumph to realize that the thread of Gair's spell had reached out and begun a sinewy path around not only Gair's own power that Thoir was holding, but Thoir's own power as well.

And then complete darkness fell.

Sarah felt panic slam into her. That fear wasn't of Gair's make, she was fairly sure. Nay, that was her own alarm, magnified beyond anything she'd ever felt before because she knew, with a certainty that frightened her, that she was going to die. Once Gair had left Thoir a lifeless husk, he would turn to Urchaid, and then Ruith, and then her. Whatever any of them possessed would be ruthlessly and remorselessly stripped from them.

She dropped her pack, then dropped to her knees, fumbling in it for something she couldn't name. She didn't think her knitting needles would serve her, even if she plunged one of them into Gair's black heart, nor the yarn Rùnach had gifted her, even if she'd managed to wrap it around Gair's head and suffocate him—

And then two things were under her hands before she realized she had touched them: the book Soilléir had written for her and the spindle Uachdaran of Léige had gifted her.

And she knew, suddenly, what she had to do.

Ruith fumbled for her and pulled her to her feet. "I'm going to release my ma—"

"Don't," she gasped. "He'll only take it."

"It won't matter if he manages to draw everything back to himself," Ruith whispered frantically. "I *know*—"

"Give me the chance to try one spell," Sarah pleaded. "The last one Soilléir gave me."

And before he could say anything else, she gathered all the hope she had in everything beautiful she'd seen with the legacy her parents had given her, and spoke aloud the words of the third spell Soilléir of Cothromaiche had given her.

The spell of Light.

The little glade exploded with the light of thousands of spheres of werelight in colors she was absolutely sure hadn't been created until that moment. They were separate, true, but somehow blended together to drive out every shadow in the glade, every hint of something that shouldn't have been there, every evil thing that lurked in the corners of Gair's garden.

Thoir had fallen to his knees, gaping at the light above him. Gair had stopped speaking, leaving his spell—and the entirety of his power—still strung out before him, like a very long, very thin thread.

A thread that could be broken, given the right amount of force.

Ruith caught sight of the spindle in her hand, then met met her gaze quickly. "Can you make that work here, do you think?"

"If I can't, we're both dead," she breathed. "What of you?"

"There's little point in having a decent sword if you can't use it now and then for good," he said cheerfully.

And before Gair could open his mouth to finish his spell, Ruith had leapt forward, drawing Athair of Cothromaiche's sword that blazed with a golden light that was immediately reflected in the innumerable balls of werelight above them.

Ruith sliced through the thread of his father's spell.

Then he released all his magic, sending glorious, singing cascades of Fadaire coursing through his soul. The glade was sud-

denly full of air that whispered as it gave them breath, trees that
sang something that sounded remarkably like a battle dirge, and
werelight that rained down refracted sunlight with the sound of
delicate snow on a bitterly cold morning.

Ruith took the ends of his father's spell of Diminishing and
threw them toward her.

Sarah would have spared a comment that he had a bit more
faith in her than she did, but she didn't have the time. So she caught
the ends of the spell with her spindle.

And she began to spin.

She reminded herself that she far preferred spinning on a wheel,
but she supposed, if she managed to consider it at length later, she
could definitely accustom herself to a more portable means of turning things into yarn.

She spun until there was nothing left to spin and the spindle
was full of Gair's power. She looked at him and realized that he
had gravely overextended himself. There was nothing left in him,
not a single drop of the power he had cherished for over a thousand
years. Thoir's was there as well, as was Ardan's, but she had the
feeling that Ardan wasn't going to want back anything she could
pull off that shaft.

She looked at the men there, all but Ruith stunned into silence,
and wondered what they would do.

Urchaid bolted first, scurrying back up his tree as a squirrel.
Thoir's reaction was quite a bit different, as was Gair's. They both
rushed at Ruith from two different directions. Thoir was undeniably mad. Gair was merely out of his head with choler.

She would have cried out to warn Ruith, but she had no time.
He backed up a pace or two to keep the others in his sights, but
tripped and went down. Sarah clicked the lever on her spindle and
the shaft fell away, revealing the small dagger King Uachdaran had
promised would be there. Thoir had snatched up a handful of arrows
and had thrown himself at Ruith, apparently thinking he could do

enough damage with those wicked metal tips. Ruith rolled out from underneath them and up to his feet, his sword still in his hands.

Sarah realized as she saw the flash of steel that she hadn't been watching the right direction. She stretched out her hands toward Ruith, watching as the dagger Gair had in his hand came down—

Into Thoir's chest.

Ruith lowered his sword. Sarah watched as Thoir staggered a bit, then dropped to his knees. He looked at Ruith, blinking in surprise.

"He took my magic."

"Aye," Ruith said quietly. "He did."

Thoir looked at the dagger haft protruding from his chest, then looked up at his cousin. "It hurts."

Ruith reached for him, but it was too late. Sarah watched Thoir fall forward, then roll slightly onto his side. Ruith reached down and closed his eyes, then rose with a sigh. He turned.

Then he froze.

Sarah looked at him, then looked in the direction of his gaze. She felt Ruith's stillness become hers.

Gair was holding on to the outer casing of her spindle that contained the tidy spinning of all his power.

"What—" she began miserably.

Ruith said nothing. He merely walked over to his father and without ceremony took the spindle away. Sarah found herself the temporary keeper of his sword as he carried his father's magic over to the well in the yard there. She almost told him to save her spindle, but he had apparently already thought of that. He slid all the magic off the wood and dropped it, wincing a little as it touched his fingers, into the well.

He fashioned a stone cover out of his imagination and power, then stopped speaking.

Sarah could see, though, that he hadn't finished with his work. The well slowly and inexorably became nothing but solid stone, encasing in its depths all Gair's power. Soilléir's spell of Alchemy, apparently. She supposed Ruith had done his father a favor by not calcifying all the underground streams for a solid league surrounding his house. At least he could most likely manage to dig another well before he died of thirst.

Ruith walked back over to her, took his sword back and resheathed it, then leaned over and kissed her cheek.

"Cheek?" she said, because she could think of nothing else to say that could possibly be equal to the monumental nature of the events that had just transpired.

"Your grandfather is watching," Ruith said half under his breath. "I'm trying not to take liberties."

Sarah looked over her shoulder to find Franciscus standing just on the other side of the little fence, leaning negligently against a tree there, his arms folded casually over his chest. He glanced next to him as Urchaid the squirrel resumed his proper shape and dusted himself off. She supposed they would keep for a bit, so she turned back to see what Ruith would do to his father.

Gair was swearing in a blustering fashion, breathing out threatenings, promising retribution. Ruith didn't even so much as glance at him as he retrieved the book of spells, paused, then picked up the ring from where Gair had dropped it. He gathered up his bow and arrows, then took her hand, towing her with him as he walked along the path back to the gate she honestly didn't remember having come through.

"Where are you going!" Gair bellowed. "Come back here and fight me! I can't believe I spawned such a coward."

Sarah looked up at Ruith but his expression gave nothing away. He escorted her through the gate, handed her his gear and the book of spells, then turned and shut the gate. He wove Soilléir's spell of Containment over it, which she knew because she watched the words pour silently out of his soul and quickly fan out to form a barrier that she could readily see was unbreachable and permanent.

"What are you doing?" Gair shrieked. "What have you done?"

Urchaid walked forward and tried to lean on the fence but only succeeded in bashing his head against the spell. He pulled back, rubbed his forehead in annoyance, then turned that annoyance on Gair.

"I believe, my good man, that he's boxed you in."

"But I'll die!" Gair cried. "You can't leave me here to die!"

Sarah looked up at Ruith. He took a deep breath, let it out, then returned her look.

"I have no more to say to him," he said quietly. "For the sake of my mother and my brothers who are dead, I can say no more to him."

"I think Urchaid's doing the honors."

Ruith smiled, a quick smile that left her smiling in return. She walked into his embrace and closed her eyes, listening to Urchaid giving Gair very timely and useful advice about saving seeds and learning to make do with what he could dry in the attic. Sarah imagined that once word got out that Gair of Ceangail was a captive audience, there would be quite a few souls braving the innards of Shettlestoune to give him other useful pieces of advice.

"Well, I say," Urchaid announced, apparently having tired of his sport, "that was a bit messy, wasn't it?"

"Let's make a bargain, you and I," Ruith said shortly, his voice rumbling in his chest. "You go away and I won't tell either Droch or your father that you're alive."

"I was thinking that perhaps I should carry off Gair's little tome—"

"No. I already have plans for it."

"What are you going to do with it that I couldn't do better?"

"Step back and I'll show you."

Sarah pulled away from Ruith and watched as he dropped his father's book to the ground where it suddenly sprang up into a far different, rather more permanent bit of rock.

Rock that looked remarkably like an owl.

"Oh, I say," Urchaid said faintly. "Well, that seems as good a thing as any to do with it. At least we know it won't be out in the world any longer, tempting mages with no self-control to thumb through its contents." He slid Franciscus a look. "No hard feelings, eh, old man? Didn't mean to clunk you so hard on the noggin."

"Well," Franciscus said seriously, "I had put an enormous rent in that very lovely lace cravat you're wearing, so perhaps we might consider our recent battle to be a draw."

Sarah watched Urchaid put his hand to his throat uneasily, as if he'd come close to losing more than a bit of lace. He nodded at Franciscus, then looked at Ruith.

"I don't suppose, my wee rustic, that you have any suggestions for locales where I might safely roost, would you?"

"I wouldn't presume to tell you," Ruith said, "but I would suggest that you do your roosting very far away from Shettlestoune. You know, you might consider a different direction for your life based on what you've seen today."

The look of loathing Urchaid sent Ruith's way was formidable. "I do not do *good works*." He smoothed his hand down the front of his less-than-immaculate jacket, then examined one of his lace cuffs. He flicked a dark spot off it, then looked at Ruith. "I'll leave all that rubbish to you. And rest assured, my dear Ruithneadh, that I will confine myself to elegant salons where you will not be. I don't imagine that will prove to be too difficult."

Ruith only watched him, which seemed to make Urchaid more than a little uneasy. He pursed his lips at Ruith, shot Franciscus a wary look, then turned to her.

"I find that I must compliment you, lady, on your work there. I daresay none of us would be breathing now without your very capable spinning."

"Thank you," Sarah managed. "You're very kind."

Urchaid recoiled as if she'd thrust a viper into his face. He patted himself for a moment or two, as if he thought he might thus find his old, foul self, then cast them all another look of disgust before he changed himself back into an owl and flapped off.

"Well," Franciscus said, rubbing his hands together, "I think we should be on our way as well. I'm not sure I can listen to Gair shouting himself hoarse much longer."

Ruith shot him a look. "Did you come to rescue us?"

Franciscus held up his hands. "I simply came to watch the spectacle, though thanks to a little tussle with Urchaid and Thoir both, I almost didn't come at all. I must say, children, that you didn't disappoint. Sarah, my gel, perhaps you should turn off those lights. I think they're beginning to hurt Gair's eyes."

Sarah looked at him helplessly. "I don't know how. That wasn't part of the spell, I don't think."

Franciscus held out his arm for her. "I'll do it for you, then teach you the spell if you like. Ruith, shall we go?"

"Please," Ruith said with feeling.

Sarah walked along with the both of them on the path that led away from Gair's house. When the path became too narrow, Franciscus released her to forge ahead, leaving her to walk with Ruith. In time, even the echoes of Gair's shouts faded. The woods were once again filled with terribly normal, everyday sounds of birds chirping, bees buzzing, squirrels flittering through the undergrowth.

She'd never been gladder of anything in her life.

She looked up at Ruith to find him watching her. She didn't smile, because his expression was so grave. "What is it?" she asked.

He shook his head, smiling briefly then. "Nothing. I was just watching you and wondering what you were thinking."

She found that she needed a fortifying breath or two before she could speak. She couldn't, however, look away from him, unwholesomely handsome three-quarter elf though he was.

An elf. She could hardly believe she was entertaining any seri-

ous feelings about such a creature, but it had been that sort of year
so far.

"I'm not sure," she managed, when she succeeded in corralling
her rampaging thoughts, "what to do now."

He considered for a bit. "We might make Mhorghain's wedding, if we hurried. Or at least the feast after the ceremony."

"At Seanagarra?" she said.

Well, she squeaked instead of speaking casually, but she was
not precisely herself at the moment. She had traveled over half the
length and breadth of the Nine Kingdoms as a bitter, terribly swift
wind, helped vanquish the most evil mage in memory, and was
now back where she had started from. Only now she was left with
trying to put her life in order when she wasn't sure where or what
the pieces were.

"I'm sure my grandfather has made a list of eligible lads for you
to look over," Ruith grumbled. "Lads who have no doubt been
allowed inside his gates for just such a purpose."

"I thought he wouldn't let anyone in for the wedding."

"I'm fairly sure he'll make an exception for you."

She looked up at him. "Am I going to be forced to dance with
them?"

"Would you rather fling yourself off the battlements in dragonshape with me?" he asked, looking far more enthusiastic about that
prospect than she was comfortable with.

She smiled in spite of herself, however, because his good humor
was contagious. "Let me see how I feel when we get there."

He stopped, turned her toward him, and put his arms around
her. The sunlight fell down onto his dark hair and lit up in a most
appealing way his bluish green eyes. She thought, now that she had
a moment's peace for thinking, that his eyes looked a little bit like
that bay Sgath had once shown her, a little piece of ground on the
shore of his lake he'd been saving for just the right person.

"I will wait," Ruith said seriously, "for as long as it takes for you to decide what your life should look like from here. I will even sit through innumerable evenings of watching you dance with every prince Sìle has engraved on that damned list he made up for you—"

"I thought you threw that list in the fire."

"I'm sure he's made another copy," he said just before he pulled her closer and kissed her. Quite thoroughly, as it happened. He lifted his head and looked down at her seriously. "I'm serious about the other. You tell me when you've thought enough."

"I'm not going to be *able* to think if you keep that up."

He chewed on something—a smile perhaps—then put his arm around her shoulders, and walked with her up the path to where Franciscus was waiting.

Sarah looked back only once. The lights were fading, though she could still see echoes of them hovering just above the treetops. She listened carefully, but could hear nothing untoward. The world was at peace.

She thought she just might be as well.

Twenty-one

※

Ruith walked along one of the porticos of his grandfather's palace, trying to decide just what he'd been doing the last time he'd walked over the same polished stones. He thought, now that he'd had the chance to give it the proper amount of thought, that he had been outrunning his grandfather with the youngest prince of Neroche. He was fairly sure a breach in the library's security had been at the root of the problem, no doubt accompanied by the report of a breaching of the pantry as well.

His grandfather's servants were, it could be said now that he was far too old to be reprimanded, a rather stodgy bunch.

He stopped at a doorway, then leaned in slightly to ascertain just what chamber he was outside and which inhabitants he was going to be eavesdropping on. He tried not to think about how odd it was that he couldn't simply identify the room from the outside, but it had been many years since he'd been in Seanagarra.

He saw his sister sitting in a little circle in front of the hearth with her newly made husband at her side. They were, it appeared, working on Rùnach's hands despite his rather vociferous protests. Ruith had no idea if Rùnach's hands *could* be healed, or even if they could be, if he would want them to be whole. His brother had changed over the past twenty years, which Ruith understood with his head.

It was his heart that was having the difficulty.

It was painful, somehow, to know he had lost a score of years with his siblings who lived still. He could only hope to make that up somehow as the years stretched out ahead of them.

He hadn't discussed his solution to their father with any of them yet. He supposed Franciscus had told Sgath who had informed Sìle who had then announced at some point, in gruff tones, that he was pleased the damned fool was seen to. Ruith had unbent enough to tell his siblings that their father was still alive but contained. He'd communicated the tale to Miach with a mere lifting of one eyebrow. But he hadn't been able to bring himself to tell anyone the particulars.

Perhaps when he'd stopped shaking as he thought about just how close he had come to killing not only himself, but Sarah.

Franciscus had spent the bulk of his time with both Sgath and Sìle discussing what Ruith had assumed were more pleasant topics. Ruith had joined them twice, once with Sarah, who had been appalled by the souls from legend they knew personally, and once on his own, simply to enjoy the company of men he admired. He had also spent a pair of afternoons with his grandmothers, Eulasaid and Brèagha, bringing Sarah along with him both times so she could be showered with the affection he knew would be so generously offered.

The rest of the time, he had simply walked along passageways, mostly the outer porticos, where he could listen to what flora and fauna had to say and watch Sìle's glamour sparkle in the fresh spring air. Well, that and keep an eye on Sarah.

She wasn't comfortable, though he couldn't say why not. His family had made every attempt to make her feel welcome, he had refrained from kissing her nearly as much as he would have liked, and his grandmother Brèagha had set aside an entire chamber full of what even Ruith could tell were marvelous things to weave with. He supposed, looking at it from his own perspective, that she felt a little displaced. After all, their adventure had begun with her losing her home, her spinning wheel, and all her gold. That had left her with no place to return to, no way to make her way in the world, and no ability to support herself until she could make that way.

He hadn't dared tell her he was more than able to provide for them both, even by using the more pedestrian means of selling the work of his hands. She knew that, and she knew he was more than willing to tuck his magic up in a trunk and go plant her garden by hand. It wasn't as if he hadn't carried on that way for years already.

"What are you doing?"

He thought he might have jumped half a foot. He turned around to find his sister's husband standing there, watching him with a bit of a smirk.

"Thinking," he said shortly. "What are you doing?"

"Stretching my legs and resting my ears."

"Is Mhorghain already vexing the latter?"

"Rùnach, rather," Miach said dryly. "I am on the verge of dropping him at Gobhann and leaving him there to weary Weger with his complaints."

"Do if you dare," Ruith said, "but be forewarned, I'll be called on to rescue him. Then I'm sure he'll want to come to Tor Neroche and tell you all about his adventures. You won't escape his carping for long."

Miach smiled. "He hasn't changed."

"Nay, he hasn't," Ruith agreed. He waited, but Miach seemed content to wait longer. Ruith finally sighed gustily. "What do you want?"

"You haven't said much about your sire."

"Nay," Ruith agreed, "I haven't."

Miach waited a bit more, then laughed, apparently in spite of himself. "Very well, keep your secrets. You come tell me all the details when you're tired of them. I'll be interested to know if any of Uachdaran's training served you."

"You should be, considering that he favored me with that training no doubt to repay me for the spell *you* filched from his solar—"

Miach made a noise of disbelief. "Ruith, *you* unlocked the door."

"And you picked the lock on the cabinet and pulled out the book."

"And we each held on to a half of it so that the blame would be spread about evenly," Miach said smoothly.

"Well, just so you know, His Majesty has a more exclusive spell of hiding," Ruith said, ignoring the way Miach's ears had already perked up. "From what I understand, what we filched was the one he leaves out for inquisitive lads who come to his hall intent on stealing things from his solar, just so they feel like they've made a proper visit."

"Interesting—"

"Nay, it is not," Ruith said firmly.

Miach considered, then smiled. "I'll go see what Rùnach thinks. When are you getting married, by the way?"

Ruith suppressed the urge to growl at the king of Neroche. "When I can convince my lady she wants to. And nay, I don't need any advice from you on how to go about that."

"Just trying to be useful," Miach said with a shrug. "As always."

"Go be useful somewhere else."

Miach only smiled, clapped him on the shoulder, then sauntered off, whistling cheerfully. Ruith cursed him silently, then turned and continued on his way. He hadn't walked another fifty paces before he found himself having to duck behind a convenient hedge to avoid interrupting a conversation he had the feeling he wasn't going to enjoy.

"You know, Sarah darling, we were thinking that perhaps we would return home."

Ruith was tempted to swear, but he would have given himself away and earned a lecture from his grandmother Eulasaid who was corrupting a certain weaver on the other side of the hedge. His grandfather Sgath was there as well, adding his encouragement to the nefarious schemes apparently being bandied about.

"I told Sgath that Ruith might be annoyed we had invited you to come with us," she continued easily, "but Sgath suspected you might need . . . less."

"Less to look at," Sgath clarified. "Sìle's hall is, I will freely tell anyone who'll listen, terribly overdone."

"It's glorious, truly," Sarah protested.

"Ah, but when compared to the wonders of my lake," Sgath said with a good deal of satisfaction, "it's just gaudy." He sounded as if he were thoroughly enjoying himself. "Think on it, Sarah. Peace, quiet, and fresh fish roasting over a hot fire. And we generally don't dress for supper, though we have been known to wash our hands from time to time before we eat."

Ruith pursed his lips. He was quite certain his mother had warned him once—very well, it might have been more than once—about the dangers of eavesdropping. He was regretting quite seriously not having taken her advice.

"Shall you come home with us, then?" Sgath asked. "You might be pleased to know I've put up a bit of a tent on that spot you fancied."

"On your lake?" Sarah asked, sounding altogether too interested in the same.

"Aye."

There was silence for a very long moment, then came words Ruith was not at all surprised to hear.

"That would be very kind."

"We'll leave when you're ready," Eulasaid said gently. "Perhaps in the morning. You wouldn't want to miss the ball tonight."

"Ball?" Sarah echoed, managing to sound with one word as if missing such a glorious occasion wouldn't have pleased her more.

"And a state dinner beforehand," Sgath said cheerfully. "Dozens of important people. Well, perhaps not dozens. It is Seanagarra, after all, and Sìle seems to always be running short of invitation letters." He paused, then made a sound of surprise. "I have a thought," he continued brightly.

Ruith imagined he did. He imagined he wasn't going to particularly care for his grandfather's thought.

"Why don't we leave this afternoon?" Sgath suggested. "You finish your walk, then meet us in the stables. We'll be ready to go in a blink, won't we, my love?"

"We will be," Eulasaid agreed. "Shall I dim the garden for you, Sarah?"

"No," Sarah said quietly, "but I appreciate the offer. I'll be fine."

Ruith started to frown, but realized he couldn't in good conscience do so. The truth was, Sìle's palace was almost more than he could look at comfortably and he'd spent more than half his childhood there. He could only imagine how many times Sarah had already dimmed her sight over the past se'nnight. That she'd remained there that long was, he supposed, something of a miracle. Perhaps it was best to let her go somewhere where things weren't so overwhelming visually. He could be persuaded to trail along after her, if she were interested in that sort of thing.

He continued to lean over in a rather uncomfortable crouch, watching the ground, until he thought it might be safe to move. He straightened with a groan, then turned to walk out of the hedge.

Sgath was standing two feet away, watching him.

Ruith looked for a plausible excuse, but found nary a one to hand. He settled for a scowl.

"I thought you wanted grandchildren."

Sgath grunted. "I won't be having any from the pair of you if you don't get her out of this garish, gilt-encrusted cage Sìle calls a palace."

Ruith refrained from commenting on the delights to be found in the little hovel Sgath had called home for centuries before he'd wed Eulasaid. Sgath would plead a poor memory and then they would be back where they started. Ruith sighed, then shooed his grandfather out of his way.

"I don't want to discuss my amorous adventures with you," Ruith said crisply. "You'll just tell me what to do."

"My advice is always very good."

"Well, you've given more than I cared for to my future wife," Ruith said pointedly. "Go saddle your horses. I have the feeling she's not going to be dressing for dinner."

"She's waiting for you over there in the garden." He lifted an eyebrow. "Her sight is very clear, you know. I daresay it extends even over hedges."

Sgath clapped him companionably on the shoulder, then walked away. Ruith watched him go, then dragged his hand through his hair. He did it again, on the off chance that it *looked* as if he'd been dragging his hand through his hair, though he supposed there was no use in hiding his thoughts from Sarah. She would see them written on his heart.

He removed himself from his hiding place, rounded the end of the hedge, then managed only a few steps into the garden before he had to stop and simply look.

Sarah was, he had to admit, glorious. She was wearing a flaming red gown he'd asked to have made for her, a gown like the one she'd worn in Léige. Her hair hung down her back in a riot of curls, though he could see from where he stood that she was wearing a very discreet circlet of gold on top of her head.

Well, he imagined that would be the first thing to go if she had anything to say about it.

She smiled at him as he wlked across the grass toward her, which he thought might be a very good sign. He drew her into his arms, because he couldn't help himself. He wouldn't keep her there if she wasn't amenable, but he wasn't about to let her traipse off to Lake Cladach without his having told her precisely how he felt.

"I want to use one of my markers tonight," she said, finally.

He nodded, because he could do nothing else.

She looked up at him seriously. "It isn't you, Ruith."

"I could come with you," he offered.

She smiled, a smile that smote him straight to the heart. "Your sister is going to be here for another few days, I think, as is Rùn-ach. Surely you want to visit with them. And I'm not going far."

He chewed on his words for a bit. "And you wouldn't be unhappy to see me in that place that isn't far?"

She closed her eyes briefly, then threw her arms around his neck and held on to him tightly. He would have enjoyed that, but she was shaking too badly for him to. And before he could say anything else, she had pulled back, kissed him quickly, then bolted across the garden.

He watched her go, then sighed as he went to sit down on a bench beneath a blossoming linden tree. The smell was glorious, but he realized after a bit that he wasn't enjoying it.

He understood what troubled Sarah. As thrilled as he was to have his siblings to hand again, it was difficult to return to a place he'd known so well in his youth whilst knowing all the years the pleasure hadn't been his. But at least he was returning to some-place known.

Sarah had nowhere to return to. There wasn't a single place in the Nine Kingdoms that she could have gone to and called home. There were many places, most notably his grandfather's hall and any number of no doubt very lovely locales in Cothromaiche, where she would have been welcomed with open arms and every attempt made to make her feel as if she belonged.

But none of those places would have felt like they belonged to *her*.

There was only one place he could think of where that might even be possible and the offer of traveling there had already been extended. He would watch her go, give her as much time as she needed to settle in, then see if he couldn't find his own way there and plead his case.

And hope that she would still be interested in listening.

Three hours later, he stood at the edge of the stables and watched as three dragons bearing a trio of riders lifted themselves with great dignity into the air and flapped off into the cloudy afternoon.

"Are you going to let her go?"

Ruith looked to his left to find his grandmother standing there next to him. He put his arm around her and smiled down at her. "Briefly."

"She told me earlier that she was using one of her get-out-of-uncomfortable-formal-dinner excuses," Brèagha said with a smile. "She hoped she wasn't offending me by doing so."

"And you said?"

"I told her that Eulasaid's garden was almost at its peak, and that it was a gentler flowering. It seemed to me that a girl with her particular sort of talents might appreciate that, especially after all she's been through recently." She looked up at him. "Don't you think?"

"I do."

Brèagha paused, then laughed suddenly. "You dreadful boy, aren't you going to tell me your plans?"

"Aye, Grandmother, I am," Ruith said, keeping his arm round her and pulling her away from the stables back to the house. "My immediate plan is to head off into the forest and chop down the most lovely tree I find—"

"Ruith!"

"Then I thought I would trouble Master Coillear for the use of his lathe for a day or two. I'll need clamps as well, and perhaps an hour or two in the forge."

Brèagha looked up at him in surprise. "Is that all?"

"You might have a chat with my horse and see if he would mind bearing a few extra burdens when we fly west."

She smiled. "Nothing from the silversmith?"

Ruith kissed the top of her head. "I'll invite you to the wedding. From what I understand, Eulasaid and Sgath's garden is almost at its peak."

Brèagha smiled at him affectionately. "We'll come. And I promise to wear flowers in my hair instead of a crown." She patted his back, then released him to walk back to the house. She looked back over her shoulder briefly. "You should leave Gair's ring with your brother."

"I thought I could," he managed, then watched her until she had safely reached the house before he went to go find the tools he was going to need.

He supposed, when he actually took a hard look at it, that there were things he still needed to discuss with his family, things that had to do with his sire and their quest and how they all might put it finally and fully behind them.

And then he would go to the place where he and Sarah could meet in the middle.

He suspected he would find Sarah already there.

Twenty-two

S arah sat on a fallen log on the most beautiful spot in the Nine
Kingdoms and watched the lake in front of her. The sunlight
laughed as it sparkled on the water, the waves sang as they lapped
against the shore, the rocks and fine sand that lay near her feet held
on to the centuries of tales they could have told her if she'd asked
them to.

She'd been happy with silence, actually.

She had been at Lake Cladach for almost a se'nnight, though it
hadn't seemed that long. She had been sleeping at Sgath and Eulasaid's house which, whilst it wasn't quite a palace, was definitely not
a cabin. It was a very lovely, large house with more bedchambers
than she'd been able to count and glorious gardens surrounding it.
Slightly less spectacular than were to be found at Seanagarra, but
she'd been very grateful for that. If she hadn' t known better, she

would have thought the whole place a fitting abode for a genteel nobleman and his wife. Modest but elegant.

She liked it very much.

She had woken that first day after a marvelous night's sleep to find a boat tied to the dock, ready for her use. She'd reached for the oars only to have Sgath come trotting down the dock with his lure-encrusted hat on his head and fishing pole over his shoulder. He'd rowed her to the other side of the lake in no time at all, left the boat for her, then whistled as he walked off to search for a decent fishing spot.

She had found herself in a particular spot Sgath had shown her the first time she'd come to the lake with Ruith. It was, as she hadn't dared tell Sgath lest she look too terribly desperate to have it, perfect. Just the right amount of shore. Room for an enormous garden, space for the grazing of sheep, and a perfect clearing in which to build a house.

She had hinted she wouldn't be opposed to another visit on the second day she'd been there, and she'd been sent out the door with a basket of supper and wishes for a lovely day. Tarbh had been waiting for her on the dock, stubbornly refusing to move until she agreed that he would be first her wings across the lake, then her . . . well, he hadn't seemed inclined to change himself back into a horse so she supposed he could only be called a watchdragon.

She looked behind her to find him currently sleeping in the sun, curled up in dragonshape. She had to admit that his preferred shape had been handy enough earlier that morning given that he'd snorted a bit of fire under her dying kettle and saved her the trouble of seeing to the blaze herself.

She wondered how difficult it would be to get a message to Soilléir, to thank him for the gift of such a lovely, thoughtful animal.

She rose with a sigh and walked back up from the shore. She paused to look at the tent she had found just waiting there in the clearing the first day—though calling it a tent was to cast aspersions on its finer qualities. It was a house with soft walls. She imagined she could have lived there quite comfortably for quite some time.

The note she'd read the week before was still pinned onto the door, a note that advised her to only let good friends inside. She wasn't sure what Ruith had said to Sgath—if anything—but the words made her smile every time she saw them, so she left the note there.

She walked over to the kettle simmering quite happily over the fire that always seemed to be at the perfect temperature, then gave her yarn a stir.

And then she realized that she had nothing left to do but stand there in the sunlight and think.

She supposed she couldn't have been blamed if her thoughts immediately went to Ruith. He would have realized a se'nnight earlier that she was using one of her no-excuse-necessary notes for getting out of that intimidating state dinner Sìle had planned. She was also fairly sure he would have realized why. As kind as his maternal grandparents had been to her, Sìle's glamour was a bit much. Not even dimming her sight had been enough to aid her much. Gair had been powerful, true, but Sarah didn't think she wanted to begin to delve into what Sìle of Tòrr Dòrainn was capable of.

Her horse-turned-dragon lifted his head suddenly and looked behind her. Sarah closed her eyes briefly and reminded herself that she was perfectly safe. Though it was unobtrusive, Sgath had his own bit of glamour laid over the entire lake. He would know immediately if something befell her.

Still, she wished she hadn't been so trusting as to leave her knives back at the house. She should have 'least have brought a sturdy kitchen knife to tuck into her belt. She looked at her horse, but he had only put his head back down on his paws and closed his eyes. Well, one eye. He was masquerading as a dragon, after all.

She took a deep breath, then turned around.

There, leaning his shoulder against a tree, stood a man clad in simple traveler's gear. There was a knife suck down his boot—she could see the hilt of it poking up—but no sword, no quiver of arrows, no enormous collection of spells hanging in the air under his hand to delight and terrify. If he were a mere traveler, he was traveling with a lack of protection that was downright ill-advised.

And on the ground next to him was a spinning wheel.

Sarah felt her eyes begin to burn, just the slightest bit.

He pushed off his tree and walked across the new spring grass, frowning thoughtfully at it, as if it were telling him to keep off it with his muddy boots. He pursed his lips, then stopped in front of her and made her a small bow.

"My lady."

"Your Highness."

"I can trot out your title as well," he said lightly, "if you like."

"Please don't," she said earnestly, then she smiled. "How was the ball?"

"I hid in the library with Miach of Neroche."

"Old habits die hard, apparently."

"Mhorghain was there as well, along with an increasing number of my cousins." He smiled and shrugged. "I think Sìle despairs of having any grandchildren with manners, though we did all make an appearance at supper the next night to trot out our good court clothes. I fear, however, that the current librarian may never recover from our antics."

She smiled. She supposed, since he had come such a long way to see her, that there was no reason not to take a step closer to him. She considered, then took another. She put her hands on his chest and looked up at him. "I needed to see less," she said, "which is why I left. But I already told you that."

"And I appreciated the difference," he said seriously.

"Did you?"

He put his arms around her. "I did." He paused, then smiled at her pleasantly. "You know, I have spoken with your grandfather."

"About what?" she asked.

"Oh, this and that."

She had to put in a bit of effort to suppress her smile. "When?"

"Several days ago at Seanagarra, then again a few minutes ago back at the house. He managed to wrest his ancient self into something with wings after I told him I would submit to his and Sìle's idea of ten handsome lads of note dancing with you before I had the chance again if he arrived at Sgath's hearth first."

"Tell me you won."

He lifted an eyebrow. "Not interested in a long line of eligible lads waiting to vie for your attentions?"

"Not particularly."

"It was, you should know," he said solemnly, "a very stormy journey. Quite the bumpy ride full of peril, lightning, and I think even a spell or two. Franciscus suggested we turn back, but I refused." He paused. "I was particularly interested in seeing you, as it happens."

"Were you?"

He nodded solemnly. "I had a particular question to ask you that couldn't wait any longer."

She looked into his rather lovely eyes for several minutes in silence, then put her hands on his cheeks, pulled his head down to hers, and kissed him. She supposed she might as well do a thorough job of it, since he'd gone to all the trouble of flying through what she, Sgath, and Eulasaid had managed to best. He was right; it had been a terrible storm.

"Is that an aye?" he managed, when she released him.

"I don't remember hearing any question."

He smiled down at her. "Wed me?"

She considered. "I might."

"I brought you a wedding present."

"Is that it over there?"

"It is. Shall we go examine it and see if it suits?"

She slipped her hand into his and nodded, then walked with him across the glade. She stopped in front of the spinning wheel and admired it, then blinked in surprise and leaned over to look more closely.

Ruith's mark was on one of the spokes.

She looked at him in astonishment. "Did you *make* this?"

He nodded solemnly.

"Does it work?"

"You'll have to try it." He paused. "I will tell you this much: my grandmother Brèagha's best spinner tried it out a time or two to point out where I might have gone amiss and she personally guaranteed that it would spin only plain wool. No dreams."

Sarah took a deep breath, then turned and went into his arms. "I don't mind dreamspinning."

"I know."

"But I would rather spin just yarn."

"I know that too," he said very quietly.

She stood with her head on his shoulder until she thought she might like to sit down. Ruith was, fortunately, seemingly very content to join her on that fallen log and look out over the water as it laughed and sparkled in the sunshine. They sat there for quite a while in silence before she looked at him again.

"I still have one state function to get out of, you know," she said with a smile.

"Which is why I'm planning to wed you in Grandmother Eulasaid's garden. It can't possibly be considered an appropriate location for a state anything." He paused. "She said she would weave you a crown of flowers."

"That is very kind of her."

"She informed me I would be wearing one as well, which is less kind," he said dryly.

"You'll look lovely."

He laughed, and his laugh was full of sunshine and happiness and the magic that sparkled as it ran through his veins. "So will you," he said, just before he leaned over and kissed her.

It was quite a while later before she simply sat there with her head resting on his shoulder. Perhaps there would be clouds in their lives from time to time, and things would not always be so peaceful or easy to look at, but she thought she could safely say that the worst was behind them.

Ruith had promised her that one day he would make sure that she had nothing but loveliness before her. She had been given many things over the past few months, but of all those things, Ruith had given her the most treasured gift of all.

And that was the mage from up on the mountain who had taken on her quest as his own, then kept her safe when that quest had become something more than the both of them. And now, he had given her the best gift of all, which wasn't the spinning wheel he'd made with his own hands.

It was the gift of his heart.

Epilogue

❦

Ruith stood on the edge of Lake Cladach and looked out over the water. It was one of his favorite views, as it happened, for the view was rarely the same. He wasn't sure if his grandmother had anything to do with the weather or it simply changed its mind on its own, but somehow the lake seemed particularly determined to show as many facets of itself and to their best advantage as often as possible.

He lifted his gaze to see his grandparent's palace sitting on the opposite side of the lake, almost blending in with the trees. That sight never failed to give him a bit of a start, given that it was a place he'd never anticipated he would see again, much less look at every day.

He shook his head at the marvel that had become his life, then turned and started back up the path toward his own house. He had to admit he wouldn't be unhappy to get himself inside and shut the door behind him. Autumn had made an appearance the night before, which had left him very happy indeed that he'd put in such long days during the summer.

The house in front of him wasn't large—yet—but it was as beautiful as he'd been able to make it with his own two hands. A library for him, a light-filled room for Sarah to spin and weave in, and a decent-sized great room that had already seen more than its share of visitors, noble or not as the case might have been.

Sìle had given them post-wedding privacy until the middle of the summer when he'd arrived on wing, changed himself into his proper shape on the path that led to the house, then considered. Ruith had watched his grandfather sigh—lightly—only once, then embrace Sàrah, kiss her hair, and invite her to show him about. Ruith had trailed along behind them, trying not to give any sign of his thoughts. He had built the house for Sarah by very ordinary means partly because he'd wanted to give her a refuge from her sight, but mostly because he was just as eager as she to live simply. They had already made journeys to several places as man and wife that weren't open to the traveler without a crown in his pack. But once those journeys had been made, he had been more than happy to hang up his crown and put on boots.

Sìle had looked at him on that afternoon in early summer, after inspecting the inside of the house, and frowned. "No magic?"

Ruith had shaken his head slightly, had another light sigh as his reward, then watched his wife and his grandfather discuss where a dyeing garden might best be planted. He'd resigned himself to a solid fortnight of building a rock enclosure.

To his utter surprise, however, Sìle had stayed to help. If the work had gone a bit more quickly than it might have otherwise, Sarah had very politely made no comment, and he had, very wisely to his mind, kept his mouth shut as well. He would admit, however, to having grown a bit misty-eyed when Sìle had helped her plant with his own two hands. And if there had been a few more plants with a less-than-ordinary character to them left behind, both he and Sarah pretended not to notice.

It wasn't that Sarah was opposed to magic, nor was he, though his grandfather would have said they were. It was just that she needed relief from her sight, and he enjoyed making things with his hands.

Though if he found himself more often than not reaching for the odd, useful spell, well, Sarah was good enough to only smile and thank him for confining himself to Fadaire.

He opened his front door and walked inside the great room—which Sìle had admitted freely had been handsomely done—then paused a moment or two in spite of himself. He didn't want to pause, but he just couldn't help himself. It would have been more reasonable if he'd been brought to a skidding halt by the beauty of his wife's face—which happened with regularity—or by the memory of the long late summer evenings spent either there or in front of the fire with various members of his family—which he often was. But he was brought up short by something else.

It was that damned tapestry hanging on the wall.

He supposed it wasn't every day that the dreamweavers of Bruadair parted with one of their creations. He supposed it was even rarer that the exiled king and queen of that land were the ones doing the weaving and the delivering. He folded his arms over his chest and scowled at the thing, knowing very well that he was wearing the exact expression Sìle had been when he'd first seen what had been sent along as a wedding gift.

It wasn't so much that the thing was unsightly, for it wasn't. That was part of the problem. Ruith could tell, even with his sight that was nothing more than adequate, that the blasted thing had a mind of its own. He couldn't say how it happened—and didn't want to investigate too closely, truth be told—but while the warp and weft held the same heroic scenes they had when the piece had been initially hung on the wall, the scene had . . . changed. And it continued to change, as if somehow he and Sarah had become a part of the weaving and the threads of their lives were altering with every day that passed what he saw on the wall.

He had begged a spell from Franciscus to turn the damned thing off, but he had to use it half a dozen times a day just to keep the weaving at bay. Sarah didn't seem to mind it, which surprised him, but she saw things he couldn't. He had found her staring at it more than once, as if she were trying to determine just how she might recreate the colors Ruith was fairly sure simply weren't found in nature.

No wonder Sìle had left a few extra things in the garden. Ruith imagined those wouldn't be the last otherworldly things that took root there.

He muttered Franciscus's spell at the tapestry on his way by, could have sworn he heard it grumble at him in reply, then carried on down the passageway to less unsettling locales.

He paused at the doorway to Sarah's weaving room and simply drank in the sight. It had little to do with the chamber itself, though he would be the first to admit it had turned out well. He'd situated it with a southern exposure, with floor-to-ceiling windows that the light might flood it perfectly. And if he had perhaps slipped in a spell that tempered the sunlight as it fell through those windows that it didn't fade Sarah's yarn, well, who could blame him? There was no point in having magic if he couldn't use it for good now and then.

He leaned against the doorframe at present and smiled to himself. Sarah was sitting at her wheel, spinning something into something else that he was certain, given the color, he might be happily wearing after it was knit up. His grandmother Eulasaid was sitting with her, spinning something entirely different onto Uachdaran of Léige's eminently useful spindle. Ruith wasn't going to comment. If Eulasaid could rid any of them of the memories of what that spindle had last spun, he would be very grateful.

She and Sarah were discussing something—the properties of

woad, he thought—and seemingly untroubled by whatever magic might be finding itself wound upon that very handy stick.

His grandmother looked up suddenly and smiled. "Ruith, my love, how long have you been there?"

"Not nearly long enough," he said honestly.

Eulasaid laughed. "Spoken like a man newly wed."

"I believe it's been half a year," Sarah said dryly. She looked over her shoulder and smiled. "Though it seems only a day or two."

"Well, darling, that's what happens when you're living a very lovely dream," Eulasaid remarked mildly. "May it always be so for you both." She set the spindle aside and rose. "I'll come back and finish that another day, if you like. I'm sure you'll find a use for it eventually."

Ruith watched his grandmother exchange a fond embrace with his lady, then come to stand in front of him. She pulled his head down and kissed both his cheeks, then smiled up at him.

"We're having guests for supper tomorrow, if you two would like to come over to the house."

"Dare I ask?" Ruith said with a sigh.

"I don't know if you do," she said with a bit of a laugh, "but I don't think you would find the evening too painful. I'll leave the choice to you. If I lived in this very lovely house, I'm not sure I would leave it."

Ruith started to offer her his arm, but she shook her head.

"I know where the door is, love, and can see myself out." She smiled at Sarah once more, then walked down the passageway. Ruith watched her go for a moment, then turned back to his wife, who had turned around on her stool and was watching him solemnly. He tilted his head and smiled at her.

"What is it?"

She rose and crossed over to him, then put her arms around his waist. "Nothing," she said, leaning up to kiss him briefly. "I'm just looking."

"And?"

She smiled. "I thought you were fishing outside."

"They were avoiding me, so I thought I would see if my luck was better in here."

She only laughed at him, which he had expected, then hugged him tightly before she pulled away.

"I'm almost done with this bobbin."

He let her go, reluctantly, though he had to admit it gave him a chance to just watch her. He sat down in the chair his grandmother had recently vacated, then closed his eyes and listened to the whir of Sarah's spinning wheel. He thought she might have been humming something under her breath, but he wasn't sure.

The truth was, he wasn't sure of too much any longer. He had begun his life so certain that it would march along a particular path, clear and well-defined. When that path had led him to a solitary house in the mountains, he'd been sure that the rest of his very long life would be spent as a hermit, shunning his birthright and avoiding anything to do with magic or dreams or family.

Until a lovely, unmagical gel had knocked on his door and changed the course of his life forever.

And now he had the gift of magic, of family, and a dreamweaving bride who saw things he didn't and who had been willing to walk with him into his darkness and stay with him there whilst he found his way out of it.

And back into the light.

It was so much more than he'd ever dared dream.